ACCOMMODATING
MOLLY

Also by Candida Crewe

Focus
Romantic Hero

Candida Crewe

ACCOMMODATING MOLLY

HEINEMANN : LONDON

William Heinemann Ltd
Michelin House, 81 Fulham Road, London SW3 6RB
LONDON   MELBOURNE   AUCKLAND

First published 1989
Copyright © Candida Crewe 1989

British Library Cataloguing in Publication Data
Crewe, Candida, *1964–*
  Accommodating Molly.
  I. Title
  823'.914[F]

  ISBN 0 434 14336 7

Typesetting by
Quorn Selective Repro Ltd, Leicestershire
Printed and bound in Great Britain
by Mackays of Chatham

For Miranda Brett

With special thanks
to Mama and James
for all their encouragement

Hope lies to mortals
    And most believe her,
But man's deceiver
    Was never mine.

A.E. Housman

PROLOGUE

When Dominic left her, Molly Almond went to the fridge. She took out a small tart in pleated wax paper, washy pink. Inside the pastry was a gooey custard. On top of it, in a dump of whipped cream, a glazed strawberry had landed like a fat man who had jumped off the roof of a building and killed himself in a pile of snow below.

It was Molly's first act of loneliness: a soft indulgence following the flurry of fury, the slam of the door.

She sat on the kitchen table and swung her legs, childlike, restless. Carefully, she licked the sticky covering of melted sugar from the pudgy strawberry. Her tongue plunged into the fluff of cream.

Molly looked at her watch. It was past nine, a summer's evening. She wondered what to do: too late for the news, too late to ring a friend and make a last-minute plan. She pushed the rest of the cake into her mouth. It was a defiant gesture. Then she slid off the table. But standing on her own in the middle of the floor, she felt the full blow of her solitude.

What now? Would she stay in the kitchen posing vacantly or wander into the sitting-room? And what then? Her thoughts hop-scotched. Wasn't it odd how literal 'walking out' could be? Dom had simply opened the door, stepped across the threshold, and disappeared: walked out. With all its implications of desertion and misery, the actual practicality of the phrase was peculiarly mundane. Now Molly was alone, she felt physically gawky because, frankly, she was at a bit of a loose end. After all, she and Dom had been going to have supper together. That at least would have entailed conversation and demanded positive action – putting butter in frying-pan, opening freezer, choosing Findus cod steaks in batter, introducing them to butter (now bubbling), dumping frozen peas in boiling water, putting bottle of ketchup beside

1

salt and pepper on table, plates, forks; chat interspersed with eating, laughter even.

It was a pity that both Molly's companion and her appetite had tangoed well away. What physical alternatives were left? (Incidentally, there was another Strawberry Sensation in the fridge. It had been destined for Dom's pudding. Now he'd never know what inspiration had gone into its choosing. A waste really.)

Four seconds, precisely, the significant walk-out. Infinitely depressing. The intimacy, built up over a matter of weeks, months, now over in such a piffling amount of time. In the circumstances it seemed inappropriate, indeed disrespectful, to opt for a passive choice and settle on the sofa, say, with a good book.

More suitable, surely, would be to pour a drink with exaggerated movements. Presumably that was what others resorted to when their lovers had just walked out on them: wave an arm, grab a bottle, spin the lid, 'fix' a large whisky, flip in the ice, create a clank.

Molly did so. She then opted to kneel on the carpet in the sitting-room. Devouring the first little cake had been a calculated move, to force herself immediately to recognise the gravity of her situation, and to be sad. Molly had hoped it might precipitate a tear, urge her to wail a bit. If only she could feel more than physical unease. A bit of self-pity at least. This present emotional indifference disappointed her. It would be far more interesting to be melodramatic – vengeful or hysterical perhaps. But, for the moment, it was still as if Dom hadn't really gone, even though she had eaten the cake. He'd just nipped down to the off-licence, would be back in five minutes.

Molly gulped at the whisky. The liquid was cold. Any minute now it would be bound to provoke some sort of emotional response. Surely.

It was time for an assessment of her physical appearance. In a moment, she would contemplate matters a little less superficial, but for now Molly would consider her body. Maybe therein lay the fundamental problem: it was not attractive to men, perhaps. It was important to be honest with herself, strictly so. No need for modesty, false or otherwise, as there wasn't anyone around to witness the egocentric summing up.

2

Still kneeling on the sitting-room floor, whisky in hand, Molly shifted into a more comfortable position. Leaning with her back against the sofa, she stretched her legs out to gain maximum view of herself. Aware that the activity she was about to embark upon was unspeakably self-indulgent, she justified it to herself: her boyfriend had walked out – quick glance at the watch – twenty-three minutes ago. This was a trauma, one of those which constitutes an undulation in the map of one's life. It required a critical going-over, a tracking of one's movements, rather than a frantic searching, willy nilly.

She started at the top. No, her head was not an object of monumental beauty. The nose was coarse, the lips undistinguished. Yet the chocolate eyes had been admired for their roundness and size, the consensus on the hair – a nondescript brown – was that it was glossy. Past comments on the complexion had ranged from 'pearly' to 'creamy' to 'peachy'. This was puzzling. A pearl, a peach, and a dollop of cream seemed to her to have little in common. Yet it couldn't be denied that, as adjectives applied to the quality of her skin, they did share a general air of flattery.

Moving downwards, Molly was forced to admit that her twenty-five years might have shown more mercy to the neck area. Wrinkles were not in evidence, thank God, as yet. But that elasticity of just a few years before was wearing.

On, on to the bosom: rounded and milky soft, if rather small. Here Molly could pause to reminisce. At sixteen she had been uncommonly in love with the son of the local doctor back at home. Hamish. He had harboured grand plans to become an architect, and, as he cupped his hand over her left breast at a barn dance, eyes closed, he had pronounced 'lovely'. At the time she had been aware it was as if he was stroking a model of the dome of St Paul's. Too modest to interpret it otherwise, she did, however, see the 'lovely' as a sort of compliment. Anyway, it would never be forgotten.

That area between the waist and knee need not be lingered upon, a certain plumpness being its defect. Others had insisted there was no problem, but Molly remained unconvinced. Consolation could sometimes be found, though. There was always a what-the-Hell-Mars-Bar, one or two happy phrases in the much-thumbed *Fat is a Feminist Issue*, or a surreptitious glance at her delicate ankles.

3

All in all, things could be summed up succinctly. On the physical side of things, the single word 'average' sprang to mind. An appropriate label. But how very dull, for to be so meant passing as one of life's blenders along with, say, feta cheese.

They definitely seemed to share the same role in life: that of a bland padding. Molly wondered if ever in a roomful of stimulating folk her physical presence could have been likened to anything more than feta in a salad otherwise populated by alluring avocado and irresistible bits of bacon? Doubtful.

All the same, she was saved from reducing herself entirely to the level of an indifferent dairy product by the acknowledgement that, in other respects, she had the upper hand. If unable to inspire physical *frisson*, fortunately she did possess *some* qualities in other respects, didn't she?

Since childhood, a certain shyness had lingered, but not crippled. So Molly was reserved, quite serious, but neither earnest nor intense. If the mood was right – a few friends, a couple of drinks – she could be quite funny, people had told her. In these circumstances pertinent observations, softly ventured, had, she recalled, sometimes prompted laughter. Coming from 'mousy' Molly they were the more pleasurable for being slightly surprising. It was this quality which people liked about her. She was unassuming but could hold her own.

So, having chiselled about a bit, scrappings of consolation could be extracted from the hollow pit of life's injustices.

Molly remembered in the confrontation before the slam of the door Dom had used the word 'pressure'.

'I feel this tremendous pressure from you,' he had thundered more than once.

What a curious accusation coming after he had made the decision to move in with her. With wry amusement, she had expressed indignation at being compared to a kind of cooker. He had snapped pompously that her remark was facetious.

'I think you fail to appreciate the gravity of what I'm telling you. Molly, I can't take it any more. You're smothering me – '

Molly glanced at her figure. Had she put on weight and not noticed?

'I'm so glad you see the humour,' he had snapped angrily. 'But I can't stand it any longer, the claustrophobia – '

'If you mention the word "space" in reference to your needing more of it, I'll throw you out before you've had a chance even to contemplate your own grand exit,' she said. That remark, she thought, was adequately dignified in the circumstances. It was, after all, extremely humiliating to be told one was smothering a man with claustrophobic pressure.

Alas, dignified though it might have been, it also exasperated Dominic. 'It's impossible to have a serious conversation with you. I'm trying to be reasonable, make you understand why I'm doing what I'm doing – '

'What *are* you doing?'

'I'm leaving you. I'm bloody well leaving you.'

And it was with that that he had swiped up his ridiculously huge coat from the back of the sofa and bloody well left her. Walked out. And she, Molly Almond, had bloody well gone to the fridge.

PART
1

CHAPTER
1

Because of the raw February day outside, the bookshop seemed particularly warm and inviting that afternoon. An observer peering in might have been reminded of a scene in a Victorian bookplate. Through the window the lights gave out a dull glow and revealed a cosy disorder within. The small emporium in Litchfield Street, off the Charing Cross Road, resembled the study of an absent-minded, dusty don.

Old shelves mounted each wall up to the cream cornice of the ceiling. Opposite the window was a stripped door (leading to a cloakroom-cum-kitchen), a small Victorian fireplace and an alcove for the desk. On the table in the middle of the square room, all the latest publications had been arranged in shiny piles, but in the rest of the shop the books, unable to be contained by the shelves alone, had belched overboard and splattered on to the floor, the desk and every other available surface. The customers, though, seemed to like it that way. It made them feel as if they were walking into a private room rather than a shop.

Molly had been working there for six months. It was her first proper job after stints as a gloomy waitress in restaurants like Pizza Express. The owner of Winter Books, Nicolas Winter, had been struck by the use of violet-coloured ink in her application letter. CVs sent in by others had proved perhaps more impressive – better qualifications, higher degrees. But Molly's spirited disregard for the more conventional black or blue ink had charmed Nick, himself a spirited man.

He was a bachelor, and very much relishing the status. The sort of person who refused to have an umbrella and wore shabby green and brown tweed suits and gold-rimmed spectacles. It did not surprise Molly that he admired her violet ink, used by her on that one occasion in an uncharacteristic fit of affectation. But she liked him, as did his customers. He treated her like a friend rather than an employee, and he treated them like guests. The regular ones would tease him about the state of the place, yet were forever impressed by the fact that, amazingly, he knew exactly where everything was. Molly enjoyed working alongside him. Although only thirty-three, he had the air of a humorous middle-aged woman and was as liable to quote Yeats or the recipe for Sussex Pond Pudding with equal enthusiasm.

That day there were fewer customers at lunch-time than usual. The cold presumably. Nick and his young assistant ate chicken and mayonnaise sandwiches together behind the desk. Then they drank milky coffee. Nick lit a cigarette.

Molly sat down on the floor and crossed her legs. Nick watched her as she pushed up her sleeves and opened a cardboard box of books with a Stanley knife, liking the fact that she was the sort of girl who obviously did not care a damn about getting the dust from the wooden boards on her jeans. Black jeans. Boyish, Nick thought, with those button flies. Still, they looked sexy on her. Her thin waist was cinched in with a tight brown leather army belt. Above it, tucked in, a thin cardigan of sea island cotton, artichoke-heart green, primly buttoned. Black cowboy boots with black stitching and pointed toes. Not inelegant. A plain watch, pig-skin strap; unostentatious gold rings in each ear. Otherwise no accessories, and no make-up.

Molly began to unpack the books. They were shiny. She appreciated their smell as she carefully cracked open the rich, creamy pages. The sight and feel of a new book by an author she admired gave a boost of pleasure. Fingering Peter Carey's latest novel, she smiled with anticipation.

Her boss was talking about death, a topic he favoured.

'Isn't it curious how an education attempts to sort out matters of a spiritual nature – all that churchgoing and Divinity? It's all very well training one's soul to aspire to Heaven and to dread Hell. But what I want to know is, *precisely* what's going to happen to me when I die. They never tell you that, do they? It's never *really* explained to us what happens to us when they lay us out, for example. From what I gather, it's a bit of a physical invasion of privacy. Now, one might crave a bit of that in life. But after *rigor mortis* has set in, frankly one's a bit past the stage when one wants to be fiddled with by a voluptuous nurse. I hope to God I'd have grown out of that kind of thing by then.'

Molly, still scrutinising the new book, sounded unconvincing in her agreement. She wasn't really concentrating.

10

'I wonder what brand of cotton wool they use to plug your orifices? I do hope it isn't Boots' pink and lilac balls. It'd be too undignified to look so colourful when one was so inert,' he added, fingering his chin.

'They put make-up on at some stage,' Molly reminded him.

'Corpse cosmetics, perish the thought!'

'Why are you so curious all of a sudden?'

'I was just thinking that a soul is rather like a love letter, the body its envelope. Because the contents are so important, that envelope should be treated with due respect. I happen to take a lot of care of my envelope – fruit, vegetables, fish, exercise. When it's been ripped open and the letter's blown away to burn in Hell or reside in Heaven's golden file, I'm keen that it shouldn't just end up in the bin. It's not an unreasonable wish.'

Molly laughed. 'You're ludicrous.'

'Simile a bit convoluted?'

'Bit.'

Molly knew Nick had secret leanings towards writing verse. Usually she encouraged him. But on this occasion she felt the world of poetry might be better off without that particular contribution.

The door opened. A customer walked inside. As he did so, a quiet bell sounded to announce the intrusion. Nick stubbed out the cigarette. Molly got up from the floor.

'Can I help you?' she asked.

She wasn't instantly aware of a presence, but of a coat. It was a huge thing which seemed to move about of its own accord. A shy voice emerged, as if through the buttonhole in the threadbare collar.

'Um. Please. Yes.' It hesitated. 'Peter Carey's new novel. I was wondering if by any chance you'd got a copy.'

Molly tried to look closer at the source of the voice, keen to see what the man was like. 'They've literally just come in,' she replied helpfully. 'Unfortunately it's not published till next week. We're not really allowed to sell it to you yet.'

His feet appeared to be winning his attention. 'Oh, right. Of course. Fine. I'll come back then.'

The voice was quiet. But there was about it a winning courtesy which prompted Molly to try and detain him. As he turned to leave, she touched his elbow.

11

'On the other hand, it seems very petty to make you wait. Take one now. No one's going to know.'

She glanced at Nick guiltily. He didn't notice. Doubtless he was still pondering the logistics of being laid out.

'Well, if that really is all right with you...' The man looked up nervously. Molly saw a red nose but an otherwise pale face. He had shy eyes that avoided more than momentary contact with hers before resorting to his feet once more.

'I don't see why not.' She bent down and picked up a copy. 'I can't wait to read it myself,' she ventured, friendly, hoping to prompt him to say something more.

'A treat in store,' he replied, before pausing to look at her. 'I'm too impatient to wait for the paperback,' he added, very quickly. At the same time, he scrunched one hand in the palm of the other so that his knuckles clicked. Embarrassment.

Molly smiled with sympathetic awkwardness. 'Would you like a bag?' she asked, ringing the price into the archaic till. Its bell made a noise like that of an old-fashioned fire-engine.

'Please.'

As she slipped the book inside the bag, he thanked her, and produced a crumpled £20 note, limp with age, the kind which smells almost damp with dirt. It caused him more embarrassment, she realised, for, having passed it to her, he set to work on the knuckles of his other hand before tentatively accepting his change. Doing so, he asked after another book he'd been trying to find.

Nick interrupted. 'As far as I know, few, if any, bookshops in London will have that. But *I* just might be able to get you one. Molly, my dear, would you care to take the gentleman's name?'

She dug into the precariously high pile of paperwork on the desk. At last she retrieved the ruffled order book. Opening it, she asked her shy customer for his name and number.

'Dominic De'Ath.'

Molly thought it distinguished, and was about to write it down but couldn't find a pen. 'Excuse me,' she said, rummaging once more into the mess on the desk.

'We are purveyors of the written word, and we cannot find a pen,' said Nick, not moving to help. 'Mr De'Ath – ' having pronounced the man's name with exaggerated diction, he paused to make way for a warm smile – 'it is a sorry state of affairs.'

12

He lit a cigarette. The customer patted the pockets of his vast overcoat, and delved into one of them to produce an old fountain pen.

'Here, use this,' he said, passing it to her.

Nick observed, amused. 'Don't forget the title, publisher, author, customer's telephone number and date of birth,' he urged naughtily. 'We should have it in about ten days. We'll call when it comes in. Molly's very efficient about that.'

Mr De'Ath thanked them both politely, smiled and retreated. When he had gone, Molly scolded Nick for gratuitously embarrassing both herself and the man.

'I couldn't help it,' he said, puffing away. 'There was such chemistry.'

'Absurd notion! Did you want me to order some more of the Tom Wolfe?' she asked, changing the subject.

'Yes. Call the publishers direct, not the distributors. We need copies quickly.'

She lifted the cream telephone on to her knee. The greasy, grimy wire was twisted.

'I'll check on the microfiche, too, in a minute, to see whether that book he wanted is still in print.' Molly tugged the sleeves of her jersey down over her knuckles in a shivery movement which hinted at excitement. It would be a pleasurable task, trying to track the man's book down. She was keen to succeed.

'I'll leave it to you,' Nick said.

Molly wondered how long it would take to find and if Dominic De'Ath would be wearing the same coat when he came to collect it.

CHAPTER

2

Helen Hardy described herself as an elderly woman of forty-two. In her heart of hearts, she knew forty-two was not exactly elderly, but she had taken the first line of Daisy Ashford's *The Young Visiters* very much to heart all the same.

'Mr Salteena,' the book opens, 'was an elderly man of forty-two.' The line would often, she found, swill round her mind like a song on the brain. There was no control over it, no means of making it go away. And with each repetition that unwelcome adjective – elderly – would bite into her consciousness, forever tormenting. Yet she had to face it: it was applicable to her and she felt it acutely.

'I feel afflicted by my years,' she had once confided to a friend, and how right she had been. 'In the company of the young, I feel a bit like a fat person in the company of the thin. Just as he's ashamed of every superfluous millimetre on his body, so am I aware of every excess year I've clocked up. Convinced we're inadequate, inferior, we share the same resentment.'

And what was there to show for all these years that so cruelly added up to an elderly forty-two? It was a question Helen often asked herself. She had spent many a lonely evening on her Pimlico sofa – oatmeal freckled with brown – pondering this one, too distracted by its evasive answer to settle with a book.

Physically, Helen felt, of course, that she had achieved, admirably, every clichéd manifestation of a 'certain' age: the texture of the face had begun to resemble a delicate linen hand-towel ruffled by use, the hair after some months of quandary had clearly made the decision to edge slowly towards a completely silver state.

Alas, these dubious 'achievements' were not the kind to be greeted with any sense of fulfilment. In fact they were exactly the sort that she could well have done without. Had the years been kindlier to her, Helen thought, they might have bestowed a little more grace, elegance even to compensate for the more outward signs of decline, to her body. She did not lack these qualities, but neither did she have them in abundance.

She must not forget the flat, of course. There was that. It was an achievement indeed. She hadn't expected an academic career to provide a roof over her head as well as such intellectual stimulation. At five, she had discovered her taste for literature and realised very early on that what was a slog to others was undiluted joy to her. Miss Rita Dobson, the English teacher with red stockings at a primary school in Salisbury, had inspired her to read voraciously. Satchel bulging, Helen would walk home and after tea retire to her room with *Treasure Island*, say, or *A Christmas Carol*. Her father, an administrator at the Playhouse, used to return at six and the rows with her mother would begin. Sitting on her bed, she could hear them downstairs, even when she blocked her ears. Sometimes it would become unbearable and she would sneak from the house. Then she would run, flat out, head down, so as to shake off that troubled feeling in her stomach. Even now, Helen could see her little grubby knees in full action under a flapping pleated school skirt, and the grey socks falling to her ankles. And even now, she could remember the relief of escaping. She would go and sit on a bench near the grass by the cathedral. Before opening her book, looking up at the awe-inspiring building she would vow, one day, to escape for good. Then, as she devoured the pages, a sense of tranquillity would trickle back and she would find the strength, an hour or so later, to return to the trials at home.

Taunts of 'bookworm' at the vast comprehensive school failed to quell her enthusiasm for literature. By fourteen she had read the complete works of Shakespeare and had become a dedicated fan of Jane Austen. Her contemporaries gained their thrills by nicking Pink in the Afternoon lipstick from Boots and having fun with the boys in the store cupboard under the stage. This was not to say that Helen was not interested in the opposite sex. No, she did have her fair share of fun. She even lost her virginity at fifteen and three months.

But popular and feverish though these thrills were to her friends, Helen remained, herself, fonder of the written word. Later, at a redbrick university in the early 1960s, she found this

15

preference still persisted, even though sex was almost as readily available as books.

Dedication and hard work paid off. She went on to teach at London and become a respected tutor. She wrote the occasional academic review for literary journals and a small Shropshire press of obscure distinction even published a collection of her poems called *The Bleaker Autumn*. Of the thousand copies printed, a mere 323 had sold. Eleven of those she had bought herself, to give to family and friends, and another nine had been bought by loyal pupils. She cursed herself for choosing such an indifferent title, for not coming up with a catchy one like *Making Cocoa for Kingsley Amis*. A collection of this name appeared shortly after hers. How clever of Wendy Cope, the author, to think of something so captivating and irresistible. Hadn't she heard somewhere it had come to Cope in a dream?

Fortunately, it was not her creative works upon which Helen relied for an income. Her modest salary for teaching at University College was dependable and regular. Hence the acquisition of a mortgage and, in turn, the acquisition of the flat.

Helen's Pimlico base was tiny. No matter, it was hers and hers alone, a tangible reward for her toil over the years. It was mainly white, or off-white – walls, carpets, curtains, even furniture. Colours, Helen felt, cluttered the mind. She relished the peace of all her whiteness, and felt safe with it as if cocooned inside a carton of milk. The only colour in the flat was in such details as the spines of books on the shelves and the plump and shiny fruit in a white china bowl in the middle of the white Formica table.

Sometimes Helen would just stand on the pale fur rug in the middle of her sitting-room and soak up the pleasure of simply being there. It was small, but there was enough space for a sofa and two armchairs near the fireplace, and a television between them. The kitchen was part of the same room, up a step running the length of it. The dazzling units were against the back wall, the little round table in front of them. Regarding its size, even the most generous-minded estate agent would have been hard-pressed to call the place anything other than 'compact'. But it was light and bright, and Helen loved it.

One solitary February evening, contemplating the flat, Helen even went so far as to congratulate herself on her colour scheme. A modest woman, self-congratulation did not

16

come easily, and the very next moment she was less complimentary.

'Wise about the white, maybe,' she thought, 'but otherwise lacking in the more general wisdom one's supposed to acquire in old age.'

Hopes, she pondered, though blighted by disappointment, still lingered vainly on. But they were more painful now. Today, they had about them a feverish air, though time was wearing them weaker every day. Surely, if she was wise, she would discard them defiantly, just as a brave widow might fling her husband's ashes into the sea. Yet even at her age she was not ready to accept a state of hopelessness.

Helen poured herself a glass of cold white wine, and sat down on the sofa. So what hopes, exactly, still lurked? She had successfully escaped from home – a hope harboured since childhood – at eighteen. And she was pleased how that initial escape to university had turned out, especially now, working at a job she enjoyed, living in her own perfect sanctuary.

The hopes that persisted were to do with men, marriage. 'That sort of thing,' she said out loud suddenly, trying her best to sound nonchalant about the matter. How she resented the importance she projected upon this aspect of her life. It coloured her reason, cluttered her mind, but unlike colour in her flat, she could not avoid it.

'It', to be precise, really meant lack of it. There had been men in her life, of course. Flings, affairs – a few. All transient, though, never long-term: a man bent on commitment was as rare as a free taxi in the rain. So, in relations with men, expectations had to be lowered, circumstances reduced.

'Can't be picky at my age. I have to accept what's on offer,' she said to herself gloomily. She recognised that for her to maintain anything remotely resembling an affair, it was essential to let a man have all his cake and eat it. Even that was better than nothing.

So Helen's eighteen-month affair with Nick Winter had run strictly on selfless lines. But had she been unprepared to tolerate his hugely advantageous share of the bargain, the affair simply would not have happened at all. Had she made even one demand, its time-span would have been nearer eighteen days.

Helen's boyfriend, a bookseller some years her junior, had a girlfriend with whom he lived. Strictly speaking, then, Helen was

17

not entitled to call him a boyfriend. It was rather too optimistic a label. But Helen could not resist using it sometimes – if never in front of Nick himself.

'I'd like a present for my boyfriend,' she had said to a salesgirl in a shop at Christmas. Daring to juxtapose 'my' and 'boyfriend' had given her uncommon pleasure. After that – despite the fact that the salesgirl had not batted an eyelid, let alone done a twirl, patted her on the back, and said 'Congratulations' – Helen had rather taken to practising the phrase on strangers. They did not know that she was elevating Nick's role in her life and, unlike friends, they had no cause to question its accuracy. So in these anonymous situations, saying 'my boyfriend' made Helen feel important for a few moments and – dare she admit it? – more acceptable in the eyes of society. Though she knew it should not, this mattered to her a great deal.

Helen was aware that people saw her as a thoroughly rational and sensible woman. They admired her for being practical and orderly on every sort of level. She could not deny she had a miraculous way with a duster, so her flat was always almost clinically clean. (Even her dreams were often finished off nicely with credits at the end of them.) And cooking was another forte. Over the years, she had learned that her physical attributes alone were not always enough to secure seduction. One of her puddings though, lovingly produced, could always be relied upon to tip the balance in her favour. But most significant, of course, was her systematic research into A.E. Housman's life and work. It was both fascinating and fulfilling, and his definitive biography seemed to be within her grasp.

On all these counts, particularly the last, she harboured a secret pride. And yet within her mind there was a pouch of irrationality. It dictated that no amount of achievement in other areas could make up for the shame of being a failure with men. She was able to make the most perfect *clafoutis aux framboises*, she was able to write about poetry in a style both original and illuminating, but she was also forced to admit to the status of spinster.

'And,' she said, pushing a chilly foot under a cushion on the sofa, 'spinsterhood's a status much abhorred.'

The very thought brought on an eggy sickness in her stomach. Her eyelids pinched her eyeballs. The whites were by now webbed with money-spider veins. Breathless, she clutched

18

the sofa's side wondering where she might find the strength to stand up and make her way, alone, to bed.

Helen was a morning person. She woke the next day feeling brighter, younger. That sadness of the evening before had subsided. Temporarily. It would be back tonight, as inevitable as the darkening sky. For the moment, though, she felt able to function, moderately content.

She swung out of bed. Her Victorian nightdress of crisp cotton had buckled above her stomach, twisted round her waist. She unravelled it so it fell to her ankles. Then she put on a white towelling dressing-gown, and tied its belt in a neat bow.

She went through to her sparkling kitchen, picking up the paper from the mat on the way. As the kettle was working up to its climax, Helen's mind turned to Housman. He was crying out for attention. She wanted to spend the day with him in the British Museum, but her timetable dictated that there were tutorials to be given, a lecture to be prepared.

'Bother,' she said out loud, pouring the boiling water into a waiting mug. 'When am I going to be able to get back to you?'

(It was not unusual for Helen to address the poet. 'People with green fingers talk to plants,' she had more than once reasoned to herself. 'I'm not so odd. I'm sure other biographers talk to their dead subjects.')

'I'm really sorry. You know how it is, Alfred.' (She felt she knew him well enough by now to call him by his Christian name.) 'All this teaching. I love it, of course, as you know. But it does mean I can't be with you as often as I'd like. Forgive me?'

Helen took her coffee to the table, sat down and unfolded the paper. 'I'm going to read this now. Will you excuse me a while? If I can make it, we'll get together for a couple of hours this afternoon. Okay?'

Housman was like a surrogate lover. He was certainly more attentive, reliable, romantic and faithful than Nick Winter. Of course, it was unfortunate that he was both homosexual and dead. 'But, there again, there're drawbacks in all relationships,' Helen said to herself.

The nature of her association with Housman was perhaps a little eccentric. But it seemed to make sense: she loved his

19

work, was intrigued by his life, felt utterly involved with him and completely in control of their affair. It was a spiritual thing they had, and was, on that level, fulfilling.

Nick knew about Housman; if not quite the extent of Helen's friendship with him. She wouldn't care much if he did find out. It would prove that there was more to her life than his brief appearances once every two or three weeks.

Alfred knew about Nick, too. Helen felt sure he didn't mind that much. He understood. But that was not to say he didn't disapprove a bit, put out that she was being taken advantage of. He turned a blind eye, though. She felt he recognised that fleeting physical pleasure, even if only occasionally bestowed, was important to a woman like her. He also saw, surely, that to secure its recurrence, she might well have to be prepared to compromise herself.

Nick was hardly a threat, it had to be said. Her contact with him was rare. Whereas she could communicate with the poet whenever she wished – and indeed did so every day – she had to wait for the bookseller to call *her* to instigate a meeting. There was no calling him. It didn't work like that. Their arrangement, if it was to survive, had to depend on his whim, his convenience – 'otherwise *c'est tout*,' Helen said.

She turned the pages of *The Times*, not entirely concentrating on its contents. She sipped her coffee and sat back in her chair, giving up any pretence of reading the paper. Nick had not rung her for fourteen days. The law of averages dictated that he was due to do so today.

Helen had done her calculations. Over the past eighteen months the gaps between calls had ranged from between seven and twenty-one days. The week-long gap had, admittedly, been a one-off miracle, but having happened once, there did exist the possibility that it could again. She remembered the undiluted shock she had experienced on hearing his voice down the line, against all expectation, on only Day Seven! Such extravagant bliss: he had rung *twice* within the bounds of just one week.

Helen went to the bathroom. Having washed, she put on a Viyella dress of Black Watch tartan, some dark blue wool tights and a pair of character shoes – Louis heels, rounded toes, a thin strap across the top of each foot.

20

When ready, Helen sat at her desk in the sitting-room in order to finish a book review for the *TLS*. She planned to go into college just before lunch.

She arranged her papers in front of her. The book was open at her side for reference. She had already written 600 words. Only 800 were needed, but there was a lot more to say. It was necessary to pare down her thoughts, and to construct the sentences with strict economy. She loved the challenge. Doing this was not unlike piecing together a jigsaw puzzle – fitting bits in, eliminating others which failed to conform. It consumed her attention utterly.

When the telephone rang, an hour or so later, she jumped. Her pen jolted out of her fingers and ejaculated a black splat of ink on to the page. Helen put one hand on her thumping heart, and with the other lifted the receiver.

'Please God, don't let it be my mother,' she gasped, putting it to her ear. 'Hello?'

'Ah, hello darling.' Familiar voice. 'It's Nick. How're you?'

'Goodness,' she said, rather flustered. Writing the review had made her forget that today she could allow herself the luxury of expecting a call from him. After all, it was Day Fourteen. Without answering his question, she automatically asked after him.

'Fine. Good to hear your. . .'

'I was hoping you'd ring,' she interrupted nervously, unintentionally. Why did she say that for God's sake? Why did she let on it had even crossed her mind, the hope? He was *not* meant to gather that. Quick cover up. 'Well, not hoping, um, more thinking, really, more thinking that you might – '

'Oh, I know, I'm sorry, I've been *so* busy,' he said, as if he hadn't taken in the implications of that 'hoping' and that incompetent retraction which followed it. 'Still, I was wondering if by any chance you were free tonight?'

Was that 'by any chance' ironic, by any chance? Of course she was free. She was nearly always bloody free.

'Er, well, actually I was meant to be seeing a friend tonight,' she said carefully, hoping she had put enough emphasis on the 'meant'.

'Oh. Well, never mind. I just thought we might have had a spot of dinner – '

'As it happens, he hasn't rung yet to confirm,' that was good, slipping in the masculine pronoun, 'and as we sort of left it open, I dare say I could skip it and if he rings tell him something came up.'

'Could you?'

'I don't see why not.'

'Well, it'd be wonderful to see you, and I'm sure you could concoct some convincing excuse.'

'Okay then, I'll do that.'

'That's great.'

'Where'd you like me to meet you?'

There was a momentary silence at the other end of the line. Then Nick mentioned something about a cosy TV supper at her flat. She said that that would be all right. She did not even allow herself to court the idea of disappointment: his wish was so predictable. Nick, a man of many faults, was not mean. It wasn't that he was reluctant to *pay* for dinner. Helen was confident that he genuinely liked being in her flat. At least he asked if he could bring anything.

'Wine? A pudding?'

Helen laughed inwardly. His offer to bring the latter was a clever way, in fact, of ensuring that she would make one. 'Don't worry. I'll make a pudding,' she said, having taken up her cue.

'You'll do that? Oh, you are brilliant.'

'You can bring some wine if you like, but there's no need really.' She knew he would.

'Okay. How about some pâté?'

'If you like, if it's not a problem.'

'Absolutely. No problem.'

'Come at eightish?'

'Wonderful. See you then. Look forward to it. Bye.'

'Bye.'

Nick hung up. Helen looked at the earpiece as a man might look at a worm in the apple into which he had just bitten. Then she replaced the receiver.

She stared blankly at the work on her desk. Any notion that she could carry on writing at this point could be dismissed without further ado. Helen was a lady who knew herself well. On the days that Nick called, her mind would – of its own determined accord – start to dance.

First, there was the post-mortem of the conversation to endure. This led to the inevitable conclusion that she had orchestrated it badly. Why did she always feel compelled to lie to him about her plans? Nick must have seen through her incompetent game-playing. After all, how many fictitious men had there been over the months who had either 'left open' their date with her, or had not yet rung to 'confirm' it? Too many, surely. He was bound to have guessed the truth. But if – by dint of amazing gullibility – he did believe her, then he was almost certainly under the impression that her seemingly endless number of male friends constituted an extraordinarily indecisive bunch.

There were, of course, a few occasions when she genuinely was busy (visiting her brother, say, or having supper with a girlfriend). But why, when that was the case, did she not tell him she could not see him? There was an inability within her to find the strength or willpower to resist him – she harboured an irrational fear he might not bother to ring and ask again. This meant she subsequently had to go through the embarrassment and guilt of letting down the person she had originally planned to see. And all for what? The privilege of cooking Nick dinner. The privilege of a chat with him about literature. The privilege of a session of indifferent sex, characterised – on his part – by an air of detachment.

Helen was an elderly woman of forty-two, and she virtually lived for these encounters with Nick. Her arrangement with Housman *was* fulfilling but it had to be said he was not always entirely responsive. Sometimes she craved a bit of come-back. And Nick was, to be sure, nothing if not garrulous. His conversations inspired her, to some extent. He would tell her dazzling anecdotes which made her laugh. And he would also listen to her talk about her boring life and manage never to appear to be bored. He was a glamorous figure: intellectually stimulating, yet intriguingly flamboyant and frivolous too. In bed he made love like a violinist who plays his instrument with perfect technique, but whose music lacks the depth of passion.

Each time he rang Helen, such thoughts would cluster in her mind for a while, distracting her from her work. Then, after about twenty minutes she would begin to panic about practicalities, preparation for the evening date – hair, clothes, food.

She piled her papers neatly on the desk and stood up, looking at her watch. Quarter to eleven. There was just time to fit in an appointment at the hairdresser before lunch with an anxious pupil at college.

Outside, Helen's clicky shoes patted the grey pavement as she trotted round the corner to Pimlico Perms. Inside, she stepped over sprigs of cut hair on the black and white tiled floor. There was a cloying smell of sweet hairspray which rasped the back of the throat.

The receptionist, Carol, welcomed her with a curly beglossed smile. 'Hello there, how are you-u-u?' she asked. Her voice was as sickly to listen to as the hairspray was to inhale. 'Will you be wanting the usual?'

A wash and set. Helen put a green towel round her shoulders and sat at a basin. She leaned back and a young man she had not seen there before came to shampoo her hair. His fingers gently kneaded her head.

'Jojoba, coconut or egg conditioner?' he asked, trying hard to sound as if he cared.

'Don't mind,' Helen replied. 'Whichever smells nicest.'

The man chuckled and rubbed in some jojoba. 'Special occasion, is it?' he asked some minutes later, turning on the spray to start rinsing.

'Yes,' said Helen, nodding slightly. A trickle of water tickled down the back of her neck like an inquisitive insect. She hesitated before going on.

'Actually, my boyfriend's coming to dinner tonight.'

'Lovely. Will you be cooking him something nice? You look like the sort of lady who can put together a delicious meal.'

'As a matter of fact – '

'I thought so. What's your speciality?'

'Puddings. His favourite's *marrons glacés bouleversés à la crème*.'

'Blimey. That sounds sophisticated. If my girlfriend made me *marrons glacés* whatsit, I think I'd ask her to marry me. She's a rotten cook, my girlfriend. Fish fingers. She's good at them. But the other day she put a tin of baked beans in a pan of boiling water. Can you imagine?'

'I don't think my boyfriend'll ask me to marry him, *marrons glacés* pudding or no *marrons glacés* pudding.' There was a wistful hiccup of a laugh as she spoke.

'I'm sure that's not true,' he responded automatically. Then he gently pushed Helen forward and wrapped the towel round her head. Smiling, he led her to a mirror to brush out any tangles

24

and pin the hair up before sitting her under a dryer. He smiled at her yet again, friendly.

'Half an hour or so. All right?', he asked, sliding his comb into the back pocket of his prim jeans. He blinked like a ventriloquist's dummy and had stumpy eyelashes.

Helen, under the hot blaring dome, scowled at him. How come he was so bloody confident that Nick was going to propose? Nick, unlike him, was not the sort of man to be lured into matrimony just because a woman could rustle up a wretched pudding. He was not the sort of man who would, of his own accord, contemplate matrimony much at all.

She glanced at the lady beside her. She had a face like the sole of a school gym shoe. Her hands were being treated to a manicure. Helen felt the woman should have saved herself the expense. The fingers were as knobbled as the gnarled bark of a tree, unlikely to be improved by the application to the nails of Rose Hip Hooray. Just as unlikely, in fact, as the likelihood of Nick proposing to her. Helen sighed, and tapped her foot once, impatiently.

Impatient to get married. At forty-two, she had waited long enough. Indeed, she had waited long enough at thirty-two. But now things were becoming more alarming. The odds were reducing.

There had been proposals, of course. Well, only one serious one, in truth. Percy. Brighton, 1966. She was nineteen. He had taken her there on a weekend trip away from university. On that grey Saturday afternoon he bought her a paper plate of plastic bacon and eggs from a joke shop on the Front. And a stick of pink rock. He was a decent man, Percy. Nervous. Rubbing empurpled feminine hands together and gently kicking a pebble with his foot, he stuttered: 'W-w-will you m-m-marry m-m-me?'

As he did so, the pebble accidentally hit her shin. He was a whirligig of hot embarrassment. Painful though her leg was, Helen was relieved because, while attending to it, he was diverted from the matter of marriage. She clutched the pain, he rubbed it, offering extravagant, agonised apologies. She never did actually have to turn him down. It was simply understood. He brought her a cone with whipped white ice-cream, a flake bar protruding from it. Passing it to her, he said he was sorry. Sorry about the pebble, and though he did not spell it out, she

25

knew he meant he was sorry about the proposal too. She felt sorry for him as well, so kissed him on the cheek, without a word. She would have liked to have said yes. But she could not marry Percy. She did not really love him, like a woman should love a potential husband. Soon a man whom she really loved would ask her. Then she would say yes.

But no man she really loved did ask her. 'Soon' came and went uneventfully. Ten years later, that teenage hope had quelled a little, given birth to a trace of realism. Soon a man whom she did not really love would ask her. Then she would say yes. But no man – even one she did not really love – did ask her. 'Soon' again passed by without incident.

And by now the hope had begun to wend its way on the course towards extinction. No man would ask her, neither one she really loved, nor one she did not love at all: neither sooner nor later.

There was a solution, of course. It had occurred to her before. The two men in her life were hardly going to do the business, so why shouldn't she? Whoever said a woman couldn't do the proposing? Stuff convention.

Helen had been quite close to plucking up the courage to ask men to marry her a couple of times in the recent past. She remembered the night she had nearly asked Julian.

Julian worked in television. He wore brown corduroy trousers and grey squashy shoes. He used to ring her and say, 'Hi, Jules here. Can I buy you a drink?' A lot of his telly friends also talked about 'buying' you a drink, never 'Can I take you out' for a drink, or 'Would you like to join me' for one? The indirect reference to monetary transaction was supposed to remind you they were doing you a favour.

Helen had an affair with Julian, Nick's predecessor, for two years. He used to invite her to his flat in Islington. They always went round the corner so he could buy her a drink in the pub; this felt like the purchase of a licence for the next part of the evening. He would then dwindle into bed and do to her what he felt she would be expecting after he had demonstrated such keen generosity at the bar. He was not a great one for sex, Julian. He went through the whole wearisome business for reasons of conscience and to gain a sense of virtue. It was as if he had set himself a task, one to be endured a certain number of times a month. He regarded it a bit as an unfit man might regard doing a self-imposed number of press-ups.

One evening, she had decided to get him drunk, so she could propose. He would have been such an unsuitable husband, she knew that at the time. But at least if she married him she could allow herself to relax in pubs in the certain knowledge that she would always be bought a drink.

First, she steered the conversation, rather skilfully she thought, towards the terrain of relationships, and encouraged him to drink four pints of beer and three vodkas. She had been on the point of suggesting, very mildly, that marriage might be the thing, using every subtle device of language known to her. She carefully planned the phrasing so as not to set herself up for humiliation: use of the passive tense and not an incriminating pronoun to be heard. Alas, as her brilliantly constructed question was about to be spoken, in a voice so controlled it had a right to sound conceited, Julian had excused himself and gone to the gents to be sick. And so the right moment passed. Helen did not try again.

She pushed up the hood of the drying dome and went to have her hair brushed out. She then paid and stepped out of the hairdresser's to catch the tube to college.

The train was stuffy and neon-lit. Helen stared at a fellow passenger. He had a puckered face like a dock leaf. There was an ad above him for some type of insurance. 'Are you looking at the next person in your life?' it asked in bold print.

Helen hoped not. It was then that she made up her mind. She would go to the market in Soho and buy some vegetables for ratatouille, and a selection of cheeses to follow her chestnut pudding. She would pick up everything else she needed at the Marks & Spencer food hall. Then she would go home, cook, have a bath with stephanotis oil, change, pour a large vodka, let the man in, feed him, and ask him to marry her.

It was a fine plan. Why the hell hadn't she thought of it before?

Nick Winter lay in bed contemplating what he was going to have for breakfast. Lying on his back, he stared up at the grubby cornice above him. What a relief, he thought, that he hadn't chosen to be one of those people who say with pride, 'I never eat breakfast.' Pure silliness to miss out on that innocent pleasure for the sake of fashion.

27

Cornflakes. Scrambled eggs on toast. Coffee. Freshly squeezed orange juice. He would not stint. He wasn't a greedy man, particularly, was he? Anyway, he certainly had no desire to comply with the trendy notions of others in this matter.

It was early. Eightish. Nick had pipped his alarm clock to the post by a good five minutes. This gave him almost as much pleasure as the thought of breakfast. He had a volatile relationship with his matt-black Scotcade, resenting its presumptuous habit of waking him with such a cheeky lack of tact: ghastly piercing bleeps with little sense of timing. That's not to say they didn't sound at the hour he had arranged for them to do so, but they had no idea when to stop. There were so many of the buggers − twenty-five to be precise.

'All right, all right. I'm awake, okay? *Shut up.*'

Breakfast lured. Quite often, before stepping on to the floorboards, he'd rub his foot down Georgia's calf. It was a useful contrast of sensations: the cold roughness of the floor helped him appreciate the warm silkiness of his girlfriend. He was afraid he was beginning to take her for granted and although the daily foot ritual was simple it seemed to do the business.

This morning, though, she was away. Had been for two days. Pity: he'd have to make his own breakfast. Still, that was another sure way of making him appreciate her in her absence.

Nick groaned out of bed. He knocked last night's glass of water over his book. The lukewarm liquid felt slimy between his toes.

'Blast,' he said, swiping up the glass. 'Blast you.'

He stumbled across the floor. It was strewn, willy-nilly, with clothes, shoes, books, all dusty. Nick liked it that way.

It was a large, square room with three big windows. They were covered by simple, thin cotton curtains, which hung precariously. On their cracking sills, more books were heaped. A forlorn, empty whisky bottle resided amongst them, along with an ashtray, the contents of which had thrown up over its edges.

There was a mantelpiece in the wall by the door. On it were more books and a few postcards; a sepia photograph, circa 1920, of a voluptuous nude; Van Gogh's *The Postman*; a picture of a kitsch 1950s' lady with scarlet lips, a pointy bust, yellow strappy shoes, a vulgar fur muff and a come-hither expression. There were a couple of stiff invitations, too, both

28

way out of date. The fireplace itself was decorated with pretty Victorian tiles of cream and brown, and had a black grate filled with tissue-paper flowers of faded pinks and yellows.

Beside it stood a crippled armchair. Its wrinkled cover hung limply and did little to conceal its concave seat. A wine glass with maroon dregs was leaning on its arm and appeared to be staring down, rather nervously, at the chair's improvised leg (more books).

Opposite was the old brass and iron bed, rickety too, but comfortable-looking. The twisted soft sheets and the squashed pillows proclaimed its irresistible comfort. On the bedside table was a large pile of letters, scraps of paper with scribbled notes, past copies of the *Spectator*, rather crumpled, and issues of *Private Eye*, yellowing with age. Occasionally, Georgia would mildly suggest he should throw them out. But Nick liked such clutter and insisted on keeping them. There had been arguments.

'You're making this room like a rubbish tip,' she had said.

'I need this stuff. It adds to the quality of my life.'

'How can you be so pompous? And so sentimental about a few old newspapers?'

'If you're too unimaginative to understand then I'm not going to attempt to explain.'

This remark had prompted extreme annoyance, he remembered. She had left the room with heavy, angry steps and gone 'Grrr!' like a character in *Beano*. Once alone, he wondered why he had not let her throw out what were, after all, just a few old newspapers. Principle, he supposed. What sort, he could not be certain. Later, he admitted to himself that it was a faintly pointless sort of principle. Originally, it might have been intended to demonstrate his authority. Not very successfully as it turned out. Georgia just thought he was sentimental about a few old newspapers – authority didn't come into it. He'd have to think again.

Evidence that a telephone lurked somewhere beneath this controversial pile was in the presence of its red curly wire. This was wrapped round a dented tin of chocolate Bath Olivers from which sprouted a black plastic tulip and an orange pencil which had been much chewed upon.

Nick swiped a pair of trousers from one of the round brass knobs at the end of the bed. He pulled on two socks, which were by no means a pair. From a pile of laundry on the

29

floor by the windows, he retrieved a white shirt which needed an iron. Nick ignored the need and put it on as it was. Once dressed, he clomped downstairs to the kitchen.

As usual, he bumped his head on the bunch of onions dangling from the ceiling. His curses caused the marmalade cat to shoot under the table from its warm nest beside the peat-brown Aga. Nick took the cornflakes from the old pine dresser, and a thick mug painted with the word 'Tea'.

'Coffee, actually,' he said to it as he placed it and the cereal packet on the table. He went to the fridge and pulled out a carton of milk. He sniffed it: a precaution which through sour experience had become habit. No good. He put it back into the fridge, and went to the front door to collect a new bottle, a copy of the *Independent*, and the post.

After he had eaten, Nick put his dirty bowl and spoon on the draining board along with last night's washing-up, still to be done. Because there was no room for it by the sink, he left the rest of his breakfast paraphernalia on the table. Then he went upstairs to find his shoes. Nowhere to be seen. So he looked in the hall. It was dark with brown William Morris wallpaper. Nick switched on the light – a single bulb hanging from the ceiling rose at the end of a long wire. He had a feeling the shoes might be near the mahogany dresser – either on top of it by its speckled, yellowing mirror (under more books and papers) or below it in amongst the torn cardboard box and mud-encrusted gumboots.

The brogues were not on top. So he removed the bike leaning against the dresser and searched through the muddle below till he found them.

'It's all your fault I'm so bloody late,' he told them.

He had a way of addressing inanimate objects, always rather resentfully. Finally, he was ready to make his way to work. He opened the door, clambered on to his bicycle and began riding down the tree-lined Hammersmith street towards Brook Green. It was a glaring morning but the cold sun did nothing to detract from the redbrick gloom of the Victorian architecture. This depressed Nick. He thought longingly of Helen's flat in a bright house in Pimlico. He suddenly had a thought – why not go there that evening, pay her a visit while Georgia was away? That *was* a good plan, very convenient. She would make him a nice pudding, talk pleasantly about poetry and allow him, after *Question Time*, to make love to her.

That idea firmly established, he continued to make his way to the West End, but now in a happier frame of mind.

When he arrived at the shop, Molly had already opened up and was busying herself with paperwork at the desk. He shuffled in with a manic air.

'Hello, hello, hello,' he said, looking about as if his eyes were following a whizzy fly. 'Where's the telephone? Must make a call. Everything all right?'

Molly found it under a dog-eared copy of *Books in Print*. She passed it to him without a word. Nick sat down and dialled a number. While waiting for it to answer, he repeated the question.

'Fine. Sold out of the William Trevor, though.'

Nick nodded, and responded to the telephone. 'Ah, hello, darling . . . It's Nick. How're you? . . . Fine. Good to hear your . . . Oh, I know, I'm sorry, I've been *so* busy. Still, I was wondering if by any chance you were free tonight? . . . Oh. Well, never mind. I just thought we might have had a spot of dinner . . . Could you? . . . Well, it'd be wonderful to see you, and I'm sure you could concoct some convincing excuse . . . That's great . . . Well, I was actually thinking rather in terms of *chez* you, cosy telly supper at home and all that. We *could* go out, I suppose . . . Well, if you didn't mind I'd love to do that. Can I bring anything? Wine? A pudding? . . . You'll do that? Oh, you are brilliant . . . Okay. How about some pâté? Absolutely. No problem . . . Wonderful. See you then. Look forward to it. Bye.'

When he put down the receiver, Nick noticed Molly had a disapproving look.

'Something wrong?'

'You're incorrigible. Whoever it was, I pity her. Outrageous.'

'Old friend. Nothing, you know – '

'Rubbish. It was patently obvious what you were about, Georgia away and all that. I don't know how you do it.'

'Wouldn't you?'

'If I had the chance! Would that I had your choice. Men are in short supply.'

'So it's not on moral grounds, you disapprove – more envy?'

31

'A bit of both, really. Even if I did have the chance I know I'd be racked with guilt and my bloody morals'd haunt me.'

'You're too finickity, that's your problem, Mol. Maybe you should be less discriminating.'

'What, lower standards just to satisfy lust?'

'You should read *Hotel du Lac*, Mol,' Nick said, not unkindly. 'It doesn't pay to be too good, you know.'

'It's not really a question of being good exactly. I just envy you your opportunity and complete lack of shame.'

'Not *complete* lack of shame. By the way, that woman's coming in this morning for twenty-three copies of *The Old Devils*. People are *odd*. What can she be wanting them all for?'

'Loved it so much, apparently, wanted to give it to all her friends.'

'How very unimaginative to give them all the same book. Did it come in?'

'Yesterday, plus the single copy for herself of *The Loved One*.'

After Molly had mentioned that title, Nick found himself, for the rest of the day, preoccupied with the subject of death. Any idea of doing the pro-forma invoices was set aside. It amused him that a customer called De'Ath happened to walk into the shop at the very moment when that particular topic was so enthralling him. The man was wearing a big coat and Molly seemed to blush in conversation with him. Such a perfect opportunity to tease her. Irresistible.

Nick did so, but she didn't take it very well. He felt a little guilty about embarrassing her in front of the man, but he didn't apologise. He was simply trying to promote the chemistry that was so evident between them, he said. Molly remained unconvinced.

Helen, Nick thought, would find the whole episode funny. Tonight he would make it into an amusing anecdote for her: there he was thinking about death very hard, there was his assistant thinking about literature very hard; she simply wasn't interested in what was so fascinating him until a man walked in and she became positively enchanted by the subject of De'Ath.

He would tell the story to Helen over dinner. He might even wait till pudding, so he could anticipate her laughter a while. That sound: haunting, sexy. It might possibly prompt him to contemplate skipping *Question Time*. He felt he had an enjoyable evening ahead. This put him in a good mood, happy enough, even, to spend the rest of the afternoon devoted to the pro-forma invoices.

Nick turned up at Helen's flat at past nine o'clock. The dinner was not ruined. She knew his habits well and had allowed for what she construed to be an affected disregard for punctuality.

By the time the doorbell rang, Helen had arranged herself on the sofa with a book. She thought this admirably casual. She was unkeen to be caught at the stove, trying too hard.

Nick appeared at the door, looking calm, handsome. Helen noticed with some amusement that he was wearing odd socks. Very characteristic, she thought.

He was obviously pleased to see her and kissed her enthusiastically before handing her a bottle of champagne and a jar of *foie gras*.

'You've gone completely over the top,' she told him. 'Quite unnecessary, such generosity.'

Nick was on the point of saying, jokily, that it helped him assuage his guilt somewhat as regards his treatment of her. But he checked himself, realising it was a remark that might prove too harsh a test for her sense of humour.

'Absolutely not,' he said instead. 'I should be taking you out to dinner. I just so love coming here,' he added, sitting down on the sofa. She gave him some champagne. Their hands touched on the stem of the glass. Nick thought he felt her trembling, though barely perceptibly. Under her shirt her nipples were poised, as if about to puncture the black silk.

Helen was nervous. She never felt entirely relaxed in Nick's presence, but tonight she was even less so. Before the evening was over she had to perform a difficult task. She could not squirm out of it now because, after all, she had said to herself she was going to do it and she could not disappoint her intentions.

It took some moments before conversation began to gather momentum. It was always tricky at first to set it on its way.

'Funny,' Nick said. 'Before I forget to tell you, guess what? The other day some girl came into the shop and asked for a good biography of Housman. I told her that no such thing existed quite yet, but that a perfectly excellent one was on the point of existing; she'd just have to wait, and it'd be worth it.'

'Honestly – ' Helen began, flattered.

'No, I meant it. She asked when it was available. That flummoxed me a bit. I told her not entirely soon but jolly nearly soon. What should I have said? How's it going?'

'Progressing, but hardly apace.'

'Ah. So, not so soon?'

'No. I have other things, you know. I'm very busy this term. An unusual number of pupils. Research can't be a priority.'

'So frustrating. I think I should go mad. Go to work to be able to afford to write. So you have the money to write, okay, but no time. Vicious circle.'

'Exactly.'

'So, is A.E.H. feeling neglected?'

Nick always referred to Housman as if he were still alive. It pleased Helen that someone else joined in her secret fantasy, even if it was unwittingly – for Nick did not know quite the extent of her relationship with the poet.

'A touch, I fear,' she replied, moving to fetch a bottle of wine. 'Would you like to have dinner?'

'Lovely. I'm starving.'

Nick went to sit at the table. As they ate, they continued to talk about work for a while, then Nick began to gossip in his irresistible way.

'Jane got a record advance for her latest novel. Makes you sick. We're talking hundreds of thousands. I do love her, but she's as mean as hell. The more she makes, the meaner she becomes. Recycles Christmas wrapping paper, that sort of thing. Anyway, I thought I'd drop a postcard to congratulate her on the sum, as it were. Hadn't been in touch for a while. And, guess what? I get a letter back saying, "Thanks for the pc. It's so nice all my friends are rallying round in this time of crisis." It has to be said, I laughed. She can be quite sharp, Jane. God, I pity that flimsy husband of hers. Just had his forty-third collection of poems rejected by Faber. You'd think by now he'd have got the hint, and gone into something more suitable like, I don't know, crocheting tea-cosies or something, wouldn't you?'

'Seriously, forty-three collections?' Helen asked, giggling.

'Well, two actually, but you know what I mean. What's more, you know who was caught with one of his editorial assistants up against the pile of unsolicited manuscripts in the post room at Bloomsbury Square?'

'F– ,' Helen said, nodding.

'Exactly. Stroking her nipples with a feather duster apparently.' Nick poured himself some more wine. 'You would've thought by now – . But no. They won't get rid of him either. Best editor in London and got a way with authors like he's got away with editorial assistants all these years!'

'How does he do it? Those gob-stopper eyes. And that vast nose like a baby's heel. I can't imagine how anybody finds him attractive.'

'The power and the intellect. Anyway, John told me he'll be dead in a year. Rumour proclaims that during the last bout in the post room he had a heart attack *in flagrante*. Gob-stopper eyes or not, you have to feel sorry for him.'

Helen grimaced and cleared the plates. Nick opened the second bottle of wine.

'On the matter of death, I must tell you about Molly.'

'Oh yes?' said Helen sitting down again. Her companion proceeded with the anecdote he had planned to relate over pudding. And just as he had supposed, Helen laughed that peculiar laugh of hers. Listening to it stirred desire within him, but he would hold off till after the pudding. In fact the very process would act as a sort of foreplay.

Helen did like his story. She had not met Molly but had heard Nick talk about her with obvious admiration. She wondered how the girl would fare with Mr De'Ath and vaguely hoped things might work out. But in the back of her mind, the imminent proposal was whining impatiently.

Carefully, she poured Nick more wine. He had by now drunk half a bottle of champagne, and nearly a whole bottle of Burgundy, so he was quite relaxed.

'That was delicious,' he told her, finishing the main course. 'Can I guess what's for pudding?'

'I expect so.'

'Oh, my God, you are wonderful. I haven't done much to deserve this.'

'True,' she said automatically, regretting it a second later. But Nick did not seem to notice.

'Is it ready yet?'

'Not quite.'

'Can I have a quick cigarette?' He pulled a packet from a faded pocket.

'Course.'

Helen lit herself one as well. This had to be the moment to start broaching the subject of marriage. But how? She quickly swigged at her drink, and puffed her cigarette with a sense of purpose. She noticed various details in the room, each so familiar – the quilted oven glove printed with the cartoon face of a laughing chef; the yellow china candlestick with the beeswax candle; the picture by Henry Lamb of the cosy sheep. In a moment of panic, fear, nerves, they all somehow looked alien, unreal, peculiarly disapproving. The chef's laugh no longer looked jolly, but hostile instead.

Helen sighed. 'I'll give it another couple of minutes in the oven,' she said.

He nodded, quite content. She watched his chin. It had a barely perceptible dimple which lent his face a look of arrogance somehow. She had it in for dimples, a bit like she had it in for the name Nick. The very word itself seemed haughty, disdainful. It was an irrational dislike. But if Nick was to humiliate her, her resentment might well focus on his arrogant dimple and his haughty name.

'How's Georgia?' she asked all of a sudden, ruffling the taboo. It was an unspoken agreement: they never discussed his girlfriend.

'Well, I think,' he answered politely, filling his glass again. 'Why?'

'Does she know about me yet?'

'Helen – ' he faltered. 'I don't know. I doubt it, but sometimes I think she might suspect.'

'Would she care?' This was dangerous ground, but adrenalin made her feel brave.

'Yes. Yes, she would. I think she'd care very much.' Nick was drunk. He sounded a little puzzled by the unexpected interrogation, even a bit defensive.

'Thinking about marrying her?'

'Marry Georgia? Whatever for?'

'Don't you want to get married?'

'To her, or in general?'

'In general,' Helen replied firmly.

'I suppose I could see a way to it. Don't think about it much.'

'Don't have to, really, do you? I mean, you've got it quite well sorted out, your life, haven't you? There's Georgia,

36

always there. Me – whenever it crosses your mind to see me – always here.'

'It's not quite like that. Anyway, we've discussed all this. I'm very fond of you both, and things are just the way they are. You don't have to put up with it. You know that.'

'Oh yes. I know all that.'

'Must we go into it, ruin the evening?'

'Of course not.' Helen glanced down at her knees. 'I just had it in mind to ask you something,' she ventured after a moment, paving the way. Nick looked at her with an expression of curiosity and dread. The former triumphed, though, and he told her to go ahead.

'It requires a short preamble.'

He nodded as if to tell her to get on with it.

'I was just wondering if it ever occurred to you to change things slightly, alter your circumstances a bit?'

'How do you mean?'

'Well, you've been sort of coasting, really, for quite a while now. Your life's never shaken by an up or a down, you just seem to cruise. There's the cosy existence in the bookshop, the secure womb of Luxembourg Gardens with Georgia thrown in. There's the social circle, too, cliquey enough to be comfortable but just adventurous enough to enjoy stimulation from outside so as not to be accused of being self-satisfied.'

'Are you getting at me?'

'No. I just wonder, as an observer, if it can be fulfilling – such steadiness.'

'You're not just an observer, though, are you? You're part of my so-called "steadiness".'

'I have a spear-bearing role, I suppose, a shadowy figure in the wings. Without wishing to push the director, I was wondering if there would be a chance of a speaking part, maybe even a dialogue with the hero, if I stuck it out a while longer? Or am I, as a spear-bearer, wasting my time?'

'What a peculiar notion you have of both my life and your part in it. Such steadiness, as you call it, happens to suit me. I think I'm content, really, as I am. Why should I need these ups and downs which you seem to think so important? I'd have thought it rather an achievement to have reached a sort of contented equilibrium.'

37

'But isn't that denying yourself the point? Don't you crave the stimulation of emotional event?'

'I'd be worn out by pushing myself through a mental obstacle course all the time.'

'But what pleasure can there be in quelling reaction – be it positive or negative?'

'I don't always. You know that, Helen. I'm not quite that resilient. I don't try to be.'

Helen suddenly decided to test him. 'How would you react to a proposal of marriage, for example?'

'Violently.'

'What sort of violently?'

'Well, I don't mean physically.'

'Violently with horror then, or pleasure?'

Nick looked at Helen and frowned. He wondered what on earth she was on about. It was such a funny question: no woman was ever likely to ask him to marry her. Women do not ask men. It doesn't work like that.

'Will you marry me?' she asked quietly.

'What?' He took a gulp of wine. His monosyllabic answer was laden with incredulity.

'I'm serious. Will you marry me?'

Nick flopped forward and snorted with shock. Mustering composure, he stared at Helen, embarrassed, amazed.

She was sitting upright in the chair opposite him. Even in the candlelight, he could detect that her mascara was blue. Suddenly the 'laide' aspect of her 'jolie laide' face appeared to be triumphing over the 'jolie'. She did not look old, exactly, but she was definitely pushing on. Nick blinked. Her stiff hair which until now he had not noticed, seemed to curl in the shape of an 'S' on either side of her cheeks. 'S' for spinster, he thought. She almost smelt of menopausal desperation.

Marry her? The notion had been so far from his own mind that for her to have even conceived the thought must mean she had the imagination of a science-fiction writer. Any 'steadiness' that she had chosen to interpret as an inherent characteristic of his existence could at this moment be completely dismissed. 'My God,' he thought, 'how could I possibly not react to an event such as this?'

His eyes continued to open wider, it seemed, as he stared at her. And all the while she sat totally still, the epitome of

38

composure. Could it be true that she was actually waiting for an answer? How could she suppose he might even contemplate the possibility of taking up the offer for one second?

'So?' she said, expectant.

Christ, he thought, the woman expects me to speak. He paused. How had Helen managed to get it so wrong? Him so wrong? Just a few moments before, she had been accusing him of too often quelling reaction. Well, she had certainly managed in just four short words to provoke in him one so extreme as to stagger him into a state of complete inner turmoil.

Finally, he forced himself to say something. 'Helen, I think you must have misunderstood,' he said. 'It's not quite like that. We had a, well, you know, more – casual thing, sort of, more – no?'

She did not answer, so he had to go on.

'I mean, we've had a jolly nice time, you and I, but . . . well . . . the nature of the arrangement, I'd have thought, would've precluded, really, any idea, really, of a long-term, committed thing.'

She nodded, urging him to say more. Thus he faltered on.

'Blimey, I'm really fond of you. No denying that. Goodness, wouldn't deny that for one minute. No, not one minute. Not a single one at that. Um, – ' He stopped. She nodded again. She wanted more? This was a hard test for his stamina. 'Over the months,' he stammered on, 'we've really enjoyed ourselves.' He stopped. How not to sound corny? This was a throbbing, bloody nightmare. 'You've taught me a lot. God knows, how would I have known so much as I do now about Housman, for instance? Ha!' A little laugh. Try and alleviate the burden of the atmosphere a bit. Why not?

'Um, and your puddings. Those – ' He shook his head, sighed and glanced upwards to make his point. 'I mean, no one can produce a *marrons glacés à la crème* like you. I mean, no one.' Well remembered. But was he sounding patronising? It was too awful if he did because he really meant what he said, even if he was hating having to say it.

'What more can I say? You've been very good to me, I haven't been very good to you. But it was our arrangement and I thought it suited us both. I had no idea – '

Helen still said nothing.

'Foolish. I've been very blind. A misunderstanding. I'm very flattered, but I think maybe I'm going to have to say . . . Helen, I'm sorry, I appreciate . . . My fault entirely. Well.'

'Housman and puddings?' she said suddenly.

It confused him. 'Sorry?'

'Housman and puddings? That all?'

'How d'you mean?'

Helen shrugged. 'Is that all? I mean, is that all you can say for an eighteen-month association?'

'Course not. I mention those as examples, merely. Two of the more tangible characteristics of it. I was always very fond of you. We had a similar sense of humour. I don't know. Other things too. Enjoyed each other's company.'

She touched her hair momentarily. The 'S' curl remained intact.

'Had? Enjoyed?'

'Well. I think so, don't you?'

'Oh. Indeed. Definitely. Lots of enjoyment.'

'Actually, I meant – ' he began.

'Oh yes?' Such politeness.

'Well, that we *did*?'

'The sense of humour's parted then? And we've stopped enjoying each other's company?'

For an intelligent woman, he thought, she must see what he was saying. Or perhaps she was purposefully making sure he would have to go through with spelling out an explanation? He had better oblige.

'No, not that. That can't change within a matter of moments.'

'No, right.'

'What I meant is, perhaps it's time we went our separate – '

'I see. We *did* enjoy each other's company. Indeed, we still would, but we won't because we won't be seeing each other any more to be able to enjoy it?'

'That sort of thing, yes, really.'

'Absolutely.'

Nick stood up and produced a shredded paper napkin from his hand. He put it on the table. Helen remained seated.

'Going? No pudding? No *marrons glacés bouleversés à la crème*?'

'I don't think so, thanks, no.' He envisaged his stomach churning with a glutinous mass of meringue, sugar, puréed chestnut – and bile. He retched at the very thought, leaned

40

over quickly to kiss Helen on the cheek and left without another word.

Alone, she sat still for a while longer. Then she stood and went to the oven. Opening it, a blast of sweet-smelling heat belted her in the face. It was strangely comforting and she smiled before looking inside. She fanned her face once with a sweep of her hand, and then took a peep.

Within was a mass of collapsed, blackened squashiness. It was hard to believe it had once been a fluffy white puff of sugary cream ingredients.

The pudding was a crestfallen failure, her first. The oven-glove chef seemed to sneer at it as Helen lifted out the bowl.

She decided, then, never to make *marrons glacés bouleversés à la crème* again.

'Last night I had two bottles of wine and a proposal of marriage. Today I feel terrible,' said Nick as he bumbled into the shop, late. 'And I suspect of the two the latter's more to blame.' He nodded to confirm his theory. 'I mean, do I *look* like the sort of unconventional man who craves proposals from women?'

Molly gave a smiling glance at his shiny black brogues.

'Am I *likely* to resent having to bend on one knee? Can you imagine *me* crawling naked over broken glass to secure for women the right to utter the words "Will you marry me?" Surely I'm not the type whose motto is "Let every year be a leap year"? Am I, Mol? So what is it about me which invites such trials?'

Molly was relieved that this morning's obsession was less morbid than that of the day before.

'I take it you turned her down?' she asked, patient.

'Turned her down? I did more than simply turn her down. After all, I'd only known the woman for two years. I turned her out, out of my life. There's no greater emotional or sexual dampener than mention of marriage.'

'Poor Georgia,' said Molly with pity, as she straightened some books on a shelf.

'It wasn't Georgia,' Nick corrected her. 'It was someone else.'

'Someone else? But you live with Georgia.'

'Yeah, but this was Helen,' he said grimly.

'Helen?'

'She's a good friend, Helen. Very sharp. Has a thing about Housman. Wears blue mascara. I'll miss her puddings, of course.

But you can't marry a woman just for her puddings, can you? Not fair. Besides, I'm not entirely sure I could manage to fancy her again. Not since that fiasco. It's really given me a turn.'

As he spoke, he had a glazed, fixed look. Molly could see it was not directed at her but at an indifferent spot, a chair-leg or the newspaper on the floor beside it, perhaps. And his words were not particularly aimed at a listener. She just happened to be there to hear his meandering thoughts which had stumbled upon a voice.

'It's a curious business. These modern women with all their intelligent aspirations allowing their fear of loneliness to engulf them. They brave humiliation with such courage. And what reaction do they get? Unsympathetic contempt. Unspeakable chauvinism. I recognise that. But far from this very recognition being half-way to solving the problem, it makes me all the more despicable for my reluctance to do anything about it.'

Nick tugged at his scruffy hair uneasily, as if trying to get rid of a tangle. He stood up and wandered about the shop distractedly. He reminded Molly, who was sitting calmly, of a desperate actor who had forgotten his stage directions.

'Her passion for Housman was very infectious,' he went on. 'I never admired him myself, but I admired that passion in Helen. Actually, it was partly that which prompted my passion for her in the first place. Yet now, in the light of this proposal, Housman is to me even more mediocre a poet than I'd originally supposed. And only the day before yesterday, the mere anticipation of one of her puddings would cause the stomach to dance. Now the very thought of *marrons glacés bouleversés à la crème* sickens my entire being. Such unforgivable intolerance.'

'You never told me about Helen,' Molly said flatly.

'I know. And you, the best confidante in the world. Forgive me. It wasn't because I doubted your discretion. I treated her badly. Fact was, I feared your disapprobation.' He paused. 'Nobody knew about Helen.'

'It's not as if you treat Georgia impeccably. Or Liz. I know about them.'

'Everyone knows about Georgia by dint of the fact we share a roof. It means, I suppose, we're an "issue", officially.'

'And have been for some years.' Molly prodded the newspaper on her knee with a pencil.

'Some years, yes.'

'So where does Helen come into the colourful kaleidoscope of your girlfriends?', she asked, starting to doodle. Triangles and circles.

'All of them play an important role in my life. Helen knew about poetry.'

'And puddings.'

'Well, yes, puddings too.'

'Helen the cooking intellectual, Georgia the caring administrator, Liz the sexually unchallenged being. They'd make a very good wife.'

'Please, Mol, spare me the disapproval. The proposal's made me fragile, so unsettled. Insecure.'

'You insecure? What about the hapless Helen?' Molly did not look up from her doodles as she spoke.

'You're the toughest sort of confidante. Your compassion's always reserved for the other party,' he said weakly.

'Maybe. But my affection's always reserved for you,' she reminded him fondly. 'Miraculously,' she added, suddenly slapping the paper on to the table.

'I don't deserve it.'

'You don't deserve the devotion of those three women. Thank God I'm not in love with you. Then my affection would be in constant combat with distrust. It'd be so wearing.'

Molly peered out of the window. The sky had a resentful air. Hanging from it was yellow-grey light, the colour of a bruise.

'Not exactly a superfluity of customers today,' she said gloomily. 'Beaten by the cold.'

'It's comforting to know one has the ability to inspire affection,' Nick said, ignoring her observation. 'Gives one a sense of purpose. I'm less sure about the distrust though. That's rather galling. The sort of person who's untrustworthy can safely throw any desire for integrity right out of the window. No hope for me thereof.'

'How about settling up your infidelities?'

'But I love them all.'

'Well, one's down. Only one to go,' Molly observed patiently.

'But be it Georgia or Liz?'

'Weigh up the priorities. Cosy, loving familiarity or *la grande passion sexuelle*?'

'Impossible!'

'Fine. You'll just never achieve the integrity. You must embrace that failure, anticipate the consequences.'

43

Nick was silent for some moments. Molly stood up and began to arrange some books on one of the shelves.

'I could marry one, I suppose,' he said at length. 'The other could be my mistress. That'd be a more acceptable arrangement than having two girlfriends.'

Nick's words forced Molly to stop a moment and clutch a book to her bosom to support her shock.

'Marriage? You, who'd emigrate to avoid it?'

'Maybe I'll just have to dwindle into it and bear it.'

'There!' she said, laughing. 'You have it. You have integrity.'

Nick frowned, puzzled. He anticipated sarcasm. 'Oh yes?'

'The integrity of stupendous self-sacrifice.'

He sighed at her mockery, then shrugged. '*Que faire?* Of course, it'd be different if I could consider you as my wife.'

'Such gratuitous flirting doesn't become you at eleven o'clock in the morning. It's distasteful before lunch.'

'Like cigarettes before twelve?'

She smiled.

'Your life is littered with limitations, Mol. Mars Bars on Mondays, flirting on Fridays, sex on Sundays. How do you remember all these rules?'

'Don't be absurd.'

Molly felt ruffled by the teasing. His words had a trace of truth. She was, after all, a creature of habit, if not quite as extreme as he suggested. It was one of her own characteristics that she least admired.

'Any luck with that book for the Coat?' he asked all of a sudden, cunningly catching her at a vulnerable moment.

She bit her lip and tightened the book to her bosom. With a toss of the head that made her hair jump over her shoulder, she told him she hadn't had a chance, yet, to look.

'Very casual,' he declared. 'I should give it a go soon. He looked like the sort of man likely to be turned on by efficiency in a girl.'

'Nick, shut up, I didn't fancy him.'

'If that's true, then my name's Susan. Don't fight it, darling. I bet you've already tried out the signature in an exercise book – Molly De'Ath.' Saying this, he wrote the words in the air with grand gestures.

She chuckled wearily. 'Deeply troubled by last night's traumatic proposal, yet you still have the energy to tease.'

'Admit it,' he urged, clapping his hands.

44

'Okay, okay. He wasn't entirely unattractive, no. You don't miss a trick, do you?'

'Passion in our book-bound, dusty midst. What extravagant fun to be had!'

'Ominous,' Molly said, faintly anxious.

'No, no. I promise not to cause any mischief – '

'What a relief – '

' – but that's not to say I won't keep an eye on progress.'

'There won't be any progress.'

Their first customer stepped inside. Both Nick and Molly jumped at the sound of the bell. Every morning it was the same. Without fail the first customer managed to catch them unawares. And every morning Nick would say, 'God, that gave me a shock,' to which Molly would answer, 'Me too'. It was as if the bell had a childlike sense of humour, loving daily to repeat the same game, because the predictable reaction of the grown-ups was so irresistibly comic.

The woman who had this morning prompted the bell to play its practical joke was middle-aged. From under a headscarf, buttercup-bleached curls protruded, neatly surrounding her oval face. It reminded Molly of those mirrors often found in the Ladies at cheap hotels, the ones with frames that have tried too hard and overdone the gilt. Likewise the customer had been over-conscientious with her dye bottle.

'Have you got the latest Jane Austen?' she asked, having browsed for some time by the history section.

Nick lit a cigarette. 'Ah,' he said, standing up and walking over to the lady. 'And which one would that be?' he asked tactfully.

'Something Park,' she barked.

'*Mansfield Park*?'

'That's the one. Saw it on the telly.'

Nick reached up to pick out a copy and handed it to her. She smiled. Orange lips. They matched the colour of the book's spine.

'Is it a good read?' she enquired, flipping the pages.

'Excellent,' Nick assured her. 'But it's not all that new.'

'Oh? Has she produced another since?'

'She wrote six novels in all.'

'All romantic like What's-it Park? Period pieces?'

Nick nodded.

'Got 'em all, have you?'

He checked the shelf and passed them down to the woman one by one.

'In that case, I think I'll take the lot,' she said. 'I love a good historical romance.'

A few moments later, the lady left the shop with a bundle under her arm. She was a happy customer. Nick and Molly smiled at one another.

'What do you reckon about this book, then, for the Coat?' asked Molly. 'Sackville Street a good bet?'

'Yes. I should wander down this afternoon, have a look. If not, I'll call David for you. He's bound to have a copy. Whatever way, I promise I'll let it be you who rings the man to tell him it's in.'

Molly raised her eyebrows. 'Perhaps you should organise your own arrangements with the same attention to detail as you do mine,' she said.

'Not a generous-spirited remark. You don't do much to aid and abet your own "arrangements" yourself. Need a bit of encouragement from me.'

'There're such things as feminine wiles – '

'Awful term – '

'Awful term, yes, but useful. They're the tricks of the game, camouflaged so expertly to the rest of the world that, if successful, they are simply seen as good fortune or happy coincidence.'

'The wily female mind, I know, is admirably imaginative,' Nick told Molly knowingly.

'Through necessity. After all, those on whom we have to use these wiles are so elusive.'

'You've so little faith in us. Such a cynic, Mol, for one so young. I'm not sure it becomes you.'

'Not really. I've got it all worked out in my mind. Have had for ages. Give me two years and the wiles will have done their bit. I'll be married by twenty-seven, say, or thereabouts. And from then on, things will be different. It all *will* be wonderful. You've got me so wrong. I'm incredibly optimistic, really. Not a trace of cynicism in me – only the weeniest whiff of realism. Quite another thing.'

'Oh dear.'

'What?'

'I'm not sure what's worse – the cynicism or the optimism. The first can only cause long-term bitterness and resentment. And the second one's sure to prompt disillusion.'

'Well, if I wasn't a jot optimistic, I wouldn't be bothering to waste my lunch hour trudging to Sackville Street.'

'Very good. Quite right. You go there. Positively turn over The World of Books to find what Mr De'Ath's after. Why not go right now?'

'All right,' Molly said, picking up her coat from the back of the chair. She flung it on to her shoulders and shrugged her arms inside. 'Won't be long. An hour or so. Will you be okay?'

'We're hardly being rushed off our feet. I can get on with this backlog of orders.' Nick stared gloomily at the pile of papers on the desk. 'I daresay I'll be able to cope.' He smiled grimly, and breathing in sharply added, 'I'm going to ring Georgie in a minute, in fact.'

'Oh yes?' Molly asked, pulling her hair out from behind the collar of her coat. 'What about?'

'To find out if she can come and see the new Simon Gray play with me tonight. I bought tickets a few days ago.'

'With Helen in mind?'

'With Helen in mind,' Nick reiterated quietly.

Molly narrowed her eyes, shook her head and began to make her way to the door. 'You're an absolute shit, you know that?' she whispered.

'I'm extremely fond of Georgia,' Nick commented. 'She's very important to me. We've come to depend on each other a lot over the years. Christ, she's one of my oldest friends. My occasional meetings with Helen were extremely agreeable, but they couldn't ever have been a substitute for what I have with Georgia.'

'What about your raucous sex life with Liz?' Molly wondered out loud, placing her hand on the chilly brass door knob.

'A mere diversion resulting from physical weakness on my part. It's very hard to resist those kind of sexual charms. Other than that there isn't much.'

Molly raised an eyebrow and turned the door handle. She watched as Nick lit a cigarette and then ceremoniously brushed off his knee. He was not a character normally to be concerned by such things. Certainly, had he not been feeling uneasy, he would not have bothered to remove a trifling bit of fluff from his trouser leg.

Without looking at Molly, he began to speak again, very slowly and with precise diction. 'I love Georgia,' he said. 'Perhaps it'd be kinder if I was to stop seeing other women.' Pause. 'I won't see Liz again. I mean as little to her as she does to me. But, if Georgia

47

found out, well, she's someone it'd mean a tremendous lot to, I suppose.'

Molly nodded.

'Perhaps I'll take Piers to the theatre with me tonight. That might be better. Then get tickets for something I know Georgie'd really like. *The Seagull* at the National, for example?' He stopped and turned towards his assistant with an open expression, keen to receive signs of approval.

The jesting bell rang as his confidante opened the door and stepped outside. As she did so Nick stared at her eyes and fancied he could detect in them a tiny smile.

CHAPTER

3

Molly found the book in Sackville Street. She decided not to ring Dominic De'Ath immediately. Four days later he came into the shop to find out if she had had any success. He wore the same coat.

Nick greeted the quiet customer. 'What did I tell you? Didn't I say we'd find it, the book you were after? My assistant here tracked it down. Isn't she wonderful?'

The two men looked at her. She was sitting on a high stool behind the desk, changing the till roll. In a short kilt of faded blue, green and lavender, and woollen tights, she seemed warm and content. The sleeves of a large floppy jersey were baggy and long. They obscured her hands up to the knuckles.

'I was lucky,' she said, without glancing up, her fingers still fiddling in the works of the till. 'Hard to get copies just like that.'

'I'm very grateful,' Dominic De'Ath said sincerely.

Molly slapped the side of the till shut, and turned to pick out the book from the orders shelf behind her. He approached the desk.

'I'd begun to give up hope of finding it.'

'Ah well,' said Molly, at a loss. 'I thought I might be able to get hold of one. It's always worth a try.'

'Indeed.' The man hesitated. 'How much do I owe you?' he asked, delving into a pocket.

'Eleven pounds.'

Nick looked at his watch. 'Damn, I'm late,' he said crossly. 'Mol, I'm going over to Bedford Square. Going to pick up some books from Piers. Might have lunch with him, all right?' He put on his coat. 'Now, you look after Mr De'Ath, and I'll see you later,' he added, stepping outside.

When Nick had gone, Molly and Dominic were left alone.

'Did you read the Peter Carey, by the way?' she asked, passing him some change.

'Finished it the night before last. Loved it. How about you?'

'Me too, though I'm not sure it was quite as good as the last one.'

'Have you read them all?'

'Yes, I'm a bit like that. Once I've discovered an author I enjoy, I tend to get all their books and read them one after the other.'

'Do you? I prefer to eke them out by reading others in between. That way you can prolong the pleasure,' he said, becoming more animated.

'I think I'm too impatient,' she admitted, giggling slightly because a conversation between them had struck up. Nerves. There followed an embarrassed pause. He looked at his feet and scratched his head. Molly straightened some papers on the desk.

'Oh,' he ventured. 'I might take a *Literary Review*. Is that all right?'

'Course. That's the new one. Came in yesterday.'

The customer moved away to browse. He walked between the high, dusty shelves, stopping to pull out a couple of thick, old volumes with faded covers. As he opened them, a musty smell swelled up from between the pages like the genie from the lamp. He read some passages to himself before replacing the books in their allotted spaces. He was warm in the cosy shop, and inside his heavy coat he felt his muscles relax: no longer did they need to stiffen as a defence against the cold wind outside.

He lingered beside the shelves, glancing over the titles stamped on to their spines. There was about him an air of reluctance: he did not want to brace the street. Here, he had the company of tempting books and that friendly girl.

Molly pushed open the small wooden door at the back of the shop. She leaned into the tiny room behind it, and flipped on a dusty kettle on a grubby formica shelf. Then she sat on the floor beside the desk in order to open a box of books delivered that morning.

'I'm making some coffee. Would you like some?' she asked lightly.

Dominic De'Ath peered round from behind a block of shelves. 'Are you asking me?'

Molly nodded.

'Sure?'

'Why not? Anything to entice a good customer.'

The good customer smiled. 'What kind of service do you call this?' he asked. His voice was gentle, kind. He moved towards her. 'Can I help with those? They look very cumbersome.'

Molly stood up, clutching a pile of six large hardbacks.

'I'm used to it,' she smiled. 'Biceps getting stronger by the minute.'

They heard the kettle flip off.

'Or would you prefer tea?' she asked, opening the door to the back room.

Some moments later they sat down together. Dominic pushed the collar of his coat away from his face. It was the first chance Molly had had to see his whole jaw. His complexion was pale but around his chin there was a bluish tinge. This was due to dark bristles which, though shaven from the surface of the skin, were evident just beneath it. His hair was brown. Cut short at either side, it was an unruly mess on top, the fringe flopping over his forehead almost into his black eyes. He was not particularly handsome, but there was a shy courtesy about his expression which made him look distinguished.

'Do you mind if I smoke?'

'Not at all. I might join you,' Molly replied. 'It'd be a nightmare not to be able to have a cigarette at work.'

'Yes. Fortunately the man I work with smokes even more than me.'

'What do you do?'

The question tripped off her tongue automatically. She knew it was a clichéd one, but there was no simple way round it.

'Publishing. I run a tiny business with a friend. There're only the two of us. We reprint rather obscure works of nineteenth- and twentieth-century literature.'

'Called?'

'Colville Books. I rent a flat in Colville Road in Notting Hill. That's where we're based. Not a very inspired name, I'm afraid. You probably won't have heard of us.'

'Rings a bell. I think Nick might've been talking about one of your titles with a customer the other day.'

'That's encouraging.'

'I don't think we had a copy, though.'

'Not very surprising. We're having problems with our distributors. So depressing.'

Dominic picked up a battered leather music case. It was brown, but there were pale scratches on it, and dark ink stains. 'I've got a couple of our books in here,' he said. 'Maybe you'd like to have a look?'

He handed Molly two large-format paperbacks. They were beautifully produced with smart plain covers in maroon. The pages were thick, the print quite large.

'They're beautiful,' she declared. 'I'm ashamed to say I haven't heard of either of the authors.'

'Not shaming at all. They *are* obscure.'

'Undoubtedly Nick'll know them both. Shall I order some copies on his behalf?' Molly asked as she scratched her elbow unselfconsciously.

Dominic looked surprised. 'I wasn't really expecting you to offer,' he said. 'I was just showing them to you anyway. But if you'd like a few, of course I'd be thrilled.'

'How about four of each?'

'I'll deliver them tomorrow.'

'Done,' said Molly, smiling.

'They're £5.95 each, less 30 per cent. What's that? About thirty something quid?'

Molly picked up the calculator on the desk. '£33.32.'

'Let's make it £30.'

'Why?'

'Well. . .' He looked at her with a friendly expression, and shrugged.

'You make a rotten businessman,' she laughed.

'Can't bear talking about money.'

'So English! I'm just the same.'

'And you're quite right, I'm no good at this side of the business. I ought to leave all the selling to my partner, Bill. He's as tough as a hazelnut!'

'Wouldn't waive the thirty-two pence, let alone the three pounds?'

'Definitely not.'

'Well, let's make it £33 so he doesn't get cross with you, okay?'

'He won't notice. Thirty.'

'All right. You win.'

Dominic stood up, putting the sample copies back into his bag.

'Good. And, as I said, I'll be in tomorrow. Probably the afternoon.'

Molly, biting the barrel of a biro, told him that that would be fine. He thanked her, said goodbye, and left.

Alone in the shop, she stood motionless for a few moments and felt curiously happy.

Nick returned from lunch a while later. 'So how did it go?' he asked.

'How did what go?'

'Well, those few Snatched Moments Alone with Mr Dominic De'Ath. You have to admire my tact.'

'I admire your self-delusion.'

'How so?' Nick feigned horror at such criticism.

'*Tact*? All that stuff before you went out. "Isn't my assistant wonderful?" Could've done without that.'

'But, Mol, I thought you'd be pleased.'

'So embarrassing.'

'Accept my apology?'

'Grudgingly.'

'Tough woman. Anyway, so how did it go?'

' "It", as you call it, went.'

'What do you mean, just "went"? That's like those ridiculous Americans who say, "That was real". Real what, exactly? "Went" how?'

'We exchanged polite conversation, which I think you'd agree is quite the norm between customer and bookseller. What did you expect him to do, produce a bunch of flowers, kiss my hand and declare passionate love in the politics section? Absurd!'

'Course not. I just thought he might've asked you out for a cup of coffee.'

'Well, he drank one here, actually,' Molly replied, with mock smugness.

'Making Coffee for Dominic De'Ath,' Nick laughed. 'I think I have a poem,' he added, and his assistant sighed loudly.

'Sounds as though it has *great* potential,' she said sarcastically.

'So, did you find out what he does?'

'Yes.' She was keen not to reveal more until necessary.

'And?'

'I'll tell you tomorrow.'

53

'I await the moment with violent excitement.'

The next morning, Molly decided she would have to tell her boss about Dominic. The Coat, as Nick liked to call him, would be coming in that afternoon, and if she did not explain why beforehand, she would be subjected to an insinuating interrogation.

Her explanation, though, had to be postponed: there was a flux of customers to be attended to. It was so odd, she thought, how some days were quiet and others so busy. There did not seem to be any particular pattern. Molly strongly believed that the weather was not a factor in people's decision whether or not to go out and buy a book. Contrary to popular theory, on some days hail and snow would inexplicably result in a crowd of eager readers waving money. And on some sunny days she and Nick would sit willing even a single customer to enter.

The cold, though, would seem sometimes to make a difference. On the whole, people stayed away when it was cold.

'It's the cold,' she would then say to Nick or vice versa. 'They don't like to go out in the cold.' Yet, occasionally, when temperatures were low, people did crowd into the shop and the pair of them would conclude that this, too, was due to the cold. 'They like to come in here and get out of it,' they would then say.

Such logic, Molly thought, was not unlike her mother's. When stuck in a traffic jam, she would state, 'They're obviously all going to the new film at the Odeon.' It never failed to irritate her daughter. Though quite funny, it also seemed so narrow-minded, somehow, so lacking in understanding. And yet, Molly was ashamed to admit, she herself obviously employed the same illogic. 'Maybe I'm becoming more like Mum,' she said to herself. 'That would indeed be a tragedy.'

By the afternoon, things still had not become less busy. People kept on coming into the shop and either wandering about quietly or demanding Nick's and Molly's attentions. She had not yet had a moment to explain to him that Dominic would be arriving later with eight of his books.

'Excuse me,' a braying voice penetrated the browsing calm. Customers looked up at the source of it with disapproving expressions. 'Can you recommend a good book? I want a good book.'

Molly moved over to a plump lady in a shocking pink jacket with shoulder pads which stuck out like those of an American footballer. Her full calves in pale green tights reminded Molly of Perrier bottles.

'What sort of thing do you like?' she asked, perplexed but polite.

'Anything really,' the woman replied helpfully. 'I've got very catholic taste.'

Molly came across a lot of people with 'catholic' taste. When she had first started in the bookshop, she had always directed them to the religious section, not entirely sure what they meant.

Then one day Nick had explained it to her.

'All these people with their catholic tastes!' he had said. 'They're a broad-minded bunch, apparently. Apparently only, mind you. Because when you get down to the business of recommendations, you discover they haven't actually a clue what they want. Have you noticed? If you've had a bad night, it can be a touch tiresome, especially when they turn down every single suggestion you make. Then if they leave the shop empty-handed, you feel like a failure – not because you've missed a sale, but because you've failed in your role as a bookseller.'

'But there again,' Nick's eyes had lit up at that point, Molly remembered, 'if you're in good humour and the customer's sympathetic and receptive – and they usually are – you welcome someone with a catholic taste. It's where the fun begins. There's very little that gives me more pleasure than seeing someone get excited about a book I've recommended. And if they then come back for more! You've succeeded in your duty, done a service, started up a rapport. Nothing like it.'

Molly had listened carefully to his speech. It was the first time Nick had told her exactly wherein lay his devotion to his trade.

'I'm very easy,' the Perrier-legged lady assured her.

'Would you like a novel?' Molly asked. Her tone was not one of contrived patience, but demonstrated a sincere desire to help.

'Oh, I think so, don't you?' The lady screwed up her nose and nodded earnestly.

Molly led her across to the fiction section. 'Or some short stories?'

'I quite like a short story, yes. But I can't be doing with that Ian McEwan fellow. Not his. Can't see the point of them at all.'

This gave Molly the kind of hint she needed. Nick had taught her that the art was not to pry, but to pick up clues to a customer's likes and dislikes, and then boldly to suggest something accordingly.

'I prefer, what, a slightly gentler read. Less gruesome, shall we say.' The lady's eyes darted over the books' spines with the same arbitrariness of direction as a fly on a window-pane.

'Yes. A bit gentler,' she went on. 'And by that I don't mean sentimental. I mean good taste, I suppose. I don't like gratuitous sex and violence, even in the name of good literature. It's not something I want to read about for pleasure. Dubious pleasure, if you ask me. Know what I mean? It's just the way I am. They can call me narrow-minded if they like – '

They? Molly wondered. Those with even more catholic taste than you?

' – but I'm not really,' the woman continued, shaking her head. 'Just not gratuitous sex and violence, that's all.'

Her fingers rested upon a thick paperback volume. She pulled it out from the shelf and looked at the cover.

'What've you got there?' Molly asked, peering over to see.

'*Ancient Evenings*. Sounds interesting. Mailer. I've heard of him. Good, is he?'

Molly nodded. The woman did not like sex and violence. Tricky.

'Oh, I was rather thinking you were keen to go after a collection of short stories?' she said tactfully.

'You're right. I wouldn't mind a change.'

Molly was relieved to see the woman replace the Mailer: spared the embarrassment of telling her it might not totally coincide with her notions of good taste.

Just then the bell on the door rang. Molly looked up to see who it was. Dominic De'Ath. She turned back to the woman, suddenly keen for her to make a decision.

'How about William Trevor?' she asked, still polite, though Dominic's presence was distracting her. 'A collection of stories has just come out,' Molly informed her, walking to the central table where the new hardback titles were piled. Nick and Dominic were talking quietly. She could not quite hear what they were saying.

The woman picked up the book and started turning the pages, excruciatingly slowly. Yet Molly remained outwardly patient, even though inside she felt like a jumble sale of frustration. So anxious to join in Nick's and Dominic's conversation.

'I loved them,' she enthused.

The woman continued to study the book. 'He's good on titles,' she observed.

'Yes, isn't he?' the younger girl replied, nodding quickly. Did she hear Nick whisper her name just then? And say something to Dominic about her qualities as a bookseller? Nod, nod, nod to the woman. 'Yes, yes, yes.'

Please make a decision, Molly thought. Coaxing smile.

A moment later the book was snapped shut. Thud.

'I'll take it,' the woman announced, smiling back and passing the volume to Molly who took it to the till. At last. Relief.

'Nick, please could you ring this up for me,' she asked, interrupting him and Dominic. 'I think it's a good choice, don't you?'

Nick did. The customer handed him some money. He placed the book in a dark-blue paper bag with Winter Books written on it in gold letters. She slipped the package under her arm and thanked him.

'You see, Mr De'Ath,' Nick told Dominic when she had gone, 'Winter Books is famed for its caring service to customers. We like to make them happy, do our best to satisfy their requirements.' He was being consciously pompous and so added a little laugh.

He was proud of his shop. He was proud of his assistant.

'Now,' he said, turning to Molly, 'I hear you've ordered some of Mr De'Ath's books?'

Molly nodded. 'I tried to tell you this morning, but all those customers, and that woman – '

'Couldn't matter less. I'm delighted. They're wonderful. I was telling Mr De'Ath that I'd been discussing one of the Colville publications only the other day. There's no problem getting mass market paperbacks from distributors, but get a beautifully produced edition by someone as small as Colville, and they're just not interested. Makes me so cross. Still, if you're round here quite a bit, you can always drop by, can't you, and check on our progress, show us your new stuff. That'd probably be best. Do you have a catalogue, by the way?'

Dominic fished a paper folder from his bag. 'It's more of a leaflet really. Not quite in the glossy league yet.'

Nick had a look. Molly tried to peer over his shoulder.

'You've got an impressive list here.'

'Small.'

'That doesn't matter. It'll expand.'

'How many are on it at the moment?' Molly asked.

'Eight altogether. It's not much.'

'But you haven't been going long, have you?'

'A year or so.'

'Well,' said Nick, 'we'll support you. Can I keep this?' He held up the catalogue.

'Of course.' Dominic looked so happy. There was about him an air of inward excitement. But he was too shy to reveal it. He shook Nick's hand, and thanked him.

'Perhaps I ought to make my way,' he said, picking up his bag from the floorboards.

'Cup of coffee before you go?' Nick asked.

'That'd be lovely, but I was rather thinking I might go to the patisserie next door. Haven't eaten anything. I quite fancy the idea of a bun.'

'Delicious there,' Nick told him.

Dominic's eyes lit up. 'It's my favourite patisserie in London. Whenever I'm round Soho, I go in. Rather too often, as it turns out. Colette's my friend. I tease her about that funny apron she wears. There's always icing sugar on her stomach.'

'She makes me laugh,' Molly said. 'I go in there most mornings with my paper and have a cup of coffee before opening up here. She calls me her angel cake.'

'Would you like to join me for a cup of coffee and a bun?' Dominic asked quietly, pushing up his coat collar to hide half his face.

The invitation was completely unexpected. As Dominic was gazing at his shoes, waiting for an answer, Nick winked at his assistant.

'Are you sure?' Molly asked. 'I'd love to come for a moment or two.'

She did not have to ask her boss his permission. He approved. She was confident about that, even if she was less so about the prospect of coffee next door with the Coat.

Nick waved his hand in a flamboyant gesture. 'Spirit her away a while, Mr De'Ath, do.'

Mr De'Ath did indeed spirit her away.

Helen folded her arms. For maybe an hour she sat completely still. The flame of the candle flickered as it consumed, parasite-like, the beeswax which upheld it. Slowly, it was determining its own suicide. But the brilliant glow looked proud, haughty even, as it sank closer towards extinction.

Helen stared at it, unblinking. Alone, she thought of nothing. Devastated. Humiliated. Stunned.

Eventually, the flame died. The darkness which fell at the moment of its death awoke her thoughts. She stood to turn on a light, and looked about her kitchen. It was a bit of a mess.

'Better do the washing-up,' she thought. Domesticity was very callous. It never let up, not even in the middle of emotional trauma. Helen contemplated leaving the dirty plates till the morning, but it would have made her feel guilty. Silly, really, to feel guilt about such a trivial matter, but she knew she did not have the strength to fight it tonight on top of everything else. So she did the washing up.

Later, her bed felt comforting. As she lay in the dark, her eyes open, Helen saw the scene at dinner with Nick all over again and once more experienced the very acute pain she had felt at the time. It was a somewhat masochistic exercise, to relive it, but she hoped that maybe things would not appear to be so bad. But they were.

'What now?' she wondered. 'Alfred, there's just you,' she added, out loud. 'Thank God, I suppose, that I have you. Otherwise, you see, I'd be totally alone, wouldn't I?'

The next morning, when she forced herself out of bed, she went into the kitchen slightly reluctantly. She feared that, having been the setting for such an unpleasant scene the night before, it might now have a hostile air.

She walked in nonchalantly, but nothing had changed. Her things remained as they had always been. The furniture,

59

the books, had not, in disappointment and shame, turned against her.

As Helen sat down at the white Formica table and spread out her paper, she realised that if anything had changed it was herself.

She suddenly recalled the sadness she had experienced as a young child when her birthdays came round. Each time, as she approached a new age with keen anticipation, she was convinced that she would somehow feel different. Yet on the day, even though it was made special with presents, friends, attention and cake, she was aware of no fundamental change inside.

It was only when she reached her seventh birthday that Helen experienced, unaccountably, an uplifting sensation inside her. Momentary. But she knew that it was that for which she had been waiting: the physical manifestation of a sudden revelation of the mind. Out of the blue, she had stumbled upon a sense of purpose, well-being even. At the time, she had pictured this feeling in her imagination and seen it as an eagle which, on a whim, had just taken off into the sky.

And now, thirty-five years later, she felt the same feeling as she sat at her table, sipping her coffee. This time, though it was in reverse. It was as if the eagle had flown well away and a vulture had returned to replace it, landing clumsily, and intent only on a kind of sickening satiation. It had come to devour Helen's last morsel of hope.

She knew now for certain that she would remain a spinster – for ever.

The little patisserie was warm inside. Molly and Dominic sat at a Formica-topped table on which were illustrated scenes of Parisian street life *circa* 1900. The chairs were equally kitsch. They each had a rounded velveteen seat of baby blue with a button in the middle, swirly gilt backs and spindly legs. The air was invisibly marbled with wafts of different smells: ground coffee, cigarette smoke, hot, sugary baking.

Colette, the proprietress, approached their table in the corner. Her old slingback slippers slapped the lino with each step. She held a small pad of paper in her hand, and a short, blunt pencil.

'Bonjour, Mademoiselle Molly. Ça va, alors? Un café au lait?' she asked, wiping the table with a greasy grey cloth and removing

a dirty cup and saucer. *'Et, Monsieur, pour vous? Un petit pain au chocolat, comme d'habitude?'*

Dominic smiled and nodded. 'The secret of my solitary brunches is out,' he told his companion. 'Would you like anything else?'

Molly shook her head.

'Just coffee?'

'Actually, I might have some orange juice as well,' she said, looking at Colette who immediately wrote *'Jus d'O'* on her pad.

'Et quelque chose à manger, mon petit gâteau de Savoie? Vous voyez, Monsieur, cette petite fille ici – elle est mon amie. Et toujours, elle commande la même chose. Du café. Elle ne mange jamais. Je t'en prie, Molly, un croissant ou une tarte aux abricots? Delicieux!'

'Merci, Colette, mais non. Je n'ai pas faim.'

The reason why Molly was not hungry was because she was nervous. Alone with Dominic, in the neon-lit café, she felt somewhat uneasy, unused as she was to having contact with a customer outside the shop. The circumstances were made trickier by the fact the she admired him and that he was almost as shy as herself.

Colette shuffled away and returned two minutes later with their order.

'Peut-être, tu es un oiseau,' she said to Molly, before moving off again, laughing.

'She's dotty,' Dominic whispered, leaning towards Molly.

'Complete fruitcake,' she agreed. 'Adores Nick. Sometimes she sneaks into the shop and brings him a hot pastry on a plate. Afternoons.'

'Does he appreciate such devotion?'

'God, yes. He goes to endless trouble to order books about knitting for her sister-in-law, and when it's busy in here he comes in and teases her in front of her customers.'

'He is funny. Insists on calling me Mr De'Ath all the time.'

Molly giggled. 'Pure affectation. He likes to camp it up a bit. He sees the bookshop as his sort of theatre, where he can perform as he likes.'

She looked at her coffee, but was anxious about picking it up to drink. Her hands, if they trembled as she held the cup to her lips, would betray her. So far she had camouflaged her nerves surprisingly well. But she was not sure she could control her hand.

'Do you get on with him on the whole?'

'Absolutely. From day one. Course, we occasionally have a frost, but that's understandable. It's an artificial set-up, if you think about it, alone all day every day with the same person.'

'I suppose you have to be friends,' Dominic said, biting into his squashy *pain au chocolat*. 'Like to try some?' he asked, holding it out to her. Molly did so, and thanked him as she wiped a flake of pastry off her chin with her sleeve. It was a childlike gesture.

'I think he really enjoys it,' she said, quite confident with the subject of Nick. Then she noticed Dominic look at the untouched coffee in front of her. 'Waiting for it to cool down a bit,' she explained quickly, and then wished she hadn't. Dominic nodded, understanding.

'How long's he been at it?'

'Couple of years or so. Used to be an editor at Carruthers & Orange, in charge of their fiction list. He was there for ten years, I think. Loved it.'

'Why'd he leave?'

'He said Carruthers was illiterate, though he had enormous respect for Orange. Carruthers became totally obsessed with sales and management, apparently, to the detriment, Nick says, of good books. He always crossed Carruthers for what he believed in, sticking up for his authors. But Carruthers wanted to make way for "sellers", phase out literature unless something was a dead cert for the Booker.'

'Didn't Orange stick up for Nick?'

'In his own way, he tried. But Nick said he was the weaker man, rather overpowered by his fat partner.'

'Is that why their list has gone downhill in the last few years?'

'Absolutely. In the end Nick just got completely fed up. That's why he left and set up the bookshop.' Molly paused and leaned back in her chair. She noticed that Dominic was nodding attentively. Indeed his expression was alive with attention. The heavily hooded eyes blinked. She now felt considerably more relaxed. Even so, there lurked in her stomach still a kind of tightness, almost as if a hand had somehow reached inside and was squeezing her guts like a lemon. She was anxious for Dominic to like her.

'In the complacent atmosphere of Bedford Square,' she began again, 'he spent all day editing and producing books to appeal to readers. But because the readers remained invisible to him they didn't seem real somehow. He wanted to meet them, the people who went out and bought them, to make the whole exercise seem worth while. He's never regretted it for a minute. Still occasionally edits something for Orange, who remained one of his best friends. So, what with that and a complicated emotional life, he's busy and cheerful.'

As Molly spoke, she picked up her squat coffee cup. The handle was inadequate, only the size of a small ring. After a few sips she replaced the cup in the saucer, and noticed it had left a little purple skid mark on the side of her forefinger.

'Has Nick got a lot of girlfriends then?' Dominic asked her shyly, taking the last mouthful of *pain au chocolat* and licking his thumbs to remove any traces of grease and flakes of pastry. Molly watched, admiring, as he then pushed aside a paper napkin and automatically wiped his hands on his trousers. Black trousers, she had observed, of thin cotton. She wondered if perhaps he had had them made abroad. India, maybe?

'Lives with his girlfriend, but there're others. I feel a bit sorry for Georgia.'

'Why?'

'She wants to marry him and, predictably, he's keen to avoid it if he possibly can,' Molly replied.

'Can you blame him? Sounds as if he's enjoying himself,' Dominic said honestly, but not with any macho bravado.

'Suppose not,' Molly shrugged. 'It's just that meanwhile she's in a Catch 22 – if she stays living with him he won't marry her because she's already almost a wife as it is. So from his point of view there's no need to go through with official commitment. And if she threatens him with leaving, he'd be very sad but also very unlikely to respond with a proposal.'

'He might. You never know,' Dominic suggested gently.

'Possibly. But it's not worth the risk. Nick'd miss Georgia, of course, especially in that big house all by himself. But she knows in her heart of hearts just as much as he does that there're plenty willing to replace her. Frightening dilemma, really. I go round there for supper occasionally. And she's so lovely. Covers up her desperation with a brave face. Dotes on Nick. And he on her, absolutely. Just doesn't want to get married.'

'It's not really fair, I do see,' Dominic said sympathetically, after lighting a cigarette. When he spoke, smoke jerked out of his mouth in short puffs with each syllable.

'That's the trouble, you see. There're all these women desperate to get married, all these men desperate to avoid it. Nick's just one who's, well, exploiting the situation, having his cake and eating it. Much though I love him, he's a bit of a bastard,' Molly said, smiling.

At that moment Colette approached them again. '*Un autre cappuccino, Monsieur?*'

'*Merci,*' Dominic replied, handing her his empty cup and saucer. He leaned back and folded his arms. His cigarette was perched between his lips somewhat perilously. When he nodded his head slowly at the French lady, the long cocked finger of ash trembled as if contemplating a clean break. But it clung on.

'*Et Molly? Du café, hein?*'

Dominic lifted his eyebrows as if to ask her if she would indeed like some more. But she declined. Colette told her in French that she was so predictable, and giggled before limping off to the counter. There followed a loud but not nasty tirade at one of the waitresses. Dominic and Molly listened and laughed. Then the swoosh of the *cappuccino* machine could be heard.

'How come you've got such a good accent?' Dominic asked Molly.

'Don't ask,' she sighed. 'I went on endless gruesome exchanges. Got pretty fluent.'

'Where?'

'Paris mostly. The longest one I went on was six miserable weeks when I was, I don't know, fourteen. A hideous suburb called Villecresnes.'

'Why was it so awful?' Dominic wondered out loud.

'Well, my so-called friend Pascale was unbearably petulant. She wore long thin scarves round her neck and had a spoilt mouth. She lived in a small apartment in a concrete block with her parents.'

As Molly spoke, she could see the parquet floor in the sitting-room, and the brown velveteen sofas. They had eaten breakfast there, she remembered, *pain au confiture*, and *chocolat chaud* in Perspex mugs. It was all so vivid, still, in her mind. She was enjoying telling Dominic. He was a good listener.

'We went into the centre of Paris a couple of times. I wanted to see the Matisse exhibition, but Pascale was keen to buy scented candles in poxy stone holders from Prisunic. She always got her way, you see,' Molly explained. She crossed her leg, putting her left ankle on her right knee. At ease.

Colette brought Dominic his *cappuccino*. A white, fluffy island floated on top of the creamy brown sea. It was speckled with chocolate powder, like dark shells on pale sand.

'One morning, she had a row with her mother,' she went on, 'and locked herself in her room. Leopardskin walls, I remember. And posters. Then she played Neil Diamond and Led Zeppelin very loudly, singing along to *Stairway to Heaven*. It sounded so odd with her French accent. Didn't have a clue what the words meant, of course, or that hippy 70s music was just a touch *passé* in, what, around 1978 it must've been.'

Dominic laughed happily, and leant forward as Molly continued. He had good teeth – sparkly.

'So I just lay on my bed and read volumes of Anthony Powell. Very homesick,' she added, continuing her anecdote quite naturally, the imaginary hand inside her stomach having relaxed its grip on her guts considerably. 'Then suddenly Pascale flung open my door and shrieked "Molly" in her aggressive French. "*Il faut que nous aillons à la soirée*" and she dragged me out of the apartment without letting the wretched mother know. We got on this grim suburban train which took us to another grim suburban flat. And a party was going on. It was three o'clock on a sunny afternoon, and the curtains were closed.'

There were about twelve or fifteen teenagers sitting on the floor round the edges of the grey room, Molly explained. Not much chat, but a lot of music and cigarette puffing. Pascale did not introduce her to anyone but put her hand down the front of a boy's jeans instead, and cackled. And she referred to Molly as '*l'Anglaise*'.

A boy in a brushed cotton shirt with a tartan pattern and the sleeves rolled up approached her and said hello. Fabrice. He had an adolescent moustache and asked her where she lived, did she have brothers and sisters? Had she heard of or been to Silverstone? He had been to England once, he told her, to see the racing driving.

They were listening to *Hotel California*. Was she acquainted with that song? Yes. Would she like to translate the lyrics

65

for him? She would try. He would like it if she would try.

Dominic laughed again. He watched Molly becoming very animated with her anecdote, emphasising her words with gestures of the hands. He was enjoying it.

'My French was still a bit dodgy then. Probably more confused by my translation than anything else, Fabrice then asked me to dance. Nobody else was. We had to push an armchair to one side. It was awful. He started by putting his arms round my neck.' Molly broke off suddenly, shivered at the memory and giggled. 'Then his tongue down my throat.' She remembered that it tasted of beer and had slid about in an alarming abundance of slimy spit. But she spared Dominic those details.

'On the way home on the train, Pascale, blowing some bubble gum, said, *"Tu aimes Fabrice?"*'

Molly had replied, *'Peut-être'* to keep her quiet. But she did not love Fabrice perhaps. She did not love him at all.

'Thank God I was spared those horrific exchanges. But I did live in France for a while when I was a child, though. After my mother died.'

Molly hesitated a moment before asking him how old he had been when that happened.

'Seven. It was pretty grim. Cancer.'

'I'm sorry,' she said, curiously unembarrassed. Dominic was very straightforward, unsentimental. Sipped his *cappuccino*. Scratched his forehead.

'Oh, one's very resilient at that age. I was okay,' he murmured, shrugging. 'I loved her very much, but children are a lot braver than one gives them credit for. Dad suffered,' he revealed, nodding.

Molly leaned forward, put her elbows on the table, and pushed up the sleeves of her cotton smock, a Coca-Cola bronze. She then picked up one of the rocky brown sugar lumps from the surgical tin bowl in front of her and twiddled it between her finger and thumb.

'Had they been married long?'

'Ten years about, I suppose. Whenever he went away for work he took her with him, locations all over the world.'

'Is he an actor?'

'Film director,' Dominic stated simply. 'I remember going too sometimes. Kenya and India, for example. America once

66

or twice. We were based in London, though. Holland Park. It wasn't so smart in those days. Very beautiful, all the same. That flat had a view right over the trees. So amazingly green in the summer. Mum used to fill the place with flowers. I'd come back from school for tea and the smell was overwhelming. I still associate cold glasses of milk with the smell of cream lilies. My stepmother never cared so much about flowers. She always let them go brown and their water get brackish.'

In his mind Dominic saw a large glass vase on the hall table of the flat he described, and he visualised the cloudy water, yellowing and stagnant around dying stems. He screwed up his nose at the memory of the stench which assaulted his nostrils whenever he was made to throw the dead flowers away, and pour the slimy liquid down the kitchen sink.

Colette came up to their table again. Dominic declined her offer of more coffee, and Molly looked at her watch.

'I think I ought to be getting back to the shop,' she said. 'Nick'll be wanting to go out to lunch soon.'

They both stood up. Dominic left some money on the table. They thanked Colette and made their way out of the café.

Outside, the cold slapped them in the face. Automatically, they hunched their shoulders as defence against it, and wandered back to the door of the bookshop. Standing there, Molly shifted from one foot to the other. Through the lighted window, she could see Nick inside with a customer. He looked warm.

'That was lovely,' she said. 'Thank you.'

'We must have a drink next time,' Dominic suggested, smiling as he said goodbye. 'See you soon,' he added.

She nodded, and thought she felt his grip momentarily tighten before he smiled, turned and walked away.

In the afternoon of the day following her proposal, Helen went to the British Museum. She worked well, considering the ordeal of the night before. But after some hours with Housman, she sat back in her chair and closed her eyes for a minute.

Last night's scene bored its way, unwelcome, into her mind once more.

She had sat motionless while Nick had stuttered his way out of their association. Inside, of course, she had not been a bit motionless. But she had had the desire to present to him at least the appearance of stillness and dignity.

There had been, too, more practical reasons for her silence. As he spoke, Helen had felt a lump form in her throat. It had been like a metal box with sharp edges and corners, lodged and gently expanding, straining the larynx. A filmy tear had nestled, too, on the ledge of each eye. Had she moved, or blinked even, they would have flooded the bottom lashes. Then she would have really cried. She could not let him see her really crying.

To cry in front of him would have meant defeat, but, worse, it would have repelled him. If a man, she thought, causes a woman whom he loves to cry, he might be moved to sympathy. If a man causes a woman whom he does not love to cry, he is invariably moved only to contempt.

Thus Helen had been determined not to give in to tears. And in this she succeeded. It was an achievement which proffered a modicum of consolation in the midst of her desolation.

CHAPTER
4

A week after the coffee *chez* Colette, Molly had a drink with Dominic in a pub in Greek Street. A few days later, Molly had dinner with Dominic in a pasta bar in Old Compton Street. A fortnight passed, and she had a night with him in his flat in Colville Road. During the following month, she saw him on several occasions.

When she went home to Oxford for Easter, Molly was able to tell her parents that she had a new boyfriend.

'I'm so pleased for you,' her mother remarked, dipping a finger into a pot of stew on the stove. 'Too many damn carrots,' she muttered quietly, prodding the energetically boiling mixture with a spoon. A delicate wrist emerged from a baggy sleeve.

Cake (she had been unable to say Kate as a child) was a typical North Oxford woman. There were details about her appearance which hinted at a former elegance: a topaz ring, a silver belt with an onyx buckle. All the same, at nearly fifty, she had almost given up. She wore a man's long grey cardigan, the pockets bulging with scrumpled paper handkerchiefs. Hennaed hair was scrunched up in a messy pile which, held together in a pink butterfly clip, seemed to defy gravity. Her feet were enveloped in frayed yellow espadrilles. At the stove, an old white cat manoeuvred itself back and forth between Cake's bare legs, coiling its tail round her calves. She ignored it.

'Is he kind?'

Molly was sitting at the dull pine table, bent over it, relaxed. One hand propped up her head, the other cupped a mug of tea. She had been doodling with a biro on a copy of the *Independent*. She felt like a teenager again, just back from school, about to do her homework. Her mother always asked if people were kind. 'Is your new art teacher kind, Mol?' 'This boy Marcus, taking you to the end of term party, is he kind?'

'Yes, Ma, Dominic's kind.'

69

'Looks after you, I hope.'

'I don't need looking after,' she replied, not indignant. Cake remained with her back to Molly. When she spoke to her daughter, she actually appeared to be addressing the stew.

'How old is he?'

'Twenty-eight, I think, or twenty-nine. I'm not quite sure. Around that, anyhow.'

Molly glanced about the kitchen, a room she so associated with her past that it almost smelt of her childhood. It was cream-coloured and cosily shabby, with curly black and white photographs and childish paintings tacked to the walls. An elderly corduroy sofa nestled in the corner beneath a large, basic clock, old and with an endearing tick. The table was rough and battered. It had been the principal setting of Molly's upbringing. It was at that table she used to sit at tea-time, after school, and eat grilled toast bubbling with butter, brown sugar and cinnamon. It was there she tasted wine for the first time. It was there she used to muddle through a geography essay, say, or perhaps discuss political topics with her parents. It was that table which had witnessed endless chats between Molly and her girlfriends about clothes, diets and boys. It was that table over which crackers had been pulled at every Christmas lunch for her twenty-five years.

As always, the ceramic fruit bowl stood in the middle of it. A couple of lemons and a withered apple were its only rightful residents for otherwise it was populated by scraps of paper, waxy crayons, a wooden hairbrush (varnish flaking) and more such miscellanea. A big white loaf sat on a round board beside it next to a coffee jar of homemade damson jam, and a butter dish. It was a familiar, unchanging still life. Over the years, it had remained constant alongside the far less still life with which it had to share its surroundings: so many comings and goings.

'Would I like him? You know I can put up with anything as long as – '

' – he's not dull.' Molly finished Cake's sentence for her.

'How did you know?'

'You always say it. Every time. He's not remotely dull.'

Molly began to tell Cake about Dominic. Her mother joined her at the table, lit a cigarette, and was interested to hear. Cake pretended not to like men very much, but – no stomping feminist, she – it was a pretence which had its limits. She loved conversations about men, and certainly in her time had admired the real thing well enough. She had had boyfriends.

Cake's mother was a dotty Russian lady, her late father had been a barrister. She was brought up in London. It was while studying at the Ruskin that she had met Rufus Almond, a postgraduate then, seven years older than herself. He was a mild man, conventional. They married when Cake was twenty. Though quite serious himself, Rufus was taken by her spirited nature.

When Molly was four, her father explained what had prompted him to marry her mother. It was a favourite story, the repetition of which she requested many times when she was little. He told her that he had asked Cake to go for a walk with him in Magdalen Deer Park, to see the fritillaries. She appeared wearing no shoes and, for some reason, he found it very funny. Together they laughed and laughed. 'She had a bewitching laugh, Mol,' he said. 'No man could've resisted falling in love with a woman who laughed like that.'

One weekend Cake took Molly, who was seven, to stay with a funny man in a house in the country. Spooky. The walls and corridors were of a dark wood.

The man was over-nice to her – sickly. He smelt of two much eau-de-Cologne and had plump fingers, one of which was squashed into a gold signet ring. It looked like a tight belt round the waist of a fat and naked woman.

There was a purple tin of wafer footballs filled with soft orange cheese on his drinks tray. 'I've a good game,' he said. And he made her stand with her mouth open while he tried to throw them into it.

Cake laughed her bewitching laugh, but Molly thought it was a pointless game.

She slept in a cold blue room.

'If you have a nightmare in the night, come and see me, I'm just down the passage,' Cake told her soothingly. Molly asked after her father. Why hadn't he come with them?

'He doesn't really like the country,' was the instant reply. She knew her mother was wrong about this, but before she had time to correct her, Cake had hurried away.

Molly did have a nightmare in the night. It was about an evil red pepper. She awoke to be confronted by a thick blackness. Uneasy, she trembled out of bed and groped along the pitchy passage till she found Cake's room and went in. It was her knees which discovered the edge of the bed first. She crawled over its expanse feeling for her mother's face. A small shaking hand roamed over the coarse texture of a blanket and the warm softness of a sheet. Then, at last, it came across a chin.

But it was rough, not like that of a woman's chin. Molly felt the sharpness of bristles. Frightened, she silently ran back to her room, wondering why the man was in her mother's bed. Maybe she had had a nightmare too and he had come to comfort her? 'But that can't be right,' she thought. 'Grown-ups don't get nightmares.'

It was a strange thing, and it troubled her. But she did not mention it in the morning.

'I think he sounds wonderful,' Cake said chirpily, pushing the white cat off the table. 'I like the idea of someone with the integrity, or imagination, or whatever it is, to publish books simply because he likes them. Is your first lot selling well?'

'Five out of the eight. Not bad.'

'Brilliant.'

'Nick wants to order more.'

'That's good.' Cake paused. 'When do I get to meet Dominic? Will you have him to stay here one weekend?'

'Not yet. I don't want him to think I'm making too much of a thing of it for a while.'

Cake nodded, understanding. 'But it wouldn't be making too much of a thing of it, would it, if you brought him here relatively soon?'

'All right. Relatively soon,' Molly agreed.

'I mean, meeting the parents doesn't have to imply you crave marriage the very next week, does it?' she teased.

It was preposterous, and she would never admit it, but Molly had in fact already contemplated marriage to Dominic. Such contemplation had not, as yet, turned into anything so strong as a craving, thankfully. But she had allowed herself to indulge the imagination, to conjecture, as to life as Mrs De'Ath.

Shameful. Yet, so what? It wasn't so unreasonable. Girls, Molly thought to herself, are, after all, brought up to think in terms of marriage. At school they are given prunes and custard and encouraged to play Tinker, Tailor with the stones. 'I wonder what my future husband's doing this very moment,' they say to themselves on a cold games pitch to pass the time. They do so, untroubled by the worry that he might not exist. And their teachers advance the conviction that marriage is inevitable. Full of prissy notions, they tell the girls they're not allowed to put their elbows on the table until they get married. Mothers, too, enhance the belief by saying to their daughters things like, 'When you're married, I'll give you these earrings.' They speak as if the possibility that they might remain single is almost inconceivable.

The wedding day, Molly felt, had a kind of magical quality projected upon it. It is a day after which one's life changes utterly – for the better, apparently. From childhood a small girl is programmed avidly to anticipate it. Experience, as a result of simple observation of couples around her, does little to quell her keenness to have her own big day.

Cake regretted marrying Rufus. Molly knew this. She sensed it early on. Her mother was a fiery woman, inconsistent. Her father was quiet. Cake became impatient with her husband. She blamed him for being weak, ineffectual, and for allowing her life to dwindle into one of 'bourgeois routine'.

'But I love just being with you and Mol, and getting on with my work. I'm not an adventurous man, Cake,' he would say.

'Oh, but you can be.' She would throw up her arms and reveal that spirited nature which had initially won his heart. 'I hate academics. With your books, in the library, you're full of adventure, lusting after discovery. You're a positive explorer then. You have this secret life, going all over the world, back in time. And I have no part of it. I stay here all day, belching with the boredom of domesticity. Then you come home, exhausted maybe, but fulfilled by your mental travels. And you ask me if you can have a bloody crumpet for tea! This house, your wife and child represent only the mundane aspects of your existence. Crumpets! There's no adventure with us!'

'You have your painting, my love. When you paint, I expect you go on sort of adventures, too, of which I have no part.' Rufus always spoke so quietly, and with such dignified tranquillity.

'Your father never bloody reacts. Damn his calm,' Cake would then seethe.

On other occasions, her temper would prompt her to fly upstairs to her studio. The door would be locked and she would remain there for hours, attacking a canvas with a paintbrush and lurid oils. Contorted faces would appear, agonised figures suffering.

Molly would be left alone at the kitchen table with her father. She used to wince within but, like Rufus, would maintain an outward calm.

'Mum's in a bit of a fluster, eh, Mol?' he always said, confiding. 'Shall we have a cup of tea? Want a game of Beggar my Neighbour?'

He remained so kind and stoical in the face of such domestic turmoil. Molly loved him so much, yet felt too jittery in her stomach to play cards. How could she turn him down, though, without hurting his feelings? This was a dilemma which made matters even worse.

At sixteen, Molly's faith in marriage was severely tested. She and her friend Lucy were watching television in the old playroom in the basement. A smell of cat pee lingered, she remembered. The two of them were sitting back in chairs, their feet resting on a mass of unironed laundry piled into an enamel tub.

Top of the Pops was bombarding them with relentlessly energetic images and music. Suddenly, Molly was aware that her friend was sobbing.

'What's the matter?' she asked.

Lucy explained that her parents were in the process of getting divorced. Their world, and hers, she said, had been desolated.

'Mum and Dad won't speak to each other. And they only speak *of* each other in terms of sheer hate.'

Lucy cried for two hours. She stopped only when she thought of Molly's parents.

'They epitomise everything that's right about marriage,' she said. 'To me, they're the ideal couple, so blissful. God, they're the only ones I know who are. After so many years.'

Cake's and Rufus's happiness, Lucy revealed, was the only thing which enabled her to bear her own parents' divorce. 'It gives me hope that at least there's one married couple who're really in love.'

Molly had not the heart to disappoint her sad friend. What would have been the point in wrenching from her her one straw of comfort? But she did not forget Lucy's misinterpretation of reality.

Molly smiled. 'But you know what it is, Ma, if you bring someone home. They automatically think one's propelling matters along, trying to make everything official. It shouldn't be seen like that, but it is.'

'Doesn't Dominic care for officialdom?' Cake asked, rising to examine the progress of her stew.

'What, you mean marriage?'

'No, no. Just the fact that you're an item, as they say.'

'Not keen to commit himself, no. But I have to give the poor man a chance. I've only known him a few weeks. He needs time to think.'

'Huh! I've no patience with men who need time to think. Why can't they be like everybody else who just thinks anyway, without having to "find time" to do so. Does he have a specific hour in his day which he specially sets aside in order to go about the business of thinking? How self-indulgent!'

'You're being unfair. We haven't known each other that long.'

'But, Mol, has he actually said to you that he needs "time to think"?'

'No. I just suspect that's what he's after.'

'I can't abide such lack of spontaneity. Surely the man can allow instinct to make some of his decisions for him?'

'You're so intolerant,' Molly said, faintly irritated that her mother had taken up this somewhat unjustified line about someone she had never met. 'He's not like that. Wait till you meet him,' she added sadly.

'Doesn't sound like that'll be for some time. There's all this thinking he's got to get through first.'

Molly resented the remark. However, she knew her mother was not being unkind, but in fact showing concern.

Cake had seen her suffer at the mercy of men before. Molly's romantic arrangements had never been entirely successful.

At sixteen, she fell in love for the first time. Hamish's father was an old friend of Rufus's. He was quite a serious fellow, Hamish, not exactly effervescing with a sense of humour. But Molly really loved him. It was funny to think of him now – those long, awkward arms, that ridiculous corkscrew hair and those earnest beige corduroy trousers. He was 'into' architecture, she remembered. Molly knew nothing about architecture, but she found herself looking at buildings more carefully as she walked to Smith's, say, in the Cornmarket, to buy pencils. Once, she searched her father's bookshelves for a volume on the subject. She discovered a thick biography of

Frank Lloyd Wright, and read the introduction avidly, before giving up.

At night, in her room, she would switch on her tape recorder and play *I will survive* by Gloria Gaynor. She would lie in bed, turn out the light and listen to the song several times while puffing on a self-conscious cigarette. Hamish had once danced with her to this record at a barn dance. Afterwards, on a hay bale in a dark alcove, he had kissed her (second ever French kiss). It was at that moment that she fell in love, and she remained so for two years.

Hamish was a Catholic and had funny ideas about associating with girls. Having kissed her that once, he told her that he felt a heavy sense of guilt. Molly knew that this must mean he was a man of real integrity. It only served to stoke her infatuation.

Alas, he never kissed her again. Once she plucked up the courage to write to him. He wrote back a week later:

Dear Molly,

I am one of those people who loathes even the thought of having to write to anyone. Yet, I have managed to find three minutes of spare time, before having to engulf myself in another of my five essays needing doing before tomorrow.

Very little has been happening here, except perhaps freezing to death at the hands of the weather.

For the past week, our school has been trying very hard at athletics (that includes me!) since we think we are rather good at it. It's incredible how some people will believe literally anything! [That bit had really made her laugh.]

I've decided to definitely try for the AA which is very exciting. Maybe I'll be a twentieth-century Wren yet.

Love, Hamish.

This was the only love letter Molly ever received from Hamish. His family moved to Yorkshire, thus geography came between them. All the same, she pined awhile.

A few years or so ago she had bumped into him at a party. He had become rather plump in the face, and stuffy.

'I'm at the AA now,' he had told her, giving a disapproving look as he watched her chewing gum. (It was during her – fortunately brief – late teenage anarchic stage. 'I can chew chewing gum at parties, I don't give a toss, and anyone who doesn't like it can lump it.') So Hamish had had to lump it. He was boring anyhow.

'Wasn't that the guy you were in love with once?' a girlfriend asked.

'If you can believe it!' Molly replied, turning from the aspiring architect. Giggles and more ostentatious chewing.

'You've had it, Mol, haven't you, with men who need time to think? I'd have thought so after Dave,' Cake asked, prodding her stew.

'Dave was okay,' Molly replied, slightly defensive. 'Just a bit pensive, that's all.'

'Mol, you have a very generous-spirited memory. He never spoke.'

'Shy.'

'Rude. I remember you asked him why once, and he just said he was "thinking". Scintillating company, he was!'

Cake was right. But it was hard to admit the fact to her mother. She had been such a success as regards the male sex. Molly didn't even pretend to dislike men, yet she had experienced only failure in her associations with them.

She met Dave while doing her A levels. He was at New College, reading history. They were introduced at the tea party of a mutual friend at Brasenose. He hadn't said much, but as far as his monosyllables would allow, he was polite. They saw each other again at the King's Arms. He drank lots of beer. Concentration on consumption left little time for conversation. But Molly liked him. She drank a Bloody Mary and decided he wasn't an unkind man.

He took her on the coach to London to see an exhibition at the Royal Academy. They had a roll and salad for lunch in a neon sandwich bar, off Piccadilly. There were three apples on a plate by the till, perennial residents, Molly thought, of such a place. They each had pale green skins, verging on the yellow, and greasy complexions freckled with blackheads. It was not a romantic spot.

'Shall I pay?' Dave asked. Their lunch cost £2.33.

'No, goodness. Let me,' she said. So polite.

'Okay,' he shrugged, giving in to her offer just a bit too easily. What was it about her that made men feel they need not even pay for a rotten roll let alone an expensive dinner? Some girls were always taken to smart restaurants, simply because they had perfected that air of expecting it. Such brazen toughness eluded Molly and, as a result, she lost out.

Dave stood in front of the pictures in the gallery for ages, looking, thinking. Molly's insides felt hollow, as if they were slipping downwards from too much standing.

Not until the evening when she lay down on Dave's bed in his gloomy digs in Jericho did Molly feel her stomach finally return to its rightful position. She did not dare ask him why he had felt the need to stare at each picture for quite so long. He might get cross, she thought. And she wanted him to seduce her.

He did so. It was her first time. She was eighteen and she was pleased, even if the circumstances were not ideal. Dave's sheets were not entirely fresh. His shyness rendered his moves a bit clumsy, but it was not an unpleasant experience all the same. Much as she had imagined it, in fact. As it was, it had not taken much imagination to guess what it would feel like, really: she had been to a gynaecologist once. On a purely physical level, his examination wasn't so far removed from the real thing. It wasn't great fun, exactly. Dave spoke less than the cheerful gynaecologist. But it was okay.

The next day when she got on the bus to go to school, she wondered if anybody could tell. Could her fellow passengers sense, instinctively, that she had done it the night before? She rather hoped they could. She wanted them to be aware that she had had The Experience, for now she could take on that air of complacency, like them, because she was also 'in the know'. This made her feel important, but otherwise she did not feel any different.

She slept with Dave a couple more times over the following month. One morning he made himself a cup of tea and got back into bed.

'Only one tea-bag, I'm afraid,' he said.

Molly nodded. 'Doesn't matter,' she told him lightly. She wouldn't have minded a sip of his.

'Molly, thing is, I need time to think.'

'Oh, absolutely,' she said, accommodating, inexperienced. 'About. . .?'

'Things.'

'Course.'

'I mean, we don't want to get into all of this too quickly.'

'Absolutely'. All of what?

'I need time to think before I can commit myself,' Dave said.

Oh, him and me. *Us*.

'I'm not sure I'm ready for an official sort of thing,' he went on.

'Official?'

'You know. Going out,' he ventured awkwardly.

Molly remembered feeling pleased that a dialogue, of sorts, had struck up. She had not had many of them with Dave.

Six months passed and Dave was still 'thinking'. At least, Molly consoled herself, he wasn't going to have to regret a spontaneous decision.

During those six months, she spent just seven nights with Dave. On one occasion, he had climbed into his bed at six in the evening and patted the duvet as an indication that she should do so too. Old socks, dirty clothes and cold cups of tea littered his rented room, and yellowing Penguin Classics lay like dead birds on the sand-coloured floorboards. Stepping over them, Molly joined her lover. He smiled and opened a foil bubble which contained an orange-scented condom. While they made love, he expertly turned on the telly with the remote control and began to watch *The A-Team*. He had spirit, Dave, she thought.

'Shall we go and get pizzas?' he enquired when they had finished, and the programme had come to an end. He hugged her and wrapped his leg round hers.

'That was wonderful,' he told her.

That was one of the nicest things he ever said to her. They went out and bought take-away pizzas and returned to bed to eat them. They made love again. This time he forgot to tell her it was wonderful, but he had obviously enjoyed himself. He trembled when it was over and smiled at Molly. She envied him his orgasms. She hadn't ever had one, not even been near one. But he so tingled after his that he shook when she touched him. Molly stared at him in the half-light and longingly wondered what it felt like to be him and to have come like him.

Molly knew Dave was selfish. But she decided it was better to contend with his selfishness gracefully, not mention it, put up with it. Otherwise she would have nothing.

Once she plucked up the courage to ask him to go away one weekend to stay with a few friends of hers. He knew the friends, liked them.

Dave had shrugged when she suggested it, and said something elaborate like 'Sure, why not?' So Molly had allowed herself to look forward to the weekend. She even mentioned it a couple of times on the days leading up to it. Dave had made noises to the tune that he was definitely going.

On the Friday morning, Molly woke up and sneaked out of bed. She made Dave a cup of tea and quietly presented it to him as he lay, an inert hump between the sheets.

'I'm going to take masses of tapes for the journey,' she mentioned casually, sitting down beside him.

'As long as you don't take the new Talking Heads.' Dave was lying face down in the cleavage of a pillow so his voice was stifled.

'Sorry?'

He forced himself round to face the bearer of his tea.

'Don't take the new Talking Heads,' he repeated. His eyes were puffy with sleep, the complexion crumpled and greenish. Hangover halitosis.

'Why not?' Molly asked reasonably.

'I want it this weekend,' he stated, leaning over to sip the tea that she had brought him, and that he had not thanked her for. He was wearing a white T-shirt that had a greyish air about it. Its ugly sleeves were like wedges. They reached only to the shoulders rather than to below the biceps, and they reminded Molly of ageing cheeses. But she didn't say so.

'Yes,' she said, 'we can take it with us.'

'I'm not coming,' he told her, slurping, blinking, smelling.

Oh? Why the fuck not?

'Oh? That's a shame. Why not, out of interest?'

'I just feel like spending this weekend with John. We want to play darts in the pub.'

Molly nodded patiently, remarkably and admirably patiently. Actually she was devastatingly disappointed. But she didn't say so, in the same way she didn't say his filthy T-shirt was hideous.

'Never mind,' she said, summoning up all her strength and telling Dave in her mind that he didn't realise how bloody lucky he was: any other girl would have hit him. She quite wanted to do so herself. But she didn't dare risk it. If she had, Dave would have said something like, 'Right, Molly, that's curtains for you and me.' Then she would have been left with nothing.

'*You* must still go, though,' Dave told her.

Thanks a lot.

'I'll see,' she said, nodding.

Of course she hadn't gone. She spent nine hours that weekend watching Dave and John playing darts in the pub. Not much fun, though at least the former had made love to her on the Saturday

80

night. But nor had that been absolutely wonderful. Still, being her, she had pretended otherwise.

She wondered if Dave ever appreciated quite how accommodating she was.

After six months' thought, Dave informed Molly one day that he had been 'doing some thinking'. She imagined he might well have done, in fact, quite a lot of thinking in that amount of time, and she nearly remembered to congratulate him.

'I've been thinking.' he said.

'Yes. I know.'

'I'm not sure it's going to work really.'

Molly said, 'Oh.'

'I find it hard, you see, to commit myself.'

'But you knew that, anyway, before you did all this thinking.'

'Yes, but I really think, now, that I can't. I don't want to hurt you.'

'I appreciate that, Dave. I'm glad you could see a way to such a swift decision. No chance of hurting me after a mere six months.'

'Don't be like that, Mol – '

'No, honestly, it's fine.'

'It was a casual thing, wasn't it?'

'Oh yes. Dead casual.'

'Are you okay?'

'Yes I'm fine, really. Very glad all that thought brought you to a definite conclusion.'

'We can still be friends?'

As it happened, they weren't great friends, anyway. Molly, like Cake, thought Dave a bit of a bore. The scanty romantic element which tied them tenuously was, to be honest, their only link. They could not still be friends, no.

'Why not?' Molly shrugged.

She went home and sat at the kitchen table and told Cake what Dave had thought. They discussed it for a while and decided what they thought. They thought it was no bad thing that it was over and, together, they ate some toast.

'All I'm concerned about,' Cake said gently manoeuvring the cat from between her ankles, 'is that you're happy, and that Dominic doesn't treat you badly like the others.'

There had not been many others, but it was true, the small amount of others there had been, had treated her badly.

81

Molly wondered if this was because she started rather later than her friends. They had gone out with boys at thirteen. Thus, they had two years' experience over her, for she had only had her first kiss at fifteen. Beery breath Fabrice. In France. Her first real French kiss.

'Well, I'd prefer to go out with a man who thinks a bit,' Molly told her mother, 'than with one who's utterly thoughtless.'

It irritated Molly that Cake was so critical about her ex-boyfriend. Her mother's criticisms were accurate, of course, but she was not entitled to voice them unprompted. That was her own prerogative: she was the girl whom he had left, thus only she had the right to complain about the man's shortcomings. Cake was only allowed to do so if Molly herself brought the subject up. Then she would make it clear she wanted her mother to agree with her own uncomplimentary observations about Dave. If, under those circumstances, Cake restrained herself and criticised him – not too emphatically – it was all right, could even make her feel better. Otherwise, her mother finding fault in Dave was out of order, and only caused Molly to be rather too generously defensive about him.

'Well, Dominic's thoughtful and not thoughtless,' Molly told her mother firmly.

'That's all right, then,' came the gentle reply. 'I suppose it's okay, if he does a bit of thinking now and again as long as he finds time to be kind to you.'

'Mum, Dominic's a kind man, all right?'

At that moment, Rufus appeared. When he saw his daughter a look of happiness filtered across his face. He gave her a kiss. 'Any crumpets?' he asked, smiling.

Dominic was a kind man. When Molly returned to London on the evening of the Bank Holiday after the Easter weekend at home, she found a postcard which had been delivered by hand.

If you're feeling cold, lonely and Sundayish when you get back on Monday night, give me a call and I'll make you some supper at Colville Road. Longing to see you, so rather hoping you will be feeling cold, lonely and Sundayish. Much love, Dom.

Molly did indeed feel cold, Sundayish and a little lonely when she arrived home that evening.

The bedsit where she lived was above an old-fashioned hardware store on the Portobello Road. Windows with grim metal frames (flaking paint) looked out on to the bustling market below. The street was permanently awash with soggy cardboard boxes and cabbage leaves coated in a black, runny grime, but Molly liked the atmosphere.

Her room was reasonably large. In one corner, there was an old cream cooker on legs. It had red Bakelite knobs. The elderly fridge said 'Frigidaire' in silver swirly writing, very 1950s, on its handle. Inside, it was that washy turquoise colour and contained half a pint of milk, two tomatoes and an egg. Beside the fridge was a small sink and a wooden plate rack.

Nearby stood an old jukebox, *circa* 1960. Molly had found it in a country junk shop, still with the original records which would play, waveringly, if an old penny was pushed into the slot.

The sofa was not exactly in its prime, but it did have length in its favour. Although covered in a bleak blue, it was at least spared having to envy a brightly-coloured rug, for the dusty specimen at its feet was of gratuitously sombre shades.

Molly's bed was behind a screen decorated with colourful Victorian pictures of posies and coy ladies with bustles, parasols and plump pink cheeks. Over it, a pair of jeans and a man's cardigan hung limply.

The room was cluttered. Books, mainly. Shelves and piles of books. But there was also an abundance of pictures, cassettes, pieces of make-up, ashtrays, newspapers, photographs, all of which contributed to the lived-in feel of the place.

Molly loved the flat for which she paid £40 a week. She lived there alone and felt happy there, on the whole. When she returned from a weekend away, though, it did depress her. This was due to the cold, mostly. The feeble gas heater always took an age to eradicate the chill. And on Sunday – or Bank Holiday – nights one or two things about it would depress her more than on other days: the dripping tap in the icy bathroom, the draught whistling through warped windows and billowing the curtains, the lack of food in her fridge, the grey crack in the ceiling above her bed.

Thus Dominic's postcard was especially welcome. How clever of him to have predicted that she might feel as she always did when returning to the flat alone. She had never told him.

Molly telephoned Dominic and then had a bath. Afterwards she put on a pair of black leggings. They flattered her legs, but she took the precaution of choosing a large Shetland jersey to cover up her bottom. The wool was rich purple, the colour of a blackcurrant fruit pastille. She stood in front of her mirror, hitched the jersey up a bit, turned round, and looked at the back of herself from over her shoulder. She tugged it down again and peered at her side view. She frowned and sighed. Then she sat on her bed to pull on some black socks and a pair of black gym shoes.

Hardly alluring, she thought. There again, it is only supper, the two of us. Leaning across to her bedside table, Molly picked up a stubby eyeliner pencil and a scratched compact. The pores of the flattened sponge inside were clogged with powder. It fell on to her lap, and formed a light brown patch on her dark leggings.

'Damn,' she said out loud, dusting it off. She held the little mirror in front of her face and screwed up her nose, thinking she looked as colourless as a frozen chicken. So she drew two black lines beneath the rims of her eyes with the blunt kohl. It made all the difference.

Then she squirted on her favourite scent. Jasmine. Distinctive. It had been a conscious decision always to wear the same scent in Dominic's presence. She had this notion that years hence he would smell it somewhere, some time, on someone else. And it would instantly remind him of her. Perhaps he would feel nostalgic. Perhaps he would feel regret. So, long after they had parted, long after he had left her, she might still retain a certain hold over him, however momentary, however distant, however insignificant.

Molly walked slowly to Colville Road, hoping the cold evening breeze would not blow the jasmine away. She padded up the stone steps of the pale pink house. It was a shabby building. The big cream window frames were flaking, cracking and the paint on the white front door was chipped in places, revealing a chive-green colour beneath it. The bell was a little black button. It was stuck precariously to a Perspex box the size of a cigarette lighter with a strip of yellowing crusty sellotape. Molly pressed it carefully but could not hear it buzz. She sniffed and blew her nose on a rose-pink paper handkerchief. After a few moments

84

came the sound of footsteps on the tiled floor in the hall. Behind the rippled glass windows in the door's upper panels, Molly could make out the blurred figure of Dominic walking towards it. Just before he opened it, she touched her nose and hoped it did not look too red.

He was looking well, she thought. His face, as usual, was pale and he did appear to be tired, but he had about him a cheerful air. The sleeves of his semolina lambswool jersey were pushed up. There was a cigarette between his fingers. He kissed Molly hello and they walked upstairs. As Dominic did so, in front of her, he put one hand in the pocket of his worn jeans. The lifted jersey revealed a crumpled beige label with red writing and just above that a black belt. She watched the graceful tilt of his body this way and that as he climbed two steps at a time.

'I was just finishing off some work,' he said, leading her into the sitting-room. It was not a large room but the white walls and big windows with no curtains gave off a feeling of space all the same. On the square table opposite the door a red spotlight lamp rose up from among the chaotic pile of papers and open books. Molly noticed Dominic's antiquated manual typewriter in the midst of the mess. A sheet of Croxley Script stuck out from its metal innards. On it he had written a few lines, but their flow had been much hampered by crossings out and strokes of lumpy Tippex.

Dominic wandered across the mangy haircord carpet and picked up the open bottle of red wine on the mantelpiece. He poured Molly a glass. She sat on a canvas director's chair.

'Am I disturbing you?' she asked tentatively. 'You're in the middle of something?'

'Not going well,' he said, pulling down the skin below one eye, looking to the ceiling and blinking, slowly. 'Trying to write the blurb for one of our books. Hang on a sec – contact lens.' He went away, still holding his eye, opening and closing it. 'I won't be long,' he called. Molly heard him run up the stairs. She stood and went to his bookshelves. She noticed many a thick pale blue volume published by the Oxford University Press. She picked out a thin green book of Betjeman poems. On the title page was an inscription – 'To darling Dominic, on your seventh birthday, with all my love, Mama.' Must have been soon before she died, Molly thought, and hastily placed the book back on the shelf. She

85

feared she had been unwittingly intrusive and immediately sat down again.

Dominic reappeared. 'Sorry about that,' he began. 'I've still got these hard lenses. Agony sometimes.'

Molly nodded sympathetically.

'Listen,' he said. 'Maybe I could get you to read what I've written so far, see if you think it's any good?'

Dominic's eyes widened in anticipation of her answer. He strode to the typewriter and pulled out the piece of paper. As he handed it to her, he took a deep drag of his cigarette. 'Do you mind?'

Molly put her glass on the floor. She was nervous about giving an opinion, worried that she was by no means in a position to do so. On the other hand, she was flattered to have been asked, and therefore felt obliged to say something. She read the three paragraphs carefully.

'I'm not sure about the end,' Dominic told her, 'but I can't seem to get it right.'

Molly narrowed her eyes at it, concentrating. Her forefinger was between her lips as she re-read the words. After a moment she made a tentative suggestion. Dominic expressed his approval. He dragged his chair to the table, put a new sheet in the typewriter, and began to rewrite his text. Molly joined him, pushed a book aside and leaned with her hand on the space she had made. The typewriter spluttered zealously. At one point Dominic momentarily broke off to squeeze her wrist, before resuming his animated activity upon the keys. As he went along, Molly made mention of one or two other adjustments he might make.

Some time later, he wrenched the new paper from the old machine and, puffing at his cigarette, re-read it out loud. When he had finished, he declared it to be perfect.

'All due to you,' he added, standing up with an extravagant smile. He thanked her repeatedly, and gratefully poured her another large glass of wine. 'Are you hungry?' he asked. 'It must be getting on. It's only pasta, I'm afraid.'

They went through to the tiny kitchen. Dominic placed a large saucepan of water on the stove to boil. Molly perched on the low window-sill. They chatted as he prepared the supper. She cut some ham into small pieces for him, and made a salad dressing. Occasionally Dominic put a fork into the pan and tried to pull out reluctant ribbons of tagliatelle. When he managed to catch one, he tipped his head back and dangled it over his open mouth. The gesture looked to Molly like a young bird being fed with a worm.

'I'm not sure if that's done. You have a try,' he suggested, passing her the hot fork, its gleam dulled by the steam which billowed from the cauldron. As she did so, he chucked some lettuce, chopped red pepper, and some watercress into a bowl. Molly drained the pasta and helpfully added the ham, some mushrooms, butter and cream to it. When the supper was all ready, they carried it through to the sitting-room. Dominic cleared the table by placing his typewriter and amorphous pile of paperwork on to the floor.

They sat down at last to eat.

'Where's Bill tonight?' Molly enquired, screwing some black pepper over her plate. She liked Dominic's partner.

'Out with Rachel, thank God. I love them both, but they kept me awake all weekend.'

'Drunk and disorderly?'

'With the emphasis very much on the latter,' Dominic said with good humour.

'I can't believe they were celebrating Easter.'

'Well, they were celebrating something in that raucous bed next door. Each other mostly,' he said.

'Noisy.'

'Very. No question of sleep. I stayed up all night reading. All three nights. Four books.'

Molly giggled. 'That bad?'

'It was just like being back at university. I think I'm going to have to move out.'

'But you like Bill.'

'Very much, yes, but since Rachel has become a more permanent feature, I'm either going to have to move out or get the Noise Abatement Society in.'

Dominic was more relaxed than when they first met. He was still a little shy, but less so. They recognised each other's shyness and it made them both feel more secure.

'Where will you go?' Molly asked.

'Who knows?'

They both knew. But neither would say so just yet.

'Perhaps I could rent a room in my brother's flat, but I think he's already got a lodger.'

87

'That wouldn't be any good, then,' Molly murmured in a matter-of-fact tone. She twisted the creamy pasta round her fork. It was like a bulky bandage wrapped round a wounded limb.

'No, suppose not. I'll keep an eye out, buy the *Standard* and ask friends.'

'And I'll let you know if I hear of anything.'

'If things get desperate here,' Dominic began, tentatively, 'would you mind if I stayed a couple of nights at Portobello Road?'

What a relief, Molly thought, that he had had the courage to suggest the obvious first.

'Of course,' she replied quickly. 'Dom, you don't have to ask. You can stay as long as you like.'

'That's really kind. Thank you.'

He poured her some more wine, then leaned forward with a confiding expression.

'I'm very fond of Rachel, but when she's at it with Bill,' he said, 'she makes a sound like a squealing pig.'

Molly giggled, and Dominic grinned a childlike grin. They were happy.

Their friendship was not characterised by that kind of ostentatious passion which both pleases and infuriates observers. Dominic and Molly were not, thank God, conducting what some might describe as 'a deep and meaningful relationship'. (They both had an aversion to the word 'relationship' anyway. It had connotations of American-style earnestness.) What bound the two of them was the fact that they had become friends. They made each other laugh. It was very simple, very straightforward. There were no complications.

If people asked Molly how it was going with her new boyfriend, she would not take on a maddeningly dreamy air. She would not talk about it in a treacly voice and make out to her friends in significant tones and in a lyrical way that never before had a man and a woman been 'so in love'. Never would she refer to the sexual side as 'love-making' and thus imply her sex life was on a higher plane than that of those who merely 'slept together' or 'had sex'. Nor would she try and make people believe that her affair with Dominic had a somehow elevated quality or was a 'beautiful thing'.

88

As it happened, she did not talk about it much. If asked, she would simply say, 'It's great, thanks'. She had no wish to bore people with her happiness. For Molly was very happy.

She admired Dominic and enjoyed his company. He was not flamboyant, but nor was he dull. There was an air about him of warm ease, of generosity of spirit, of honesty and intelligence. He was good, but not pious.

'I think I might find it quite distracting if you were to squeal so,' Dominic laughed, slouching back in his chair and crossing his legs. 'Maybe that's why Bill's got such a loud voice – to let Rachel know he's there. Anyway, the combination makes for many a sleepless hour.'

'Do they know they're keeping you awake?'

'I thought it'd be tactless to say anything. Embarrassing for them.'

'You'll have to be more assertive. You only need mention it in passing, as it were, in the form of mild teasing. They'd get the hint.'

'There's no need now, really. If Rachel's moving in that's reason enough for me to move out. Too small here for three. It's a bad idea, anyway, living and working with Bill in the same flat.'

Molly quickly agreed. She did not, after all, want to deter Dominic from staying with her. It was an exciting prospect and surely indicated official recognition that they were together. Such a sign of security pleased her.

When they went to bed that night they silently tangled themselves together in a tight hug. Wrapped round her he felt warm.

Sex with Dominic was quite different from sex with Dave. For a start, Dominic, unlike Dave, did not opt to watch *The A-Team* while he was in bed with Molly. Nor did he have a hungry expression on his face which revealed a deep desire, not for her so much as for a pizza (mozzarella, mushrooms, double pepperoni). What's more, her present boyfriend flattered and thanked her in a way which proved it seemed to matter to him that it was *she* who was there as opposed to anybody else.

'I'm very lucky to have somewhere nice to go,' Dominic told Molly appreciatively as they lay in the affectionate embrace. 'Very lucky it's you too,' he added quietly. He was conscious of the fact that it was hard not to make such a statement sound both insincere and corny.

After they had made love, Molly lay on her back and glanced up at the ceiling. She pulled a pillow under her neck and her eyes began slowly to wander about the room. She studied the sombre form of the mahogany wardrobe at the end of the bed. It was a huge thing. The top of it curved at either end. Elephant's shoulders, Molly thought. The silhouette of a high, wooden ironing-board rose up in front of the window. She fancied it, too, was a wild beast, a gazelle perhaps. Beside it stood a delicate wicker table with spindly legs like a giant stick-insect. On the stringy coconut-matting heaps of clothes relaxed like snoozing dogs.

Animal life abounds in Dominic's bedroom, she suggested to herself, not for the first time. The view over this domestic wild-life park had already become so familiar. The white expanse of bed was a sandy patch, upon which she and he always rested in the shade of a hatstand tree.

Molly laughed inwardly at her elaborate imagination. She stared at the sleeping figure beside her, and wondered why she had tolerated Dave so patiently for so long: Dave in his stale and claustrophobic cell, Dave with his clumsy and impersonal notions about sex.

Thus it was that when Dominic pitched up at Portobello Road a few days later, with a bag of clothes and a suitcase of books, indeed when Dominic *moved in*, Molly felt considerable pleasure.

And as to whether or not she had been sensible in allowing him to come, in her mind at least, there was not even the prospect of a doubt.

'I hope,' said Nick, the morning after Dominic moved into Molly's flat, 'that you'll restrict such intimacy to just this one customer.' He sat back into his chair and lit a cigarette. His pose reminded Molly of an elegant character in a Max Beerbohm drawing.

'As it happens,' she replied airily, 'I had plans to take in Mr Jones, Harry Turner, oh yes, and the one who's got a thing about books on Sociology – what's he called?'

'Mr Freeman – ?'

'Yes, him, and Daniel Johnson, of course. I find him so attractive. The eyes.' Daniel Johnson always bought books on religion. He had blond eyelashes and a squint.

'Don't mock me, Mol.'

'How could you suppose that because I share a bed with one customer I'm going to want to with all the others?' Molly began to straighten some books on the table. As she did so, Nick noticed that in the soft grey material of her skirt there was a tear. It was at the hem which loosely swung just above her knees when she moved.

'You silly ass. I was teasing. Couldn't resist,' he said. He knew Molly would have spotted the little rip. It pleased him that she had clearly been too unconcerned about such a trifle to do anything about it.

'You flirt with customers far more than I ever do,' she laughed.

'That's not fair. Who's the one who's actually having an affair with one? I've never taken my respect for them that far.' Nick smiled. 'It didn't take too much for you to be seduced by Mr De'Ath. What, a cup of coffee at Colette's and a week or two? You're easy, Molly Almond. I'm far more of a challenge.'

Molly protested. She had met Dominic in February, she reminded him, and had only been seduced by him a few weeks before Easter.

'That's perfectly respectable,' she said.

'But now he's living with you – '

'It's a temporary measure, till he finds somewhere. Makes sense. It doesn't mean we're getting married next month.'

'I never suggested such a ludicrous idea. Please.' Nick fanned his face with a book as if quite overcome. 'I think Mr De'Ath is a very charming fellow, just a bit precipitate, that's all.'

'He's only staying a while,' Molly pleaded.

'That's what you think,' Nick replied knowingly.

'Well, he can't be there for long. The place is too small for a start.'

'I'm sure your desire to have him under your wing will outweigh the disadvantages posed by your flat's confined dimensions.'

Molly looked at her boss. He had an air of one who had just said something a little daring. Recognising that he had a point, she was cross with herself for underestimating Nick's powers of perception.

'You're all the same,' Nick went on. Molly assumed he must be referring to women. 'All crave a set-up before you even learn how a man likes his coffee.'

'It wasn't my idea.'

'Ah, but when – by miraculous good fortune – it presented itself, you were there, poised to seize the opportunity of taking him in.'

'What about practicality? Dominic had to move out of Colville Road and had nowhere to go. Solution: he comes to stay with me, with whom he has stayed quite a lot in the past three weeks or so, anyway, till he finds somewhere of his own. It's really very obvious and logical. And, of course, I don't object because, if I did, I'd be going out with the wrong person.'

'Okay. But, Mol, promise me you won't make an issue of it?'

'What do you mean – issue?'

'I don't know. Ask him where's he been if he comes in late.'

'Course not. Why should I?' Molly's voice sounded defensive. She had finished straightening the piles of books, and was now standing beside the table, awkward.

'Because you might be tempted to become couply all of a sudden,' he said.

'Give me some credit.'

'The freedom mustn't be threatened, that's all. Scares 'em off.'

'Absolutely. If he starts giving me a hard time about my arrangements he'll be out like a shot,' Molly said, retaliating with a smile.

'Quite right,' he said, agreeing even though she had twisted his words to suit her own sentiments. 'Course, the funny thing about having freedom is one's less tempted to take advantage of it.'

'Yourself excluded,' Molly reminded him.

'Possibly,' Nick admitted with a wicked smile. 'But perhaps Dominic has no such urge. He's an honourable fellow. Got integrity.'

'I think so,' Molly beamed, pleased that Nick recognised those characteristics in her boyfriend which she so admired.

'I see qualities in your boyfriend which, alas, I myself lack,' Nick admitted honestly. 'I might lightly boast about my infidelities, but I don't feel proud of them. There's no pride to be gained from deceiving someone you love. Only guilt.'

'So why d'you do it?' Molly asked genuinely curious.

'Weakness,' he stated, shrugging. He placed another cigarette between his lips. Molly silently observed that his hand shook a little as he held a match to the tobacco tip. 'Dominic's not a weak man. I can tell that, even though I don't know him very well. I like him, Mol. Knows precisely what he's about, seems to me. Shy perhaps, but absolutely straightforward.' Nick emphasised the 'absolutely', pausing before he said the word, taking a long puff of his cigarette, exhaling hard, and only then finishing the sentence. 'You know what I mean?'

Molly indeed knew what he meant and nodded humbly, bit her lip. She was grateful to Nick for being so frank. She smiled and went over to him. Momentarily, as she sat down beside him, she rested her hand on his shoulder by way of an unspoken thank you.

At that minute a bouncy rep appeared with a bag of books, a spotted bow tie and a hooray grin. He was from the Sand Press, an old rival of Carruthers & Orange. Nick did not care for him.

'Nick, my dear fellow, I come bearing the Summer/Autumn list. A lot of fine stuff we have here too. I think you'll find that Sand has excelled itself. We have the new novel by our greatest living writer!'

'Hello, Adam,' Nick said grimly. 'Sit down,' he added, pulling up a chair to the desk and pushing a newspaper from it on to the floor. 'I can't offer you tea, I'm afraid.'

An explanation did not seem to be forthcoming. Molly, who thought Nick was being a touch rude, stepped forward and told the rep that they had run out of PG Tips. 'But,' she said, 'we do have some coffee.' The man nodded appreciatively.

'Well,' he began, settling down to his business, 'let me show you our big lead title for the autumn.'

'The anticipation's unbearable,' Nick commented.

Molly frowned at him disapprovingly as she stepped into the back room to switch on the kettle.

'It's his best book yet,' Adam assured the bookseller. But Nick remained unmoved.

'I'm sure, but alas I shall have to temper my inevitable enthusiasm, I'm afraid. It's a curious thing, but Sand titles have a habit of remaining steadfastly attracted to the shop shelves. Our customers are an undiscerning bunch, no doubt.'

'But surely no. You mean you've got returns?'

'Returns, yes, quite a few,' Nick said, folding his arms.

'I'm sorry to hear that,' Adam told him earnestly. 'It's the time of year I'm sure.'

'Possibly,' said Nick.

He looked the rep in the eye. It was not kind to be unfriendly, but Adam's eager manner and silly notions irritated him. How could he respect a rep who referred to that snivelling pseud from Islington as England's greatest living writer? Everyone knew Sand's most important author had penned one supposedly shocking novel in the 1950s but had produced only flaccid, deeply pretentious rubbish ever since.

'You'll be wanting twenty copies, at least, I'm sure,' Adam informed Nick with infuriating emphasis, opening his black plastic file with see-through leaves inside. Into each he had slipped book jackets and press releases.

'The cover alone is a masterpiece,' he said, pushing it under Nick's nose. 'We've got major interviews in all the papers, and a three-page profile plus pics in the *Sunday Times* Colour Supp. Can't really do better than that, can you? We're all wild with excitement in Bloomsbury Place.'

Smug little shit, Nick thought. This man had a physical effect on his stomach not unlike that experienced when watching operations performed on television.

'I must come round soon,' he mentioned cheerfully. 'I should like to witness such wildness.'

'Yes,' Adam replied, with a feeble half-laugh. 'So, how about thirty then? Fifty?'

'Five.'

'Fifty-five. A wise decision.'

Nick shook his head and held up an opened hand – five. Adam registered and blushed: colour washed over his face, darkening it like water seeping through the soil of a freshly sprinkled plant.

Molly reappeared from the back room bearing two cups of coffee. She passed one to Adam, and plonked the other in front of her boss on the desk, somewhat aggressively.

Molly is cross, thought Nick. Perhaps I've been a bit rude to Adam. Well, not perhaps. I have been rude to Adam. Uncalled for.

Molly leaned against the desk facing the visitor, her back to Nick. She folded her arms and shook her head. Adam's eyes took in her short skirt. She thought he looked a little prissy, but he had a face which illustrated a desire to please. Father Christmas cheeks, a rounded, friendly sort of nose. Molly was keen to make up for Nick's dismissal of him. She was also anxious to order some Sand Press books. Her opinion of them was different from that of her boss.

'I think we could do with taking more than five,' she suggested, polite but firm. 'Let's see. Maybe not as many as fifty. It's quite an expensive hardback, after all. But I reckon we could easily sell twenty-five.' She addressed herself to Adam.

'I think that's maybe nearer the mark,' he ventured, tentatively. 'After all, there's a lot of people who'll buy it automatically for the author, regardless of the publicity he's going to get.'

'Absolutely,' she agreed, turning to Nick to see his expression. It was surprisingly placid. 'I certainly would,' she asserted. 'I happen to love all his books. Nick's just a bit sniffy about them because the more recent ones have tended to be less funny than his first few. And,' Molly added, teasing, 'he's suspicious of people who live in Islington.'

The two men laughed.

'That's probably part of it,' Nick admitted, prepared graciously to accept a remark against himself. 'All right, Adam. Molly's won me over. Forgive me if I seemed a bit prejudiced. We most likely will sell twenty-five.' He nodded and smiled with good humour. 'So, we'll take them.' As he relented, he put his hand up to scratch behind his ear, just beneath the arm of his spectacles. Doing so, he managed to tilt the glasses to one side. They became lopsided on his nose, but he did not bother to re-adjust them.

'Well, that's wonderful,' Adam declared, beaming, more relaxed. 'Can I tempt you to anything else?'

Molly replied that he certainly could.

'Shall we have a quick look through the portfolio, then?' The rep was unsure to whom he should address the question.

'Why not?' Nick murmured agreeably. 'But can I leave you with Molly?' he said, standing up, looking at his watch. 'I ought to make my way to Bedford Square. Meeting with Orange. She can take the order. You'll be better off with her. She doesn't have any silly notions about Islington.' The words were spoken with humorous good spirit. 'Will you excuse me?'

Adam stood up, clutching his portfolio to his knees like a cartoon character. When he took one arm away to shake Nick's hand, various sample book covers took advantage of his awkward stance and escaped to the floor. Watching him, Nick wondered why he had so taken against the man. Molly had

95

made him recognise that Adam was all right, really. He was just as vulnerable as anybody else.

Nick bent down to help him gather up the shiny sheets.

'We have to be a bit careful, though,' he confided as he stood up straight again. 'I hope you'll understand. As you say, it's a difficult time of year.'

Adam quite understood. He was grateful that Nick Winter, a bookseller whom he admired, was actually friendlier than he had supposed.

Nick lifted his jacket from the till. Cheerfully, he patted his pockets, in the characteristic way with which Molly had become so familiar, to reassure himself that his cigarettes lay therein.

'I'll leave you both to it, then,' he told them before saying goodbye and making his way.

Left with Adam, Molly sat in the chair behind the desk and went through the new Sand titles with him. Such responsibility gave her tremendous pleasure. As she sat there, deliberating on how many to take of those she had chosen, she realised quite how much she cared about the bookshop and loved her job.

Alone in the shop when the rep had left, she involved herself with the laborious, but not unpleasant task of decorating the window with fans of new publications and display cards. As she was doing so, she noticed a lady peering inside, an intent expression on her face. Her complexion had across it a grey film of gloom.

After some minutes, the woman entered the shop. The hem of a Black Watch dress hung below her coat.

Molly extracted herself from the window display shelf, climbing over the books she had chosen to arrange upon it but which, for the time being, were strewn willy-nilly. The customer looked lost, frightened almost. Molly asked if she needed any help.

'No thank you,' the lady replied quietly, tentatively. She paused, looking round with agitation. After a brief moment, she changed her mind. 'Actually, yes please. Where might I find your poetry section?' she asked politely. 'I was looking for Professor Field's new essay on Housman.'

CHAPTER
5

There's many a cliché, Helen thought, on the subject of time, but none more fatuous, surely, than 'time heals.' It made her cross.

Two months – more even – had passed since the proposal and Helen's misery was proving admirably persistent. Bugger time. When would it start to do its bit? There was *still* so much humiliation, *still* so much loneliness.

Such was the ostentation of the former that Helen saw it not as a dowdy scarf discreetly coiled round the neck, but more like a vulgar mink coat enveloping the whole body. It was the kind of humiliation which pinched the shoulders and made one stoop. So, in the same way that people could apparently spot a virgin by her gait, they could surely spot, likewise, that a man had made her suffer. Walking on the street, Helen felt she could recognise those knowing looks and hear the windy whisper: 'There goes a spinster spurned.'

See reason, Helen, she told herself. Paranoia plays havoc with the imagination. Nobody cares. When they glance at you on the pavement, they don't really see you or think about you at all. And certainly they don't acknowledge the impression you think you're giving, because they're too busy trying to give their own impressions. It's a bit like a teenager who smokes, Helen reflected. He puffs away, thinking he is cool. But he forgets his friends are too involved in their own smoky cool to notice or care about his. Indeed, does he notice or care about theirs? Does she assume a girl on the tube is perkily promiscuous because she has a breezy air? Or a man is full of regret because his head is bowed? No – so nor do they assume that she's a spinster spurned.

All the same, the mink coat humiliation did seem to have about it a conspicuous quality, even if she was rational about it.

The loneliness was more private, but no less excruciating. It was like an out-of-order tone which sounded inside the head –

on and on. No one else could hear it. Sometimes, even Helen herself forgot it was there. But never for long, because it wouldn't really go away. And there was no hope of it doing so until she happened upon the only cure – companionship.

Of course, at work in the British Museum, Helen had Alfred still. But he came home with her more rarely now. Occasionally she told him important things.

'The last time I saw Nick, he sat on this chair, here, that I'm sitting on. You know what he said? He said I'd taught him a lot about you, far more than he'd have known about you otherwise. And now it's over, he'll never have me, but he'll always have that, that knowledge I gave him about you.'

Although she did talk to Alfred from time to time, the mornings and evenings were spent in her flat, essentially alone. Her tangible companions were the newspaper, the television, a book, a boiled egg. The telephone was another, but on the whole it remained a fair-weather friend, ringing only rarely and hardly ever to impart stimulating information.

'Hello, Cyril Bailey here,' it informed her sometimes. Cyril Bailey was the administrator at college. 'Miss Hardy? I'm organising various members of the English department to club together for the Head's leaving present prior to his taking up his post at Warwick. Might we be able to expect a contribution from you, Miss Hardy?'

About once a week, it would be Mother. 'Your father's been elected Secretary of the Cricket Club. I think a note of congratulation's in order.'

Fascinating things like that.

The telephone's tendency towards inertia left Helen plenty of time simply to contemplate. Thus it was that in the weeks leading up to Easter, she was able to project on to Nick certain qualities he had never attained when she was actually with him. She now viewed that dimple – which she had once seen as a purely arrogant feature – in a more generous light. It gave character to his face. Distinguished. And he made her laugh so, didn't he? So much more than other men. And his horizontal performances: surely such elegance of technique must have demonstrated *some* kind of passion?

In her mind, she saw his naked body, sinewy, and watched the image of it make love to her. She blinked. The image changed, like a slide in a projector. There was again the same naked body, but it was upon an unfamiliar bed and with a female companion with lithe legs, taut flesh, young milky breasts.

Was it Georgia, the girlfriend? Or could it be Molly, the girl in the bookshop? Who was the faceless creature who recurred regularly in the imagination and sickened the sweet throb of longing inside her?

It had to be one of these two women. Ostensibly, Nick's closeness to the latter was entirely platonic. This young girl had the luxury of his confidence, his friendship, his respect, and the joy, every day, of such proximity to him. Yet, whether she loved him as a lover – did she? – or just as a friend, how could she appreciate such a privilege? While the spurned spinster had to make do with relishing mere memory, there was Molly Almond by his side daily and yet probably not even appreciating it. The injustice mocked and taunted.

In the weeks following the proposal, Helen's contemplation opened the way to an almost obsessive desire to see Nick again. And she could so easily. Her keenness to do so could be satisfied by such a simple act: a trip to the bookshop. She traced the familiar route of her possible trip to the Charing Cross Road. It was so inadvisable, so imprudent – he would not want it – yet the very idea excited her sense of danger.

'I can go to a bookshop if I want. It is there as a service to the bookbuyer. I am a bookbuyer, and, as it happens, I want the new essay about you, Alfred.'

Helen informed Alfred that Winter Books was conveniently close to the British Museum. 'So no doubt I'd go there anyway,' she said, 'whether Nick was there or not.'

At Easter, Helen went home to Salisbury for the long weekend. On Easter Sunday she and her parents went to the service at the Cathedral. Her mother wore a raffia hat, glossily dark blue and with red crocheted cherries. During the lesson, Helen struck up conversation in her mind with Alfred. He was uncharacteristically responsive. Perhaps this is the right atmosphere to bring him out of himself, she thought, staring at the altar.

'So, do you think I should go?' she asked him.

'No, my dear. It would not be wise,' she imagined him replying.

'But you don't understand. I have to see him again. It's the only hope of exorcising my love for him.'

'Why?'

'Because I suspect I've elevated him in my mind out of all proportion. A glimpse of the reality might change all that once and for all.'

'I fear that is unlikely,' came the clear response in her head.

At lunch, the three Hardys ate a sherry trifle from a cut-glass bowl. The elder two talked about the erratic bowel movements of their ailing, nicotine-stained poodle. Helen decided that Housman was wrong. Death had removed him somewhat from reality. Women could be assertive today. He was out of touch.

On the Monday after the Easter Bank Holiday, Helen took the tube to Tottenham Court Road. From there she walked to Winter Books.

'Of course, let me show you to the Poetry Section,' Molly said helpfully. 'I seem to remember it came in only last week.'

'Oh, so you ordered some, anyway?' Helen asked carefully.

'Well, I didn't personally. I think the manager did, though. Now, let me see.'

On reaching the relevant shelf, Molly ran her finger along the book spines.

'Oh, I can't seem to find it.'

'Is the manager about?' Helen asked tentatively.

'Afraid not. He's just gone to a meeting at a publisher's. Don't know how long he'll be.'

At once, Helen felt both major disappointment and major relief.

'I was almost sure we'd got copies,' Molly went on. 'I'm terribly sorry. They should be coming in if they haven't already. Maybe Nick's put them somewhere. Anyway, I can order one for you, if you like.'

'Not to worry,' said Helen, watching Molly intently. This was the girl who every working day was so close to Nick. No wonder she smiled so.

Helen thought, this girl must be in love with him.

She wanted to ask her about him. She wanted to know if the faint smell of cigarettes was because he had been smoking. She wanted to know if he had about him the troubled air of regret. She wanted to know if he had ever spoken to his assistant of a lady he once knew who told him about Housman. She wanted to cry out and tell this girl how much she loved him in order

100

that she might extract a comforting word or smile from the one that was so close to him.

But, restraint. She wanted to say so much, but she said nothing.

Molly came back to the desk. 'I'll tell Nick you came in asking for it,' she began. 'Let me take your name.'

Helen shook her head, suddenly afraid.

'Are you sure?' the girl asked kindly. 'We can easily get you a copy. Probably by the morning. It's no problem.'

Molly's voice was thick with kindness. Laden. She liked the customer and wanted to help her. The lady seemed vulnerable, somehow.

'How's Nick?' Helen ventured unexpectedly. Molly's kindness had given her sudden courage.

'Very well.'

'I haven't seen him for a while,' Helen said, fingering a button on her coat.

'He's as spirited as ever. How do you know him?'

'Friends for quite a while. We met at a party, what, a couple of years or so ago now, must be.'

'Before my time,' Molly said.

'How long have you been here?'

'Only a matter of months. What a pity he's not here. I'm sure he'll be sorry to have missed you. He's always very annoyed when friends drop by and he's out.'

Helen doubted that. Any annoyance he might feel would be directed only at the presumptuous visit she had made. Apart from that, he would feel pleasure – pleasure at not having been about when she came.

'Unfortunately, I'm not sure it's worth your while waiting for him. I don't know how long he's going to be. But if you'd like to stay a bit on the off-chance, have a cup of coffee?'

Helen thought, this girl seems so happy. Was it Nick who was making her so happy?

It was a curious thing, but her desire to see him had, in the last few moments, begun to dwindle, feel less urgent. There was a sweetness about Molly which made it all right that Nick was not there. And the girl clearly had such affection for him that just to be near her was enough. Vicarious pleasure. What's more, this way she was spared the agony of his curtly polite disapprobation.

'How kind of you. Are you sure I'm not disturbing your work?'

'Any excuse,' Molly said, confiding. 'I'm trying to do the window at the moment. I want to surprise Nick by finishing it. But I suspect that he won't be back for ages. He's gone to see his former boss. Orange. Wants to cheer the old man up. They'll be getting drunk together and doubtless cursing Carruthers.'

'I remember stories about Carruthers.'

Molly indicated that Helen should sit down and then went into the back room to switch on the kettle. She kept the door open by cocking her foot round it and carried on talking.

'Did you ever meet him? Hugely fat. Comes in here sometimes and is very grand. He puts on that Jeffrey Archer face which sort of says, "Do you know who I am? I'm a hugely important person and you should consider yourself extremely privileged that I have addressed you." Dead patronising. Know the type?'

Helen nodded.

'Milk?' Molly asked with the beak of a carton poised above a mug. Helen said, 'Please, no sugar,' so Molly tilted the carton and the white liquid plopped into the coffee. She passed the mug to the lady.

'By the way, I'm Molly,' Molly said boldly, sitting down behind the desk and taking a sip from a cracked yellow cup with faded violets.

Helen introduced herself.

'Nice to meet you.' The girl's voice was still warm. Maybe Nick had never mentioned her name to his confidante after all.

'I never met Carruthers, no. Never met anybody Nick knew in fact. We only saw each other, really.'

Molly sensed a certain sadness in Helen's tone, and felt a bit embarrassed.

'Not very often, of course,' Helen went on. 'It wasn't like that, you see. It was more a periodical thing to tell the truth.'

'You've been out of touch for a while?'

'In a sense. Goodness, what is it? Nearly three months must be.'

'Not too long then.'

'Feels longer.'

'Have you been away?' Molly asked innocently.

'No,' came the reply along with a brave smile. 'He's been away. It's that way round.'

102

Molly looked at Helen, puzzled. She wondered who she was, what part she played in Nick's life. A relation? Hardly. Had he ever spoken about her? She stared at her trying to gain inspiration. The woman had a handsome face. Must be in her mid-forties. Her eyes, despite being decorated with blue mascara, appeared to be dulled by sadness. Maybe her husband was unfaithful to her? Maybe he loved her still, but she did not love him?

'Well, he hasn't been *away*, as you know. But he's been away from me,' the sad lady explained.

Suddenly it dawned upon Molly. Housman. Blue mascara. This was no cousin or sister. This was the woman who had proposed to Nick a few weeks before Easter. Of course. The one he had turned down.

'We were together, kind of, you see.' Helen, emboldened, felt she could tell the kind girl. 'Came to an end, though, like all good things.' She sighed.

'I'm sorry.'

That was all Molly could think of to say in response. A little feeble, she owned, but she was at a bit of a loss.

'Actually, I'm not altogether certain it was a good thing, but it came to an end anyway. My fault.'

'Takes two,' Molly suggested sympathetically. She felt both sorry for Helen and faintly awkward.

'But I precipitated its demise. Some silly notion I had about marriage.' A little laugh.

'He was off before the pudding. Couldn't even stick around to eat his favourite pudding.'

The pudding, Molly remembered, the very thought of which, Nick had said after the proposal, had sickened his entire being.

'Rejections never get any easier to bear. If anything, when you reach my age, they're worse. One's misery is enhanced by added desperations. One's time is running out.'

'I'm sure that's not true.'

Women, Molly thought, are curious creatures. Such intimate confidences so soon, despite their lack of actual intimacy. Maybe all women are automatically intimate even if the foundation of friendship has not been laid and, indeed, might never be. They simply sympathise with their own lot, understand it, and commiserate about it with one another, willy-nilly. Men, though, don't. Perhaps there's no need. Perhaps their lot's okay, doesn't require mutual commiseration for, after all, you rarely catch them bemoaning matters of a personal nature within moments of meeting one another.

In Helen's mind, on the other hand, was the realisation that she was not usually so forthcoming with a stranger. But she sensed an affinity with Molly. They both harboured an affection for Nick, and because of this she could talk about him to her. It was, admittedly, uncharacteristic to lay herself open in this way. That was the tendency of women with naturally chatty dispositions. The sort who, she had observed, could babble away comfortably to people they hardly knew about private things. That kind of behaviour was quite common among younger, women's magazine reading types, but she found all that sort of thing plain embarrassing. With Molly, though, it was different. She was able to confide in her.

'Modern feminist ideals mean well, I'm sure,' Helen said, sceptical, 'but they conflict, you see, with that fundamental feminine instinct. We all bleat about independence, but we all want to be loved by men deep down. Our bodies, our minds, crave freedom, apparently. But they also ultimately crave security, husbands, children. Modern life is a sore test.'

Molly had not bargained for this. It was surprising, but she went along with it, nodding politely. Helen had a point, but the window needed attention before Nick's return. Dilemma. She ran her hands through her hair and ruffled it.

'There're some, though, aren't there, who don't necessarily want the independence? There's no conflict then. They simply crave marriage,' Molly remarked.

'Isn't that rather an unfashionable view these days when most women are trying to keep quiet about the desire for a husband? They're superfluous, less important than careers apparently, and it's considered undignified to long for one. So we conceal such desires and people look at us and think, she's all right, she can cope. But we're not really all right, not underneath. We cope, yes – there's no choice. But we're never all right.'

The two women sipped their coffee, both perplexed by the fact they were holding such a conversation. Molly looked at Helen all the while with concern. There was truth in what the older woman said, and she sympathised with her sentiments. Occasionally she, too, had pondered upon the possibility of ending up alone. But she had always imagined that time, in the end, would probably see to it that she didn't. For Helen, though, there was a certain urgency. And Molly felt strongly for her. But she felt something else, also. Much to her shame, there lingered inside her a mild disgust. Disgust for such desperation, even though she understood it. Please God, she thought, may I never experience desperation such as this.

'Don't ever let anyone try to make you believe that life's all right on one's own,' Helen went on. 'Lack of companionship makes the very soul feel tetchy. Everything, however seemingly settled, isn't in fact really so. Because even if work's flourishing, say, and there's fulfilment in all other aspects of one's existence, there remains a fundamental *lack*. The reason? Because nothing's properly settled until one's achieved companionship. Only then can life take on that elevated quality of true contentment.'

Molly wondered about this. There was no doubt before she and Dominic had been together she had never known real companionship, and since she had discovered it, she had never felt so happy.

Certainly, in the past, she had seen happiness only as a momentary thing, brought about by a particular event – a clap of inspiration, say, or a magical party. Until she met Dominic, Molly had never believed in the possibility of a period of happiness. Happiness was only ever transient. It was sadness which was characterised by periods.

She had heard some people, of course, lay claim to having experienced extended happiness. But, she had observed, they usually only acknowledged it in retrospect. Molly had always felt that to be an entirely false kind of happiness, enhanced to supposed perfection only by an imperfect memory. People said, for instance, that their school days were the best of their lives or, on the subject of their teenage years, 'I was happy then'. Indeed, they remembered, vividly, a sporting triumph or the sweetness of their first kiss. But they always failed to recall the torturous terms when they were bullied, or the doubts and insecurities which, throughout adolescence, lingered on.

'I know what you mean,' Molly said after a pause. 'Companionship and contentment definitely seem to go together.'

Repetition of what Helen had just said really, but it was hard to know what to add. She was reluctant to voice her own thoughts to this desperate lady.

'Nick can't be said to have been much of a companion,' Helen admitted. 'But when he was with me – infrequent as that was – I loved him just being there. Constant vivacity.'

'He's a good companion, Nick,' Molly agreed.

Helen wondered if she meant 'companion' or just companion.

'Makes me laugh a lot,' Molly went on, unaware of the conjecture within Helen's mind. 'Never get bored with him around, that's for sure.' She was trying to make light of the conversation, bring it to an end, even. The window needed doing. She felt sorry for the woman. But for the moment, she herself was happy. She didn't really want to dwell on despair till the time came when it affected her. There would be plenty of dwelling then. Was this selfish of her? Possibly. But Helen's desperation, to be honest, frightened Molly. It indicated that her own present period of happiness – twenty-five years in the dawning – would end too, just as those moments of it had done in the past. And another one might not dawn again. She did not want to think about it, and the sad stranger was making her think about it. She wished she would go away.

'He ought to be back soon,' she told her, hoping it might prompt Helen's departure.

'I won't wait,' came the abrupt reply. 'Let me just say this. He's not an unkind man particularly. He's just a normal man. Enjoys bachelorhood. And why not? It's a happy state. But just a word of advice, enjoy it for the present, but don't hope for the future.'

Helen had decided that Molly had meant 'companion' as opposed to merely companion. Companion in the significant sense of the word.

Molly smiled. The lady had got it all wrong. 'We're just friends,' she explained. 'Nothing more.'

Helen pretended not to hear her, or chose to ignore what she said.

'Not really much point with men like that. Their charm transports us initially. But ultimately it deceives us. Hankering after security we misinterpret flirtatious attentions. This encourages false hopes, misplaced optimism. What they're after is adventure.'

Molly had heard enough. Too sympathetic to be impatient, though, she resorted to polite hints. She nodded, looked at her watch, apparently casual, and sighed.

'The wretched window. It's one of my least favourite chores. Would you forgive me – '

Helen stood up. 'I am sorry. I've kept you – '

'Not at all,' Molly told her quickly. Her tone was entirely without sarcasm. 'It's just I suppose I ought to get it done before Nick reappears or else he'll tell me I'm dozy or something.' She laughed. Helen put her hands in her pockets.

'Best to get it over and done with,' she said.

Molly grimaced, but with good humour. 'There's only a limited amount you can do with books. Spread them, fan them, pile them, stand them. That's it, really. I sit here sometimes, and I think – how can I make this window more interesting than other bookshop windows? I thought of old-fashioned mannequins in wacky clothes sitting in pensive poses with the latest publications in their hands. That'd be good, don't you think, except some people might think this is a clothes shop or something and come in asking for trousers.'

Helen smiled.

'Then I had this other idea. I thought perhaps I could construct a huge house of books. A skyscraper of books, like a vast Lego building.' Molly's eyes brightened as she turned to the window and swept her arms from the floor to the ceiling.

'Trouble with that, though, we couldn't spare the necessary stock to make it with. Nick said the customers would invariably come in asking for the foundation stones. I don't know, big books like the Shorter Pepys, say. In order to sell it, we'd have to pull out a copy and the whole thing'd collapse. Pity really.

'Alternatively, of course, I did suggest we bung a few authors in there. Now, that'd intrigue the customers, entice them in. But Nick said, no, he couldn't think of one author who'd be prepared to suffer the indignity of being stared at like a monkey in a zoo. I said there were enough who were prepared to go on *Wogan* and plug away, so why not the window of Winter Books? We could guarantee lots of sales, I told him. But he didn't get my point. There's not much room for window ingenuity in a bookshop, you see. So that's why I'm reduced to fans, and more bloody fans.'

'I think I'd better leave you to them,' Helen smiled.

Molly stood still in contemplation of her window. 'I had such plans for it,' she remarked after a pause. Then she turned to Helen. 'Would you like me to tell him you came?'

107

'I think probably not. In fact, far better not.'

'I won't breathe a word.'

Molly was discreet. She did not know Helen, and Nick was a great friend, but she meant what she said.

'Thank you for the coffee. And thank you for putting up with me,' Helen muttered.

'Any time,' Molly replied rashly. Did that sound rude? Was it acknowledgement of the fact that it had been a case of 'putting up with' Helen's company? 'A pleasure,' she added hastily. It had not, after all, positively not been one.

'Do you still want me to get the Housman?' she asked.

Helen began to make her way to the door. 'Not to worry. I think maybe it'd be wiser if I gave Dillons a try. Thank you all the same.'

Molly did not press her, and they said goodbye. Once alone, she took up her position in the window again and began to arrange various new books into fans, and more bloody fans.

Nick stepped inside the elegant house in Bedford Square, the offices of Carruthers & Orange where he used to work. He smiled at a bepearled girl sitting below a chandelier at a reception table in the hall. Then he sprinted up the wide stairs. They were covered in a dull carpet so his footsteps did not sound.

Reaching the first floor, Nick knocked on a cream-panelled door and opened it without waiting to hear the statutory 'Come in'. The room was large and light. His friend and former boss stood opposite him by a big casement window, talking on the telephone.

A bowl of oranges was sitting on Orange's scruffy leather-topped desk. It was his thing, his little joke. Orange's oranges. He brought in a fresh bag of them every morning, but they were rarely eaten, except by those authors whom he discovered and admired. They could all recall having signed their first contract under his watchful eye, and remembered that immediately they had done so Orange had congratulated them and offered them a piece of fruit. This little eccentricity was known throughout the publishing world and was considered to be a great honour. All those on whom it was bestowed (fewer nowadays due to the decline of standards within the house, perpetrated by Carruthers)

108

knew that it was Orange's acknowledgement of their talent and his way of saying that a wider literary distinction would invariably come their way.

Orange was a tall man in his late fifties. He wore a 1930s suit. It was dark and double-breasted. His grey hair was uncombed and stuck out in unkempt tufts. That and his protruding eyebrows gave him the air of a jovial but absent-minded academic.

On seeing Nick he raised one finger to indicate he would only be a moment.

'Christ,' he bellowed into the receiver. 'What's the matter with our bloody proof-readers? There're three such glaring mistakes on this cover I begin to wonder if the whole bloody lot of them are illiterate . . . Yes, the art department sent it up this morning. How can those idiots have allowed it to get through! It has to be changed . . . What do you mean, too late? Look, I'll have to discuss this with you later, I've got someone with me. But nothing is to go ahead till I say, all right? I'll call you back.'

Orange put down the telephone and slumped into his chair.

'God, what a relief to see you, Nick,' he said with a weak smile. 'I don't often get cross, but just look. Look at this.'

He passed the offending book jacket to his friend and sighed. Nick shook his head sympathetically.

'How about a drink?' the older man asked, getting up again and walking over to the tray of bottles on a table in the corner. He poured out two glasses of whisky.

'Where's Carruthers?' Nick asked, sitting down.

'In New York for a week trying to convince some bestselling hackette that we are the publishers for her over here. I think John's gone completely mad. All he can think about is getting bigger and more expensive bloody sagas. The more abortions and incest the better. It depresses me beyond measure. Yet, what can I do? If I tell him that we're a publisher whose reputation is based upon producing books of a certain literary calibre, he bombards me with wretched figures and tells me it's the sagas that pay. His priorities have gone out of the window.'

'Well, don't lose heart completely,' Nick told him. 'I've got something up my sleeve for you.'

'Oh yes?' Orange's voice lightened.

'It's a bit of a shot in the dark, but I think you should certainly look into it. I haven't read it myself, and I doubt now

I'll be able to until it's finished and on sale. All the same, I've reason to believe it'll be excellent.'

'Come on, out with it,' Orange encouraged. 'A novel?'

'Biography.'

'How exciting. Who?'

'Well, actually, someone I'm not a tremendous admirer of, but who does have many admirers all the same.' He paused. 'Housman.'

'You mean *A Shropshire Lad* Housman?' Orange asked, smiling.

'Exactly. The definitive biography of A. E. *Shropshire Lad* Housman.'

'How very interesting. Our poetry list could do with just that sort of boost. He's very fashionable at the moment, isn't he?' Orange asked, rubbing his chin.

'And becoming more so.'

'So who's the author?' Can you bring him in tomorrow?'

'Ah, well, that's a little more difficult. I'm not entirely sure she's speaking to me,' Nick said. Cigarette in hand, he let his arm fall casually to his side.

'What do you mean?' Orange was intrigued.

'I turned down a proposal before Easter and things might just be a little tricky.'

'What sort of proposal, Nick?' Orange gave him a puzzled, sidelong glance.

'Marriage.'

'You're not serious? It becomes more and more intriguing. Who is she?'

'Her name's Helen Hardy. She's very intelligent, very nice. A bit lonely. Teaches English at University College. I met her originally at some party, then she came into the shop.'

'And you were taken with her?'

'She had such enthusiasm, such passion for her subject, I was rather taken by her, yes.'

Orange raised a quizzical eyebrow. Nick nodded.

'I had an affair with her. I liked her a great deal. We didn't see each other very often. Both busy. But when we did, we always had a good time. As I said, I'm not a great fan of Housman, but she made some progress with me, began to make me see his point.'

Orange asked about the proposal.

'Most unexpected,' Nick explained. 'And I can't lay claim to having handled it at all well. I saw no alternative but to bring the thing to an end, really.'

'What with Georgia as well!'

'Not fair on anybody. So, anyway, that's why Helen and I don't see each other. I reacted rather violently. Molly was rather tough with me about it, I remember. Quite right, I suppose. She is a wonder.'

'Indeed,' Orange agreed. 'And what effect did it have?'

'It made me think that perhaps I'd been a bit extreme on the poor woman. I thought it wouldn't be a bad thing if I was to do her a good turn. When I last spoke to her about it she hadn't got a definite publisher, you see. One or two were interested. I always told her that when it was finished I'd show it to you. The fact that she's probably not speaking to me doesn't stop me from telling you about it now, even if I can't exactly produce the typescript.'

'Do you think it'll be any good?'

'Piers, I wouldn't be here if – '

'Quite, my good fellow, just checking.'

'I'd go so far as to say that I think it'll probably be brilliant, and I promise I don't say that out of a sense of guilt about the author. I do have my reputation to preserve.'

Orange laughed. 'Nick, I don't doubt you. So, how do I get hold of this lady? University College?'

'I think that'd probably be the best.'

'You know, I'm going to write to her this afternoon. I'm so excited. Are you sure she hasn't a publisher already?'

'Pretty. And if she does, she certainly won't have signed – '

'Gazump!'

'Precisely.'

'Nick!'

'Piers, you're running a business. It's either that or more sagas.'

'You're a hard and ruthless fellow,' Orange told his friend affectionately.

'Anyhow, we don't know that she has, so send her a letter quickly.'

'I will, I will.' Orange wrote down a note to himself, beaming. 'The definitive biography of Housman by an intelligent, lonely spinster.'

'A handsome academic lady,' Nick added.

'Speaking of which,' Orange sighed, 'I think I've had enough of the handsome academic lady in my life, or rather not in it.'

He was referring to his ex-wife. 'She's more demanding now, I'm convinced, than she ever was when I was married to her. What is it about divorce which renders the really quite reasonable quite unreasonable? I seem to remember she accused me of being the one who lacked reason!'

Nick laughed. 'And Isobel?' he asked. Isobel was the lady to whom Orange was currently attached, but not married.

'I think I'd better have another drink,' he said, getting up with a naughty smile. 'Will you have one?'

Nick mentioned that he ought to be making his way back to the shop, but accepted all the same.

'Isobel,' Orange sighed, 'is proving somewhat tiresome. It's these divorced women. She keeps harking on about her ex-husband. Not that I'm a jealous man. No. It's just he was such a dull character and therefore so's her harking on about him. I pity Julia's poor man if she spends as much time banging on to him about me.'

'You need to find a younger lady,' Nick suggested with a wicked grin.

'Actually, I'm very lucky really, with Isobel. She's not so bad. A man my age can't complain. Rotten cook, of course, but she's a good friend.' As he spoke Orange began to tap his earlobe with his finger. Nick had noticed Piers doing this once or twice before. It was an almost childlike gesture which Nick found oddly endearing.

'Good company, makes you laugh, interests you?'

'Not really.' Orange scratched his chin. 'It has to be said, she's not terribly interesting.'

'Wants to marry you?'

'There is that, yes, which is a mild irritation. Not that I'm averse to it. Just not to her.'

'Doesn't sound like an entirely satisfactory arrangement to me.'

'It isn't,' Orange admitted gloomily. 'A lot of things aren't entirely satisfactory at the moment.' He fingered the book jacket which had earlier made him so cross. 'Isobel and her harking, John and his wretched sagas, bloody book covers,' he added, poking the latter. 'It's a jolly good thing you came by with this proposal. There's nothing like the prospect of a decent new book to cheer me up.' Orange took a swig of his whisky. 'Thanks a lot, old thing. I like the sound of this Housman lady. I like the sound of her a lot.'

CHAPTER

6

The water was tepid, greasy, grey. On its surface small bubbles made patterns like delicate lace which had torn. Molly plunged her hand into the sink and fished about for any remaining things from last night's supper to be washed. Her fingers felt a cold, flabby lump of rice and a stray pea. Quietly squeamish, she shivered a little and plucked out a teaspoon before tugging the plug out. She didn't much care for washing-up.

The flat was uncharacteristically warm. She had returned from work an hour earlier and flicked on the heater full blast.

Molly wiped her hands, kicked off her shoes, and contemplated the mess. Dominic's things. But she didn't mind them being there. Not a bit. His mess was fine.

She plonked herself down on the sofa, feet up, and shut her eyes. I wonder where Dom is, she thought, but wasn't troubled by the wondering.

Switch on the telly. *EastEnders*. Switch it off again quickly. Book. Three pages. A soft snooze. Content.

'Hi there, Mol.'

Dom's voice. Her eyes blinked awake.

'What's the time? How long've I been asleep?'

'Don't know. I only just got in. I went to the Warwick with Bill. We needed a drink. Bad day.'

'Oh dear. Why?'

'There was this book I really wanted to do. I thought I'd got it, clinched the rights from Gallimard. But what do I hear today? I've been pipped at the post. I won't go on about it. It's just so annoying. Anyway, how're you?'

'I feel like I've been out for hours.' Molly held her head and sat up.

'It's only eight. When did you get back?' Dominic asked gently.

'Hour or so ago.'

'Had you forgotten, we were going to go and see *Jean de Florette* tonight at the Gate?'

'No. No, not at all. I hadn't. What time does it start?'

'Nineish. Do you still want to go?'

'Very much so,' she answered, slapping her cheeks to dismiss any remnants of sleepiness. Dominic kissed the top of her head and went to the fridge for a can of beer. Then he sat beside Molly on the sofa and pulled a crumpled brown paper bag from his coat pocket.

'Here,' he said, passing it to her. 'I thought you might like this. Found it today in a dank shop off the top end of Shaftesbury Avenue. It's a second-hand bookstall, really, but they have the odd this and that too. What d'you think?'

Molly took out a floppy beret of deep red velvet. It had a Morris-Minor-green lining, rather grubby and fusty.

'Put it on,' he urged.

'It's great,' she enthused, standing to look at herself in the mirror. 'I love it.'

'I imagine it's an old theatrical one. There's a little black hoop on the side, see, for a feather.'

Molly thanked Dominic and gave him a hug. 'I'm going to wear it all evening,' she pronounced proudly.

A while later, the pair of them left the flat to walk to the cinema. On the way, they didn't speak much. But it wasn't because they had nothing to say to each other. It was because they didn't feel any compulsion to make conversation.

The film was long. Molly loved it. Watching it, she forgot herself entirely, was sucked into the Provençal world it so beautifully depicted. At the end, when the lights woke up, it felt almost peculiar to be back in Notting Hill, surrounded by normal London folk with Coke cans in their hands and with such prosaic concerns as, 'Where did we leave the car', 'Indian or Chinese, what do you reckon?'

Normally, Molly went to films with girlfriends. They would go and lap up chirpy romances set in New York apartments, where the characters would lead Technicolor lives. The heroines always did things like attempt (in vain) to hail a yellow cab on a wet and crowded Fifth Avenue while tripping over the flapping wings of their shiny shopping bags. More often than not the Unlikely Hero would appear (in bright sneakers, say, or wacky trousers), trip over and shout at her before winding up, twenty-seven minutes later, in her white apartment under the huge duvet of her vast bed. There they would eat 'take-outs' from red cartons and say witty things like 'I had a dream so boring it woke me up' before that familiar but glamorous noise – the American telephone – would invariably interrupt their sound-effected kiss. The statutory happy ending would always, needless to say, prompt Molly and Co. to sigh and wish together afterwards over a hamburger that they, too, could find a U.H.

Now she had Dominic, though, it was different. In his company, she still wrapped the fantasy of the film around her as she always had, but when she emerged from the cinema into the cold Notting Hill night, her heart did not feel burdened by wishful thinking.

'How about Tootsie's?' he asked on the pavement. 'Why not?' said Molly, and they walked a few yards along the street to the small hamburger restaurant.

It was dimly lit inside. They sat at a brown Formica table by the window. Around them on the rough brick walls hung tin advertisement posters of the kind found in American bars. They were of varying colours – ketchup red, Colmans yellow, Hershey's brown. There were candles in little glass domes on the tables. Molly had often been to this place with friends and she had sometimes fiddled with the wax over coffee.

Supper was good, ordinary. But Molly recognised that precisely because it was normal, it was special. She was not one to hanker after the taut linen tablecloths and the sparkling glasses on stiletto stems of smarter restaurants. Instead, she preferred to project an element of romance on to the familiar. There was not much romance about Tootsie's. Yet she was particularly happy to be there with this particular companion. This was the kind of happiness she had thought about when Helen had spoken to her of companionship.

They talked about the film and agreed it made them both want to go to Provence.

'Never been,' Molly said.

'Really? I lived there for a while when I was a child,' Dominic told her. 'In the Luberon.'

'How old were you?'

'Eight or nine, I suppose. It was when my father was making a film in Avignon.'

116

David De'Ath was a director of somewhat lugubrious low-budget films. He was much respected by critics and frequenters of the NFT. But he made little money because, alas, a wider audience was yet to appreciate his productions.

'We were there for a good eleven months,' Dominic went on. 'I went to the local school. It was after my mother died, when my father met Cecile who brought me up, really, from then on. He married her when we returned to England, but we used to go back there every summer to stay with her family. It's just like it was in the film.' Dominic yawned.

'Tired?'

'Not really,' he said, pushing his plate to one side. 'Just fed up about not getting those rights. It was a book I really wanted to do. French novel. Brilliant translation by some unheard-of Victorian woman who died because her husband was jealous that she worked so hard. He was an alcoholic. He forced lots of gin down her throat and threw her in the Thames. Amazing story. I found out quite a lot about her. She didn't have any money but was the mistress of a French aristocrat who read lots of French books to her. When she drowned he took to his bed and never got up again.'

'How do you know all this?' Molly began to fiddle with the candle wax. Momentarily it felt hot and gooey on the tips of her fingers. Then it formed into a hardened cap like that on a matchstick.

'Libraries. When things aren't going well at the office I go to libraries. When things weren't going well today, in fact, I went off. Found a book I'd been after for ages. I just hope I'll manage to get the rights for that. If I do, it'll make up to a small degree for losing the French one.'

'Was Bill pleased?'

'He hasn't read it yet. He will be, though, I'm sure. But when I got back he was full of excitement about the fact that Hatchards had placed their biggest-ever order with us. Forty or so, I think, five of each. So we're both feeling rich today.'

Molly laughed.

'Shall I get the bill?' Dominic asked, smiling at a passing waitress. Some moments later it was placed on the table and he rummaged around in his pockets for his wallet. Molly opened her cheque-book.

117

'No you don't. As I said, I'm feeling rich today, Mol. I'm going to do this.'

She began to protest.

'Come on,' he said. 'Let me take you out for a lousy hamburger.' He pushed her cheque-book aside. 'Put that thing away,' he ordered, and then put £15 on the saucer. She thanked him, and they made their way back to the flat.

Molly took off her hat.

'So you're not going to sleep in it?' Dominic asked with mock pain. Smiling, she wandered to her bed behind the Victorian screen. Dominic made two cups of tea and joined her, giggling about the beret.

For God's sake, Molly, she told herself, appreciate the present, moments such as these. It may not last. It's an attitude which might make others impatient. They might well believe you're too self-conscious and would do better just to get on with it, rather than think about it all the time. Understandable. Yet it's too good just to 'get on' with it, and not think about it. It must be relished *now*. If not, the regret when it's over will be greater, more acute. For, added to the sadness that it no longer exists, will be the bleak realisation that while it did exist, it wasn't fully appreciated. Yes, then the regret will be even more intolerable.

So when Molly and Dominic sat up in bed drinking tea, she watched him telling her his plans for the next day. And she thought of Helen, and thought, 'How lucky I am.'

'So what're you up to this weekend?' she asked, as he turned out the light.

'Not much. Thought I might try and find a book I've been wanting to get hold of for ages.'

'Like to come home to Oxford?'

'I'm busy on Friday night.'

'Saturday morning?'

Pause. 'Why not? That'd be lovely,' he said, wrapping himself around her.

'Will you marry me?' she asked him in her mind. Nick had run off before the pudding.

'I'd like to meet Cake and Rufus,' he replied out loud, still there, still lying beside her.

Bringing him home doesn't mean you crave marriage the very next week, Cake had said.

118

'And I could go to the Bodleian. Still got my pass,' he went on, calm.

Of course not. Of course not the very next week. Absurd notion. Give her some credit. She had more patience than that.

'The window's great, Mol,' Nick announced to her the next morning. 'You're brilliant.'

Molly gave him a sceptical look. 'It's only a few fans.'

'Ah, but you have a way with a fan. No one can do fans like you.'

'It's not very difficult. I'm going to get up to date with the orders today. We're rather behind.'

'My fault,' Nick said, plonking his newspaper on the desk. 'I meant to do them yesterday, but this meeting with Piers – '

'I forgot to ask, how did it go?'

'Very well. I took him this idea for a book I think he should publish.'

'And?'

Nick sat down and lit a cigarette. Looking for the ashtray, he placed piles of books and clutter from the desk to the floor.

'Remember I told you about a woman who proposed to me?'

Molly remembered.

'Well, she was writing this book on Housman, and I've told Piers that Carruthers & Orange must buy it.'

'To assuage your guilt?'

'Molly! No!' Nick protested loudly. He paused and added in a quieter voice that that was, perhaps, a small part of it. 'But only a very small part, mind you. The book's bound to be good and it's just what C & O need at the moment, a decent biography.'

'And you feel you must do the decent thing?'

'I didn't have to tell him about it!' he claimed.

'I suppose it indicates you've some conscience,' she said.

'You know I felt bad about it,' he muttered grimly.

Molly shook her head.

'All right. Maybe I didn't make it obvious. But that's not the reason I told Piers. It's not as if she's going to have problems getting a publisher anyway. Doesn't need my help.'

'That's fair. As long as you weren't doing it entirely out of charity,' Molly said.

'Certainly not. I wouldn't recommend a book I didn't think would be any good. My pride's too strong for that.'

119

A man walked into the shop. He asked about a recently published thriller. He had a slightly pompous, self-satisfied air.

'Let me have a look,' Nick said, leaping up from his chair. 'I'm not sure that we do,' he admitted in a concerned voice, leading the man to the crime shelf.

'And why not?' The customer sounded indignant. He was wearing an olive-green felt trilby and an Inspector Clouseau mackintosh.

'I expect we've sold out,' Nick replied quickly.

The man brightened. In a less aggressive voice, he asked whether that was really so. He seemed pleased. His tight mouth even relaxed into a sympathetic curve.

'Oh yes,' Nick assured him. 'I'm sure that must be it.' He checked the shelf again. 'Sorry about that.'

Molly, sitting at the desk, looked surprised. She could not recall ever having had it in stock.

'Are you sure we had copies?' she wondered out loud. Nick smiled at the man, put his hand behind his back against the pocket of his black moleskin trousers, and surreptitiously gestured to his assistant. He fanned his fingers at her in a manner which told her not to say any more.

'Absolutely. We definitely did,' he stressed meanwhile. 'No question.'

Molly could not understand what her boss was on about. She knew she was right, yet kept quiet all the same.

'Can I order you a copy?' Nick asked the customer helpfully.

'Oh. No, no. Thank you,' came the flustered reply. 'Just checking,' the man added, mumbling, and swiftly made his way to the door.

When he had gone, Molly interrogated Nick. 'You knew we didn't ever have that. I even think I remember you specifically telling me not to order it, that you doubted it would sell here,' she stated. 'Why on earth did you tell him we'd sold out?'

'Ah,' Nick began, tapping his nose. 'Couldn't you tell?'

'What? He was the author or something?'

'Precisely,' he answered excitedly, walking round the central table with almost dance-like movements, and poking the air with his finger to emphasise that precision which he acknowledged.

'How did you know, though?'

'Experience,' Nick replied chirpily. 'You can spot an author, "just checking" to see if we've got their books a mile off. It's that contrived nonchalance which gives them away.'

'But he wasn't very nice. Why did you tell him we'd sold out when we'd never had it in?'

'Feel sorry for authors,' he explained. 'It must be so frustrating and depressing once you've gone to the trouble of writing a book and, more often than not, struggled to get the thing published, then to go into bookshops, and find they're not even stocking it.'

Molly smiled and nodded. 'Oh, I see,' she said.

'Well, I think perhaps I should order a couple of copies now.'

'You great sentimentalist! We're not running a charity, you know,' she told him, uncharacteristically tough.

'No, maybe you're right. I don't think it would sell here to be honest,' Nick agreed resignedly. 'It's so agonising, though, don't you think? Poor man.'

'He's probably doing okay. I expect lots of other bookshops have got it on their shelves.'

'Hope so,' Nick said, and paused. Molly giggled at him, and playfully ruffled his hair. 'Hey, Mol,' he went on, 'you didn't think what I did about Helen's book was purely for selfish reasons, did you? You didn't really think I only did it to make myself feel better? I'd hate you to think I was that self-motivated.'

'No, not really,' she said kindly. 'Just checking,' she laughed. 'Just checking.'

That evening, as Nick bicycled home, he felt cold.

Georgia was in the kitchen feeding the marmalade cat. She wore jeans and a yellow T-shirt. No make-up. He walked straight to the Aga and put his hands on the rail. His girlfriend greeted him warmly. Loving. As usual.

'How was work?'

'Not too bad.' Automatic response.

'Lots of customers?' she asked, tapping the enamel bowl with a fork. The jellied cat meat, released from its tin, stank of preserved blood and packaged offal.

'Quite a few,' Nick replied defending his nose with the back of his hand. His girlfriend did not appear to mind the smell.

'Takings good?'

She had a scintillating line in questions, Georgia.

'About two hundred, I think.'

'Average then?'

'Average.'

'How about a drink?' she asked, opening the fridge to put in the remaining half tin of cat food.

'A glass of wine would be lovely. Thank you.'

'I got us some steak for supper. A treat.'

'Lovely,' Nick said again. He was feeling irritable and didn't know why. Georgia deserved better than this.

'I thought you'd be pleased,' she said sadly.

'I am. I really am. Sorry.' He took her hand and looked at her. 'Tired, that's all.'

But that wasn't all. He was tired. But he was also feeling claustrophobic. The cosiness, though he cherished it in some ways, was suffocating him. The questions, feeding the cat, steak for supper. It all spelt security, and it frightened him.

He looked at his girlfriend as she poured him some wine. She was good, Georgia, perfect really. They had known each other for a long time. And they were friends. He loved her in a way. She looked after him, spoiled him. He didn't deserve her. Yet, sometimes, he was beastly to her and he didn't know why. Unforgivable.

Perhaps he did know why, come to think of it. Perhaps the reason was because she loved him so much and, perversely, he wanted to punish her for it. It didn't make sense, of course. But he couldn't help it.

'I love steak. Thank you, Georgie,' he said, but not without effort.

'I thought of asking a couple of people for supper, but then decided it'd be nicer to be on our own,' she informed him. 'That's why I got steak.'

Bloody steak. 'Quite.' How much longer could his enthusiasm for the steak hold out?

'Darling, would you forgive me? There're various telephone calls I ought to make. Can I do anything first?'

'No, no. You go ahead,' she said lightly, not a trace of resentment. Such goodness!

'I never asked you about your day,' Nick said, making his way to the door. 'Was it okay?'

'Fine, thanks,' she replied, pleased he had asked. Too pleased. It annoyed him, so he left hastily, even though he cursed himself for his intolerance.

Supper was a trial. The two of them sat at the table in the kitchen. It was warm, cloyingly so. Nick looked about him. The cat was stretched out beside the Aga. In the open cupboards he could see a packet of rice, a yellow and red box of suet, a jar of home-made jam, a sinewy bottle of raspberry vinegar. A bunch of onions, one of the endless bunches of onions hanging from the ceiling, dangled above his head. It was like the illustration in a children's book of a cosy, domestic scene. Stifling domesticity.

'Isn't it funny,' Georgia began as she dipped her knife into the mustard (there was some case the other day, wasn't there, Nick thought, when a man killed his wife over a pot of mustard?), 'how you can really tell a person by the contents of their supermarket trolley. I mean, I was in Sainsbury's today, waiting in the queue. You honestly only have to glance into that trolley and you get a complete picture of someone's life.'

I love you really, Georgie. My thoughts are wicked from time to time. It's not your fault. It's like when you're at the theatre and there's a melodramatic moment of silence. You have this overwhelming urge, all of a sudden, to cry out 'Fuck', ruffle the order of things for the hell of it. But it doesn't mean you're not enjoying the play, it's not to say you're not enjoying the play.

'The saddest ones are those buying for one. I feel sorry for them,' Georgie went on. 'You know, it's the pint of longlife milk gives it away. Then there's always the complete TV supper in a foil box with the gloomy photograph on the cardboard lid: a sensible blob of steak and kidney, spoonful of peas, one or two carrots, a scoop of mashed potato. Misery.' She shook her head.

'The one can of chicken soup,' Nick offered, helping her along. She was trying so hard, and he was being so cold. Bastard. Don't let me be so unkind, he pleaded with himself. It's because she really loves me, and I don't really love her. I'm not really so unkind. Circumstances. I love you, Georgie, in a way. But I love someone else more. I'm in love with someone else.

Georgia laughed. 'You're absolutely right, the one can of chicken soup! That's a real tell-tale sign.'

I'm beginning to enjoy the play less and less. I'm getting closer and closer to crying 'Fuck!' It's becoming harder and harder to stop myself.

'Georgie?'

'Um?' Nervous smile. Nick sounded serious. He had something important to say. Silence.

'Any good manuscripts recently?' he suddenly asked.

'Is your steak all right?' she suddenly asked.

Simultaneous questioning. Awkward giggles.

'No, no – you – ' she said. Accommodating.

'It's fine. Lovely. Just done enough.'

Georgia smiled at the approbation. Then she told him about the manuscripts. She worked part time for a publisher, reading unsolicited submissions, and editing occasionally.

'They say, what, 55,000 books are published a year? Well, by my reckoning, there must be about five which remain unpublished to every one that does make it into print. You cannot believe the amount of scripts which arrive every day! More and more. I expect C & O are getting the same.'

'Probably,' Nick said.

'I think they say it's only one unsolicited manuscript gets published every five years. Well, we've certainly never done one in the six years I've been there. We've received on average ten a day. So depressing.' Georgia took a mouthful of her steak. She had a young face – she was thirty – but an anxious expression.

'Georgie – ?'

'Each time I read one I hope it's going to be the new discovery and as I open the first page I'm thinking perhaps – Yes?' Georgia sensed something was amiss. Nick did indeed have something important to say. Instinctively, she was putting it off. She looked down at her plate. Slowly, she pushed her knife and fork together. Half the steak remained uneaten. Georgia's appetite had gone.

'I don't think I can marry you, Georgia.'

There. He had done it. He had yelled Fuck.

Nick's girlfriend bit her lip and stood up. She cleared the plates away. Order miraculously still intact. She sat down again. She lit a cigarette. She raised her eyes to look at her ex-boyfriend.

'I'm sorry,' he whispered, putting out a hand to hers. She took it, squeezed it, and shook her head without a word. The funny thing was, she was the one who looked apologetic.

'Have I done something wrong?'

Nick shook his head, not unmoved. 'You haven't done anything wrong. It's not a question of right or wrong.'

'I thought I'd covered it up so well. I thought you had no idea.'

'Georgie, don't.' This time, Nick squeezed her hand.

'I must never let him really know, I said, mustn't let him be aware of my longing. In the end, he'll come round. But till then don't say a word. It'd put him off, I thought. He'd run a mile. But I obviously didn't do a very good job of it, did I?' Little questioning laugh. 'All that restraint, yet you knew all along.'

'Not all along, no.'

'Not since the very beginning, then?'

Nick shook his head. 'Promise.'

'Since when, then?'

The bachelor glanced about his kitchen, shrugged. 'All this,' he murmured, his eyes alighting upon the well-stocked cupboard. 'Little signs.'

'Would it have made any difference if you hadn't guessed, if I hadn't been so transparent?' Trembling voice.

'I loved you, Georgie. Still do – '

'So why – ?'

'Circumstances can be so cruel.'

'I did so much for you – '

'And, my God, I did really appreciate it, my love.'

'Why, then, the – ?'

'I'm sorry.' Nick turned his face away from her. He was sad.

'There's nothing I can do to change it?' She paused, and then added that, no, she supposed not. 'Just tell me one thing, honestly, yes?'

'What?'

Georgia breathed in sharply. 'Is it that you don't want to get married, or,' she faltered, 'that you don't want to marry me?'

Nick looked at her pleadingly. His silence answered her question.

'Please. Tell me the truth, Nick.'

For almost a minute, he said nothing. Then his voice dabbled the silence with a shaking whisper, barely perceptible, like a toe dipping into the water of a chilly pond.

'There's somebody else I love.'

He heard Georgia swallow hard. A tear darted from one eye.

'Well, I did ask,' she said, gently stubbing out her cigarette. 'My fault.' Quieter now. She stood up. 'I think I'll go to bed.'

125

Her hand made a small gesture towards the washing-up piled by the sink. 'Don't worry. I'll do it in the morning. Shall I make up the spare bed?'

Nick closed his eyes. An extended blink. No.

'Are you sure?' Hopeful voice. Maybe it hadn't come to that: separate beds.

'I'll do it,' he muttered.

Hope splintered.

Georgia kissed him on the forehead, told him to sleep well. Then quietly she withdrew.

Alone, Nick leaned over to reach for a bottle of whisky on the dresser. He poured himself a glass with slow deliberation.

What he had just done was undoubtedly unkind. But he was not, really, an unkind man, was he? It wasn't easy: Georgia wanted to marry him, he didn't want to marry Georgia. Bare facts – which could only be called unkind. Kindness, after all, is hardly intrinsic to rejection. Was there such a thing as a person who could reject a lover kindly? Was there such a thing as a murderer who could kill a victim sympathetically?

Nick put his head in his hands and closed his eyes. How, he wondered, could he have done it any other way? He had tried to be gentle, but the truth wasn't gentle. It was like slugging bullets into somebody, but wrapping each one in cotton wool first.

Perhaps he should have set selfishness aside, married Georgia though he was not in love with her. But would not that too have been unkind? Perhaps he should have just let them carry on as they were, letting her think he would marry her one day? Also unkind.

Nick sat up straight, removed his gold-rimmed spectacles and rubbed his eyes. 'The facts being what they are,' he whispered to himself, 'there's no such thing as a kind alternative.'

He stood and walked to the window behind the sink. It was black outside and he could see his muted reflection clearly. He was tall and thin, but not spillikin-like. The legs could do with being just a fraction longer, he decided. The suit wasn't bad though, not bad at all. There was definitely a certain elegance about it. He took a step forward and bent over the sink, the more closely to inspect his face. Handsome, no, but it was what people called a 'nice face', pleasing and sparky. He tried out a frown, then a grin. The smile was soft.

126

It was all okay, but who was he to deserve the love of such a good woman as Georgia? She, he reflected, is capable of inspiring the admiration of many men. What had he done to distinguish himself in her estimation?

He peered hard into the pane. 'I do love her,' he mouthed, 'but it's not enough. We were together under false pretences.'

Nick returned to the table and to the whisky.

She had remained calm, seemingly calm. Always so stoical, Georgia. But he knew well he had crushed her heart like a pill in a pestle and mortar. It upset him that he had upset her, made him unhappy. He was troubled by it because, he told himself, 'I have this power I don't really want or understand. Where does it come from?' He was reluctant to exercise it.

But he had. He had in the past and was continuing to do so. Take Helen, for example. He had not enjoyed her proposal. But neither had he enjoyed turning it down. Maybe it was an arrogance to suppose he had made women unhappy by rejecting them, patronising even.

'Yet,' he said, out loud, 'if I have, I don't like it. If I've done it before and I've done it just now, what's to stop me doing it again?'

Perhaps it meant he was selfish and callous and essentially unmoved by the fact that he could affect others so? This he found frightening. Why should he continue to be loved by women when what he actually deserved was to be rejected by them?

Nick had been spoiled. He was by no means physically devastating. Still, there had always been about him a certain flamboyance which had enabled him to behave as badly as his vanity desired. Having discovered early on that he had the luxury of opportunity, he had exploited it. Who wouldn't?

Yet had he been happy? Had he enjoyed taking advantage of the choice?

The answer, ah well, was a resounding not particularly. Served him right, really, he supposed.

Nick sighed and put the glass to his lips. He drank. The alcohol, though the soothing colour of honey, was bitter. It sizzled his tongue.

Nick rose early the next day. Sleep had been fitful and he had woken easily, without the aid of his hearty alarm clock.

He rather wished Georgia had not remembered to put it in the spare room. In the circumstances, he did not feel he was entitled to be the recipient of such thoughtfulness. Because of this, the satisfaction he usually experienced when he managed to pip the wretched thing to the post was, this morning, denied him.

Making his way to the bathroom, Nick noticed that the door to his and Georgia's bedroom was firmly closed.

The black and white bathroom tiles were cold under his feet. Nick shivered and turned on the taps. The water crashed loudly into the deep Victorian bath. He stood to watch it fill, his mind blank. After a while he climbed inside.

The water was hot, but Nick did not enjoy his bath. He lay back in order to relax but he was unable to. So he washed quickly, and stepped on to the pink mat.

He wrapped a towel around himself and went to the basin. The mirror was steamed up, but he did not wipe it for he did not wish to see his face. He cleaned his teeth, and managed to shave without cutting himself.

Beside the tooth mug he spotted a squat bottle: Georgia's deodorant. On the label it said 'Blue Mist'. This struck Nick as a bit odd. He wondered about the character who had been inspired to christen it thus. Whoever had done so must, he thought, have a very fanciful imagination. Not many people would be able to equate a light fog with a roll-on. And where had there ever been a *blue* mist exactly? He had only seen the gloomy grey kind. It was perhaps lucky, he concluded, that he had not been inclined towards a job in the BO business.

When he had finished in the bathroom, Nick strode out on to the landing and automatically headed for his own room. It was just as he touched the white china door handle that he remembered this was not a normal morning. Contemplation of the Blue Mist had distracted him. He could not simply burst into his room as usual, and hum while he dressed.

Nick put his hand on his chest, and thanked himself for not making an insensitive entry. All the same, his clean clothes were in there and, more important, he very much wanted to see Georgia before he left for work.

So he knocked on his own bedroom door. He did not enter until, after a moment's pause, he heard a muffled 'Come in'.

Georgia was lying in their – his – brass bed, on her side of it. Her eyes were open, but she was very still. Nick went over to her.

128

'Can I?' he asked, indicating that he would like to sit beside her. She nodded and shrugged at the same time.

'I didn't sleep much either,' he said gently, guessing by her pale face that she had been awake most of the night.

She smiled bravely, but said nothing. Nick took her hand in his.

'Not great consolation, eh?' he remarked with sincere concern.

Georgia swallowed hard, lump in the throat.

'You'll be wanting a clean shirt,' she muttered at last.

'I came to see you.' Nick squeezed her hand. 'Wanted to talk to you.'

'Won't you be late?'

'Bugger the bookshop, Georgie. Are you all right?' Pause. He shook his head and looked away from her. 'Silly question.' It was a whisper.

Two tears suddenly varnished her eyes. 'I was thinking I'd go to Sarah's,' she mumbled.

'There's no hurry,' Nick told her. But they both knew that there was.

'I'll start to move some of my stuff out today. Is it all right if I leave the rest till I get myself sorted out?'

'Georgie – '

'There's no need for me to be here when you get back tonight. I think it's best if I don't hang about.'

'But if Sarah can't – '

'Sarah's my sister: she will.'

'I can't believe it's happening,' Nick murmured. Georgia raised her eyebrows.

'What did you expect?' she asked, not with sarcasm but with genuine curiosity.

'I hadn't really thought about the practicalities. I hadn't really envisaged the move out, somehow, the tangible change.'

'You thought I'd stay?'

'No, no. Course not. I just sort of thought everything'd be the same. It'll all be so different.'

'Different. Yes. Suppose it will.' She looked about the room. 'Well, you not here, your things.'

'I'm not staying, Nick. I won't "just be your friend" either. Not for a while, at any rate.'

'Quite. No question ... Georgie, I'm sorry. I will miss you, you know.'

'I'm sure,' she replied patiently. 'But I won't bother you,' she added, dignified. 'Only about the things, my stuff.' There was a pause and an intake of breath. 'Do I know her?'

Nick closed his eyes. Of all the things he owed her, it was an answer to that question. Unfortunately, it was that question which was going to be impossible for him to answer. The guilt was too much.

'I do, don't I?' Georgia asked huskily.

Nick's face, though expressionless, expressed a lot to Georgia, who knew him so well.

'Not only do I know her, but I like her too. I've had her here for supper, haven't I?' Georgia knew.

Nick closed and opened his eyes slowly by way of an economical nod.

'I'm very fond of her,' she said, too generously.

Nick bit his lip. The guilt retched inside him. He was, he said to himself, a complete shit, but he was, he added, again to himself, in love.

The green and maroon checked bus seat was slightly warm from somebody else's bottom. Molly crossed her legs and looked out of the window. The weather had not bothered much this morning, she thought. It was a nondescript spring day. Cold.

The conductor speedily turned the handle on his meat-mincing machine and issued a flimsy ticket. Molly put it into her pocket and plugged in her Walkman. She normally read on the way to work, but today she felt like listening to music. Ruth Etting's 'Mean to me'.

Although she was happy, the song made her feel sad. Through the glass she stared at a red traffic light. And all of a sudden she experienced a momentary nostalgia for sadness. There was something strangely compelling about it. It was so familiar, comforting even, that she found she almost enjoyed it: a frightening realisation.

She quickly poked the Stop button and rummaged in her bag for her book. Don't tamper with your period of happiness, she warned herself. Such wilful melancholy is unforgivable.

Molly arrived at the shop before Nick and stood outside looking at it a moment. The facade – glossily painted in dark blue and with dull gold sign-writing saying Winter Books – was old-fashioned but distinguished. She decided that, thus framed, her window display did not look too bad, after all.

She went inside and switched on the lights – lamps with black card shades, and unobtrusive spotlights – then sat at the overflowing desk and began to open the post. The usual sort of stuff: publishers' catalogues, a copy of *The Bookseller*, an invitation to a book launch, a bill or two, and a postcard to Nick from a friend on holiday in Portugal. The telephone rang. It was a customer asking for a learned German volume which would involve a pro forma invoice to the publishers in Hamburg. This reminded Molly that they were again behind with the orders and she began not to look forward to her day. She made herself a cup of coffee and set to work.

Nick arrived mid-morning. He had a distracted air.

'I'm not early,' he said. It was a euphemism he often employed. He felt that to avoid use of the word late somehow made him less so. 'Bloody tube. Okay, so I didn't exactly set out on time. Exactly. But then when I do get on the bleeding tube it makes me even less early. It deigns to go along a bit but then it stops. No reason, just stops. Great. And all these dozy people they just sit or stand there in silence as if they're quite happy to be stock still in the middle of a bloody tunnel for hours. They smile as if to say, "Fine, yes, this is our idea of a good time." But I can't bear the way they just accept it, carry on reading their papers or chatting as if it's some kind of privilege to be there, as if they deserve to be delayed. Makes you sick.'

'What do you expect them to do?' Molly asked blandly.

'Shout a bit, stamp their feet, I don't know.'

'What good would that do?'

'You see, I bet you're one of them, aren't you?' he asked excitedly. 'You sit there, lapping it all up, the inconvenience, thinking, "It's my due, I've no right to get angry." '

'There's no point getting angry. It doesn't make the train move.'

'That's a bloody typical attitude,' Nick protested, not nastily.

'So you shout and stamp, do you? I'm glad I don't travel to work with you,' Molly laughed.

Nick paused before answering, then admitted, a bit deflated, that he didn't do that exactly.

'So what do you do, then, exactly?' she asked with a mischievous smile.

'Well, I think about it, certainly, at any rate.'

'You think about it, you mean shouting and stamping?'

'Well, yes, of course. I think that's what I would do if – '

Molly raised a questioning eyebrow, but found Nick was unable to say precisely what 'if'.

'At least I contemplate making a fuss, not like the rest of them who just sit there like doped chickens.'

'Ah, so it's all right that you're just sitting there too, then, because you're, after all, contemplating – '

'All right, all right, don't tease me. I'm not happy,' he said, suddenly more serious.

Molly put down her pen. She had continued to write out the invoices while the conversation was going on. Nick's latest statement, though, forced her to stop. She looked up, and her concerned expression seemed to ask why, even though she didn't say a word.

He shook his head and lit a cigarette.

'Georgia,' he said, sitting down.

Molly waited. Nick inhaled slowly and deeply. After blowing the smoke out, he bit his lip.

'I haven't been very kind,' he said at last. 'I told her I could never marry her.'

'Not very kind, no,' Molly agreed. 'So another one bites the dust.'

'You mustn't think it gives me pleasure. But I suddenly realised it wasn't fair on either of us, the pretence.'

'Quite.' Molly paused. 'So, who is she?'

'What do you mean?'

'The pretence has been going on for some time, and would've gone on going on. It must be someone really special for you to have brought it to an end.'

'Molly – ' Nick's voice sounded surprised.

'What else would've precipitated your getting rid of her, like this, so out of the blue?'

'It was doing neither of us any good. I was taking advantage of the situation. We were both unhappy with the arrangement.'

'And?'

'All right. I won't deny other elements.' Sounding a little nervous, he sat down and fiddled with his spectacles.

'Tell me who it is,' Molly said.

Nick stared at her and said no.

'Do I know her?'

132

Georgia had asked the same question. 'Depends what you mean by know,' he replied.

'I see. What cunning evasion.'

'I'm not going to tell you.'

'I'll get it out of you in the end.'

'I feel wretched. Have we got any drink next door?' he wondered, standing up again and going into the back room.

'It's eleven-thirty in the morning!'

'Now, I don't want you getting prissy. There was something else I wasn't allowed to do before lunch the other day. What was it? Ah yes, flirting. Life's becoming intolerable. I need a drink.'

In the cloakroom-cum-kitchen, Nick poured himself a shot of Scotch, then re-emerged to resume his conversation with Molly.

'I daresay I'll regret it. Georgia meant a lot to me.'

'I hope you're not going to become self-indulgent.'

'You're very harsh,' Nick observed, leaning against the desk and taking a swig of his drink.

'I liked Georgia,' Molly told him.

'You like me.'

'Can't think why,' she remarked, smiling. 'And what of Liz, number three? Will she go the same way as Georgia and Helen? Or has she done so already?'

'I haven't seen her for a long while.'

'Oh. This girl must be having a great effect on you. You'll be contemplating marriage next. Now that would be something. When do I get to meet her?'

'The whole thing's deeply unsatisfactory,' Nick told her. 'It's hopeless. It'll never work out.'

'It sounds like you've got rid of your girlfriend on excellent grounds. Georgia's no longer around and by the sound of it this new one won't be for long. You have organised yourself well.'

'The "new one", as you call her, isn't around at all. I love her from afar.'

'Oh, that's marvellous. You really have landed yourself in it, haven't you?' Molly's tone was not unkind, just mildly impatient. She picked up her pen again, and began to chew the lid.

'If you tell me I've only myself to blame, I'll make you do the stock-taking all on your own!' Nick said, trying to humour her.

'I wasn't going to say that.' In a gentler voice, she told him she was sorry. He looked at her appreciatively, and shrugged.

133

'How're the orders going?' he asked, in a near whisper.

'I'm slowly getting through them.'

'I forgot to tell you, I sold the last of Dominic's books last night after you'd gone. Will you ask him if he could bring round some more copies?'

Molly brightened. 'That's wonderful,' she said excitedly. 'I'll tell him tonight.'

Nick watched her face. It seemed so happy.

'How is he, by the way?' he asked faintly.

'Very well,' she enthused.

'Good, good,' came the quick reply. 'Now, I must just call Piers and get on. All right?'

Molly nodded and resumed her work.

CHAPTER
7

Molly liked trains. And she was particularly fond of Paddington.

On Friday evening, she arrived at the station with time to spare before the 19.03 to Oxford. This enabled her to roam what British Rail were inclined grandly to call the 'platform concourse', and to take advantage of the 'facilities' it offered. She went to the Travellers' Fayre Buffet for a foam well of Coke, John Menzies for copies of the *Standard* and the *Spectator*, and the Sock Shop for a pair of tights. She was just the sort of person that BR should really appreciate, she thought.

The modern train had vulgar turquoise seats and that white neon lighting that makes everyone look dead. Molly found herself a place by a window and marked out her territory by putting her papers on the table in front of her.

After some minutes the train moved off imperceptibly. Molly thought of those tiny projections in her ear which gauged movement and balance which she had learned about in biology. 'Bet that's foxed you,' she told them silently. 'Didn't realise we were moving, did you?'

Slithering through the darkness, the train made little noise. Molly stared out of the window into a blackness which was only occasionally alleviated by shining amber polka dots.

Molly turned on her Walkman and was reminded of train journeys she had made in the past. There had been something so melancholy about the combination of music, motion and travelling alone. It had always prompted self-indulgent reflections about isolation and longing.

Although the present combination of music, motion and travelling alone brought back to her all those former thoughts, Molly was now able to dismiss them. Temporary solitude was no longer a trial for she was not solitary any more. Now she could feel inside her a comforting warmth which would not let her forget that she was part of something that made her happy.

Rufus met Molly at the station. She spotted him before he did her. He was standing by the metal shutters encasing the closed John Menzies stall. Queuing with other passengers for the privilege of handing her ticket to the nicotine-fingered guard with his greasy hat, she stared at her father.

He was a tall man, late fifties, and distinguished-looking even though he had on his perennial, somewhat grubby, corduroy jacket. Light brown. Beneath it he wore a thinning cashmere jersey of dark blue, and a pair of baggy grey trousers. He was not a great one for co-ordination of colour, Molly reflected affectionately. Clothes, or indeed shoes (scuffed black brogues with soles which flapped like cows' tongues when he walked), were not his thing. On a don's salary, which was unremarkable to say the least, Rufus liked to spend as little as possible on such necessities so as to allow for the more pleasurable expenses.

'My tastes in luxury can hardly be said to be original,' his daughter remembered him once declare. 'Books and good wine wouldn't exactly rank among the wittier or more memorable choices on *Desert Island Discs*.' Rufus was a shy man and utterly unmoved by the desire to be exposed in the media – he occasionally reviewed history books for the *Sunday Times*, but had declined every request to speak about his subject on television – nevertheless he had always harboured a sincere wish to be on this particular radio programme. Molly could recall countless times when her father had openly revealed this fantasy.

'For my fifth record,' he would say, for example, 'after a *lot* of thought, and considerable deliberation, I've decided against Beethoven's Piano Concerto No. 3 played by Wilhelm Kempff. I'm afraid I think it might have to be dropped to make way for Mozart's Sinfonia Concertante in E flat played by Spivakov.' After making such a remark, he would pause, nodding pensively, the decision clearly agonising him. Cake and Molly would then laugh lovingly and tease him with his earnest dilemma. He used to protest at first, insist it was a very serious matter, but would then invariably break into a smile.

'You never know, one day I might be asked for all you know, then at least I'll be prepared,' he would claim, laughing too.

Rufus's face brightened as he spied Molly stepping through the ticket barrier. She walked over to him and gave him a kiss. He had a smooth complexion, and prominent cheek bones that would have made any sculptor happy. Although somewhat gaunt, he did not look old. The skin around his brown eyes had little wrinkles, but they only really showed when he smiled, so Molly took them to be lines of happiness rather than of age.

Perhaps what gave Rufus's years away more than anything else were his teeth. Molly had seen pictures of him when he was young, laughing, and revealing a perfect ivory smile. Now, though, they had thinned, parted slightly, and were shadowed by a barely perceptible tinge of grey. He had lots of gold fillings. He had a thin tongue, bright pink with very white taste buds: icing sugar on a raspberry sponge cake. And very sweet breath, never anything but the sweetest breath.

His pale lips were curvaceous. Like a Renoir nude lying on her side, Cake always said. As a child Molly had thought the comparison rather rude. But from her mid-teens, though, she realised it was more a sexual thing for, since then, her mother had taken to referring to her marital sex life quite a lot – 'bloody amazing, the best', apparently. Molly was slightly astonished by this, considering her parents' tumultuous emotional disparities, but she was pleased all the same, even if she did prefer not to hear or think about it too much.

Rufus was obviously pleased to see Molly. In the car on the way home he asked after the bookshop and Dominic enthusiastically, but she sensed something was amiss. His hands were tight on the steering wheel. The backs of them were marbled with veins, and his eyes had dulled.

They drove back to Warnborough Road, the quiet tree-lined street where they lived. The house was typical of many in North Oxford: large, Victorian, with pale stone, and windows big enough for the neighbours to play soap operas. At the back there was a garden surrounded by a red-brick wall – appealingly blunted, and encrusted with lichen. The neglected lawn was as shabby as those hairy rugs which were so popular in hippy households of the 70s. There were two cherry trees in the middle of it, between which sank a lugubrious grey hammock.

The dark hall was warm. The wallpaper, a brown striped design, was tatty, being over twenty years old. The Almonds had bought it in their more extravagant days, when they were first married. They had been richer then, or perhaps just less careful. The antique mirror with the elaborate frame by the door had belonged to Rufus's grandparents, and the rows of pictures had been collected over the years. Cake only ever

137

wanted to spend the odd bit of spare money on pictures. And her husband encouraged her. One of her favourites was an early Craigie Aitchison. She had loved it so much that in order to buy it, she had sold a necklace given to her by her first lover. Another, also acquired soon after she married, had been paid for with the proceeds from the sale of Rufus's first car. He had, of course, been sad to part with his much cherished old Mini, but he thought the painting – a reclining nude by Tony Fry – as irresistible as did his youthful and persuasive wife.

The sitting-room door was open. It was in there that the paintings hung. Walking past, Molly glimpsed them and the small pencil drawing by Augustus John – of his wife Dorelia – for which she had a particular fondness. She also saw the lighted fire. A low tapestry table squatted in front of it. That was covered with piles of books, in the middle of which stood a vase of sweet pea. Cake's Dalmatian, Currant, was asleep on one of the squashy white armchairs, his front leg limply hanging over the cushion.

Cake herself was to be found in the kitchen crouched into the sofa, on the telephone. She was wearing a pair of old jeans and no socks or shoes. Her legs, though not especially long, were thin and she had tucked them beneath her. The hand which wasn't clutching the receiver was fiddling with her toes. She had on a collarless shirt of thick cotton, white with very thin black and dark blue stripes. But for the fact that it was encrusted with splodges of different coloured paint, it might well have belonged, Molly fancied, to a large old fisherman. The buttons were not done up very high. When Cake inhaled or sighed she could see, through the open neck, her mother's papery skin smooth over the ribbed bones in her chest, like a delicate leather glove being coaxed across the knuckles of a lady's hand.

Her dark brown hair had been wrapped up in a scarf, almost turban-like at the back. The style was reminiscent of that worn by the nude depicted in Ingres's 1808 painting, *Bather*: an unlikely choice for a woman in the late twentieth century, but none the less appealing for that. Molly had always admired Cake's sartorial quirks.

When her husband and daughter entered the room Cake did not look up. By her, on the small telephone side-table, was half a glass of red wine.

Molly sat at the big table and eased the cat from its snoozy position next to the bread board on to the floor.

'Drink, Mol?' Rufus asked, going to the dresser.

'I just find it extremely annoying that he takes yet another painting on trust, as it were, and he never comes up with a cheque,' Cake said loudly into the receiver. 'I suppose I should've learned my lesson by now, but I can just never believe someone has the gall to behave that badly. God knows, he's been a friend for fifteen years.'

Molly nodded at her father, and whispered that she would like some wine. Otherwise, they did not speak: Cake was not in good humour and they both knew that their voices, sounding while she was on the telephone, might incite her temper.

'Well, I'll be seeing him on Monday so I'll just demand that he either writes a cheque then and there or gives the painting back. I think that's fair, don't you? Yes, okay. Me, too. Molly's just arrived . . . Monday. You too.' Cake replaced the receiver and stood up.

'Scrambled eggs for supper, I'm afraid,' she said, kissing her daughter. 'It'll have to do.'

Rufus and Molly simultaneously said, 'That's fine', with more enthusiasm than Cake's statement perhaps warranted. Trying to please.

'When do you want them?' she asked, plainly bored by the whole idea of supper.

'I'll do it,' Molly said, accommodating.

'Well, there's something I want to watch at ten.'

'Plenty of time,' Rufus said, looking at his watch. 'Mol and I'll do it. Won't take a minute.'

'When's Dominic coming tomorrow?' Cake asked, pouring herself more wine.

'Depends if he comes by train or car. The car's a bit dodgy at the moment. In time for lunch at any rate,' Molly informed her brightly. Cake was an expert at creating atmosphere.

Rufus wandered into the larder and could be heard scrabbling about.

'What are you doing in there?' Cake called impatiently.

'Looking for the eggs.'

'For God's sake, where do you think they are?' she huffed.

'Mum – '

139

'Well, they're where I've always kept them,' she told Molly, and then added loudly, 'Second shelf down on the left.'

Rufus reappeared a moment later with a half-dozen box.

'Couldn't see them at first,' he muttered. 'Must be blind.' His voice was apologetic. Cake sighed.

Molly felt vicarious pain, agonised for her father in a way she knew only too well. Cake had no tolerance for people who could not find things. She used to send her young daughter upstairs to fetch a book, say, having instructed her where to look for it. Such requests always caused the child's guts to flip over like clothes in a washing-machine at the end of its cycle. Fear. Fear on so many counts – that she wouldn't be able to find what had been asked for and the shame of having to return downstairs empty-handed, to admit to the failure. Her mother would huff and throw a saucepan into the sink. And would insist on dragging her to the very spot that had been pinpointed. The fear inside Molly was then of knowing that the book, so definitely not there moments ago, would have been placed there by a bogey man, in the interim. Thus, invariably, Cake could spy it instantly and tell her she was stupid.

'Are you blind, or don't you know your left and right? What about the difference between up and down? Got that yet?'

Panic. Shame. Fear.

Was Rufus now feeling the same fear, or was it a more grown-up sort of fear he felt? Perhaps his was more concerned with Cake's inability to forgive such trivial things as not spotting a box of eggs in the larder. Did it not demonstrate, much more significantly, that his wife was devoid of compassion? Did it make him question the nature of her love for him?

Hard to say. Maybe not. He had spoken recently of 'the core' in their marriage. The reference had been breezy, oblique, for Rufus was not a man who enjoyed discussing matters of an emotional nature. But he had spoken once more openly. When Molly was young, he had revealed to her a simplified version of his way of seeing things.

Marriage was like a great ship, he had said, deliberately using a simple image so that her youthful mind might understand.

'You sail a few small boats, then you meet the right person, like I did, and you just know that the next voyage is on a huge big ship.'

'Like the QE2?'

'Exactly,' he had said, pleased he had successfully appealed to the childish imagination. 'And when it leaves the port, everything's exciting. The horizon positively dazzles your eyes. A while later, as the journey progresses, the ship begins to come across choppy waters, and later even terrible storms.'

'So it might be shipwrecked?' Molly recalled she had asked this question wide-eyed, thrilled and frightened by the idea.

'Might be wrecked, yes. But in your heart of hearts, you know it won't be really. And you know why? Because you've put so much into that ship, all your belongings, everything you have in the world. And in amongst them is your true belief that your ship will survive, because it's such a special one. You have real faith in it, you see, the reason being because you love it so much. And you know the minute you let anything slip overboard the ship'll sink. So you can't let that happen because then you'd be left with nothing.'

'And if there wasn't a little boat to pick you up and save you, you might even drown?'

Rufus had raised a gloomy smile at that, and had kissed his daughter without answering.

The young Molly had never told Cake about the ship afterwards. She was not absolutely sure she would have been able to make her mother understand.

Molly asked after her painting. It was more than Cake deserved, but she could always be relied upon to be forthcoming on the subject of herself. At least it might defuse the tension.

'I haven't told you my news. Remember Amy, my friend from New York? She's got a small gallery now in the Village which is apparently doing terribly well and she wants to give me an exhibition.'

'That's wonderful!'

'In the autumn. Of course, Rufus is half-hearted. Never liked Amy.'

'Cake, you know that isn't true. I just said she was a touch humourless, that's all.'

'Which is rich coming from someone who's a laugh a minute.'

Rufus was visibly annoyed but contained his anger. 'Like milk in your scrambled eggs, Mol?'

'Don't worry, I'll make them,' she said, standing up. 'Go and watch the news, if you want. I'll give you a shout when they're

141

ready.' She looked at her mother and added defiantly that she would cook him some bacon as well.

Rufus turned to his daughter. He was grateful to her, and smiled by way of thank you. Then he retreated next door.

'That was an unnecessary remark,' Molly pointed out when he had gone. Over the years she had become bolder.

She remembered another scrambled egg supper. When she was about eight, the three of them had been eating at the green baize card table in front of the telly. There had been the same tension then. Being younger, though, she had been more frightened. Holding a knife and fork which were too big for her small hands, she had silently trembled and been unable to cut her toast.

'What's the matter with you?' Cake had enquired.

At first she had just stared at her mother, unable to speak, completely still, unblinking. The skin below her huge, sad eyes was as translucent as the wax spilt from a milky-coloured candle. If she didn't move, she thought, perhaps her mother would forget she was there, wouldn't demand an answer. Alas not.

'So, Mol?'

'I'm cold,' she had lied.

'Well, then, turn up the heater,' Cake had suggested unsympathetically. Molly had looked at Rufus and under the table he had put a hand on her knee because he had understood.

'What do you mean, unnecessary?' Cake asked her daughter. 'I can't bear it when he criticises my friends. Amy's an extremely old friend.'

'He didn't criticise her, Mum.'

'She's giving me an exhibition, and Rufus said she was humourless.'

'You're being rather humourless about it yourself, if you don't mind my saying. He probably didn't mean it,' Molly told her.

'He didn't say he was pleased for me, or congratulations, or anything like that. Nothing. When I told him I had a show at Amy's, his response was, "You mean, your humourless American friend?" '

'You know Dad. He's proud, really. You know that. Come on.'

Molly put some bacon in a pan to fry and beat up some eggs in a little pudding basin. She added some salt, pepper and milk.

142

Cake sat at the table. She scrunched her hair with her hand and lit a cigarette.

'Well, why the hell doesn't he ever say so then?' she asked, puffing away.

'If you were after a man who went in for declarations, why did you marry Dad?'

'I'm beginning to wonder.'

'Beginning!' Molly remarked. She saw a man throwing cheese footballs into her mouth, but she didn't mention it, even after all these years.

Cake leaned forward, her elbows sliding over the table. She put her head in her hands. Molly looked at her mother and wondered if it was the burden of regret which so weighed her down. She felt pity and contempt and love.

Turning back to the stove, she struck a match, lit a gas ring and bludgeoned the prim blue flames with a buttered saucepan. She sloshed in the eggs.

Cake got up lethargically, cut a couple of slices of bread and dropped them into the toaster. She leaned back against the dresser and watched Molly stirring the sloppy yellow mixture.

'Here,' Molly said, pushing the wooden spoon still in the pan towards her. 'Keep an eye on this. I'll go and get Dad.'

Cake took over at the stove. Molly found her father watching the news as she had urged.

'Supper,' she told him lightly. He stood up immediately and rubbed his hands appreciatively.

'I can smell you've made me bacon,' he said, putting his arm round her shoulders. 'I'm a spoilt man.'

'Hardly.'

'Have you managed to cheer Mum up for me? She's been a bit low,' he whispered, trying to make light of it with a brave smile.

'Er, not exactly.'

'Well, let's both have a go at supper, shall we?'

Molly nodded, and they went through to the kitchen, bound not only by firmness of purpose.

On Saturday morning, Molly slept late. She was woken by the cat who had sneaked into her room and proceeded to walk across her face. Her eyes opened to that grey-yellow light which comes of sunlight through skimpy curtains. They wandered about the room, alighting upon all those familiar objects of the past. There was the chest of drawers, which Molly and Cake had painted with bright fish and sea shells long ago. There was the crumpled poster for the RSC's production of *Julius Caesar*, which she had seen on a school outing to Stratford. There was her red dressing-gown with piping, an old one of Rufus's, which she always left at home.

Also familiar was the dim ache of nausea in her stomach. Whenever her parents were not getting on it was the same. The fact that she was was older made no difference.

Supper had been strained. There had not been a row, but Cake had made various snide remarks which Rufus should not have allowed her to get away with. Perhaps, if they had been alone, he wouldn't have. But Molly doubted it. 'Anything for a peaceful life,' he would say, and so Cake would continue to go on at him, and he would continue to take it.

Although Molly, like Rufus, preferred to avoid an argument, she did, all the same, sometimes become impatient with his tolerance. She wanted him to assert himself occasionally, fight back. That was, after all, what Cake seemed to be after. If he gave it to her, it might quell her a little. But he never did: Cake for all the importance she placed on kindness, had married a man who was perhaps too kind.

And it was her bad luck that she loved him so much. She might curse his kindness, perversely test it with great shows of intolerance and by flaunting her lovers; and she might fantasise and threaten to abandon ship, but despite everything, twenty-five years or so had passed and Cake was still Rufus's wife.

'Why do I love that father of yours so much?'

The question had been asked during an unguarded moment as much as, what, ten years ago now? Cake in tears. Molly could picture the scene clearly.

Early evening. Cake's studio. She had been up there for hours, working. Rufus, back from college, had poured a glass of wine for his teenage daughter to take up to his wife.

Molly had done so. Knocked on the door. No answer, so she opened it very slowly and quietly.

The room at the top of the house where her mother retreated to paint was large. The walls and the floor were white and they were both covered in paintings. There was

144

virtually no furniture except for an old easel and a small wooden stool. When Molly went in she found Cake with her back to the door, standing at the easel. Paintbrush in hand, she was poised in front of a big canvas. About her feet, and in fact splattered all over the floor, was the perennial chaos of drawings, scrumpled papers, squelched paint, old coffee cups, flattened cigarette ends. The smell of oils was almost sickly, but very familiar, evocative, and Molly loved it.

Cake did not hear her enter.

'Mum, I've brought you up some wine,' Molly had said going across to her, tiptoeing through the mess. Cake had thanked her, but continued to stare at her picture. When Molly reached her and handed her the glass, she had noticed that tears were tripping down her mother's face. Still without turning to Molly, Cake had taken her wrist and squeezed it. There was a dash of blue on her cheek.

'This is the best I've ever done. Ever,' she revealed.

It was quite abstract, the painting, and of deep colours – black, dark blues, purples, greens. But it was possible to make out two figures – a man sitting with what seemed to be a pensive, sad expression, and a woman whose questioning stare seemed to bore into him, trying, perhaps, to understand something. Neither looked happy. But in spite of their sombre faces, and the sombre colours, there appeared to be a curious radiance about them all the same. It would have been hard to explain. Impossible. But Molly thought the painting very beautiful, and, like Cake, was able to recognise that it had a special quality.

'I can't sell it,' Cake had suddenly stated blankly. 'Because it has to be given to your father. I want only him to have it. It's for him, you see. No one else in the world.'

More tears, but no sobbing. 'Why do I love that father of yours so much?' she had then asked calmly.

It was a rhetorical question. She followed it with a brave smile and by kissing her daughter on the forehead – regretful, apologetic, loving.

Molly had told her sincerely that the painting was beautiful, and that her father would think likewise. 'He'll love it so much,' she had said, and then, spirits uplifted, tactfully she went away to leave Cake to work out the answer to her own question.

Rufus did love the picture. Still did. It hung in his room in college just above his desk, so he saw it every day, and he never looked at it, he said, without recognising and appreciating its beauty.

Molly snapped herself out of her nostalgic thoughts and pushed aside her blankets and primrose-coloured sheets. She sloped downstairs for some coffee in her dressing-gown.

Cake, cleaning some paintbrushes at the kitchen sink, was cheerful.

'Dominic rang,' she said. 'His train gets in at 12.50. I told him you'd pick him up, but he said he'd get a taxi.'

'He couldn't get the car to start?'

'Dead, he said. What sort is it?'

'Clapped-out Morris Minor.' Molly took a mug from the dresser. 'Where's Dad?'

'Gone to New College to get some wine. He'll be back in a minute.'

'Is he all right?'

'Fine. Why?'

'Just wondering.' Molly paused. 'You won't do any of that when Dominic arrives, will you?'

'Any of what?' Cake asked innocently, as she shook her brushes like a thermometer to get the water out.

'All that stuff last night.' There was no response so she decided to make herself clearer. 'Getting at Dad.'

Her mother blotted the brushes on a drying-up cloth and joined Molly at the table, her eyes a little red. She hung her head and rubbed her hands on her knees.

'I'm sorry, Mol,' she said, after a moment. 'It's not good.'

'Not good,' Molly repeated, trying to add weight to her mother's understatement.

'I promise . . . when Dominic comes. . .'

'I don't want him to feel awkward. It's difficult enough as it is without you giving Dad a hard time.'

'Why's it difficult enough as it is?'

'Well, coming here, first time and all that.'

'Did he have to give it a lot of thought before he could come?' Cake asked sarcastically.

'Yes. A lot of thought,' Molly replied, even more so. It's better, she decided – unlike her father – to drive into the skid, than to veer away from it.

146

Cake immediately apologised. 'I'm looking forward to meeting him. He seems to make you so happy which makes me like him already.'

'That's good.'

'And everyone tells me how nice he is.'

'Who?' Molly asked, pleased.

'I spoke to Nick the other day. At the bookshop. You'd gone out for a minute and we had quite a long chat. He said how much he liked him. But I detected in his voice a certain regret that you'd found yourself a boyfriend. Diverts your attention from your work apparently,' Cake smiled.

'Typical,' her daughter muttered with good humour.

'And from him, he said. Told me he likes you all to himself.'

'God forbid,' Molly giggled. 'I wish he wouldn't say things like that. So embarrassing. I'll get him for it on Monday,' she added, with a naughty grin, and they both laughed.

Cake went into the larder and brought out a bag of potatoes. Over the sink she began to peel them. The vigorous movements were such that her whole body seemed to vibrate, and the hem of her flowing skirt appeared to dance. Cake could attack a potato with a singular ruthlessness.

In the past she used to ask her young daughter to do them for her. Molly had never dared refuse, but she had seen it as a test of her competence, and clearly recalled being made to stand on a chair so as to be able to reach the sink. The sleeves would be pushed up, and the cold, murky water would chill her forearms. The metal peeler used to dig into her small childish hands. She was unable to make it function properly, and it hurt her. So the task was laborious, slow and painful. Humiliating, too, because Cake could whip the peel off in long strips, whereas she could only ever manage pathetic scrapings, the size of fingernails.

To this day Molly had a thing about potatoes, and if cooking them herself would only ever bake them. Fortunately, whenever she was at home nowadays, Cake no longer asked her to do them. Some years ago Molly had had the courage for the first time to resist giving in to her mother's request. By then, of course, her more grown-up hands had mastered the peeler, but it was an instrument which still had bad associations. Cake had clearly cottoned on to the message because since then she had always done them herself without a word. To Molly this was a sign of her ability to stand up for herself, and to assert her adult strength over Cake. For as the years had passed she had learnt no longer to love and fear her mother blindly, but to love and judge her rationally.

A while later Rufus returned from his college.

'I'm making your favourite lunch,' Cake told him fondly, still peeling away. Smiling even. When she finished she wiped her hands on her skirt, sat down and began to tell her husband and daughter a funny story. A natural raconteuse, Cake was able to make an anecdote out of the most mundane experience. She related an encounter she had had in Broad Street the day before with some ridiculous figure who had been madly in love with Rufus for years and was a family joke. They all laughed. Cake's laugh still had that winning ringing quality. It prompted Rufus and Molly to exchange a glance: no wonder they admired her so.

Afterwards, Molly went upstairs to dress. From her small overnight bag she pulled out a pair of khaki shorts from an Army Surplus store, and put them on over black wool tights and tatty Converse sneakers. Then she quickly flung on a black jersey which she had swiped from Dominic. It was big and baggy and not short of a hole or two. There was something extraordinarily pleasing about wearing it – a piece of clothing that belonged to him, was loved by him and even smelt of him. In it Molly felt a secret sense of privilege that she was really part of him. Putting it on enhanced her good mood. Thus it was that when she looked at her face in the mirror she was able to wonder, with good humour, what it would be like not to have a nose which possessed all the shiny qualities of a snooker ball. Cheerfully she dabbed on a little foundation before going downstairs to the kitchen again to join her parents.

'Dad's done brilliantly,' Cake enthused. 'He's got our favourite wine. Extravagant thing.'

'Felt we could all do with a treat,' Rufus remarked. 'I hope Dominic likes drinking. We've got lots here.' He put one of the bottles on the table, opened it and poured each of them a glass.

'To Cake's New York exhibition,' he said cheerfully, raising his glass. His wife put her arm round his waist and thanked him. Molly's anxiety began to subside. The relief was considerable, but she was not so complacent as to expect it to last.

Dominic and his coat arrived at half-past one. He had missed his train, and apologised, embarrassed, but then seemed pleased when he realised that they were all so relaxed about it.

'I was in such a twit this morning,' he said. 'Bloody car. Here,' he added, taking a crumpled paper bag from his pocket. 'I brought you this.' He handed Cake the package and she pulled out one of his books.

'Excellent,' she said sincerely. 'Thank you.' Rufus had a look at it and poured him a glass of wine.

'I look forward to reading that. Wonderful,' he said.

A while later Cake indicated they should sit down for lunch. Fortunately, she stuck to her promise so Molly's queasiness had no cause to return.

In the afternoon, Dominic went off to the Bodleian and Cake told her daughter she liked him 'a lot'.

'He's so attractive and intelligent and polite,' she enthused in the way mothers do. Molly realised her mother probably had a picture in her mind of The Dress. It was a claustrophobic realisation, but a curiously pleasing one too.

'I think he's very kind,' Cake went on, and Molly knew she was fantasising about the future. But she couldn't blame her. She had herself, after all, had similar fantasies.

At supper, Molly's nausea presented itself again, and not in protest at the fish.

'Of course, Dominic,' Cake said, drunk, flirtatious. 'You can't go on expecting your husband to take an interest in your work when you've been married as long as I have.'

She was wearing a black crêpe dress, a little tatty, from a second-hand shop. Her hair was messily scrunched into a precarious pile. Her lips were red. She looked good, Molly thought, proud but uneasy. Perhaps a bit too good. It was hard to acknowledge to oneself that one's middle-aged mother was still attractive. The threatening older woman. Molly wondered if Cake had a younger man who appreciated her paintings.

'Rufus isn't interested any more. You know,' she cheeped, 'I don't think he appreciates what I do.'

This is so excruciating, Molly said to herself, and closed her eyes in an exaggerated blink. She opened them to look at her mother with a pleading expression which said, 'You promised'.

'She's got it all wrong, of course,' Rufus imparted. 'I think her paintings are wonderful. Can't keep saying so, though, can

149

I? Otherwise they'd be meaningless, my comments.' His voice had a persuasive tone. He was trying, in a dignified way, to quieten his wife. Alas, in vain.

'Well, bugger that,' Cake protested. 'Useless, rotten critic you are. Silent most of the time. A painter needs constant encouragement. It's a solitary existence. The least one can expect is for one's husband to show an interest – '

'Cake,' said Rufus, firmly, by way of a polite shut-up.

'Don't you think, Dominic?' she went on.

Dominic looked at Molly, who in turn looked at her plate.

'Damn your reticence, Rufus,' Cake spat. This was familiar territory, but because Dominic was witness to it Molly felt more wretched than usual.

'Mum, it's not true,' she suggested soothingly. But her mother was not soothed.

'Not true? Why's he never talk about my work, then, let alone praise it?' Cake gulped more wine ostentatiously.

'I toasted your exhibition before lunch, remember?' Rufus whispered.

'Oh yes, the champagne really flowed,' she said.

'I thought you were pleased with the Muscadet.'

'Thrilled. Just the thing for a celebration.' She reached for the bottle.

'Come on, Cake,' he coaxed quietly, indicating she had already had enough to drink. She pulled a couple of hair pins out of her hair and shook her head. The tangled mess fell to her shoulders. Defiantly, she poured another glass.

'Terence likes my paintings,' she taunted.

'Like some more, Dom?' Molly asked, standing up, interrupting her mother.

'Now there's a man who really appreciates my work. Dominic, shall I tell you about Terence?'

Molly would have paid to die.

'I don't think *I* want to hear about him,' Rufus remarked crossly.

'Perhaps I ought to tell Molly about Terence,' Cake said. 'She's not the only one blessed with an admirer – '

Rufus stood up. The chair legs screeched on the floorboards. He took his wife's wrist and firmly led her from the room.

150

'Get upstairs,' he ordered, 'and don't come down till you're sober.'

Molly could hear her mother's laugh and her dull footsteps on the carpeted stairs. She flinched with shame and helped Dominic to more fish pie.

A moment later, Rufus reappeared with pained eyes.

'A little too pleased with the Muscadet,' was all he said, before he changed the subject.

Molly bit her lip, agonised for him. Even if she could manage to forgive her mother for this, she would never forget it.

Rufus began to question Dominic about Colville Books. Molly maintained facial attention, but was actually thinking about Cake. And Terence? Who was Terence, exactly? What kind of an admirer? An admirer of painting? An admirer of women? Did Terence merely love Cake's work, or did he love Cake herself?

Molly watched her father in conversation with her boyfriend. Rufus was calm. Only his bleak eyes betrayed the fact that there had just been a scene with his wife. She had severely tested him. Molly marvelled at his serenity. What kind of love or faith in marriage enabled him to stick by a woman who treated him thus?

'More wine, Mol?' he asked, flicking her out of her thoughts. She thanked him and held up her glass.

Later that night, Dominic sat on the end of Molly's single bed. He seemed huge, somehow, in her small, childish bedroom.

'Exhausted,' he said, pulling off his shoes. Then he put out his hand to indicate she should sit beside him. 'Not entirely sober,' he smiled. 'How about you?'

She shook her head. 'Thank God,' she said.

'What's up?' he asked. 'Cake?'

Molly nodded.

'Don't worry about it.'

'Why? I can't stand it when she behaves that way to my father. In front of you, what's more. It's almost as if she does it on purpose, to humiliate us.'

'Don't be silly. As Rufus said, she'd just enjoyed a little too much Muscadet.'

'You don't know her. She's always doing it. God knows why he puts up with it. I'd divorce her.'

'He loves her,' Dominic remarked.

'Can't think why.'

'Come on. You do too.'

'Perhaps.' Molly's voice was a whisper.

There was a hole in Dominic's old Levi jeans. With her thumb she began gently to rub his protruding knee, staring blankly at it as she did so.

'Yes you do,' he told her.

'But she's such a cow. She doesn't deserve him.'

'They've been married a long time. People don't give these things up lightly.'

'Lightly? It wouldn't be lightly. She's been sleeping around for years.'

'How do you know?'

'Don't tell me Terence, whoever he is, simply admires her brushwork. I know my mother. She's been having affairs since I was a child. And she doesn't even bother to keep it a secret from Dad. God, no, it's like as if she's almost proud of herself for having lovers.'

'I'm sure you're being unfair.'

'What I'd do for a conventional mother. She's meant to disapprove of my behaviour, not the other way round. I hate the trendy middle-aged who feel that just because they smoked what they call "pot" in the 60s, and dyed their hair green, that they're Bohemian and liberal and can treat people like dirt. My father doesn't want his nose rubbed in her extra-marital sex life. All this open marriage bit, it doesn't work.'

'It can if both parties go along with it.'

'Would you want your wife to sleep around for kicks, and publicly announce the fact?'

Dominic admitted he would not.

'Well, then. I know for certain when I get married I don't want to endure the kind of thing my father's had to. Mum's example isn't exactly an encouraging advertisement.'

'I'm surprised you still want to get married in that case.'

'The triumph of hope over observation.'

'I'm sure your husband will appreciate such faith.'

Molly looked at him closely. Would you appreciate such faith, she asked him in her mind, if you were he? Will you be he? Why do you speak so definitely in the third person as if discounting the possibility that you could be he?

'I hope he will,' she muttered glumly, complying with Dominic's choice of pronoun. 'Perhaps I'm a bit naïve.'

'Why?'

'Well, seeing them and still wanting it, still having such faith. It's an instinctive thing, I suppose. If I'd had brothers, I don't reckon they'd be so daft. Mum's behaviour would've put them right off the whole idea.'

Molly struggled out of her jersey and leaned against the bedhead.

'It takes two,' Dominic suggested. 'If it's really not working, they're probably both to blame.'

'Of course it's really not working. It hasn't almost since the day they got back from their honeymoon. I'm not sure how long Dad can go on.'

'Look, Mol, this really has nothing to do with me.'

'What do you mean? It has a lot to do with you. You've a lot to do with me, so you are involved.'

'I don't want to be – '

'It's affecting me, and if you care about me – '

'Of course I do, you ass. But I can't be drawn into private family matters.'

Molly looked at him quizzically.

'It's honestly none of my business,' he went on. 'I barely know them.'

'You know me. You might at least be a bit sympathetic.' Molly hugged her knees to her chest.

'Molly, I'm sympathetic, okay?'

She slowly began to rock a little to and fro, pensive.

'I'm sorry if your parents are having difficulties, but I can't be inveigled into it.'

'I'm not trying to inveigle you into it,' she remarked reasonably and quietly. 'It's only that you were here, you saw it going on, I wanted to discuss it with you.'

'I'm very tired.'

'Me too. I'm sorry. End of discussion.'

She was very accommodating, she noticed. 'Anything for a peaceful life,' she thought: her father's philosophy.

If she said what she really felt, if she said, 'Bugger your reluctance to become inveigled', there was the risk he might wander

153

away, a knell ringing in his ears to the tune of claustrophobia. 'Suppress the spontaneous outburst,' she ordered herself, 'and you preserve much more.'

End of discussion.

They undressed, and manoeuvred themselves into the single bed. But it was awkward. Dominic kissed Molly good-night – warmly?

'Too squashed,' he whispered gently. 'To be honest, I think we'd both sleep better if I slept in my room. Do you mind?'

Molly watched as he slipped away. But, left alone, she did not sleep better. To be honest, she did not really sleep at all.

At breakfast, mid-morning, the sun brightened the colour supplements and Rufus's eyes. The book section of the *Sunday Times* was spread out before him. A globule of marmalade gingered Anita Brookner's hair and a flake of croissant obscured her shoulder.

'Morning, Mol,' Cake said. She was in her towelling dressing-gown, smoking and leaning against the stove, waiting for the kettle to boil. 'Sleep well?' Rufus enquired.

'Like a log,' came the reply.

'Dom not awake yet?' her mother asked, not disapproving. 'Let him sleep. Lunch won't be till two,' she went on.

The kettle whistled. Cake made three cups of coffee.

'Might go back to bed for half an hour,' she said. 'Bit of a hangover,' she admitted, smiling. 'Serves me right, I rather overdid it on the Muscadet. Bung the beef in the oven whenever you think, would you, Mol? It's all ready. I've just got to do the pudding.'

She put her hand on Rufus's shoulder. 'Can I nab the *Observer* if you've finished with it?'

Her husband nodded and said 'Do' in a friendly tone. Cake kissed his hair, took the paper, and went upstairs.

Molly sat down opposite him and leaned forward over the table, her head in one hand.

'She apologised,' Molly commented, sipping her coffee.

'In her own way,' Rufus smiled. He had a particularly good smile, so full of expression. Molly always knew what it meant.

'You're too forgiving,' she told him gently.

He shook his head. 'Not really. Foolish more, perhaps.'

'Magnanimous.'

154

'Better to ignore.' He paused. 'Anyway, I'm sorry.'

'Why should you be sorry?'

'I hate to put you through all that.'

'Used to it,' Molly admitted, not grudgingly.

'Alas,' Rufus said with regret. 'Still, Cake and I should have restrained ourselves in front of Dominic.'

'Mum's the one who should've restrained herself,' she corrected. 'Anyway, Dom can handle it.' Her voice lacked conviction.

'Sorry, Mol.' He put his hand on her knee, as he had in the past.

She acknowledged the gesture with a smile, and felt strangely comforted.

The train back to London was crowded but Molly and Dominic managed to find seats. On their sticky table were three empty beer cans and a couple of dishevelled paper napkins smudged with ketchup and mustard. The girl opposite them was about nineteen. She was wearing a neat jersey with T-shirt sleeves, peach-coloured, and had a thin, flat slither of a gold chain round her neck. A copy of *The Puzzler* was occupying her attention.

Dominic opened the *Observer* and began to read. Molly was quite content, in his presence, simply to stare out of the black window.

The girl stood up and headed down the aisle, to the buffet. Molly watched her bare legs and white stilettos step over the various knapsacks and bags in her path. She returned a while later bearing a Max-pax tea with an inkwell of milk, a bag of crisps and a Penguin. As she sat down, she looked at the pair on the facing seats, and smiled at Molly rather weakly.

Was it wistful, that smile, Molly wondered. The solitary girl on the train, a Max-pax her only companion. Was she seeing her and Dominic as one of those coupled entities to be envied? Presumably. She could pity the girl now from a complacent distance. In the past, she had spied couples on trains (what was it that was so poignant about trains?) and had pitied herself.

Molly smiled back and did not immediately rustle her boyfriend's attention away from his paper. No need to rub it in.

The girl got off at Reading.

'It went okay, lunch, I thought,' Molly remarked eventually.

Dominic did not look up. Um, he said.

'Mum was being fine. I like it when she gets going like that, telling funny stories about me and Dad. I loved her on Dad's old girlfriend. What did she say? "The kind of woman who thinks *broderie anglaise* is an art form". She was in a much better mood.'

'Very good,' Dominic said, the *Observer* still winning his regard.

'Makes everyone's life so much easier.'

'Mol, I'm trying to read the paper,' Dominic pointed out crossly, tapping it.

'Sorry, you don't want to get inveigled,' Molly remembered, suppressing a sigh.

'No, and I do want to read the paper.'

'Can I borrow the Review section?'

Of course, he said, and handed it to her.

'You liked them, though, didn't you?' she asked.

'Very much.'

And there the conversation came to an end: they read the rest of the way to Paddington.

Because she was not alone when she returned to her flat, Molly's Sunday evening gloom was not quite as ferocious as usual.

Her companion switched on the heater and went to have a bath while she opened an envelope which had been slipped under her door.

It was a letter from her landlord.

Dear Molly,

      As you probably know, Toby's moving out of the first floor flat and I thought I ought to offer you first refusal on it. As it's a bit bigger than your bedsit, I would have to charge an extra £20 a week if you decided you wanted to move in. Let me know.

      Love, Sam.

The prospect excited her. Fond though she was of her bedsit, it was small and becoming smaller with the Addition and his editions. The increased rent worried her considerably, but Dominic was generous and she could probably muster the courage to ask him to help out.

156

'I've got a letter from Sam,' she told him when he emerged from the bathroom.

'Who's Sam?' he shivered.

'The man who owns the house,' she said, looking about her room. 'Really nice. I thought you'd met him. He's about forty but looks younger. A bit of a 60s relic. Wears black jeans and leather waistcoats. Hasn't got any money. Gets very drunk. Actually I used to quite fancy him.'

Dominic sat on the sofa and rubbed his long, thin legs with the towel. She watched him gently dry the backs of his knees, and wondered why she found such ordinary movements so sensual. It was an indefinable thing, but because of it she trembled a little inside.

'What's he do?' Dominic asked before looking round at her sitting on the sofa beside him, and seeing that familiarly desiring expression on her face. It was a winning expression which he loved. He wanted her too.

There was a flicker of indecision in his eyes. He hesitated for a moment before smiling and kissing her cheek. It was as if to say, regretfully, that just now he did not have the time. Even though he hadn't actually said anything, Molly knew that that was what his promising gesture meant.

'Not a lot,' she said, continuing the conversation that they were having out loud. 'Ostensibly produces an art magazine. But it appears less and less because he hasn't got the backing. It's meant to be quarterly, but I don't think it's come out for eight months. Anyway, he's offered us the flat downstairs.' Excited voice.

'Offered you,' Dominic corrected her, not unpleasantly.

'Well, yes,' she replied, a bit deflated. 'I really want to do it.'

'Then why don't you?'

'Well, it's another twenty quid a week. That'd really be stretching me, but I think it'd be worth it. Have you seen it down there? It's lovely.'

Dominic said he had not.

'So what do you reckon?'

'Molly,' he said, in a gentle tone. 'It's your decision. I don't live here.'

Molly looked at his papers and books on the table and floor. She looked at his vast coat on her chair. She looked at the half-drunk bottle of beer at his feet. She looked at the

157

towel round his middle. Finally, she looked at him, his languid post-bath limbs, his head sleepily lolled to one side. He looked so at home.

'Absolutely,' she agreed. 'But bearing in mind you're, well, what? staying here, really, sort of, would you think it was a good idea?'

'It's your decision.'

'Advise me, then, as a completely disinterested party. Do you think it's a good idea or not?'

'Can you afford it?' he asked.

'Course not. You know I'm broke.'

'Well, obviously, I'd pay half, or as much as I could – more if Bill and I sell a few books. But that's only a temporary measure, as you know – '

'Yes, I know – ' she whispered.

'So, when I move out – '

'When you move out?'

'Well, will you be able to afford it then?'

'What I meant was, when you move out, when's then?'

'You know, when I find somewhere.'

'Oh yes. Course.' Molly's voice was bleak. 'You could always stay on – '

'I want somewhere of my own.'

Molly nodded some quick nods to show she completely agreed, and saw his point. Completely. But of course.

'So what then?'

'I'd just have to find £60 a week somehow. Maybe Nick'll give me a pay rise. Cut down a bit, I suppose, not that I'm exactly extravagant.'

She put a finger through a hole in his black jersey which she was wearing again that day. Then she fingered the little rip in her skirt.

'Could do with a new one of these,' she laughed. 'Mum must have bought this years ago. Still, I better resist if you're not going to be around for long,' she said, lighthearted.

'If Nick orders some more books, I'll buy you a new skirt,' Dominic suggested, 'and jersey, even, so you don't have to keep borrowing mine.' He did not sound resentful.

'You mustn't,' she said generously, but relishing the offer all the same. Well, certainly not a jersey anyway, she thought. I *want* to keep borrowing yours.

158

'When's the guy downstairs moving out?' Dominic asked.

'Sam didn't say in his note, but I imagine a month or so.'

'So I'd better start saving.'

This euphemistic confirmation that he would move with her gave Molly great pleasure. 'You'll come then?' she asked, to make sure.

'For the time being,' he replied, standing up. 'Where did I leave my trousers? I'm meant to be meeting Bill in the Warwick in five minutes.'

'Oh,' said Molly.

'Do you mind?'

She shook her head. No, as it happened, she didn't mind at all. Not in the least. After all, Dominic was moving in with her downstairs, and going to help out with the rent.

Elation.

'Come along a bit later if you like,' he suggested, swamping himself into his coat.

'I might well,' she replied happily. 'About an hour.'

'See you then,' he said, in a cheerful voice, and went on his way.

The pub was crowded. The atmosphere was clammy with smoke, beery breath and the deep hum of Sunday night voices and laughter. Tired figures were slumped on dark chairs or squat stools, pints in hand. Others stood on the bleak lino: white T-shirts, distressed leather jackets, old worn jeans, earnest cigarettes.

Molly squeezed her way through. Familiar faces. The odd smile. A friendly wink or two. She passed a man at the bar whose extravagant buttocks in light brown trousers enveloped the stool like sacks of grain over a donkey's back. His fingers clutched a tall glass of Guinness – black treacle topped with a layer of stiff cream.

'Seen Dom, Jack?' she asked the fat man. Jack was a printer, a friend of Dominic's partner, Bill. Molly did not know him well but had seen him there often before. He seemed to be permanently fixed in that seat, and she could not be absolutely sure the glass of beer had not been superglued to his palm. She liked him, with his cheerful disposition and ready laugh.

'Playing pool, love, I think. Can I get you something?'

'Thanks. Don't worry. I'll get one the other side of the bar.' Molly patted him on the back and carried on inching her way through the crush.

Dominic was, as Jack said, to be found playing pool. Molly spotted him bent over the green table with a cue in hand, his right elbow sticking up behind him. One eye was half closed, partly, Molly guessed, with concentration, and partly to avoid invasion by the billowing ribbon of smoke emanating from the cigarette between his lips.

Bill, his opponent, was standing, hands on hips, at the other end of the table. He had a grey polo-necked jersey and a worried grey look to match: he was losing.

Rachel, his girlfriend, about twenty-seven, was sitting cross-legged on a chair nearby. Arms folded, with her head resting against the wall, she had a lonely air. The mouth was like a staple in a pin cushion. Fed up.

Molly walked over to her and sat down, having kissed Bill hello on the way.

'Bored?' she asked her sympathetically. It was necessary to raise the voice considerably to be heard above the exuberantly drunken hum.

Rachel shrugged and smiled, pleased to see Molly. 'I'm glad you've come,' she told her. 'This game's been going on for hours. Nobody really to talk to.'

Rachel's voice was quiet. Funny, Molly thought, that this was the one who apparently made so much noise in bed. She had met her before one evening at Colville Road with Dominic. The same thing had struck her then. Rachel had not said much, and when she ventured to speak she had done so almost in a whisper. All the same, she had appealed to Molly as a sympathetic character. She was a theatrical lighting designer, and had a penchant for bare legs and gathered cotton skirts with floral prints, *circa* 1950. Otherwise, Molly knew little about her.

Rachel had nearly finished her glass of beer, so she offered to buy Molly a drink. When she stood up to go to the bar, her black leather jacket squeaked.

'What'd you like?' she questioned soundlessly. Molly lip read and asked for some lager. Rachel took her time for she wasn't very assertive with the barman. But she eventually returned bearing two glasses. There was a crumpled £5 note between her teeth. Molly relieved her of one of

160

the drinks so Rachel had a spare hand to put the change in her pocket.

'Thank you,' Molly said.

'The others can get their own,' Rachel remarked reasonably as she sat down. 'How do you know Dominic and Bill, by the way?'

Molly sipped at the amber liquid. Its froth made a fleeting appearance as a moustache above her lip. She licked it off, rested the glass on the floor by her ankle, and answered the question.

'Oh, so you haven't been going out with Dominic for that long, then?'

'No. Couple of months.'

'I really like him,' Rachel told her. 'Very straightforward, nothing malicious about him. He's not dull, though, is he? Sometimes one can be a bit impatient with people who're too nice, but he's got an edge too, hasn't he, so he's definitely not got that problem.'

Molly agreed, pleased.

'And mad about you, of course,' Rachel went on, warmly. 'But you probably know that anyway. So obvious.'

'Well, sort of,' Molly said. 'He's not a great one for putting things into words.'

'But you can tell by implication, can't you? I mean, the other night he and Bill and me were slobbing around at Colville Road, having a bit of supper. Dom kept talking about you, saying a lot of nice things. Well, being him he didn't actually *say* much directly. But I very much got the impression he's extremely in love with you.'

Rachel, as she spoke, was fiddling with the zip of her jacket. Molly thought the acutely gratifying remark deserved a less nonchalant physical accompaniment. So she squeezed her own fingers till they went white and purple and hurt.

'Yeah,' Rachel continued, sliding the metal tongue up and down the metal teeth. 'He showed us this blurb you'd helped him write. Very proud he was, I could sense it.'

Molly rejoiced at Rachel's sensibility.

'And later, we all got into a long discussion about sex.' Rachel broke off to take a gulp of her drink. 'It started because Dom was teasing Bill and me about the fact we tend to make a bit of noise,' she said, her voice becoming even quieter towards the end of the sentence. She laughed, somewhat embarrassed.

So, Molly reflected, he had found the courage to broach the subject after all.

'Anyway, I very much got the idea that things were absolutely satisfactory on that score. More than. Maybe I shouldn't be telling you this.'

'No, go on,' Molly urged.

'Bill told me later that Dom had said to him the sex life was absolutely amazing.'

'That's encouraging. Sure he meant with me and not someone else?' Molly wondered with humour enough to giggle.

Rachel smiled. 'You joking? Dominic's congenitally faithful to those he's in love with.'

'Did you know his last girlfriend?'

'Mary? Or rather, Merry, as Bill called her.'

'Oh, was she very cheerful?'

'No, quite the opposite. It was a joke. She was so glum. Glum as an undertaker. Not a bit like you. Billy was really glad when Dom got rid of her. Me too.'

Rachel ran her hands through her straight red hair.

'Was he in love with her?'

'Merry? For a bit, maybe, at the beginning, but not for long. Couldn't possibly have been for long.'

'Why not?' Molly wondered, intrigued. She unclenched her fingers and reached down to the floor to retrieve her drink. She took a few more swigs.

'Well, she wasn't exactly scintillating company, I'll tell you that much. I think he stayed with her because he felt sorry for her. All that glumness. But he can't have respected her that much. If he had, he'd have left her a lot earlier than he did. I'd hate someone to stick with me just because they felt sorry for me.'

'So, if Dominic walks out, at least I'll know he respects me,' Molly mentioned cheerfully.

'He won't leave you,' Rachel remarked. She dismissed the notion in a way which Molly found comforting.

'Because he feels sorry for me, too?'

'No, no, no,' her companion replied, laughing again. 'Course not. It was a whole other story, Dominic and Merry. You and he are an entirely different matter altogether. Believe me.'

There was a sudden cry from Bill: he had lost the game. Molly and Rachel looked up, startled. He and the victor came over to them.

'You two all right for drinks?' Bill asked gloomily.

Dominic kissed his girlfriend on the forehead and momentarily fingered her hair.

'Now, I've got to play Neil,' he whispered. 'You don't mind, do you? Promise we'll be very quick.'

Molly shook her head and smiled brightly. Dominic resumed his position at the green baize table beside a tall man with long thick dreadlocks and a large woollen hat in Rastafarian colours. Neil smiled and waved at Molly before he patted her boyfriend on the shoulder and started the game.

Bill brought them all some more drinks and sat down with Molly and Rachel. He leaned over and suggested that Dominic must have cheated to have beaten him.

'I've known him for a long time,' he murmured, shaking his head, falsely grim, 'and I always knew he was a cheat.' Pause. He then chuckled to indicate that, really, he thought no such thing.

'I hear you're going to be moving to a bigger flat downstairs,' Bill said. 'That'll be good, won't it?'

'I can't wait,' Molly nodded enthusiastically.

'Dom sounded pleased. He was telling me about it before you came. Said he hadn't seen it yet, but that you'd said it was nice. Seems to trust your judgement,' Bill added, smiling.

'It's only a temporary thing, until he finds somewhere else,' said Molly.

'That's what he says,' Bill confided, winking, friendly. 'A bit like that guy Davies in *The Caretaker* saying he's got to go to Sidcup to get his papers – he'll never get round to it.' Bill offered Molly a cigarette and lit one himself. 'He likes living with you, I know. Only says all that 'cos he can't quite admit to himself that things've turned into, well, a proper arrangement.'

'He seemed very adamant about it only being a short-term measure.'

'Maybe he meant it then,' Bill remarked, sceptical. 'But I reckon once he's got a few of his books on the shelves he won't be in much of a hurry to move them again, find somewhere else.'

Molly laughed. 'He'll hang around, then, because I can accommodate his books?'

Bill shook his head, smiled, and put his arm round her shoulders.

'No, you silly thing.'

'He'll hang around 'cos he's very fond of you,' Rachel piped up.

'Exactly,' muttered Bill, before standing to check on the progress of Dominic and Neil's game.

Half an hour or so passed. Rachel described her job to Molly. Molly was interested, but beginning to feel very slightly drunk, and a little tired. She was happy about what Bill and Rachel had revealed, and in a good mood. All the same, there was a sudden keenness to go home, to go to bed.

'Do you suppose they've nearly finished?' she asked Rachel, bending her head in the direction of the pool table.

Rachel supposed that they had.

Some minutes later Neil declared he had won, and asked them all what they wanted to drink.

'I think I might go back, actually,' Molly suggested, but turned to Dominic to tell him to stay.

'You don't want a last one?' he asked.

She shook her head. 'Do you mind?'

He did not. He would like to take her home, he whispered. The two of them said goodbye to the others.

Dominic put his arm round Molly's shoulders, and they wandered out of the pub and slowly back to the flat.

Molly told Nick her news the following morning before the shop opened.

Unfortunately, she found, enthusiastic was not the appropriate adjective with which to describe his reaction.

'I think you're mad,' he told her, flinging notes and coins into the till as he prepared for the day.

Disappointed, she asked him why.

'It's obvious, Molly. You can't afford it. I thought you found the £40 that you're paying at the moment crippling enough.'

'I do.'

'Well, then. And now you're opting to pay sixty?'

'Half that. In fact, my rent'll go down.'

'Yes, for a while, but when Dominic leaves it'll effectively double. Then you're really going to be pushed. Much though I'd like to, I can't increase your salary at the moment. Turnover is slow, as you know.'

'I'm not asking for a pay rise, Nick.'

'It wouldn't exactly be unreasonable if you were. You work hard for little reward.'

'I like what I do,' Molly assured him.

'All the same, I feel guilty about it,' he said, pushing the till drawer shut a touch aggressively.

She told him he shouldn't. Nick shrugged.

'Anyway, I think it's a bad idea.'

'I like the flat. I'll find a way to afford it. Give up smoking, for example.'

'Some hope,' Nick replied encouragingly. 'Besides it's not good that Dominic's going to be living with you.'

'He is already. We're only moving down a flight of stairs.'

'In order to accommodate him?'

'Well, I admit it is rather cramped in my flat at the moment, but I've always had my eye on that other one. Even before Dominic. Nothing to do with Dominic. It's a nicer flat.'

'Yes, but he'll be paying rent there so it won't be a question of him simply being a guest any more, like it is at the moment.'

'It's only a practicality. And to help me out. It'll still be mine. He's told me he has no intention of sticking around.'

Nick crouched down to the grate and lit the fire. 'I remember voicing my reservations when he first moved in to stay with you. This is one more step to manoeuvring him under your wing, isn't it? Camouflaged in the name of practicality. He can see through it as easily as I can. Come on, if he was as happy as you are about it, he wouldn't be so keen for the arrangement to be temporary.'

'He wants somewhere of his own.'

'Why?'

'I don't know why,' Molly admitted.

'Because he's scared you're trapping him, that's the reason. You're only setting yourself up for being hurt. Once he's living with you on an official basis, it's going to be all the more painful for you when he does move out.'

'No, because I'm expecting it.'

'That doesn't make any difference. When he says to you in a few months' time, or whenever it is, that he's found his own place, you'll be extremely upset.'

'No, I won't.'

'You will, Molly, I bet you. That's if you're still together, then, anyway.'

'What do you mean?' she asked sharply. 'We're very happy.' Defensive voice.

'Everyone knows that the process of disintegration speeds up when people live together.' Nick's hand began to scrabble through the papers on the desk. He found his packet of Marlboro under a crumpled letter. Having extracted a cigarette, he tapped it on a book between his finger and thumb, and placed it between his lips. As he spoke it moved up and down like an oar.

'I can't understand why you're being so pessimistic and discouraging,' Molly said, passing him a box of matches.

'You'll see,' Nick remarked ominously, shaking it and taking out one of the pink-capped matches. He lit the cigarette before blowing out the flame with unnecessary vehemence.

'Well, you haven't changed my mind.'

'I didn't think so,' he replied. 'What's the time? Damn, five past ten and I haven't opened the post yet. You'd better unlock the door. There's a customer outside who has an air which suggests he might even want to buy a book.'

'I'll welcome him with open arms,' Molly said gloomily as she turned the key. 'There aren't many of them about,' she added, and the man who had been loitering at the window stepped inside.

'Hello there, you two. How're you?' It was Harry Turner, a regular customer. 'Something up, Nick? You've got a face like a stomach cramp.'

The bookseller raised a weak smile.

'Well, at least Molly's looking well. Now, you don't by any chance have the new Tolstoy biography? Reviews have been marvellous.'

Nick set aside the letters. He drew on his cigarette, stood up and handed the man a copy from a pile on the central table. They began to discuss it. As they did so, Nick's pained expression relaxed. Whenever he was not in good humour, Molly noted with admiration, he was able to disguise it when dealing with a customer. In fact, the very process of gossiping with them, exchanging opinions, making suggestions and selling books gave him so much pleasure that it was often enough immediately to put him back into his more usual, cheerful mood.

Molly sat at the desk to take over the business of opening the post. Although Nick had lit the fire, she felt a little cold in her white Fred Perry T-shirt. It was of thin cotton, the texture of which reminded her of close-knit goose pimples. She shivered and put on her blue suede bomber jacket.

As she was opening the bookshop telephone bill – always alarming – the telephone rang. She searched for it beneath the various books and papers on the desk, and lifted the receiver.

'Winter Books,' she said automatically.

'Molly, darling, Piers here. Nick about?'

'Got a customer with him at the moment. Shouldn't be long. Shall I get him to call back?'

'Just wanted to know if he's coming to the Pilgrim launch on Tuesday week?'

'Don't think I've heard him mention it. Hang on a second.'

Politely, she interrupted Nick's conversation to ask him.

'Definitely,' he told her. 'And tell Piers I'll speak to him later.'

Molly relayed the news. Then Piers asked whether or not she would be at the party.

'I didn't know I'd been invited.'

'But of course, my dear Molly, you know you're automatically asked to all the C & O parties. We sent your and Nick's invitation together.'

'Hopeless thing must've forgotten to show me. Would it be terribly rude to ask if I could bring Dominic?'

'De'Ath? That fellow who runs Colville Books? Nick told me about him. I hear you and he have struck up a friendship?'

'Well – '

'Certainly he must come. Bring him along. Delighted. I've been wanting to meet him. Knew his uncle. Cambridge together. Very clever man.'

The conversation came to an end and Molly resumed the task of going through the post. She was beginning to feel warmer.

Nick and Harry Turner approached the desk, laughing. The former passed her the Tolstoy. She rang it up on the till and put it in one of the smart blue and gold paper bags.

When the customer had left, she told her boss that she, too, was going to the party.

Nick's mood had taken a turn for the better, and he said he was sorry he had failed to show her the invitation.

'But we'll both go together,' he enthused. 'I think it'll be good. Pilgrim's a fascinating man. You must read his book.'

'I will,' Molly assured him. 'I asked Piers if Dom could come,' she added, tentatively. 'He said yes.'

'Very good,' Nick said quickly, picking up the telephone bill. He raised one of his eyebrows. Molly did not know if this was the shocked response to the large sum he apparently owed British Telecom, or due to the prospect of Dominic accompanying them to the C & O party.

She could not tell, and even though she wanted to know, she did not ask.

For most of her life, Molly had had to endure the unhappy trial of entering parties alone. She put this unfortunate state of affairs down to the fact that she was an only child. Others, if not with a boyfriend or girlfriend, could usually rely on a sibling to escort them. There was something monumentally lonely about turning up at parties on one's own. She had seen some people carry it off in a manner which was admirably grand and self-confident. Alas, that was an art she was yet to master.

Molly did not much care for parties. As a child, she had probably been more gregarious than she was now – urged by Cake along to tea parties in the dubious name of fun.

Her mother loved parties. Always. Molly remembered evenings at Cake's dressing table as she prepared to go to them, watching her put on masses of make-up: black round the eyes, plum-coloured lipstick.

She would squirt her wrists and cleavage with scent. Sometimes she even used to squirt some on to Molly, too. The fine spray would tickle her neck, and she would recoil with the joy of it. Then they used to laugh together. Endless giggling. And she would be allowed to choose which earrings Cake was to wear. She usually picked her favourites: the dangling Georgian bows. French paste. Molly always used to believe they were diamonds.

Rufus would join them, after his bath, and take Molly up to bed. Sometime later, Cake would appear in the lightened doorway of her daughter's attic bedroom, looking unimaginably beautiful in the child's eyes. She would usually have done her hair up like an Edwardian lady and put on a black clingy dress; often decolleté and short, it would invariably reveal a good deal of peachy bosom and stockinged legs in shoes with heels as thin as daffodil stalks.

In the darkness, Cake used to walk over to the small bed. She would offer up a powdery cheek and, unkeen to smudge the meticulously applied gloss, would kiss the air above Molly's ear.

'I'll tell you all about the party in the morning,' she always promised sincerely.

But the next day she never remembered to do so. Molly therefore had to make do with imagining women in colourful dresses, music, and laughter.

It was only when she grew up that she realised parties were never quite as magical as Cake's appearance before going to them had led her to believe. People did not really dress or dance or laugh like she supposed. Quite often they – and indeed she – just wore jeans, and sat and looked bored or sad. They were almost always disappointing, parties, but Molly did occasionally make the effort to go to them, spurred on by the hope that one day she might stumble upon one which fulfilled her fanciful notion.

Launch parties at Carruthers & Orange were better than most. They happened about once a month. Molly quite enjoyed going to them, escorted, as she usually was, by Nick.

Sometimes he would take Georgia along too, and say how lucky he was to be able to accompany his two favourite women.

Molly had liked it when Georgia joined them. Nick's girl-friend was sympathetic, comforting, someone to turn to if she was ever stuck and alone. She was sorry Nick had put an end to his association with her.

A week and a day after having discussed the party with Orange on the telephone, Molly found herself, Dominic and Nick, walking up the front steps of the Carruthers & Orange house in Bedford Square. She wondered if the latter remembered similar occasions when Georgia had been with them. Was his expression one of regret?

Molly watched Nick look at her boyfriend as he took off his enormous coat in the hall. Wistful? She was the one with a partner now.

Although Nick was the last person who would wish to invite sympathy, Molly took his arm in a friendly gesture. Dominic followed closely behind as the bookseller and his

169

assistant sauntered up the stairs. At the top, the three went into Carruthers' vast office. It was crowded but, with her two friends, Molly managed to summon up more confidence than usual.

The party was to celebrate the publication of a book by a historian called Thomas Pilgrim, a friend of Nick's. It was a typical publishing gathering.

There were about 150 people in the tall room, huddled beneath its dignified ceiling. A side table had been cleared and a white cloth laid over it. Glasses, like suspended bubbles, had been set out in formal rows – red wine on one side, white on the other. Ladies with stiff hair, and in black dresses with white collars and cuffs carried round large silver plates with superior canapés. There were smoked salmon roll-ups with cream cheese, midget sausages with a spicy sauce, and upturned thimbles of pastry with innards of chicken and cheese. The food never varied. Not that anybody did nibble at them much. Nick was one of the few exceptions. 'I don't care a jot that it's not fashionable to be seen eating at these parties,' he claimed, stoking his mouth with one of the stunted sausages which came his way. Dominic, following Nick's lead, risked a pastry parcel.

'Very daring,' Nick said, as he watched him put it into his mouth. 'Lucky you've got Molly and me to tell you if you get a flake on your chin!'

Dominic swallowed.

'No, you're all right,' Nick whispered charitably. 'Now, shall I introduce you to Piers?'

Molly looked about. She recognised a few faces – various employees of C & O whom she had met with Nick; one or two agents, several writers. Piers Orange approached the three of them. He kissed Molly, shook hands with Nick and greeted Dominic enthusiastically.

'You must be Dominic De'Ath. Here,' he said, passing him a glass of wine. 'Have this. Or would you prefer white? Mol, how about you?' he asked, handing her one too. 'Nick can get his own, lazy fellow,' he added, smiling at his friend affectionately.

At that moment, a lanky woman in her forties sidled up to Nick and dropped one of her arms round his neck so her hand hung limply at his chest. She gave him a luxuriant kiss on his chin, rather too close to his mouth. Drunk. Her buttercup curls were like loose purl-stitch knitting. She had a slit in her skirt and her good legs shimmered in white tights which wrinkled at the knee. A pink handbag with a mean strap had fallen from her shoulder and was clinging to the bend of the other arm, which was poised on her hip.

'Nick, I've just read Thomas's book, and hear you're responsible for it,' she twittered. 'You are a star.' Another fat, glossy kiss.

'Not really, Edie,' Nick said, sighing and surreptitiously making a desperate face at Piers. 'Have you met Dominic De'Ath?' he asked her, his neck cricking from the strain of her mole-spotted limb. 'Dom, this is Edie Carruthers.'

'Wife of the boss himself,' she slurred, and winked at the young man. 'Tell me, do you like books, Dominic?'

Molly shivered with embarrassment. Her boyfriend smiled at the woman, but it was a question he could not, however polite, bring himself to answer. No matter: Edie Carruthers did not appear to notice anyway.

'Nick, darling,' she began loudly, 'you're so clever, did you know that? Come with me. Let's get a drink together, shall we? I think you need one. I certainly do.'

I wonder, Molly wondered, whether Edie's in love with Nick or just fancies a quick fling? She noticed her hand lightly brush his shirt above his nipple. Nick flinched, barely perceptibly, and smiled weakly as the woman drove him away in the direction of the drinks table.

Either way, thought Molly, I think she's going to be disappointed.

Dominic spotted a friend, excused himself, and moved off to talk to her.

'Eager Edie,' Orange whispered in Molly's ear, smiling. 'Alas, I fear she may be on to a lost cause. She's been trying to sleep with Nick for years. He's terrified of her. Thinks she'll eat him for breakfast. She's a powerful woman.' Orange laughed at his friend's grim predicament. 'Thank God I'm not within the age limit. In fact, one more year and Nick'll be in the clear. He's pushing on. Once he hits thirty-five, she won't be interested any longer. I'd lock your friend Dominic up if I were you,' he said jokily.

'I don't think he's glamorous enough for her,' Molly commented.

'That doesn't bother her. She's turned on by intelligence. That's her thing. Pity she isn't blessed with huge sums of it herself. Unfortunately, she seemed to be able to spot it in your

171

friend immediately.' Orange's tone was not entirely serious. Glass in hand, he rubbed his chin with his forefinger. A drop or two of wine splashed on to his yellow tie in the process. He chuckled, not seeming to mind.

'I've heard very good things about Colville Books,' Orange began again. 'Impressive list they've got, haven't they?'

'Not making much money though, yet,' Molly revealed, sipping her drink.

'They will. Apparently Dominic's got plenty of talent. He'll make it work.'

'How do you know?'

'Publisher's instinct, Mol, publisher's instinct,' he said, tapping his nose in a knowing gesture. More wine on the tie. Another good-humoured chuckle.

Nick, having managed to relieve himself of the lanky Edie, reappeared at Orange and Molly's side. He looked flustered, cross even.

'What happened to you?' the publisher asked, laughing.

'Thanks a lot, Piers,' Nick snapped, sense of humour unusually inconspicuous.

'Oh dear. Did she spit you out?' More teasing and laughter from Orange. Molly could not suppress a giggle.

'Not funny,' Nick said, frowning. 'She dragged me to the cloakroom.' Pause. 'She grabbed my flies and tried to – ' he added in a quieter voice.

'Such is the excitement of a C & O launch party,' Orange declared.

'Bloody embarrassing,' the bookseller remarked huffily.

'Here, have another drink,' the older man said kindly, leaning to catch a full glass from the tray borne by a passing waitress. 'I've got good news,' he went on. 'I wrote to Helen Hardy about coming to see me about the Housman. She rang and spoke to Emmy, who made an appointment, sometime in the next couple of weeks.'

'Really? Oh good,' Nick said, perking up.

'Yes, I'm looking forward to it. Grateful to you for that. Thank you. As Edie so accurately observed, Nick, you're so clever, such a *star*,' he teased.

'Oh, shut up, Piers,' Nick managed to raise a smile.

'I should've asked Helen along tonight, really. Wish I had. But I thought it might've been a bit awkward, my not having met her yet, and what with you being here and so forth.'

'Probably right. I think you'll like her. She's an impressive woman.'

'And you got rid of her.'

Nick shrugged as if to suggest that maybe he had been a fool.

'Your loss, sounds like,' Orange suggested, putting his hand on his friend's shoulder. 'Listen, I better go and do some duties as host. Have you spoken to Thomas yet? I'll see you in a while.'

Left with Molly, Nick turned to her and asked if she was enjoying herself. She nodded.

'You don't seem as though you are,' Nick said, glancing at her. She looked elegant in jeans. And was that a nipple, he wondered, beneath the white linen shirt, or merely a shadow? Hard to tell. Loopy earrings, silver, gypsy-like; weren't they very heavy? His eyes reached her face – slightly paler than usual, wasn't it? And the expression, though smiling, betraying a certain strain? He could be wrong, of course.

Molly pushed her dark fringe away from her eyes, revealing a gentle widow's peak, hardly noticeable. Nick quickly brushed her forehead, now bare, with his hand.

'Cheer up,' he said casually. 'Here, have a cigarette.'

He opened his packet and pulled one half-way out for her. He had first done so in the same manner when she had just started working in the bookshop. Even then, when they had known each other less well, she had teased him about it, saying it was a rather officious way of offering someone a cigarette – 'like an over-conscientious waiter in a pretentious restaurant,' she had told him.

He had taken the mockery very well, and declared his intention always to continue to offer cigarettes likewise in the future. It developed into a joke between them, and it had become with him, though uncharacteristic, an automatic habit, now almost unconscious.

The room was steadily beginning to fill with people, and to overflow. Elbows had started to knock each other. The noise level – increasingly drunken voices – was rising. Molly felt the uncomfortable sensation of a woman in a silk dress squeezing past behind her. Two pointed breasts made their way across her back.

173

She pretended not to notice, and patiently suggested to Nick that it was 'getting quite crowded'. She wondered what had happened to Dominic. Could not see him.

A tall man with a nose like a baby's foot bore down on Nick with exuberant greetings. He had a very bright tie, gas-flame blue. It was Alexander Bird of Bird and Swift, the literary agency in Charlotte Street. He had a squeaky voice, and his laugh, like an extended hoot, was somewhat disarming. Nick introduced him to Molly. The handshake was boisterous.

'My dear, you're the one that works with Nick. I've seen you in the shop, haven't I? You must be a woman of admirable tolerance to be stuck with him all day.' Extended hoot. 'Is he really as ludicrous as his friends have been led to believe, or is that only when he emerges at night from his Litchfield Street lair?'

Party conversation. Nick thrived on it. Molly, though quite well practised, did not.

'There is no better companion than myself,' Nick declared. 'I make jokes, a lot of jokes, and I refrain from embarrassing and blinding her with such, well, sartorial fluorescence,' he added, staring at Bird's tie.

Another extended hoot.

'My ties are famous,' the taller man asserted.

'No, Alexander, infamous.'

After this preamble, the two of them began to discuss work. For a while Molly attentively looked from one to the other as they spoke. But her attentions were interrupted by the noisy approach of a pretty girl with long hair, ostentatiously red.

'You're Molly, aren't you?' she asked. 'Hello. I'm Liza. Friend of Dom's.'

Molly said hello, puzzled but warm.

'I've just been having a chat with him, and he was telling me all about this new girlfriend of his. Pointed you out to me from over there.' Liza waved vaguely in the direction of a far corner. 'Said he was keen to introduce me to you. But we lost each other, and I seem to have found you before he has.' She talked so fast that Molly was only just able to catch her words. Liza had green eyeliner. Her buxom lips with freckles reminded Molly of one of those varnished shells only ever found in expensive souvenir boutiques at seaside resorts.

'I worked with him when I was Publicity Director at Rubinstein's, and he was a junior editor there. I can't tell you how infatuated I was with that man!' she cheeped. 'Don't worry,' she added quickly, putting her hand on Molly's shoulder, 'I'm married now. He came to my wedding, in fact.'

Molly noticed a small ruby ring on her fourth finger. She wondered if the choice of stone had been wise, what with Liza's gingery colouring, but did not come to a conclusion. It was a fleeting speculation only.

'I do love him,' Liza sang on. 'He was by far the sexiest man at Rubinstein's. Not the best looking. I think Simon Duncan won that title. He was the Sales Director. I don't know if he's still there. But Dominic's got charm, hasn't he? I was constantly making mistakes on my press releases: never was good at grammar or spelling. But I don't think he ever got cross, not even if he saw them after I'd sent copies out to all the literary editors. So shy and modest, but always so kind.'

A squat man, head down, pushed his way past Molly. He made a path through the crowd by holding his hand out in front of him and flapping it from side to side like the fin of a fish swimming through water. A journalist, Molly assumed, seeking out literary gossip. Or perhaps he was from a tabloid and was cruising for stories with a sexual slant. She hoped he had not spotted Edie and Nick in the cloakroom.

'Bruno!' Liza shrieked, grabbing at his sleeve as he went by. He turned back to look at his captor. He attempted to smile, but his cheeks appeared to be puffed up and bulky like badly distributed cellulite on a fat woman's bottom. The lips parted, revealing a soggy grey mush squashing through the many gaps between his teeth. Grease oozed on to his yellow chin. Molly estimated he must have at least four sausages stuffed in there, and probably a pastry thimble or two as well.

Liza introduced him as her 'favourite hack'. So Molly had guessed right. But she was not supplied with a surname. Bruno the Journalist thrust a porky palm into her hand. She felt a sharp pain at her wrist. Then she noticed that half a dozen cocktail sticks, which he had obviously tried to hide up his shirt sleeve, were protruding from his cuff. It was one of those dubious social situations, she decided, which, had it happened to Nick, would have been exploited as the perfect opportunity for a *bon mot*. She chose to ignore it, and say nothing. As was always the way with her, she knew the appropriate witty remark would suddenly present itself much too late, in the bus, most likely, on her way home. There was an official term for that, wasn't there? *Esprit de l'escalier.*

Molly's mind was wandering. It was time to find her companions. With a polite smile, she extracted herself from the Bruno/Liza knot, and jostled her way into the midst of the crowd.

Shoulders. Calves. Necks. All anonymous, animated, ubiquitous chatter. Party frivolity. Quite fun, really.

She was Alone in a Crowd. Pity that phrase was such a cliché. It was rather an intriguing concept. Hadn't it been one of the choice of subjects for her Art O Level, the painting section? As far as she could recall, she had done a solitary figure at a party, an elegant lady, beautiful in black. Funny how inspired the idea had seemed at the time, and how corny and obvious it appeared to her now. She smiled at the thought, and felt quite happy.

Of course, she wasn't really Alone in this Crowd at all. Dominic was there somewhere. It didn't really matter that she had lost him temporarily. He had come with her. He would leave with her. Such luxury to be spared all that doubt as to what she was going to be doing 'afterwards'. At drinks parties, people always asked, 'Are you going out to dinner?' She rarely was, of course, but she sometimes lingered till the end in the hopes of inspiring an invitation from somebody. More often than not, though, other people's evenings had been planned and it was necessary to resort to the humiliation – worse than arriving alone – of leaving alone. And all the while brave smiles, laughter even, and the cheerful wave goodbye. To be seen to be in good spirits was imperative until one had gone outside, turned the corner, and passed from view. Only then was it permissible to relax the face into the grim, more genuine expression of the solitary figure wending its way home at 9 p.m.

Molly shivered at the recollection and looked about her. The large Carruthers was only two or three people away from her, wheezing as he spoke to a woman on whom had been bestowed an unjust number of those qualities more commonly associated with the guinea-pig – long body, bulbous hips, coarse caramel-coloured hair. The old publisher caught Molly's eye and winked at her. She did not want to wriggle herself into his conversation, so cheekily she winked back and turned away.

176

Jostling through the crowd, she spoke briefly to a few friendly acquaintances. Talking to C & O's pearly receptionist, whom she knew from her various visits to the offices on errands for Nick, Molly suddenly felt a hand on her upper arm. Then she heard Dominic's voice in her ear.

'Found you at last. Been having a good time?' he asked. 'There were quite a few people here I know. I was keen for them to meet you. But I think most of them have gone now.' He looked about him, over the landscape of heads.

The receptionist made a polite excuse, said goodbye cheerfully, and went off in pursuit of someone else to talk to.

'I met Liza,' said Molly.

Dominic said, 'Oh, right,' giving nothing away, no clue as to what he thought of her. Men can be so curiously discreet at times, Molly thought.

'You worked together at Rubinstein's?'

'She was in publicity,' came the simple reply.

Did you have an affair with her? Molly asked him, not aloud so an answer was not forthcoming. Even if it had been, he would not necessarily have told her in full.

What was it like to kiss that glossy shell? Did you fancy that between her lips it was possible to hear the breathy sound of the sea?

'Do you suppose Nick's still here?' Dominic's question was chirpily unaware of the conjecture within his girlfriend's mind. He was enjoying the party, enjoying seeing his friends, enjoying being there with her. Not thinking about Liza.

Relief: sexual jealousy – which had, rapier-like, pierced the navel moments before – now, fortunately, subsiding.

'I'm sure he is. Finds it hard to drag himself away from these things till the end,' Molly informed him, inner wound – though still in the process of healing – completely obscured from view by (absolutely essential) brave cheer.

Then her boyfriend, in the middle of the crowd, loosely put his arm around her waist and guided her towards the door. They found Nick leaning on the drinks table, his hand in a bowl of small black olives. Rabbit droppings, Molly thought. He was half-heartedly flirting with a woman who had a plastic bangle, Barclays Bank turquoise.

'Mol and Dominic, hello! I was just saying to Suzie here, Suzie Heron – you've met? – that the buckle of her belt was

177

rather wonderful, don't you think? It's a silver lion's head and that bit's its tongue sticking out.'

'He's just told me it looks like a cat being sick,' Suzie Heron revealed, giggling.

Nick threw three roasted peanuts into his open mouth, like balls into a bag. A fourth missed and trickled its way over the bumpy terrain of his shirt front, tie and trouser leg. He suddenly thrust himself forward to catch it before it could reach his knee.

'Are we off then?' he asked, straightening himself up again.

Dominic turned to Molly. His considerate look seemed to quiz her about what she wanted: supper with him alone, or with others too? She smiled: she did not mind at all.

They decided to go to an inexpensive restaurant in Soho with Nick, Suzie the Accessory, and a few others, including Thomas Pilgrim whose book the party had been in aid of.

Walking round Bedford Square, Molly fell into conversation with Suzie, who was the literary editor of a glossy magazine.

'He wouldn't get away with remarks like that about my buckle, would he,' the latter said of Nick, 'if it wasn't for that infuriating charm? It'd even be all right if he was really good-looking,' she added fondly. 'Is that Dominic De'Ath by the way?' The question took the form of a whisper in the ear because he was walking directly in front of the two of them. 'Colville Books, isn't he?'

Molly regarded Dominic's back view: the huge expanse of dark coat she knew so well, hands in pockets, head tilted back a little, laughing quietly, happy presumably.

She nodded proudly, and quickened her pace, excited. It was almost ten o'clock, yet she was in on a plan, and so much of the evening still lay ahead.

CHAPTER
8

Helen woke up, as her sweet-sherry drinking mother might say, 'all of a dither'.

It was no ordinary May morning.

Some weeks ago, she had received a kind letter from a distinguished figure in publishing.

Mr Piers Orange, Chairman and Editorial Director of Carruthers & Orange, had expressed a desire, in writing, to meet Miss Helen Hardy.

Miss Helen Hardy stepped out of bed and stood beside it. She put on her dressing-gown.

Miss Helen Hardy.

She said the words out loud to herself. The carpet felt bungy under her feet. Funny, Mordechai used to call her Miss Helen Hardy. Mordechai had been her, well, bit of rough trade.

Yes, people might well see her as a rather conventional spinster. But she had had her fair share of experience, just like anybody else, all those people seemingly more worldly than herself.

Mr Piers Orange might very well write to her as Miss Helen Hardy. And he'd very probably have an image of her in his mind. A touch stiff and grey. Red lipstick or fuchsia pink, perhaps. Yes, most likely fuchsia pink. Brown lace-ups, too, this spinsterish biographer of Housman no doubt had in the publisher's eyes. And how was she coping with the poet's homosexuality? Skimming over it, dismissing its significance.

Well, she wasn't in the least bit like that, in fact, was she? As it happened, she had one or two friends who were gay and she didn't mind a bit. She also had a surprisingly modern flat in Pimlico. Lots of white. Not nearly as old-fashioned as he might assume. He probably saw a low mahogany table between two brocade armchairs. And mother of pearl coasters. But there wasn't a coaster to be seen. He'd never guess from the name,

Miss Helen Hardy, at the truth: that she was actually in possession of an oatmeal sofa. And the little abstract sculpture on the floor (by the oatmeal sofa) which could very well pass for avant-garde – how would he explain that? Nick Winter had been convinced it was meant to be a couple copulating. Now, that wouldn't fit into Piers Orange's picture at all, would it? No school-marm would want to see that every day voluntarily, would they? Yet she, Miss Helen Hardy, did, and she thought it very beautiful besides.

What's more, Helen went on in her head, some people had even been known to hear the occasional expletive pass her lips. Not many. And not often, it must be said, but every now and then. Fuck, for example, was a word not totally alien to her. She did use it when something really riled.

Helen, standing in her dressing-gown, rested her hands behind her in the small of her back. Then she leaned backwards to stretch her torso.

'Mordechai fucked me,' she proclaimed, her voice straining slightly as she forced herself up into an upright position again.

Mordechai had entered her life in the summer of 1974. He had favoured Brutus jeans made up of a mosaic of denim squares. Really not attractive at all, even then, when flares and navels were still the thing. He was 'in antiques'. Gathered fireplaces and doors and so forth from old houses. Repaired them, sold them. Very good with his hands. Wrote a bit of poetry on the side, apparently. He told Helen he was an athlete's foot sufferer. They met in Camden Town. He was quite nice looking, a bit Michael Caineish, shorter, but he had halitosis, she remembered. Chillies. Yes, he'd been keen on Indian takeaways.

Keen on sex, too, as it turned out. Never had she come across such an imagination. Baby oil and Nestlés milk. It was the combination that was so puzzling. He was rough trade, though, Mordechai. Perhaps that best explained it.

He picked her up in a pub. Yes, definitely, Camden Town. What she was doing there it was hard to say. Being stood up by someone else most likely. He had asked her her name, bought a few drinks and said, 'So you're on for a good going over? Shall we load my ledge of love together?'

She had thought it rather an obscure way of asking someone to go to bed with them. Luckily the reference had not been lost on her, and, it had to be admitted, it had proved curiously irresistible. She had never done it before with someone she did not know at all. Surprisingly exciting, the prospect.

They had gone back to what Mordechai referred to as his 'place' — a bedsit round the corner. Not clean.

Spread on the white enamel table top: half a pint of cheesy milk, one stainless steel knife scummed with margarine, Mother's Pride toast crumbs, two empty baked bean cans. In the bathroom: damp tiles, a loo still manifestly rich from an earlier occurrence, greying bath patterned with grit, and the odd pubic hair, perfectly curled.

Mordechai and Helen had smoked a joint on a big cushion covered in an Indian cotton of purple and yellow, and mirrors the size of halfpennies. Then they had graduated across to the unmade 'ledge of love' and proceeded to 'load' it.

And all the while he insisted on calling her Miss Helen Hardy. She hoped this was for reasons of humour, but never asked in case Mordechai was being serious. The two of them met quite a few times, and he never did stop calling her that. Perhaps he felt that their arrangement, being quite so casual, might benefit from this one note of formality. Curious character, Mordechai.

Would Piers Orange ever guess that the Miss Helen Hardy to whom he had written had had such an association?

Definitely not, she decided, and was pleased that her life had been more mysterious, and more unlikely, than some might assume. In fact, she thought, no one could have imagined some of the things she had experienced. Perhaps Mordechai hadn't inspired tremendous happiness at the time. But at least the memory of him enabled her to feel, years later, a certain glow of private satisfaction: she had a past. Oh yes, incongruous as it might seem, she had seen a bit of life, had one or two experiences. Others, prissier than herself, might go so far as to call them unsavoury. But not her. Helen was proud of her past. It was almost colourful.

And she wanted Piers Orange to know it, to be aware that the woman whom he had addressed as Miss Helen Hardy was by no means a pent-up spinster. She would go out and out to rumble any such prejudices.

Suddenly inspired, she began feverishly to untie the towelling belt round her waist and take off her dressing-gown. Then she went to the bathroom. Washing at the basin, she told her reflection in the mirror that she would dazzle him in red.

'I shall jolly well be the scarlet woman,' she declared out loud, and smiled.

Back in the bedroom again, she flung open her chest of drawers. There, lying on top of a pile of sombre jerseys, was her best cardigan: Campari-coloured cashmere.

She undid the buttons and put it on. The thin wool felt extravagantly soft on her bare skin. She shivered at the pleasure of the sensation. It was a piece of clothing she wore rarely. Special occasions only.

Standing at a bus-stop in Knightsbridge twelve Christmases ago, she had spied it in the window of a smart shop. The price had been beyond the bounds of reason. Yet she fell for it and despite every principle she had about her self-indulgence, she knew she had to buy it.

So she began to save. Weeks later, she returned to the shop able to pay for it. To this day she could still see the powdery face of the helpful saleswoman, her half-moon spectacles and the tape measure round her neck. Helen's hand had shaken as she wrote out the cheque for the vast sum. No purchase, she thought, could have been less characteristic. Never before or since had she spent so much money on one item of clothing. Lack of both interest and inclination. Nor had anything so bright been submitted to her wardrobe. Until that moment, it had only known dark colours due to her desire to remain as inconspicuous as possible. At the time she must have been in love.

Anyway, it was the perfect thing with which to dazzle Orange, along with a black skirt, perhaps, so as not actually to blind him. Helen stepped into a simple Viyella one which reached to just above her ankles. After putting on a little make-up, she felt completely satisfied with her appearance. It was a rare feeling, and was possibly because the adrenalin was firing. When ready, she went through to the sitting-room, and over to the desk.

In a pile she found the vital piece of correspondence. It was a folded bit of paper, thickly cream. The letter heading was of a shiny orange typeface, very elegant below the illustrated logo: a cluster of oranges in an upturned C-shaped bowl.

The recipient was anxious to re-read its contents for the umpteenth time – just to make sure. Doing so, she was able to confirm, yet again, that Mr Orange would be given 'great pleasure' if she were to visit him at his office to discuss her work on A. E. Housman.

As it happened, 'her convenience' had turned out to be very accommodating: she had rung his secretary immediately and arranged an appointment for Monday, 18 May, three o'clock.

She looked at her watch to check: it was indeed that very same date.

No wonder the adrenalin was flowing.

The elegant grandeur of the building in Bedford Square was somewhat daunting. In the hall, Helen went up to a young girl whose pearl teeth matched her pearl necklace. She wore patent shoes, but they had prissy bows which tempered their powerful shine a little, and her manner was friendly enough. She directed her to Orange's office.

He opened his door and greeted Helen with that confident public school civility which is guaranteed to put a nervous middle-aged lady at ease.

'I'm so pleased to meet you, Miss Hardy,' he said sincerely as he shook her hand.

His grip was firm. Helen noticed a gold signet ring on his little finger. 'Do sit down,' he added, pulling a chair nearer to his desk. 'Can I get you anything? Coffee, tea, a drink?'

'I won't, thank you very much,' she replied, placing her handbag on her lap.

There was about him a very generous-spirited air, she thought, and a warmth which she would have been unable to guess at from his formal letter. Although she supposed he must be almost sixty, he looked younger than she had imagined he would. He was not particularly handsome but he had one of those 'very nice' faces. His cheeks were slightly puffy and pink. But it had none of the fatness or breathiness that is normally associated with puffiness and pinkness.

'Are you sure, my dear? I think I might have some tea. Certain you won't join me?'

Helen nodded, and said thank you. Orange pressed a button on the telephone. There was a cheeky blip noise which then went dead.

'Damn. We've just had these new ones put in. Can't get to grips with them at all. High-tech fangled stuff. Can't see the point. I have to use digits now to call my secretary whereas before

I just used to shout. She gets very cross with me for being so fogeyish. Emmy!' he shouted suddenly. 'Whoops, that'll get me into trouble,' he whispered with a good-humoured chuckle.

The door opened and a girl in her twenties entered, laughing. 'You're hopeless,' she told her boss. 'Did you remember to press the blue button first?'

Orange's guilty smile said no. 'Ah well. I'll get the hang of it one day. Would it be possible for me to have a cup of tea? This is Miss Hardy, by the way, the authority on Housman.'

Emmy nodded: yes, she would bring him a cup of tea, and yes, of course, hello, Miss Hardy. She smiled and left the room.

Orange pushed his bowl of oranges to one side of his desk and leaned forward to talk more closely to Helen.

'I hope you didn't think my letter too presumptuous, out of the blue like that?'

'Not at all. I was delighted.'

'It was just that when I heard about your book I thought I shouldn't waste any time in expressing my interest.'

'Nick Winter told you?'

After a barely perceptible pause, Orange said that that indeed was the case. It was a delicate admission in the circumstances. Nick probably did not rank high on her list of favourite people.

'Very enthusiastic report, he gave, of course,' he remarked tactfully. 'But it was merely a case of him letting me know about your biography. I myself am very interested.'

'I'm very grateful to him,' Helen said. 'It was a thoughtful gesture on his part.'

Orange was surprised and impressed by her dignified response.

Helen wondered if Nick had told him about the proposal. She slightly hoped not. These things were private matters. It was more likely, though, that he had. Still, she didn't really mind. The publisher was a kind man, and seemed to respect her all the same.

Emmy reappeared briefly with the tea and a pile of letters for Orange to sign.

'I'm very interested, you see,' he went on, 'because I fear our poetry list is rather weak at the moment. I had a vague plan to launch a new poetry imprint – special uniform format and design – that sort of thing. I'm a fan of Housman, and I

184

feel such an addition to our biography list would complement the poetry one well.'

Orange sipped his tea and looked at his guest.

'I'm very pleased that you're keen on the idea. Housman's not particularly fashionable at the moment. I just hope you like the book,' Helen ventured shyly.

'Ah. You must think me very precipitate,' he declared, putting down his cup. 'But publishers take risks. At least good ones do. I have a feeling about your book, Miss Hardy. Of course, Nick was the person who told me about it and I respect his opinion utterly. It's hardly a question of taking risks with his recommendations. But, also, I have something else. It's that indefinable thing, no reason for it – instinct. I have an instinct about your book, you see? Does that sound improbable?'

'I'm amazed,' Helen told him.

'Some might think it unbusinesslike to go about obtaining books in this way, unprofessional even. But I'm not a business-man, you see, I'm a publisher. The two don't necessarily go together,' he laughed, 'at least as far as I'm concerned.'

'But wouldn't you like some kind of synopsis, outline, the first few chapters – ?'

'If you like. It's not essential though, before we decide what you want. Either we just make a gentleman's agreement that when you've finished it you give me first refusal, or you can show me whatever you've done that you think's appropriate. Then, if I like it, I could give you an advance and we could settle on a reasonable date for completion and delivery of manuscript.'

'Lord, I don't know when that would be.'

'Couldn't matter less. I've waited ten years for books, or more. I have the instinct, you see, and I'm a patient man.'

Orange watched for Helen's reaction. In her eyes there was excitement, but otherwise she maintained a serene air.

He wondered about her in her baggy cardigan, sleeves rolled up, winningly casual. It suited her, that colour, he thought. The brightness of the red cashmere reflected, he fancied, a definite brightness of spirit. It seemed to flatter her skin – a slightly duskier tone than he had imagined it would be. For some reason he thought the complexion of an unmarried university lecturer would be paler. Some foolish old-fashioned notion, perhaps. The unsullied English rose? But

185

this lady must be in her late thirties, even forty. Just because she was officially a spinster – a word which traditionally seemed to imply frustration – did not mean she hadn't had her fair share of fun like anybody else. He stared at the good-looking face. Who was to say she hadn't, in fact, had even more fun than most? All the same, Orange detected a certain sadness lurking beneath the polite shyness. She was a clever woman, he knew that, but also vulnerable and alone.

'I've done a lot of work on it already,' she told him. 'It's always been worth while, of course. I never really worried about publication because I considered it more as an academic exercise. I felt even if my research came to nothing, it wouldn't be wasted. Because maybe someone in the future might happen upon it and in some way find their little discovery fulfilling, and want to make something of it.'

Orange nodded, fully attentive.

'I had obviously harboured secret hopes that one day it'd be published, but it's a great bonus and boost that someone's showing encouragement at this stage. I've occasionally – not very often, admittedly – but there have been one or two occasions when I've found myself flagging and asking myself the question, why?' Helen crossed her legs and sat back, more comfortable now. 'Why am I doing this when I'm not even certain anybody'll want to publish it?' she continued. 'But I always found I had this overwhelming desire to write it. It was something that had nothing to do with reason or consequences.'

Orange slapped his hand on his desk. 'Oh, that's wonderful,' he enthused, 'because it would have been terrible simply to have given in to such trifling notions as practicality and good sense, don't you think, Miss Hardy? I can't tell you how excited I am. Are you?'

Helen laughed. Of course.

'And now you've got me and my instinct hanging over you, you'll have practical and sensible reasons, after all, even if you did find they were superfluous.'

He stood up and walked jauntily to the window.

'Now, let's see. What shall we do? I expect you'd like to go away and think about our options – whether you'd like to let me see it so we can think in terms of an advance or whether you'd like a less formal arrangement. What do you prefer?'

'I think I'd like to let you see it and we can go from there,' Helen suggested. 'I've done over 50,000 words. I could get a copy of the manuscript sent round in the morning. You mightn't think it's any good at all.'

'I'm sure I will. I'm terribly looking forward to reading it. I suppose I should advise you to get an agent though. Would you like me to help you there?'

'I wouldn't know where to begin,' she admitted.

'Well – I've got this great friend, Alexander Bird, of Bird and Swift.'

The Housman expert nodded. She knew the name.

'I'll put you on to him. He's wonderful, the best. You'll like him.' He paused. 'I'm sorry. Am I being too enthusiastic and unfashionably keen?'

Helen laughed: a sparkling sound, and promptly assuaged his anxiety.

'So then, very soon, you could meet him and he'd help you come to a decision and very soon after that we could have lunch and another discussion. Perhaps towards the end of next week? What do you think, Miss Hardy? A good idea?'

Miss Hardy smiled. What she thought was that it was a very good idea indeed.

May the eighteenth already, Molly thought on the bus into work as she opened the *Independent*. Could it really be that she had met Dominic four months ago and he had been in her flat almost as long? It hardly seemed possible. Felt more like four weeks.

It was a gloomy Monday. When Molly put the key in her door later that evening she found herself looking forward to a quiet evening with Dominic in front of the television.

She put her bag on the chair, washed her hands because she felt filthy and sticky and poured herself a glass of orange juice. He wasn't back yet. Probably still at Colville Road or at the Warwick.

Molly lay on the sofa, put the telephone on her stomach and rang home. She hadn't spoken to Cake and Rufus for a while. Her father answered. He was pleased to hear from her but his voice sounded heavy.

'How're the two men in your life?' he asked, trying to disguise the heaviness.

'Fine. Dom's really well. Got the rights to a book he was after. Compensates a bit for the French one he lost.'

'And Nick?'

'Okay. Seems a bit gloomy though. Probably worrying about the takings. He won't admit it, but I think he's missing Georgia. Says he's in love.'

'With her still?'

'No. Someone else.'

'So why's he missing Georgia?'

'It doesn't appear to be working out with the someone else.'

'Lonely then, and regretting giving the girlfriend the push?'

'Seems so. What's your news?'

Rufus explained that his work wasn't going well. His daughter, concerned, asked why.

'General exhaustion, I think,' was his reply.

'And how's Mum?' she wondered. The question was not a *non sequitur*.

There was a pause.

'Very high spirits. The New York exhibition seems to be going ahead.'

'With the scintillating and witty Amy?'

Rufus laughed at Molly's naughty remark, but was loyal enough to his wife not to comment further on her friend's qualities or lack of them.

'When are you moving downstairs?' he asked.

'A week or so now, I should think. I'm going to be broke, but it will be lovely.'

'There's an exhibition I'm quite keen to see at the RA. I was thinking of coming to London next week. Do you want me to bring your bicycle? Could save you a fiver or so a week if you rode to work?'

'I suppose so,' Molly replied. 'Rather grim in the winter, but you're absolutely right. Good idea. I'd be very grateful. When are you coming?'

'I don't know. Friday, Saturday maybe. I'll call you. We could have lunch.'

'That'd be lovely.'

'Hang on. I think Mum wants a word. Lots of love, Mol, see you soon.'

Cake's voice took over.

'Darling – ' Extravagant tone.

'Is Dad all right?' Molly asked immediately. She had a feeling he was not.

'Oh, he's fine. How are you? Good to hear your voice. You've heard my news. The show seems to be going ahead. I sent over a transparency of my painting – you know, the one called *The Fall*. They're going to reproduce that one on the invitation and Amy rang from New York to say she loves it and it's so exciting, isn't it?'

Molly agreed.

'So, anyway, I'm going over there in a couple of months. You should come with me, Mol. I'll take you, why not?'

'Thank you. I'll have to think about it. Very generous of you. I might not be able to get off work though.'

'No. Rufus said the same. Got a lot on. Pity. Anyway, you must try. I'm sure Nick'll let you.'

'You could take a friend.'

'Who?'

'I don't know. Terence maybe. Would he like to go?'

Not a flicker. 'Possibly. And he'd be very supportive, I'm sure. But I'd much prefer to take you.'

'That's good,' Molly replied, polite, sceptical. Did Cake not know she knew, or was it simply that she did not care that she did? Was that why she was so blasé about her association with Terence?

Molly wondered at her mother's extraordinary capacity to hurt her father. It was not gratuitous malice. Her unkindness was due to simple thoughtlessness, total self-absorption. Cake had hurt her, too, for the same reasons. But daughters were less vulnerable than husbands. They could not so easily be shed. Thus it was that the pain she caused Molly as a child had not been so urgent. Nowadays, Molly could shrug it off even, relatively unmoved. Perhaps, this time, Rufus would find the strength to do likewise, be able finally to dismiss it.

Yet, Molly could envisage her father's face as, at the other end, he overheard the conversation, knowing he knew. The pain dulling the eyes. What kind of fortitude could endure this latest blow? As before, she supposed: the determined, sincere desire not to lose Cake, not to let the weakening ship finally sink.

Of course, Rufus had always known, hadn't he? From the man with the cheese footballs to Terence, as well as all those in between. Such resilience.

It had paid off in the past. After all, she had never actually left him.

But was it any longer worth while for him to hope? Would Cake ever return to him completely, give up her lovers for good? Maybe he had made the decision not to struggle forcibly to extinguish the hope? Possibly, he believed that if he allowed it to persist it might, along with the desire to win her back, eventually fade and expire of its own accord.

'Take care of Dad, okay?' Molly told Cake, not unaware of the irony of the order. 'I'd better go now,' she said.

The conversation came to an end and Molly replaced the receiver. She stood up to refill her glass. As she did so, she noticed a piece of paper on the table, a message. Dominic's handwriting.

Mol,

Work not going brilliantly. Suddenly fed up so have decided to go away till the end of the week. Sorry not to have let you know yesterday. It was a last-minute thing. Promise to be back in time to help you shift the stuff downstairs. Tell Nick I'll bring in some more books for him next week. We'll go out for supper when I get back. Take care.

Love, Dom.

It was a nice enough note but Molly shivered all the same. The sudden disappearance. No real explanation. It alarmed her.

'Work not going brilliantly,' she re-read out loud and nodded. 'Work.'

She picked up the telephone. Something, indefinable, was niggling inside. She needed a friend, she didn't know why, she just needed a friend.

Unkeen to be alone, she arranged to go to some American film with one. Set in New York it had plenty of Manhattan street life, Manhattan gloss and Manhattan emotion to distract the mind.

Yet the niggle went on and neither the film, nor a hamburger, nor a friend could do anything to exorcise it.

Molly went home alone and wondered if it signalled the imminent end of her period of happiness.

'Dominic told me to tell you he'll be coming in next week with more books,' Molly told her boss the next morning.

'Very good,' Nick replied, running his finger down a list of titles on the microfiche screen. 'Damn,' he muttered to himself, 'I thought it had come out in paperback.' He turned round and asked if she was all right. 'You sound low,' he observed.

'Bit,' she shrugged, putting her coat over the chair. 'Dom's gone off somewhere. Left a note.'

'Has he? Where?' Nick's tone was casual but not bored. He sat back and put his knee up against the edge of the desk. His black linen trousers were a little crumpled.

'Didn't say,' Molly replied.

'Been a bit of marital strife? You never mentioned it.'

'Not as far as I know. Said it was work making him feel fed up.'

'Well, there you go. No need to feel grim.'

'I think there is. Plenty. You don't just bugger off like that, without telling someone.'

'He did tell you. In the note.'

'Yes, but he might have rung,' she said, stepping into the back room and switching on the kettle.

'Why? He was a bit fed up with work, like he said, and probably just wanted to be on his own for a while. Perfectly reasonable.'

'It might seem so to you,' Molly declared. 'But it indicates a basic lack of communication to me.'

'Don't be ridiculous. You're imagining a significance quite out of proportion to reality. I thought you promised you weren't going to be keeping tabs. Just because he's staying with you doesn't mean he can't go off as and when he likes.'

'I never suggested that. I just thought he might have told me, that's all, rather than leave a mingy note,' she said, spooning some Gold Blend into a couple of mugs.

Nick shook his head. 'You haven't a leg to stand on,' he said gently. 'Why should he have rung you? You should be grateful he left a note.'

'He didn't even say where he went or precisely when he was coming back.' As she spoke Molly stood with one knee bent to keep the back room door open.

'Molly. You're doing a Georgia.'

She sighed. 'I just feel uneasy. I think he was wanting to get away not only from work.'

'Very unlikely, and anyway, so what if he was? He'll come back and things'll be back to normal, I bet.'

'It's funny. I never feel this need to get away from him.'

'That's just the way it works,' Nick remarked, turning back to face the microfiche. He peered into the blue-green screen.

'So when he does from me, I feel I'm losing my grip.' Molly poured the boiling water, some milk and sugar into the mugs. Then she placed one beside Nick. He nodded by way of saying thank you and said that she didn't, or at least she shouldn't, have a grip.

'All right, I feel he's slipping away.'

Nick shrugged, stood up and walked to the shelves. 'One moves on,' he said. 'Now, listen, I want to shelve some of the stuff that came in yesterday,' he announced, changing the subject. 'Would you check in *The Bookseller* for me to make sure I haven't missed something vital. Oh God, and there're all those bloody job application letters to reject. Could you face it?'

Molly nodded. What did he mean – one moves on? Had Dominic told Nick something she didn't know about? She sat at the desk, picked up some writing paper and decided to keep quiet about it.

The telephone rang. 'My dear Molly – ' Orange's voice – 'how are you? Is Nick there?'

'Standing on a stool, with a pile of books in his arms.'

'Bad moment? I do so want to talk to him.'

'Hang on a second.'

Nick stepped down and she passed him the receiver. 'It's Piers,' she whispered, 'sounding very excited.'

'I'm very excited,' he began when Nick came on the line. 'I saw Miss Hardy yesterday.'

Nick laughed. 'You're so predictable.'

'I think the book's going to be marvellous. The first few chapters arrived by bike this morning. More here than I thought. I've been flicking through them. Can't wait to read it all properly in the next couple of days. You were absolutely right to put her on to me. I told her I'd get her in touch with Alexander. Good idea? And it looks like we'll go from there.' Orange's voice was full of enthusiasm.

'I'm very pleased.'

'She's an intriguing woman, Nick. She knew it was you who prompted me to write the letter. No bitterness there, though. Poor lady, I like her.'

'Me too,' Nick agreed quietly.

'Anyway, I was just ringing to thank you. I suggested to her that we should all get together for lunch – her, Alex and myself. Perhaps you'd like to join us?'

'Perhaps in a few weeks if it all works out. A bit more time.'

'Just so. And, by the way, if you have any more women whom you've rejected and who're as nice as Helen, and who happen to be writing books, let me know.'

The two men chuckled.

'I think Mol might've tracked down that book you wanted,' said Nick.

'Seriously? She is brilliant. I didn't think she ever would. I'll come in tomorrow, pick it up. Tell her I'll take her out for a drink for that. I wonder what on earth you'd do without her?'

Nick wondered likewise.

'Amazing,' muttered the publisher.

'Amazing,' repeated the bookseller, and the conversation came to an end.

That evening Nick stayed late at the shop catching up with the accounts. He arrived home at about nine.

The house lacked the warmth of company and he felt gloomy. He wandered into the kitchen and turned on the lights. The cat purred hungrily. God, when did he last feed the cat – yesterday or the day before? The responsibility.

Nick was hungry so he poured himself a drink. Since Georgia had gone there hadn't appeared to be much food in the house. Nor washing powder, come to that. Odd. He seemed to spend his life in the supermarket. What, three times since she had gone, how many weeks ago was it now, four? The tedium of shopping. Flummoxed by the Technicolor choice of packages, he had only managed to come back with countless cartons of Alpen, and tins of chicken soup.

He was fed up with Alpen. He was sick of chicken soup. Yet he was hungry.

Nick retrieved the unwashed cereal bowl he had used at breakfast from the draining board and poured some fresh Alpen into it.

'I am muesli,' he told the cat and groaned. He took one spoonful and was so bored by it he pushed it aside.

He opened that morning's paper which earlier he had not had time to read. Some moments later when deeply involved

193

in Foreign News and his glass of whisky, he was shaken by the sound of the doorbell.

'Who the hell could that be, cat?'

It was Georgia.

'I've borrowed Sarah's car,' she told him on the doorstep. 'Hope I'm not disturbing you. Rang earlier. There was no answer, but I came on the off-chance anyway. My stuff. I've come to get the rest of my stuff.'

Nick hustled her inside enthusiastically. 'Lovely surprise. Course. Your stuff. Come in. Time for a drink?'

Georgia, thinner, looked at her watch. 'Quick one,' she said. She was wearing a floppy viscose skirt which fell to just above her ankles. It outlined her jutting hips. And a faded grey sweatshirt. No bra. Her hair was tied back in a white butter muslin scarf. Nick remembered having sex with her one Sunday afternoon upstairs. They had been too excited to unknot that scarf. He had bitten it like a rabid dog and they had laughed.

Nick kissed her on the cheek. She smelled of tuber rose. As always. Always had. Always would. Never changed her scent, Georgia. It took him back.

They went through to the kitchen.

'Looks like you need a washer-upper,' she remarked regretfully, sitting at the table.

'Don't you want to take off your jacket?'

'Cat seems smaller. No, I won't be staying long.'

'No, I never was much of a one at the kitchen sink, was I, Georgie?'

Nick's ex-girlfriend shook her head. 'How's Molly?'

'Fine,' he nodded. 'Yes, she seems fine.'

'Any progress there?'

Nick shrugged.

'I'm sorry,' Georgia said sincerely.

'Dominic,' he replied.

'You still – ?'

He looked at her blankly, without moving. Only a blink. 'Alas,' he whispered at last.

'I don't know what to say. I'm sorry.'

'Nothing to say. Fact of life. Come-uppance for the way I treated – ' He stopped abruptly and held out his hand to her.

'You don't deserve it – ' Georgia remarked generously.

'I do really,' he replied. 'Every bit of it. Serves me right.
I could've stopped it happening.'

'You can't decide not to fall in love with someone any
more than you can decide to do so.'

'Oh yes, you can,' Nick said firmly. 'There comes a point
when you bloody well do choose to let it go one way or the
other. After the choice has been made then it's more difficult
to reverse it, but beforehand it's definitely all a question of
calculated decision. Mine happened to be a selfish one and now
you're suffering for it, and so am I. I wish I'd never let myself.
It was pure self-indulgence.'

'You're being too harsh on yourself. I don't agree with
you about it being in one's power. Meet someone and fall
in love with them instantly or gradually, there's nothing you
can do about it. It just happens one way or the other. It's not
something that can be controlled.'

'I can remember the moment,' he began slowly, quietly,
after a pause, 'when I decided to fall in love with Molly. I knew
I shouldn't, I knew it'd bugger things up but I did decide all the
same. And,' he stopped a moment before going on, 'I know I
could've stopped myself. I know I could.'

Nick bit his lip.

'But I didn't, Georgie. I fucked it up. And now,' he said,
gesturing towards his uneaten bowl of cereal, 'I go to the
supermarket and I'm a buyer of the single serving and the
chicken soup. I exist on Alpen and I'm alone.'

Georgia watched him carefully. She might well have been
pleased that he who had hurt her so was miserable. But
she was not.

'Is there nothing in the house?' she asked, standing up
and going to the fridge as if she were still part of his life.

She thought she was again for a moment: there in his
kitchen as if it were any normal Tuesday evening. Nothing
much had changed there – except, perhaps, abnormally dimin-
ished supplies. And she still loved him.

'No, no,' Nick said briskly, uneasy, seeing her so automatically
slotting back into her former role. 'Nothing much.'

Georgia opened the fridge door. Bare. 'I see what you
mean,' she sighed. 'You're not looking after yourself properly.'

'I'm okay,' he assured her hastily.

'Hadn't I better quickly make you something?'

'There's no need, really,' he said, standing up quickly. 'Let me give you a hand with your stuff.'

'No, honestly, I think you should eat something.'

'I have. Alpen. Fine.'

'Not Alpen,' she said, almost bossily. 'Look, I spy some rice and a tin of tomatoes. Couldn't I just – ?'

'Better not,' he said gently. 'Thank you, though. Now, what's left for you to take? I think we ought to get your things together.'

'Absolutely,' came the speedy reply. Georgia realised her offer had been misplaced, inappropriate.

The two of them gathered her various possessions from about the house: a chair, a few records, a couple of prints, a suitcase or two of clothes. Nick helped her load the car. As she was leaving, she kissed him goodbye and said she hoped things would 'work out'.

'Send her my love,' she added, driving away. A little way along the street, she pressed the horn.

Nick felt bleak. It was an ugly sound, like the squawk of a tortured bird.

Radio 4's *Today* programme woke Molly abruptly and informed her it was Tuesday, 26 May.

Dominic had been away now for over a week. A week and a day to be precise. She did not know why he had gone, really, or where. Nor did she know when he was coming back, indeed . . . if. Garrotte that thought, she told herself quickly, or you won't be able to get out of bed. What she did know did not amount to much, actually. He would be back in time for the move, apparently. But he was not sure when that was. She herself had only heard yesterday: Sam had rung and said that the flat would be free on Saturday. If only he would call, just to say when he was coming back. It wasn't that much to ask.

But maybe she was missing the point. Maybe Dominic was making one, the very nature of which precluded such secure communication.

On her way out of the flat, Molly picked up the post – a bill and a dentist's appointment confirmation for her, and a letter for Dominic. She would have liked a letter, she thought, and locked up before walking to the bus stop.

The day in the bookshop was long: the customers were demanding and Nick was irritable. By the time she returned home, Molly felt tired and gloomy. She ought, she supposed, to start putting her possessions in boxes in order to carry them downstairs at the weekend. But she procrastinated, for her gloom made her lethargic. She flunked on to the sofa with a can of beer and a cigarette in front of the television.

It was one of those solitary evenings when even a moderately interesting programme can be made into an event. She looked at her watch. There was half an hour before a documentary about an imprisoned bigamist who had several illegitimate children, one eye, a phobia about plants and, what's more, was dying of AIDS. So Molly planned a quick bath, the hour-long stint with this particular unfortunate (just one of the BBC's seemingly endless supply), the *News at Ten*, maybe even the weather forecast, bed, a few chapters of her book, sleep.

But it was not to be. Just before the final 'light' item on the news, Dominic appeared, looking well. He was wearing his old jeans. There was something about him in them that Molly had always found winning. The long legs? The softness of the pale, worn denim? She noticed grains of sand round the rims of his tatty brogues and on one sleeve of his holey blue jersey.

Molly was pleased to see him, and he hugged her. That familiar smell, his smell, beer shampoo, clean sweat, French cigarettes, faint aftershave. Unchanging. Unique.

'I missed you,' she said, jumping up from the sofa. Her voice was light, not laden with important reproach.

Dominic missed his cue and did not reply in kind. Perhaps this was a good thing. It would have been much better if she had given him a chance to speak unprompted. Too late now.

'How've you been?' he asked, opening a can of beer, smiling.

'I've been fine. More to the point, where've you been?' Her tone was studiedly ungrudging.

'Norfolk. To stay with a friend.'

'Who?' Obvious question.

'Old friend called John. He lives in Brancaster. We went for long walks on the beach.'

'Looks like the sea air did you some good. Got a bit of colour in your cheeks.' Molly tightened the bulky belt of her towelling dressing-gown and sat down on the sofa again. She put her feet on the cushions, and scratched her ankle.

197

'I only meant to go for a couple of days but once I got there I couldn't drag myself away.'

'Thank you for your note,' Molly remarked, generously, but hoping he might apologise for not having rung. He did not.

'That's okay,' he shrugged, looking at the television. 'God, it's odd to be back,' he added, sitting down beside her.

Oh?

'I should've stayed, really,' he went on.

'Why didn't you?'

'Work.'

Of course.

'I expect it was good to get away from it for a bit though, wasn't it?'

'I really needed it, yes. I like just going off on my own. I like being on my own. Very important.'

'But you weren't on your own,' she pointed out reasonably.

'You know what I mean. I was a lot of the time. John was working. What's important is a bit of solitude, being away from the norm – work, London – '

'Home, the girlfriend,' Molly suggested, putting her feet on his lap.

'Yes, that too,' he agreed honestly, but not nastily.

'It's funny. I don't have that.'

'What?'

'I love being on my own occasionally. But when I go away it's to get away from work and home, but not people. Not you, for example.'

Dominic nodded. 'That's where we differ then,' he said quietly. 'It might be a defensive thing on my part, I suppose. I don't want the pressure. When I go away, I like to go away from everything familiar, and to be completely free and independent.'

'That's fair,' Molly said, then paused and drew breath. 'Did I drive you away this time, something I did?'

Dominic looked up at her. 'You didn't drive me away, no. But work was getting me down, and things, yes.'

Things?

'I don't know,' he went on, 'you know how it is.'

No.

'Well – ' he sighed. 'I don't want to talk about it now.'

That thing of avoiding the issue.

'Come on, Dom. What?'

There was a pause. He rubbed her shins affectionately. Nervous.

'Oxford. Your parents. You know, becoming embroiled.' He sounded uneasy: keen to be honest, not keen to be unkind.

Molly nodded, rather patiently, she thought.

'I'm sure it's a sort of fear on my part,' he faltered on. 'But one has a certain degree of nervousness about being . . . wound in.'

Use of the pompous pronoun.

Wound in?

'Wound in?' Molly repeated, questioning.

'That's maybe not the right phrase,' Dominic admitted, taking a gulp of his drink. 'But you know what I mean, we've discussed it. It's just that being involved in the private family bit – ' He stopped, put the beer on the floor and wrapped his arms around himself, shivering a little, as if being enveloped by a warm blanket.

'I know. The involvement makes for the claustrophobia of "commitment".' There was only a barely perceptible hint of sarcasm in Molly's tone as she put his gesture into words for him.

'That sort of thing,' he nodded. 'Any more beer?'

'I don't think there is.' Molly stood up and went to the fridge. 'We've got some wine,' she said, peering inside.

'Don't worry. I might go out and get a couple more cans of this stuff in a minute.'

Returning to the sofa, Molly picked up the letter that had arrived for Dominic that morning.

'By the way, I forgot to give you this,' she said casually, glancing at the television as she handed it to him.

'What is it? A letter? When did it come?'

'This morning. Why?'

'It came here?' Dominic slapped it on his knee. Molly took the gesture to be one of annoyance.

'Course. What are you on about?'

'Why, why?' he asked, opening it and reading it quickly. 'Bloody hell.'

'Bad news?' she wondered out loud, concerned.

'No. Why did they send it here?'

Molly was puzzled. 'What do you mean? What is it?'

'Only a note from a friend. But he should've sent it to Colville Road.'

'I don't understand,' she said rubbing her eye with the back of her hand.

'And he sent it here.'

'So?'

'This isn't my address.'

'It got to you, didn't it?'

'That's not the point. I don't live here.'

Molly sighed, and shook her head in amazement. But she didn't say anything. The point she would have liked to make was that she was sorry to inform him that, alas, it rather appeared to her, and now obviously to others, that he did live there. But Dominic's extraordinary revelation indicated that he was under the impression he did not. So her point would have been pointless.

'See what I mean?' he said.

Yes, she said. No, she meant. Somewhat nervously and foolishly, she added she was sorry. It was an apology that was entirely misplaced, for presuming to suppose that Dominic lived in her flat when, if anything, he should have done so for insulting her by denying it.

'I'm hungry,' he remarked quietly, standing up and rubbing his head. 'How about a Chinese takeaway? It'll still be open, won't it?'

Molly nodded.

'What would you like?'

'You choose,' she told him, staring at the television.

'Right. I'll be back in a minute.'

Alone, Molly shut her eyes, pensive for a moment before opening them to look about her. What she saw were Dominic's things – his books, his clothes, his small table beneath the window. And yet, according to him, he didn't live there. It was a curious delusion.

Hugging her legs to her chest, Molly put her chin on her knees. In her mind, she told him he was ridiculous. You great idiot, who are you trying to fool? What's the point of denying it?

Yet, what had she said in reality? I'm sorry. I'm sorry for being so tactlessly mistaken in supposing you to be a fellow resident of this flat.

Mad.

Still, like Rufus, she was unkeen to prompt a silly row. It would achieve nothing, only tension. It was unlikely any kind of protest would change Dominic's mind. Drop it, much better, and eat the Chinese takeaway happily, forgetting the slight difference of opinion.

When, some minutes later, Dominic returned, the two of them were in better humour. They laid the silver-foil packages on the low chest in front of the sofa. Molly sat cross-legged on the cushions and balanced her plate on her calves. They began to eat and he told her about his trip.

'I walked every day for hours,' he said. 'The beach was deserted because, although it was sunny, it's still cold. Brancaster's got these amazing dunes where you can sit in a hollow of sand. You're shielded from the wind by tough tufts of grass. I slept there once or twice. Dreamed so vividly. The sleepy air, I expect.'

Molly listened attentively, the difference of opinion forgotten.

'About half a mile out there's a skeletal wreck. Black. It's very haunting from afar. But when the tide's out you can walk to it. It's covered in barnacles and slimy algae, and isn't nearly so spooky when you're close up. I went with John.'

'What's he do?'

'He's got an incredible converted barn across the marshes where he sculpts. It's so beautiful there. I must take you one day.'

His remark was met with an enthusiastic nod. Molly took a mouthful of chicken with beanshoots and cashew nuts. Dominic had chosen well, had remembered her favourite. He spooned some more fried rice on to his plate.

'Pity I had to come back so soon, really,' he went on.

It was a remark to be overlooked, the one immediately preceding it having been so encouraging.

'Still, I'm glad to see I'm back in time for the move, or else I might've got myself into trouble,' he smiled.

'Yep. That would've been it,' Molly said with a teasing chuckle.

'When can we go ahead?' He put a shaving of beef and a chip of green pepper on to a prawn cracker. When he bit into it there was a noisy crunch.

'The weekend, Sam said. I'm going to start putting some of this clobber in boxes.' A few minutes later Molly stood up, threw the greasy cartons away, and put the dirty plates in the sink. Ah, the security of domesticity. As she did so Dominic pushed up his sleeves, lit a cigarette and smoked it, inhaling slowly. When he stubbed it out she noticed that a little muscle twitched in his slightly brown forearm, just beneath the surface of the skin. It was like a minnow in still water.

It was late. In bed Molly lay on her back looking up at the inky ceiling. She was unable to sleep, while various thoughts grappled with each other in her head.

He had slipped away and all the while her mind had been distracted by questions. How long? Why? And anxieties – he had voluntarily stepped out of her sphere and perhaps he had no intention of returning. The control is ebbing, the grip is loosening, the period of happiness is over, she had thought.

Now though, thank God, he was back. Questions answered, anxieties dispersed. But never again such complacency.

The restaurant in Charlotte Street buzzed with the high-spirited exuberance of the Friday lunch-time customers.

Piers Orange, Alexander Bird and Helen Hardy sat at a small, round table in the window looking out on to the bright pavement. On the other side of the glass, pedestrians jostled briskly past in front of them.

Inside, a selection of knives, forks and glasses gleamed on top of the white cloth. The linen was so stiff, Helen noted, that it might have remained suspended in the air even if the table itself suddenly collapsed beneath it.

The elderly agent – pressing sixty-five? – popped open a Cellophane condom of Grissini. He then snapped off an inch of the long stick between his teeth and began to chew, mouth slightly open. Helen, directly opposite him, was able to sample the sight of the churning sawdust paste therein. Alexander Bird was wearing a tie, blatant pink. On it, a small canary of a comparatively discreet yellow, had been painted. It sat in a bare tree of two simple brown lines – one of them a trunk, the other a branch. She had seen ones like it for sale in the shop at the Royal Academy.

Piers flipped open his napkin and laid it on his lap. He asked Helen what she would like to drink. Something light, she felt. Did not want to fall asleep in the afternoon: work to be done. A spritzer. He chose a Campari and orange juice. The waiter brought their order on a small silver tray. Orange sipped at the exotic orange liquid, the ice clanking in his glass expensively like semi-precious stones.

He looked happy. Helen watched him. There was something sympathetic about his bushy eyebrows. Her slightly nervous glance was admiring, and excited. She straightened her napkin – of almost sheet proportions – over her stomach and thighs. Thus covered, she felt strangely secure. Here she was, an author, being taken out to lunch by her new agent – whom she had only met last week – and her potential publisher. Her experienced forty-two years had not prepared her for the peculiar sensation she was now feeling – something akin, she imagined, to being hauled up in a bucket and rescued, having passed a long and involuntary sojourn at the bottom of a dank well.

The waiter handed them each a menu.

'I don't see why I should be cool and try to hold out my enthusiasm till later,' Orange began honestly, smiling. 'Bugger restraint. I want to say right now how much I admired the chapters I've read. Helen,' he added slowly, looking at her, hoping she would not mind the use of her Christian name – Miss Hardy was too spinsterish, formal, didn't suit her – 'it would give me tremendous pleasure if I could publish your book, and if you and my dear friend Alexander would consider accepting the offer I have in mind.' He stopped, took a swig of his drink, folded his arms, and sighed. 'There you have it. I've laid myself open to you.'

Helen gasped almost girlishly. She fingered the silky folds about the collar of her new yellow shirt – crêpe de Chine, daring neckline. Swigged at the sparkling spritzer. Overcome.

'Well, that's very good news,' Alexander Bird remarked, happy, but – more used to such declarations – not as ruffled as his new author. 'If we're buggering restraint, I might as well go ahead and immediately ask what sum it is you have in mind?'

'But, Alex, that's downright vulgar. In front of the author, and we haven't even ordered yet,' the publisher joked. 'Let's decide what we all want to eat first. Then you see,' he said, turning to Helen to explain the procedure, 'for the rest of lunch we can talk about different things entirely, gossip for example. And afterwards we go our separate ways and make endless telephone calls to each other all afternoon. I start by making an offer and Alex rings you for your reaction and a consultation. Then we all call each other again, haggle a bit and so on. That way we manage to maintain a bit of propriety. At least we think we do,' Orange added with a jaded but good-humoured laugh.

They all opened their menus. Helen did not want to eat. Her stomach was currently being wrenched upwards about a hundred feet on the end of a piece of rope – not exactly the ideal circumstances to inspire an appetite.

'A quick choice, then,' Alexander said excitedly. 'The watercress soup, followed by the calves' liver for me. What would you like, Helen, my dear?'

'The goat's cheese and olive salad, please.'

'Just one course?' Orange asked her, concerned. 'Not tempted by the monkfish and sorrel sauce? I think that's what I'm going to have, after a spot of sweetbread terrine.'

Helen shook her head.

'I'm very worried that won't be enough for you,' he told her kindly.

'Plenty,' she assured him, and the waiter came to take their order.

'All right, then, Piers, now we've dealt with the basics, let's move on to the gossip,' Alexander remarked, winking jovially at Helen. 'Then we can all rush away and hurry along with the third stage, the vulgar bit.'

'Okay,' Orange said and paused. 'But while we're at it, why don't we bugger restraint entirely and order some champagne? How about it?'

The agent and the author nodded with glee.

Champagne.

Matters augured well.

'How does ten sound to you?' Orange asked Bird on the telephone later that afternoon.

'Twelve,' Alexander responded in a deep and serious voice.

'Eleven.'

'I'll ring you back.'

'How does eleven sound to you, Helen, my dear?' Alexander Bird asked his author when he rang her in her flat moments later.

Eleven what? Helen wondered. Eleven hundred? Lovely.

'I might be able to wangle twelve,' his voice went on before she could reply.

Do people say 'twelve' when what they mean is one thousand two hundred? Could he really be saying pound sign, one, two, comma, nought, nought, nought? Twelve *grand*?

'Helen?'

I hadn't thought about money, she thought. How funny it is, the idea of my actually being paid by publishers to write, when somehow it seems more logical for me to pay them.

'I happen to know Piers thinks there's a distinct possibility that it might fare well in the Hills Lager Biography Prize,' Alexander continued, 'so I don't see any reason why I couldn't bump it up to twelve.'

What did she think of twelve?

Frankly, she did not think very much as it happened, the staggering proportions of the sum having momentarily numbed the mind.

'Fine,' she said, 'whatever you think.'

'But if I can't get more than eleven, bearing in mind he originally offered ten – '

Yes, he's definitely talking in terms of thousands. People certainly don't refer to one thousand simply as 'ten', short for ten hundred. My God – thousands!

'Would you go with eleven?' his voice continued. 'First book, and that. I think you'd be wise. I mean, I probably could get it up to twelve, maybe even twelve and a half, at Rubinstein's or the Sand Press at a pinch. But I don't think you'd ever find another editor like old Piers. Worth a lot, really, having someone on your side from the start, rooting for you to succeed. What do you say?'

Helen thought, what a luxurious problem this is, so removed from reality.

She could picture Orange in her mind. The friendly eyebrows, the almost childish excitement in his eyes at lunch when he had come clean and declared his admiration for her book. The publisher was definitely on her side. Alexander Bird was right about that. And he appeared to have faith in her too. Champagne! It was a winning formula indeed.

'No question,' she said at last, calmly.

Would that all decisions were so easy, so pleasurably arrived at.

'Great. Lovely. I'll ring you back in a few minutes,' Alexander Bird enthused down the line.

True to his word, the man with the dazzling neckwear called Helen back moments later.

205

'Well, my old friend Orange seems to have agreed to settle for twelve,' he told her. Even his voice, that of an experienced agent who had seen it all before, sounded excited. 'Excellent news, isn't it?' he went on. 'I'm so pleased. They'll be drawing up a contract for you to sign in no time. Wonderful, wonderful. Congratulations.'

Telephone still in hand, Helen fell back into the sofa, kicking off her shoes. She cried out with delight.

And for a heavenly moment, she not only forgot she was a woman of forty-two, but also that she was a solitary spinster.

That perennially gruesome fact, for a second or two, quite deserted her consciousness.

CHAPTER
9

Molly sat on a packing case. A stubby nail dug into her thigh. She stood up quickly and in revenge gave the box a kick. Then she thumped it with her fist to ensure it didn't delude itself and think the first blow a mistake.

'What *are* you doing?' Dominic asked, laughing. 'Want some pizza?' he added, sucking his finger like an over-conscientious character in a commercial keen to impress the sceptical that his hot-dog was 'finger-lickin' good'. He held out a flabby triangle to her. She recoiled from it in mock horror.

'You're forgetting, I used to *be* one of those before I worked in the bookshop,' she said, remembering her stint as a waitress at Pizza Express. 'I never want to see one again. Hey, where d'you think the table should go?'

Dominic put his supper aside and lit a cigarette. 'There's not exactly a huge choice,' he teased.

'Okay. It may be small, but it's very exciting,' she remarked, looking about the room. 'A kitchen. A real, proper kitchen. It's not much to ask for, is it?'

He shook his head.

'Won't be long before I get everything sorted out. It's going to be brilliant. An extra twenty quid a week. I'll be broke, so who cares?' Molly declared happily, relishing the scene. 'You're covered in dust,' she observed.

'I'm exhausted. Think I'll go to bed. We've got all day tomorrow to do this.' He stood up and went next door.

'I'll join you in a minute. God, I can't get over the novelty of having a separate bedroom,' she enthused, peering through the door. 'So grand.'

'It'd be more so if I could find the wretched pillows,' Dominic pointed out patiently.

Molly, in her excitement, just smiled. She turned back to the kitchen and spied the old crusts of pizza which he had left uneaten in the tomatoey carton. And she suddenly felt a rush of appreciation for her change of circumstance. So Dominic, like Dave had, harboured a fondness for pizzas. But that was all right. At least her present boyfriend restrained himself from the urge to gorge on an American Hot while still panting from the effects of an orgasm.

She had a lot to be thankful for.

The next morning, a Saturday, Molly's keenness to sort out the new flat meant that she awoke early. Anxious not to rouse Dominic, she crept into the kitchen in her dressing-gown and made a cup of tea. She sat by the window at the table and glanced at the familiar market below. It was beginning to throb. Through the glass she could hear the muted cries of the stallholders and suddenly wanted to be among their colourful wares – everything from scarves to bananas.

Tiptoeing back to the bedroom, she picked up her clothes from the floor and dressed stealthily. She put on jeans and an old blue sweatshirt. Then, in a pair of flat shoes, she padded downstairs and on to the vibrant street.

Molly would buy breakfast to celebrate her kitchen. She could treat Dominic – who usually had to make do with milkless tea – to her speciality, originally perfected for Rufus, of sausages, bacon and eggs. The works.

Meandering through the slow crowd, she felt the fresh sun on her cheeks, and it warmed her and her intentions. She passed the boxes of fruit and vegetables, the piles of cheap cosmetics in garish packages and the racks of hippy skirts. Along her way, she collected a few brown paper bags. They bulged promisingly with the things she bought. An old man, blind, was playing a mouth organ outside a dowdy chemist. A few copper moles blemished the bottom of the dented biscuit tin at his feet. Molly stopped and dropped in 50p, and the man smiled gratefully as he swayed to his music. She turned towards Woolworth's and entered the haven of pale salmon neon, suddenly remembering she needed light bulbs. Then she ambled out and over to the supermarket to buy washing powder.

Standing in the check-out queue, she didn't feel the usual queasiness of impatience. In fact, she was so relaxed that the gathering of these supplies for her new flat was a pleasure. The eagerness to make everything perfect left no room for such concerns as wasting time on mundane details.

Slowly wandering back, Molly stopped outside the window of the Body Shop. Her fingers were becoming stiffly purple due to the user-enemy handles of her heavy carrier bag. Meanwhile, her mind was wistfully trying to justify her supposed urgent need for some moisturiser (the ingredients of which might have been more appropriately listed in the recipe for an exotic pudding than a cream to rub into the face).

Dominic might accuse me of extravagance, she thought. There again, he might like to borrow it himself. . .

The voices in her head, both with their rational arguments, went on for some moments, privately facing temptation and weighing up the pros and cons.

After a while, she stepped inside the shop. A rainbow of warm smells arced around her – spicy oils, fruity soaps – luxuries for the nose.

'Molly!' A chirpy voice interrupted her internal discussion. 'Goodness, how're *you*? Haven't seen you for ages.'

Familiar voice behind her. School? University? Not now. Please.

She turned round. Neither school nor university, but a friendly regular customer at the bookshop: Lucy.

'Haven't see *you* for ages,' Molly repeated. 'Where've you been? Given up buying books?' she joked. 'Or getting them elsewhere?'

'Neither,' Lucy beamed. 'Been away for a while. Cheshire.' Loaded tone implying that she had found more in Cheshire than cheese.

Molly said, good. Lucy wore yellow shoes.

'I'm getting married,' she enthused.

'Congratulations!'

'Thank you.'

Who is he? What does he do? When's the wedding? Stock questions. All answered with enthusiasm.

But the enthusiasm was only slightly infectious. It got Molly down a bit. Still, she was interested enough to ask where the wedding was taking place. A lovely little church in Cheshire. And the dress?

'Off-white, I thought.' The information was imparted in a significant voice. 'My aunt's making it for me. It's going to be so beautiful.'

There followed a precise description, enthusiastic, of the details.

Molly said, 'It sounds wonderful.' It didn't.

Why are you getting married, she asked Lucy in her mind, staring at the spot on Lucy's chin, the colour of which matched Lucy's shoes. Why you and not me? Okay, so I'm not cross to have missed out on a picture framer in Nantwich, and I don't want pearly beads in the shape of a rose on my bodice, but I do want a husband.

But I'm not going to tell you that. I can, say, Lucy, I'm very happy for you.

'Lucy, I'm very happy for you.'

I am. Really. But I'm not going to admit that I, too, want to be a wife. You don't admit things like that. Not ever. The rule is you don't let on. Not ever. Women in the latter part of the twentieth century have feminist ideals. They don't think about marriage, unless it slaps them in the face. They certainly don't tell people that in fact marriage is the thing they aspire to more than anything in life.

A husband. Children. Security.

It's not asking much. But one must never ask for it, all the same.

'How about you, Molly? Any developments on that front for you?' Lucy asked. Predictable. Intrusive.

Keep up the pretence. You're cool about it. Play the game. The game is you're fine as you are. Take it or leave it, frankly.

'No plans.' Nonchalant little shrug.

'But you've got a man?'

Got a man. Unspeakable expression. The scented rainbow suddenly seemed rather sickly. Got a man, indeed. Molly chose to answer the question by using a phrase where the juxtaposition of verb and noun was slightly less offensive.

'There's a boyfriend, yes,' she said.

'So, when're you going to tie the knot?'

Molly did not care much for Lucy and her fiancéed air.

'Oh, we're not, as far as I know. Haven't really thought about it. No need, really, except if one wants children. And even then – '

'Oh, I so disagree,' Lucy disagreed.

Molly said, 'Do you?'

'Marriage is what it's all about, really, don't you think?'

Yes.

'No. Not really. There's more to life than – '

'Sure. But let's face it, it's jolly nice to have a husband.'

Molly shrugged. 'Yeah, I guess,' she said, but very casually. She found the conversation depressing.

Yes, of course it's 'jolly nice to have a husband', you silly woman in your silly shoes, but some of us aren't as lucky as others, you tactless creature. I don't want to hear about your cream lace veil. I want to marry Dominic and to have my own cream lace veil and to talk about it beside shelves of ice-blue shampoo and white musk powder on Saturday mornings, too.

'Is that the time?' Molly asked.

Go away and sneeze in your own confetti, Lucy, why not?

'I think I'd better be making my way. Dom's breakfast,' Molly said, out loud.

I may not be getting married to him, but I look after him just as well as you do your future husband. What's more, I bet I make better bacon and eggs than you do, engaged or not engaged.

'Duty calls,' Lucy remarked. She had a good line in original phrases, Lucy.

'Well, good luck with it all. I hope it goes well.' Molly did mean what she said.

She excused herself with a polite goodbye, and made her way out of the shop, the moisturiser forgotten. Marriage was on the mind, now, and wretched weddings. All this talk had quite flustered her, sapped her of all those earlier feelings of relaxed contentment.

Walking quickly, she began to head along the block towards home. The street had become more crowded. Faces bobbed about her like ping-pong balls in gently flowing water.

She imagined herself in some lovely country church, in her off-white dress and her cream lace veil. And the featureless ping-pong faces of the market crowd suddenly became those of her wedding guests.

211

She tried to think of Dominic's supper and she stopped at a baker's stall. But she fancied the man behind it was wearing a morning coat and had a carnation in his buttonhole. Didn't he? In his hand a service sheet was poised – or was it a white paper bag?

'Yes, dear? What do you want?'

It was a white paper bag.

And spread out was fruit cake with yellow marzipan and white icing, wasn't there?

'I've got banana bread, walnut slices, chocolate chip cookies, hazelnut biscuits, blueberry muffins, lemon tart, vanilla creams, jam doughnuts, maple syrup waffles, Battenburg log, strawberry sensations,' the man boasted.

Molly looked at them all at once, a blur of deliciousness, even though in reality there was no wedding cake.

Which would Dominic like best of all? She wanted him to have a memorable pudding tonight. She wanted to make the perfect decision. She wanted to seduce him with her choice.

'Come along, love, I haven't got all day,' the man urged.

Her eyes alighted upon the opulent crimson of the strawberry sensations. The pair sat plumply on a square plate, their pink paper holders like upturned tutus.

'Please could I have those,' Molly asked, pointing meekly.

'Good choice, love. One twenty,' he said, gathering them up and darting open the bag with a flick of his finger. Molly watched the baby shark's teeth of the paper's white edge swallow them up.

A good choice indeed.

'Like some breakfast?' Molly asked, sitting on the bed. 'I've been shopping.'

'What's the time?' Dominic, waking up, groaned. He sat up and put his arms behind his head on the pillow. Molly looked at his biceps. The night before they had held her so tightly.

'Elevenish, I think. I thought I'd cook you a proper brunch,' she said, watching him appreciatively. This is what it's all about, she thought. Mundane, real-life happiness.

'How long've you been up?'

'Oh, ages. I went to the market. Got various things we needed. And sausages. What d'you reckon?'

212

'Really, there's no need. I can do it,' Dominic suggested, missing the point.

'No, no. I'll shout when it's ready,' Molly said, standing up. Although she did not eat breakfast herself, she was keen to make it for him. She went into the kitchen.

'I won't be a minute,' Dominic called sleepily.

About half an hour later, the pair of them were sitting at the kitchen table. The May sun beamed in, revealing a glittering dust silently floating, like plankton in the sea caught by the light of a diver's torch.

Dominic crunched on fried bread bathed in saffron-coloured egg yolk, and Molly sipped her coffee.

'Bumped into this woman in the Body Shop, a customer at the bookshop. She's getting married.' Irresistible topic, marriage.

'Oh yes?' Not very interested.

'I got the whole thing about the wedding, down to the last bead on the silk train.'

Dominic tipped his eyes upwards as if to say, God forbid, poor you.

'I mean, I can't be doing with that sort of thing,' Molly lied, hoping this reaction would reassure him. 'All that stuff, honestly.'

'Better to do it in a registry office, no one knowing about it, get two witnesses off the streets,' Dominic said, smiling. 'I'm not into all that church bit. If and when I get married, I reckon the thing to do is to keep it a secret till afterwards, then tell everyone. Avoids all the family hassle.'

'Quite,' Molly lied again. 'I mean, I had this woman banging on about where she was buying her wretched shoes, and the precise ingredients of the bloody canapés at the reception. As if I care. I don't want to get into any of that.'

'Well, there's no immediate danger, is there?' Dominic said, chewing away, good-humoured. A gentle tease.

'Thank God,' Molly lied, yet again.

Well, that's settled that one, then, hasn't it? she thought. No danger of you sweeping me off to some gloomy registry office for your secret ceremony.

Damn your secrecy. Damn the woman, whoever she turns out to be, who wants to partake in it.

I want it to be me, Dominic. I'll forsake the church, the family, the dress, the bridesmaids, the veil, the shoes, the champagne, the canapés, for you and your effing secret ceremony.

Who wants a white wedding, anyway? Me? Course not! When I could have you and your registry office?

I want a white wedding more than anything. I always have, always will. I've been brainwashed since I was a child to yearn for it with every element of yearning in me, and now you're telling me it has to be a secret ceremony in a registry office without all those traditional details I've always dreamed about.

Yet, if you'll have me, I'll go along with your plans. I won't have any of the things I've longed for, because I'll have you.

And yet you won't have me, will you? It won't be me at your grim, impersonal little ceremony, will it, despite my unvoiced sacrifices? They make no difference, do they? You won't be changing your mind. No amount of cooked breakfasts will have you contemplating tripping up the registry office steps with me.

No, no. That doubtful privilege is reserved for some distant, future, faceless woman who's hard and beautiful and clever and sophisticated and loves registry offices and anonymous witnesses and secrets.

And I am not she.

No. No.

Molly Almond wants the white.

You can tell, can't you?

So I am not she. I can't be she. The she spurns white, and is perfection.

No. No. Not me.

By mid-afternoon books were on the shelves, china was in the cupboards, furniture had been arranged. It had taken longer to sort out than anticipated, but the place now looked lived in. Molly had just sat down at the table, satisfied, with a cup of tea and Dominic had gone out to buy a plug and some beer, when the doorbell rang.

It was Rufus. He had an old custard-coloured bicycle and a long face.

Molly welcomed him with a hug.

'I was very keen to see it, and I promised to bring the bike,' he said, stepping into the communal hall. 'Is this a bad moment?'

'Not at all,' Molly assured him happily. 'I've just made a pot of tea. Here, leave that against the radiator and come and have a look round.'

'See,' she said, when they were upstairs, 'I've got a separate kitchen and bedroom.'

Rufus approved and told his daughter she had made a wise decision.

'I do hope so,' she said. 'By the way, thanks for bringing my bike.' Molly poured her father some tea and asked after her mother.

Rufus said, 'Ah,' and at that moment Dominic returned.

Warm hellos.

Molly's boyfriend offered Molly's father a cigarette. Then he joined them at the teapot.

'We must've shelved so many books this afternoon,' he told Rufus, smiling. 'Exhausting.'

'Any room for this?' Rufus asked, pulling a large catalogue from a plastic bag. 'I've just been to the RA. Thought you'd like a copy, Mol. You saw the exhibition, didn't you?'

Molly accepted the present with enthusiasm.

'And while I remember, I must give you one of your mother's invitations for her show. They arrived from New York a few days ago.'

He passed her a folded card. It had a grim picture on the cover, beautifully reproduced. Under it 'The Fall' was printed in grey letters. Lower down, it said 'An exhibition of paintings by Cake Carlisle'.

Her maiden name.

Molly turned to her father with a quizzical expression. Sad.

'Let's have a look,' Dominic said. She handed it to him. 'They've done it terribly well, haven't they?' he asked, missing Molly's and Rufus's significant glances at one another.

'Why did she do that?' she asked, after a moment. The question was directed at the older man.

'Why did she do what?' Dominic wondered out loud, looking up from the invitation.

'Use Carlisle,' Molly said flatly.

'She has a high regard for her independence, Mol,' Rufus remarked by way of an unconvincing explanation.

'But she's never done it before, not used Almond on her work. Why this sudden bid? I think it's very insulting to you

215

that she calls herself Carlisle suddenly, like it's denying your existence at an important turning point in her life.'

'I understand it.'

'You're more understanding than me, then, Dad.'

'Her work's her own thing. I'm not a part of it. As a painter I think she wants to be known by her own name. There're considerations regarding the' – Rufus paused to indicate the word he was about to use was not his own – 'identity.' The syllables were uttered with reluctant deliberation.

'Oh yes, and I dare say when she goes to America she'll be overcome by a desire to find herself too, no doubt. Needs to retain her own identity as a painter! I've no patience with such earnest self-consciousness. It's a load of vacuous rubbish, pseudy nonsense.' Molly aggressively plonked her cup of tea on the table to demonstrate further her contempt.

'You're being a bit harsh, Mol,' Rufus muttered.

'I'm not. It's just I'm not interested in a mother who's concerned with things such as her wretched identity, for God's sake. She paints pictures, she's married to you, her name's Cake Almond. Why not just get on with it?'

There was a pause. Dominic lit another cigarette, awkward. He did not look at either of them, but stared at the back of his hand. He puffed away uneasily.

Rufus sighed miserably. Molly watched her father. He had about him an air of resignation. His jersey had holes, his hair was ruffled and his pallor betrayed despair.

'I don't think she wants just to get on with that,' he mumbled quietly, eyes cast to the floor. Ominous admission.

'What do you mean?' Molly asked, gently, sensing a revelation was imminent.

'I'm sorry, Mol.' Rufus shook his head.

Ah. So that is it.

I understand now. You have come to tell me that she has gone. That she really has got on with it. Just not the 'it' I was referring to – the painting pictures, and the being married, and the just being Cake Almond 'it'.

No, Mum is getting on with another 'it' – the painting pictures and the retaining her identity and the being Cake Carlisle 'it'.

An altogether different 'it'.

One which spells the end of it.

There were silent tears in Molly's eyes. Dominic put his hand on her shoulder and left the kitchen without a word. Rufus stared at the teapot. The sun beamed on, unsympathetic in its brightness.

'Terence,' Molly said at last.

Rufus nodded.

'She's already gone to New York. Earlier than planned,' he informed her.

'And he went too?'

He nodded again, tapping his thumb on the side of his mug of tea.

'What's he like?' Molly asked.

'An extremely nice man,' came the answer, devoid of bitterness.

'Which hardly makes things any better. If only you could hate him.'

'No, Mol. I wouldn't want to hate him, and I don't.'

'Her then,' she suggested.

'I shall always love her.'

Of course. And so shall I. Damn her. Damn you. Damn me.

'What'll you do? Sell the house. Move back into college?'

'Unless she wants it.' Rufus spoke softly. Molly wondered at his dignified restraint.

'You'd give it to her?' she asked.

'I'd like her to be happy. If that made her happy.'

'What about him? Will they get married?'

Rufus said he didn't know.

'I'm worried about you, Dad.'

'Oh, no need to worry about me, Mol. I'm a man of some resilience.' He smiled, weakly resilient, as he spoke. 'I'm thinking of you.'

'My God, look at me! I've got all this,' Molly looked at herself, at her kitchen, at her view. And Rufus knew that her 'all this' meant not so much all of that, but the presence of Dominic in her life.

'And there's Dominic,' she confirmed. 'I'm sad for you, Dad, but I'm okay. You're not to worry about me. It's you.' The lump in the throat was sharply painful.

'We'll be all right, won't we?' he asked. He put his hand on her knee, as he used to when she was a child. She recognised the reference: us against her.

Molly nodded with a stoical smile. She was scared to talk, fearing her voice, forced through the lump, might also squeeze out the dormant sobs. But then Rufus gave her a hug, and that prompted them anyway. Molly cried unrestrainedly.

Her father comforted her a while privately, and then called Dominic.

'Look after her for me,' he whispered to him as he was leaving.

Dominic put his arms around her, sat her on the sofa in the sitting-room, gave her a drink and told her, sincerely but awkwardly, that he was sorry.

His efforts did not pass unappreciated.

'I feel much better now,' Molly announced an hour later. It was odd, she was almost pleased. Her parents' separation had been so close for so many years. There was about her, suddenly, a sense of relief. The inevitable had finally happened. Molly was unhappy and happy.

Dominic, in the armchair opposite her, drank his beer.

'Don't you think it's probably a good thing really?' she asked him.

Probably, he said. Non-committal.

'I mean,' she continued, 'it had to happen some time. It couldn't have gone on. In some ways, I think Dad'll be better off. I imagine when your wife stops loving you and before she decides to leave you, it's a bit like when your child goes missing before you know for certain that it's dead. You go on hoping. The process of recovery can only really start when you find out the truth. It takes time and it's agonising and hellish, but till then the healing can't begin.'

'I expect you're right,' Dominic remarked.

'Don't you think he'll be better off now?'

'I don't know, Mol. If you say so.'

'You must have some opinion. Isn't he well shot of my mother? No?'

'I don't know,' he repeated. 'I can't honestly say.'

'Why? I'd have thought you'd've agreed. I mean, you saw the way she treated him in Oxford, and that was just one weekend. It's been going on ever since I can remember.'

'I can remember in Oxford telling you it was none of my business.' The voice was quiet, not grudging. 'It's a private matter between you and them.'

'And you don't want to get, what was it? Inveigled, I think you said.'

'Inveigled. No. No, I don't. You're right.'

Molly nodded, pensive. The crisis of her parents' divorce, and still he wished to remain detached. It was understandable. It was also unforgivable.

But Molly forgave him. Predictably.

'I'm sorry.' Another superfluous apology. 'I suppose 'cos it's just happened I want to talk about it, that's all. I can't help thinking about her in New York, glittery with the excitement of just being there with her bloody lover, and her bloody independent identity as a painter. And him, all alone in Warnborough Road having to deal with all the oppressive associations and memories.'

'Try not to think about it,' Dominic urged, quite warmly.

'I'll try,' she said, brightening in response to the warmth. 'Maybe I should do something to take my mind off it. That pile of washing next door.'

'You needn't bother to do mine, Mol.'

'Why not?'

'Well, I can do it,' he volunteered cheerfully.

'No, it's fine. I don't mind at all.'

'Look, just because I'm here doesn't mean to say you have to do my washing.'

'I never said it did. It won't take long.' Molly thought he would be pleased if she did his washing, and she was keen to do it for him. She would not say so, though. 'Honestly, I don't mind. I've got to do mine anyway, so I might as well. You haven't got much, I seem to remember – '

'I'd prefer it if you didn't – '

'What are you talking about? Why?'

'I just would.'

'Don't be silly. I can do it. It may not be my favourite occupation in the world, but as I said, it'll take my mind off things.'

'I don't want that kind of pressure, Mol, okay?'

What? Washing a couple of pairs of socks – pressure?

'What do you mean, pressure? If I bung a few of your things in my wash, that's pressure?'

219

'Couply. Homey,' he said simply. 'You know what I mean.'

'Dom! Come on. It's nothing to do with that. It makes sense. I'd do it for a girlfriend if she was sharing the same roof.'

'I don't like it.'

Molly sighed. 'You're daft,' she said with considerable good humour, but only just concealing that she was crushed within. 'Okay. If you'll excuse me, I'll go and do my own washing then,' she added, heading for the door.

'Of course I'm sorry about Rufus and Cake splitting up,' Dominic mumbled suddenly. 'And I'm sorry if I won't talk about it. But it all gets a bit much, all right?'

Molly, humbled by the unexpected apologies, bit her lip. 'All right.'

She went into the bathroom. She heard Dominic switch on the television. She turned on the taps of the basin. But it was not 'all right'.

Kneading the clothes, soppy in the slimy, milky water, the tears began to well again.

He's slipping away, she thought. I'm losing my grip, she thought. And there's absolutely nothing I can do about it, she knew.

The sound of the television voices tell me he's here. But he's not really here. He's on his way.

Like Mama, he's gone.

Perhaps because of Mama he's going, he's almost gone. God, don't let him go. I don't want him to go. I want him to stay for ever. But he won't, will he?

I pressurise him, you see, because I talk about my mother, and I offer to wash his socks.

It's because, really, I want him to be involved, to be part of my life. And though I try not to show it, he knows. And he doesn't want to be involved, to be part of my life.

I hate my mother. I hate washing socks. But I love him. And he feels pressure.

What can I do?

When Molly went back into the sitting-room she made sure she was cheerful. And Dominic was there, after all, in front of the television.

'Hey,' she said lightly. 'Have we got any more beer?'

'There're two cans in the kitchen,' he told her.

'Good. Do you want another one?'

'That'd be lovely. Thanks.'

She went next door to fetch them, and reappeared and plonked herself down on the sofa. 'Have you seen the *Independent* anywhere? I want to see what time that film's on.'

'Here,' Dominic said, keeping his eye on the screen, and he passed it to her.

They were silent. The telly wittered on. His fingers tap-danced on the remote control box which was sitting on the arm of his chair.

'When would you like supper?' she asked perkily after some minutes.

'Don't mind.'

'Nineish be all right?'

Dominic ummed.

'I got us some fish. And peas.' Trying a bit too hard, perhaps.

'Very good.' Disinterest.

'And, what's more, I've been very extravagant and bought a bottle of special wine, and two little surprises for pudding.'

'Very good.' Repetition of disinterest.

'A house-warming surprise.'

'I saw them in the fridge,' he said, vaguely, still looking at the television. He didn't want to be surprised.

Molly said, 'Oh.' Disappointed. 'Never mind. They looked good, didn't they?'

'Mol, I'm trying to watch my programme. Sorry. Do you mind?'

'Oh, sorry. I'll let you get on with it. Just very quickly, would you like some of the wine I bought?' she whispered.

'I'd love some. Thank you.' He turned to look at her a moment and winked affectionately.

She went into the kitchen to fetch it, came back, sat down and opened the bottle. The cork made a rasping squeak, as uncomfortable to listen to as a finger rubbing the surface of a balloon. Eyes still on the television, Dominic lifted his shoulder to his ear for a second and grimaced.

Molly passed him a glass of wine. She was not particularly interested in the programme he was watching. She slouched back into the sofa cushions, folded her arms and stared at the screen without really taking in the flickering images. A little bored, she wanted to start a conversation, but instinct told her that she should not.

Dominic laughed suddenly. Molly had not registered precisely what it was that prompted him to do so. But she laughed too. She wanted him to think she was concentrating and for him not to guess what she really wanted to do. But during the advertisements, unable to resist, she asked him if he thought she ought to ring Rufus.

Dominic sighed in response and then told her that maybe she should, if she thought that was a good idea.

'Well, I don't know. Perhaps if I call, it'll just remind him of everything. But what if he's lonely?'

At last her boyfriend turned his face to her.

'Molly, please. I don't know.'

She nodded. 'I think it'd be best if I just gave him a quick ring, make sure he's all right.'

'You do that. Good idea.'

The programme began again.

'I'll take the telephone into the kitchen, okay? Does it reach?'

Dominic said that it would. Molly went with it, and her wine, into the next room and shut the door.

'Dad? When did you get back? An hour ago only? What happened, the train was delayed?'

'It was lovely seeing you. I thought the flat was great,' he told her.

'What're you doing tonight? I think maybe you should go out.'

'I've plenty to be getting on with. Work.'

'I don't want you to be lonely,' she told him.

'I promise. You all right?'

'I'm fine. Dom's here. Watching telly. We're going to have a quiet evening in.'

'Probably best,' Rufus remarked.

'Do you think she'll ring me? She hasn't rung me to tell me herself yet. She might at least ring me.'

'I expect so, Mol.'

'Do you have a number?'

'She didn't leave a number.' Rufus's voice sounded disappointed rather than angry.

'Typical.'

'Listen, if you do speak to her, promise me you won't be unkind,' he implored.

222

'That's her line, Dad. Always on about kindness. Look at her! Hardly the personification of it herself. Hypocrite.'

'Promise me, Mol.'

'I can't promise, I'll try. But it'll be against my better nature.'

'Don't. I'm to blame too in all this, you know. It's not all her fault.'

'Ninety-nine per cent.'

'Well, whatever you think, my love. But you're not to get at her if she rings. Promise.'

Molly sighed.

'As I said, I'll try, but it won't be easy.'

'For me, eh?'

'I'll try. And if you feel low, you promise you'll call me. I'll be on the very next train if you like,' she assured him.

Rufus promised.

When the conversation was over, Molly informed Dominic that her father had sounded 'pretty low'.

Half an hour later, the telephone rang. It was a transatlantic call. Cake in New York.

'Darling, how are you? I'm sorry I didn't ring before. It was all such a rush, my coming here earlier than planned. I didn't say goodbye to you. I'm sorry.'

Molly, she told herself, you promised Dad.

'It doesn't matter, Mum. How are you?'

'Confused, Mol. Dad's spoken to you, has he?'

Molly answered in the affirmative.

'What can I say? Only that I'm sorry.'

'Me too. How could you do it to him, Mum?' Molly took the telephone through to the kitchen again but did not shut the door. She sat on one of the two yellow wicker chairs she had picked up in the market for a fiver. On the wooden floorboards her bare feet felt cold and exposed. So she swivelled round and rested them on the white plastic pedal-bin.

'Don't think it was easy. I swear it wasn't easy,' Cake was saying.

'Nor was it exactly kind. It's you who always went on about kindness.'

'I thought, maybe, in the circumstances, it was kinder to go. He knew about Terence.' The voice sounded remote. Molly wondered if it was the literal distance only.

'He knew about all the others, too,' she informed her mother.

223

'What others?'

'Come on, Mum. I'm twenty-five years old.'

'I dare say he knew about the others, too,' Cake admitted. 'You're right. So perhaps it was kinder for me to bring the pretence of our marriage to an end.'

'It wasn't a complete pretence, was it? He loved you all the while, and you him in your own way.'

'In my own way, yes. Still do.'

'So why did you do it? Couldn't you have gone on for his sake?'

'I don't think so, Mol. I'm sorry.'

'What'll you do then? Marry Terence?' There was a flatness about Molly's tone which was very uncharacteristic.

'Who knows? Maybe.'

'He's with you now in New York?'

'We're staying with Amy. The show's soon. We all want you to come out. There's a room for you here. Amy says you must come.'

An offer which could be refused.

'When're you coming home?' Molly asked, refusing the offer but avoiding doing so directly.

'Not long. After the exhibition. Few weeks. It's not like real life here really.'

'No. It wouldn't be.'

'I'm as confused as you.' Cake had her emotional voice on. No doubt when the call was over, she would be off finding herself before tea. It was curious, Molly pondered, that a woman so impatient with 'the self-indulgence of those who need time to think', should be so concerned with the introspective notion of her own identity.

'I'm not confused. Expected it sooner actually, you giving up. Surprised you held out so long.'

'Don't be like that. I didn't exactly enjoy doing what I've done,' Molly's mother moaned.

'If that's the case, perhaps you should've spared yourself a joyless task.'

'It's hard for you to understand.'

Molly said that it was not. 'I understand it perfectly,' she assured her mother.

In as much as I understand, it's very simple: you're to blame. You are selfish. That is all there is to understand.

Molly, you promised Dad you'd try not to be unkind to her.

'As it happens,' she said, resisting the temptation to abuse, 'I don't want to discuss it on the telephone.'

Cake and her guilt complied by changing the subject.

'How's the new flat?' she asked flatly.

It was 'fine' she was told.

'And Dominic, how's he?'

Ah, my boyfriend. I expect you'd like to put a dampener on that one, too, wouldn't you, like you did all the others? Well, you're not doing too bad a job on that score. Yes, I thought you'd be pleased to hear. Because, you see, though you are however many thousands of miles away, your influence still lurks here. It's a pity you couldn't have taken it with you, really, packed it in your suitcase along with your identity as a painter.

It's not only Dad you affected. You managed to upset me, too. Fortunate, isn't it, I've a kind boyfriend to turn to. Time of crisis, bit of support never goes amiss.

Alas, as it turns out, things are proving rather tricky, Mum, if you're interested.

Dominic is a kind man. You were rather anxious about that, I seem to remember. But the kindness could just recoil because by upsetting me, you're causing me, in turn, to pressurise him, apparently.

A mother so keen that my boyfriend should be kind. A mother so devoid of kindness herself. Ironic, really.

I hope Terence is very kind.

There again, he better not be as kind as Dad. Fatal, that.

'Dom's fine,' Molly responded automatically.

'Things going well there?'

'Oh yes. Very well. Thank you.'

'I'm glad. Listen, darling, I promise to write, and ring again. Lots. And please change your mind about coming out, okay?'

Molly said, okay, because that was what Cake wanted to hear. That, too, was what Rufus would have wanted her to say. But she didn't mean okay.

'I'll ring soon. Take care of Dad for me,' Cake urged. Then she and her daughter sent love to each other.

The conversation came to an end.

'That was Mum,' Molly informed Dominic without moving from her comfortable position between the kitchen chair and the pedal-bin.

'I think I'll make supper,' she said eventually, standing up.

'Hang on a second, Mol.' There was a pause before the voice coming from the sitting-room added, 'I've been thinking.'

Ominous.

'Um?'

'Come through here a minute.'

The invitation was accepted with pleasure. Indeed, encouraged by his hospitality, Molly took it a step further and went to sit on Dominic's lap. He shifted in the armchair to accommodate her not heavy weight. She clutched his knee and felt the softness of his jeans in her hand. Then she peered into his face. She remembered seeing it that first time in the bookshop partly obscured by his coat collar. It was all the better for the full exposure that was now so familiar to her. The round eyes blinked less, the shyness having given way to affection. And he smiled more, the affection – due to the warm ease he had come to feel in her company – better able to manifest itself openly. Beside his pale complexion, the colour of his lips appeared to be especially rich: almost purple, like a stain made by blackcurrant juice on bleached pine.

There was a long silence.

Molly and Dominic just looked at each other. She could not construe the meaning of the expression on his face. It was a face she knew so well, but an expression she did not know at all. The eyes and the lips were completely still. Melancholy? Troubled? Moved?

'I don't think this is going to work,' he whispered at last. Then he pressed the 'Power off' button on the remote control panel.

What? Questioning eyes.

'Me here.'

Oh?

'I have to admit, Mol – ' Pause. ' – I've started to feel this sort of – pressure from you.'

Ah. That. Light response essential if you're wanting to eliminate any such notions.

'Hey, you're making me sound like one of those cookers, Dom,' she smiled lightly pressing his chest with a weak fist. 'You don't think of me as a cooker, do you?'

226

'Mol, that's a facetious remark.' Remarkably gentle, the voice.

'Well, I'm sorry if you think I pressurise you. I don't mean to. You're talking about the socks, eh?' she spoke quietly, coaxingly, not angrily.

'Among other things.'

'My mother's separation from my father?'

'That too. Yes. You talking about it. It's as if you're trying to make me part of your family.'

'I wouldn't say that. It happened. You're around. So I talk to you about it. I'm sorry if you see that as pressure.'

'Living here, becoming involved, don't you see?'

'Not really.'

'Washing socks – ' Dominic said with a pained smile.

'We've been through that. I didn't wash your socks, okay?'

'But it shouldn't have come up in the first place.'

'If you feel so strongly about a couple of pairs of socks, honestly – '

'And all that talk this morning of marriage.'

'That? It was hardly an in-depth discussion. I was merely telling you, in passing, about this girl I saw who bored on about her wedding dress. Don't flatter yourself it was any kind of hint.' Defensive.

'No, of course not. I just feel this tremendous pressure from you.' Dominic's voice was becoming uncharacteristically loud.

'I'd call it paranoia,' she said.

'I think you fail to appreciate the gravity of what I'm telling you.'

Molly thought for a moment and did not say anything.

'I think perhaps you're right, I do,' she admitted at last.

'Molly, I can't take it any more. You're smothering me.' Gently he began to manoeuvre her from his lap. She stood up reluctantly. He then did likewise.

Was this some reflection on her size? Molly glanced down at her figure. Had she put on weight?

'Are you telling me I've got fatter?'

'I'm so glad you see the humour,' he snapped. Up until then, he had remained calm, but now he seemed cross. 'All this commitment you seem to be after – '

'Have I ever requested your commitment? Would I? Come on, Dom.'

'Not in so many words maybe. I'm aware of a sense of claustrophobia, though. I can't take it, Mol, any more.'

'Don't even think of mentioning the word "space" in reference to your needing more of it. Spare me that. If you say that, I'll throw you out of here like a shot, even before you've had the chance to contemplate it yourself.'

It was good to maintain a certain humour, wasn't it, in circumstances such as these? More dignified. After all, many a humiliating accusation had been levied – pressure, claustrophobia, smothering. Surely it was best to rise above them all with a bit of good humour?

Alas, the tactfulness of Molly's reaction only seemed to fire Dominic's exasperation further.

'It's impossible to have a serious conversation with you,' he told her.

'You know that's not true.' Feeble protest.

'I'm trying to be reasonable.'

'I respect your endeavours. But they're misplaced. How can total unreasonableness even attempt to be reasonable? No one else sees me as a pressure cooker.'

'You've obviously failed to understand what I'm doing.'

Confused and anxious, Molly turned to face Dominic squarely and dared herself to look him straight in the eye. She thought him strangely appealing, ruffled as he was by frustration. Awkward. His stance reminded her of an artistically perfect statue, seemingly accurately fashioned, yet one which, when very closely scrutinised, does not actually correspond to reality. His hands, though elegant, appeared suddenly to be too big. He scrunched one with the other. A nervous habit of his. The knuckles made a cracking sound like walnuts. And were the eyes a little bloodshot? Hard to tell because they were partly closed in a frown of anger and agonised concern.

'I've tried to make you understand what I'm doing,' he uttered.

Molly took a sharp breath and held her head high.

'What are you doing?' she asked quietly.

She knew, of course, by now. Had to hear it though. From the blackcurrant lips. She would be absolutely certain then.

'I'm leaving you. I'm bloody well leaving you.'

Confirmation.

Dominic swiped up his huge coat from the back of the sofa and bloody well did just that. Walked out and left her.

The door slammed.

And it was with that that Molly stepped into her new kitchen and bloody well went to the fridge.

PART
2

CHAPTER
10

'Alfred, I've decided a visit to Winter Books is in order,' Helen told Housman as she woke on Monday morning, the first day of June. 'I have to talk to Nick.'

There was a silence.

'Look, I'm going anyway and care not a jot whether you think it wise. Much though I respect you, I don't need your approbation. I'm not changing my mind.'

An expression of almost cheeky defiance filtered across her face.

'Come on, Alfred,' she went on as she emerged from her bed and started to dress. 'It's only courteous. How so? Well, you must see it's only polite to thank him. He recommended me to Orange. If he hadn't, you never know, others might never have seen our book. As it is, we've been blessed with a most distinguished publisher.'

Helen went into her white kitchen and made some coffee.

'No, I'm not deluding myself. It's not just an excuse. This afternoon I shall be going to Winter Books not to ask after some book I could easily obtain elsewhere, but expressly to see Nick. To thank him, and to go away again. That is all. I need justify myself no further.'

As she spread her paper before her, Helen sensed her poet friend might at last be convinced, and some hours later she entered the little bookshop with a jaunty air.

It was warm inside. The room simmered with the treacly glow of the late afternoon sun. Helen found Molly staring closely at the microfiche screen, and jotting down details of various books to be ordered. She was wearing a pair of men's black jeans and a T-shirt, the colour of which reminded Helen of a copper beech tree. Over the back of her chair hung a dark blue bomber jacket. It was made of suede and looked soft and worn with age. Helen wondered if it had come from one of those shops which sold

233

second-hand clothing from America and had an alarming name like Jolt. Maybe she had borrowed it from her boyfriend.

'Hello, Molly,' she said, uncharacteristically bold. Last time she was there, she had twittered 'Excuse me' in a nervous whisper. The girl looked up, startled. Her face had a greenish tinge.

'I'm so sorry, I didn't mean to give you a fright. How are you?'

Molly responded with a feeble 'Fine', and asked Helen the same question.

'I'm very well. I've come to see Nick. To thank him. He told Orange about my book.'

'Yes. He said,' Molly stated glumly.

'Did he? That's nice. Is he around?'

'Won't be long.'

'Out again? I don't have much luck, do I?'

'A meeting. At the paperback suppliers. East End. Said he'd be back by four-thirty.'

They looked at their watches simultaneously.

'It's nearly that now,' Helen remarked. 'Do you mind if I wait a while?'

'Not at all,' Molly replied before offering Helen a chair and making some tea.

She remembered how vulnerable she had seemed last time. Then there had been a curious dullness in the woman's eyes. Her face had been gaunt, as if all elements of hope had been sucked out of it like guts might be from the slit belly of a dead rabbit.

But time had passed. Wasn't there now about Helen Hardy's cheeks a peculiar quality, and about the eyes a faint, faint glow, barely perceptible?

Perhaps it was a trick of the light? Or perhaps it was a trickling of hope which, as a trickling drip might slowly begin to nourish a desperate anorexic, might have slowly begun to revitalise the desperate lady?

Helen had spoken of longing, of disillusion, then. And Molly had felt pity and disgust for she had been happy then, and merely feared such desperation.

'I can't remember the last time I came in,' Helen said. 'It must've been April some time. You told me about your plans for the window.'

Molly nodded. 'Just plans,' she said.

'It's good to have plans,' Helen told her. This time the girl seemed sad. Last time she had been cheerful.

'I had plenty. Perhaps it's better not to.'

Helen asked why.

'So much scope for disappointment,' came the gloomy reply.

'You mustn't think in those terms, at least not yet. Leave that to old spinsters like me.'

'Too late. I'm disappointed already.'

'The window?' Helen asked, trying to be light-hearted.

'Not that, really, no. Other things.'

The older woman said nothing, unwilling to pry.

'Remember you talked about rejection?' Molly went on. 'You said it didn't get any easier.'

Helen understood suddenly wherein lay Molly's disappointment. Perhaps the jacket wasn't her boyfriend's after all. 'I'm sorry,' she said. 'Not very consoling that,' she added.

'And you said I wasn't ever to let anybody try and make me believe life's all right on one's own. Well, that's a pity.'

'You won't be for long.'

'No, you see, I don't agree,' Molly murmured. She was sitting upright, very rigid, and clutching the arms of her chair so hard that her knuckles looked like white chocolate buttons. She stared at the feeble steam rising from her cup of tea on the desk in front of her.

'Once you get over – '

'How long'll that take? Maybe I never will. And let's just say I do, the whole process has to start up all over again.'

'How do you mean?' Helen asked softly.

'The wait, first of all, before you meet someone. Then when and if you do, the decision as to whether or not you like them. The speculation as to whether or not they do you.'

'That doesn't take so long.'

'Okay. So you've got over the tentative first meetings. But then maybe things go wrong, so you have to start again. You wait, then maybe you start again, if you're lucky. But after a while you might not think the new arrangement's working either. Even if you do, what's the guarantee he does? It all takes so much time, and one's growing old.'

Helen looked at Molly's sad face. The creamy complexion. Not a line to be seen. No make-up except a smudge of brown kohl beneath the eyes. And the whites of the eyes had a pure, bluish quality about them. No pink tinge due to ageing veins. Helen regarded the smooth neck around which a glossy brown pony-tail curled. She did not say so for fear of sounding patronising but, Helen thought, Molly was not growing all that old.

'It's all experience,' she said instead, trying to reassure her.

'All right. So just suppose you are lucky enough to meet a person in your life, another you know you could marry. He might not feel the same.'

'There again, he might.'

'Yes. He might. But even if he does, marriage remains for a long while only an unspoken possibility. Nothing definite. Without saying a word, one's got to try and convince him it's a good idea, all the while appearing to be the model of casual indifference. This can take a long time. I'm talking about years. I don't want to wait years and even then not be sure he mightn't baulk at the idea.'

'It won't happen to you.'

'How can you be so sure?' Molly looked at Helen, sceptical.

'I was one of the unlucky ones, and things may change for me yet.'

'Who's to say I won't be an unlucky one? Anyway, I can't conceive of life without this particular person. In an ideal world I couldn't have imagined someone I'd wish to be with more than him. Now he's gone, I don't want anyone else, even if, years from now, someone does come along and happen to want to marry me.'

'It might seem like that at the moment,' Helen told her.

'You must know the feeling. I know you know the feeling. You said last time.'

'I do, yes. But I promise it's one that numbs. It's all-encompassing at first, but time really does eventually start to ebb away the pain. I know that Nick was all I wanted and I wonder, still, if I'll get over him. But it's already, through necessity, less piercing now than it was. You'll find consolations.'

'What consolations?' Molly asked, at last letting go of the chair's arms. She gently picked up her cup in both hands and when she held it to her lips her knuckles resumed a healthy colour. The tea was lukewarm now, and slimy on her tongue.

'Well, I've begun slowly to see that other factors in one's life can bring happiness. I've been lucky with my book,' Helen said.

'That's wonderful, but that's not companionship.'

236

'I had lost all hope of companionship, I admit. But with the book, I've discovered the renaissance even of that hope, one which I thought had died on me for good.'

'Why does getting your book published make you feel things might change, you might find someone after all?'

'Because it reminds me that after all I can be the recipient of good fortune, just like anyone else.'

'At the moment, I can't imagine how that feels. I'm just aware that I've not only lost Dominic but I've also lost that sense of hope. I'm sure I might be able to bear the first loss more easily if it wasn't for the second.' Molly's tone was totally matter-of-fact. Helen admired her ability not to sound self-pitying.

'Believe me,' Helen urged.

It had been the woman's desperation before, that had disgusted Molly. Of course she pitied Helen's lingering sadness about Nick, but she despised, now, that rediscovered air of faith. How dare a middle-aged spinster be capable of any hope, when she was capable of none?

And Helen watched the young girl. Her very eyes betrayed her sadness. She recognised that desperation. She, like Molly, was bearing the pain of the loss of a man she loved. But she, unlike Molly, had begun to detect the tiniest hint of hope. It was beginning, miraculously, to bloom again, and she was old. In Molly, it seemed to have died. There was no such bloom, and she was young.

'Even when one's old one can meet someone, suddenly, you know. It's never too late for the process you were talking about to begin,' she assured her hopefully. 'Something can always slap one in the face when one's least expecting it.'

Molly watched Helen carefully as she spoke. She had a kind face, kinder than her mother, though Cake was more beautiful. But Cake, who had married, was hunched with regret. Helen, who had not married, was serenely sad, but she was not hunched with regret. It is regret which scalpels the brows, while serene sadness merely shadows the forehead with dignity.

'I've had one or two such slaps,' Molly revealed with a slight laugh. 'Turned out to be wet kippers.'

Helen smiled warmly, and stretched out an elegant hand to put her mug on the desk. Then she pushed up the sleeves of her cable-stitched cardigan. It was of a spirited green, and had leather buttons, and big pockets. Molly doubted old paper

237

handkerchiefs were stored in Helen's pockets, like they were in her mother's.

Helen leaned back in her chair. She was wearing jeans and crossed her legs, relaxed. Almost youthful, Molly thought, but not in the studied way Cake was. Cake seemed to resent her years. She had contrived to shake them off by adopting a progressive manner. But Helen's nature was more genuine. Dignified. And Molly respected her.

'Oh, I've had my fair share of them too,' Helen admitted, laughing at herself. 'A positive overdose of wet kippers.'

'Not mentioning any names,' Molly smiled.

'Not mentioning any names,' Helen reiterated. 'Had enough to feed the five thousand,' she added lightly.

The pair of them sighed with good humour. Molly seemed to have perked up a little. If Helen was in any way responsible, she was pleased.

'And not mentioning any names – ' she repeated, looking at her watch, 'it's five o'clock already. Where do you suppose he's got to?'

'Not punctual,' Molly reminded Helen.

'I remember.'

'He'll be back in a minute. Another cup of tea?'

'Lovely. Thank you.'

Helen stood and browsed around the shelves a while. A number of customers entered, and Molly attended to them helpfully. A quarter of an hour or so later, Nick returned.

'They didn't half go on,' he said, striding across to the desk. 'Everything been all right here? I am sorry it took so long. Have you been all right, Mol?'

'Better than I was this morning. Someone to see you,' she said, indicating Helen who was standing in a corner, studying an open book in her hand.

'My God,' Nick declared, rather shocked. 'Helen. Goodness. Ages. Lovely.' He strode over to her, admirably restrained in his surprise, and kissed her hello.

'How've you been?' An innate courtesy left no room for him to be at a loss. Any embarrassment he might have felt was well concealed.

'I came to thank you,' she told him. 'It's good to see you.'

'And you. Goodness. Are you well?' Nick removed his spectacles and appeared to scrutinise the lenses for non-existent specks of dust. Then he wiped them on the bottom edge of his grey linen jacket before replacing them and blinking twice very deliberately.

Helen nodded. 'I just wanted to say thank you very much.'

'What for?'

'Orange. Thank you for putting him on to me. I appreciated it.'

'It was a pleasure. Least I could do.'

He had always been charming, Nick.

'Well,' Helen shrugged. She was not quite sure what to say next, so smiled to fill the gap.

'Look, can I offer you anything?' he asked, tapping his pockets in an automatic gesture familiar to both women. He was looking for his cigarettes. Without a word his assistant passed him one of hers, and he thanked her with a smile.

'That's very kind. Molly very sweetly made me some tea.'

'Nothing?' Nick rubbed his hands, curiously cheerful. In a funny way, he was pleased to see her. The upset was some weeks ago now. Quite forgotten, he told her in his mind. He had always been fond of Helen.

'I must let you get on,' she said.

'Oh no,' he asserted, persuasive. 'We like diversions, don't we, Mol?'

Molly agreed. She was pleased Nick was being kind to Helen.

'Why don't we get something from Colette's? I'll go and get us something from Colette's, why not? We can have a proper tea. I want to ask after A.E.H., you see. I'm keen to know how he's progressing. How about a rum baba, Helen? Do stay for tea.' Nick's enthusiasm was genuine. Helen was an old friend.

'No tea for me. Thank you.'

'Not a rum baba? A *pain au chocolat*, even?'

Helen shook her head, and thanked him again, smiling. My God, how she had loved Nick. She had really loved him. Funny to see him, now. There he was, that familiar suit, those familiar enthusiasms. The endearing dimple.

Same man. Same Nick. Did she love him still?

'Mol, would you like a *pain au chocolat*? Helen, stay while we have one?'

But Molly did not want a *pain au chocolat* either. Associations. Dominic. That first patisserie tea together. Unwanted recollection. But Nick, and his kindness, they could not have known.

Had she appreciated it then, their little tea together *chez* Colette? No recollection. Let me have appreciated it then, she thought.

'Rejection all round?' Nick asked, deflated. 'Oh dear. Helen, stay at least the time it takes me to have a cup of tea? Mol, is there still some in the pot? Come on, tell me how Housman's progressing.'

Helen put on her coat. 'He's progressing fine,' she told him.

'Apace even?'

'Even apace, yes. I think I can say that.'

'Piers told me you had lunch last week, and he'd introduced you to Bird. What've you decided?'

'We had a lovely lunch. We didn't talk much about the book, contracts, advances. I haven't really decided.'

'Oh.' Nick sounded surprised. 'But Bird took you on, didn't he?'

'He did. I feel very privileged to have got such a respected agent.'

'So he'll advise you.'

'I've got a meeting with him tomorrow. He says we'll decide then for definite about the advance. He thinks I should take it.'

'I think he's right,' Nick assured her. 'And if the book's really progressing apace, why not?'

'Why not?' Helen smiled.

'Any minute you'll be signing that contract. Wonderful.'

'Well, thank you.'

'Not me. Thank Orange, thank yourself.'

'All right,' she said, and stepped forward to kiss him goodbye.

Nick embraced her happily and congratulated her. 'I'll sell them like hot cakes,' he added as she stepped out of the door. 'Did you hear that, Helen? Hot cakes.'

As she walked from the shop, she looked back at the window, and the man she had loved was mouthing 'hot cakes'.

Helen laughed, and hastened away. There was about her step a lightness, a lightness which until that moment she had long forgotten.

That night, Molly was slapped in the face.

Unhappy, and unwilling to be alone, she went home with her best friend. Nick.

And he asked her an unexpected question. It was just like a slap in the face.

By the time Helen left the bookshop, it was almost closing time.

'You look miserable, Mol,' Nick observed. 'What can I do? The man was a shit. I liked him, yes, but the man was a shit.'

'He wasn't a shit. I mucked it up.'

'You did nothing wrong. You can't blame yourself.' He sat at the desk beside her. As they spoke, Molly was cashing up. Rather slowly.

'I don't want to go home to my bloody flat. On my own.'

'You don't have to go home to your flat on your own. I'll come with you, if you like.'

'But he's all over it. His things and everything. I don't look forward to them going, I can't bear the idea of them not being there, him taking them away, demolishing our flat. But neither can I stand the idea of facing them. Not tonight.'

'Here, let me do that,' Nick took over the task of cashing up. 'Come and stay with me,' he suggested. 'Good idea?'

Molly declined.

'Why not?' Nick asked.

'Imposition.'

'Molly! Don't be silly. I want you to come. I'm not going to let you go back to Portobello Road.'

'Are you sure?'

He was sure.

So Molly relented.

Nick took her in a cab back to his house, and sat her in the kitchen with a huge drink.

'This is very kind of you, Nick.'

I am not kind, he thought. In many ways I'm not kind at all. You are here, he said to her in his mind, because you are unhappy. I hate to see you unhappy. But that's not because I'm kind, I don't think. I hate to see you unhappy, Mol, for other reasons.

'It's selfishness, more, really. I hate to see you unhappy,' was what he said out loud. 'Not much I can do to comfort you.'

'This drink'll help,' she said, taking a gulp, grateful. 'I'm glad I'm here. I keep thinking about Saturday night. Can't believe it's happened. You warned me it might. If he moved in. Of course, I didn't take any notice.'

241

'I thought that it could, possibly. But not so soon,' Nick admitted quietly.

'One day. Not long, huh?'

'Not very impressive, Mol, no.' Nick was trying to sound light-hearted.

'Guinness Book of Records,' she suggested.

Nick nodded, and smiled sympathetically. The pair sat at the table a while, and drank, talking.

'Now,' Nick said, standing up after a while. 'Why don't I make us some supper?'

'There's no need, really. I don't want to put you to any bother. I'm not very hungry, to be honest.'

'Come on, Mol, do you good.' Nick pranced to his shelves. 'Now, what've I got?' He looked into a cupboard or two. 'Not a lot really. Alpen? No, that won't do. Chicken soup. Warm you up.'

Molly watched him take down a couple of tins, and told him, gently, that she was not cold.

'Well, I could do with some. Have just a bit with me, go on.'

'A little, then.'

Saucepan. Match. Flames. Bowls. Spoons.

'Toast?'

Toast. Butter. Salt. Pepper.

Better than Saturday night, Molly thought. On Saturday night, Dominic left me, and I had nothing to do.

Tonight I'm with Nick, and I can watch him prepare supper. Thank God for domestic diversion. I have something to do.

'Since Georgia left, I've overdosed on chicken soup,' Nick laughed.

Like Helen on wet kippers.

'Can't be doing with shopping,' he went on.

Hate shopping. Love Molly.

'That was my trouble,' Molly told Nick. 'Too fond of shopping for us, I was. Too homey, apparently.'

'I thought that too once,' Nick admitted.

'You hated shopping, yet you thought it too homey if she did it?'

Nick said, yes. 'Not really fair, I know. What's more, I carried on and let her do it, didn't I? But she bought supplies. Like a wife. Washing powder. Things like that. Washing powder's for married couples.'

242

'Nothing wrong with washing powder.'

'No, nothing wrong with washing powder. But I didn't want to be married to Georgia.' If you bought washing powder, it would be different, Nick told Molly in his head.

'I bought washing powder, and Dominic didn't want to marry me.'

I do, Nick told Molly in his head.

'The peril of Persil,' she sighed, with a hint of a laugh.

The two of them ate their soup and they stared at each other, and felt strangely comforted.

That night, Molly slept in Nick's bed.

Nick, too, slept in Nick's bed.

It was after the soup, and after finishing off the bottle of whisky, that the decision was made. Of course, she could have spent the night in the spare bedroom. But they were both drunk, and they were best friends and, as it happens, neither of them wanted to be alone. There was no embarrassment or awkwardness. Nick, sensing Molly's loneliness, simply asked her. She, keen if possible to exorcise that loneliness, complied. Logical.

Nick's bedroom was no less cluttered since Georgia had moved out. The piles of papers and periodicals had increased, the dust thickened. And the bed was unmade. It looked inviting.

Molly sat on it and glanced around her. She wondered about Nick's life, his other life, outside the bookshop, outside his life that she knew so well, the one she was a part of. Was he, in his bedroom, a lonely bachelor since Georgia had gone? Or did he cherish the solitude?

She imagined him there alone at night, sitting in the broken armchair by the fireplace, drinking whisky, smoking, thinking. What did he think about then, late at night, all alone? Books? Loneliness? Women?

Her eyes alighted upon an empty Scotch bottle on the windowsill, and she was unable to answer her silent question. She thought he was happy though, in his own company, with his carefree clutter all about him. Perhaps he really likes being on his own, she thought, and wondered what she was doing there.

Nick sat on his armchair and lit a cigarette. He stared at Molly, and he wondered what she was thinking.

It was so strange having someone there, with him again, in his bedroom – the first time for some weeks. Molly.

He knew her face so well. He had seen it day after day, and studied and learned its expression, the way the colours were projected upon it. Depending on where she was in his little shop, her face was altered by the different lights: the playful orange of the fire, the sturdy white of a spotlight, the calm yellow of a lamp.

They had seen each other, of course, outside the confines of the bookshop. Indeed, Molly had been to Hammersmith before, more than once, and not so long ago, to have supper, entertained by himself and Georgia.

But there, on his bed, in the semi-darkness, she was quite different. Her look was shadowed by a new sadness, and it was a look he did not know. In the bookshop, even in his own sitting-room, he was familiar with that more characteristic brightness about her. It pained him to see the change, and he longed to comfort her.

'I'm tired,' she said, after a while.

'We must go to bed,' he declared, standing.

'Is it really all right if I sleep here?'

'I want you to,' Nick replied.

Molly went to the bathroom and returned to undress while he went to clean his teeth. She climbed into bed, and looked up at the ceiling. He must know the contours and the details of the cornice so well, she thought. Georgia, too. As Georgia missed Nick, did she long to see that sight once again, the grubby little flattened roses, with one or two chipped leaves? Now Dominic had gone, she knew she would certainly miss the view from her bed of his things, his clothes, his books.

'Your bed's very comfortable,' Molly told Nick when he reappeared and joined her between the sheets. They lay on their backs, side by side, not touching, rather still.

'It's very old,' he said. 'I've had it for ever.'

When Nick turned the light out, it still did not occur to Molly that they would make love. But in the darkness, they moved into each other's arms and chatted a while.

Nick said that her being gloomy made him gloomy. She told him that that was silly, and he shouldn't be. He said it was infectious, gloom. She told him that it needn't be, that it was pointless the two of them feeling low.

'We won't sell any books tomorrow,' she remarked, 'if we've both got long faces.'

244

They smiled at each other, and without another word, they made love. There were no questions. It was just as simple as that.

It was afterwards that Molly was slapped in the face: Nick asked her to marry him.

She had never been proposed to before, though she had often thought about it. Often. Hearing the four words for real, they sounded strangely normal. Five syllables.

I hate washing up.

A slap in the face.

I miss Dominic.

Those phrases all had five syllables, too. That was funny.

'Okay,' she said.

It was just as simple as that.

Molly did not go home, except to pick up clean clothes, for the rest of the week. As usual, she spent her days in the bookshop, working alongside her fiancé. But in the evenings, they would travel back to his house together, and she would stay with him.

It was not like real life. Molly felt strange, having so long anticipated what it must be like to be loved by someone so much that they actually wanted to marry her. Only other people got married. People like parents and that ludicrous Lucy in the Body Shop. Now it was she, who had always wanted to be a wife, who was, in fact, going to be one. It had happened at last.

And yet, did she feel so different? She was still Molly, after all, the same Molly as she had always been. Brown eyes, shapely hips, long fingers. Things hadn't really changed so much. Everything looked as it always had. Buses were red still, and strangers didn't congratulate her in the street, and she was in love with Dominic De'Ath still.

On Friday night, Molly told Nick that she wanted to go home to her flat. She needed time to think. He said he thought that a good idea. He was an understanding man: she had not so readily tolerated lovers and their needs to think.

When she returned to her flat, after the familiar bus journey, Molly felt very, very lonely.

It smelt of Dominic: French cigarettes, lime aftershave.

All around his things were strewn, like ghastly layabouts. Some of his books remained still in boxes from the move. No need to unpack them now, she thought. He would come to collect them soon.

She sat on the sofa, not knowing quite what else she should do. She was there, ostensibly, to think. The sofa was as good a place as any.

The deep silence in the room was ruffled by the sound of his voice in her head, calling her. Mol. She had loved the intonation he had, all of his own, when he called her Mol.

Looking about her, she spied the velvet beret on the chair. A present, given during the late period of happiness. It was a cliché: the treasured object spotted at a bad moment, gratuitously bent on inviting tears. But Molly did not give in to its tempting cue. She was there to think about other things, not there to cry.

Molly had forcibly to shove her thoughts in the direction of other things — namely marriage, namely Nick.

She was full of doubts. She loved Nick, certainly. He was her best friend. But she did not really love him, did she, as a fiancée ought?

Yet how dare she doubt? Molly chastised herself. Surely she should be grateful. It was all she ever hoped for. All her life, the warm anticipation of her very own marriage had ferried her over the trials of that of her parents, and she had managed — just — to maintain her faith. And now that anticipation had graduated into reality. There was a man who really loved her. Nick really loved her. And she had doubts.

Anyway, she told herself quickly, she had accepted. It was too late now to have doubts. The man she really loved did not want to marry her. Who was to say she might really love another man again? And even then, who was to say he would really love her, and want to marry her?

'Here's your chance,' Molly said in her head, 'to marry. What's more, to marry a man who really loves you, even if you don't really love him. You might not get that chance again. You mightn't get the chance to marry again at all. Even to someone you don't really love or even to someone who doesn't really love you. Dominic's not coming back.'

She decided, after all, to ignore the doubts. There were no doubts. She would marry Nick.

Having had time to think, Molly went to Hammersmith in time to have lunch. It was a sunny Saturday.

Nick hugged her when he opened the door. They went inside and sat at the table and drank wine.

'I bought us some very special wine, Mol,' he enthused. 'I went shopping. I must be a new man.'

Molly smiled. Helen was right, she thought, watching her future husband, the process need not take quite so long, one could be slapped in the face, after all. And Nick was not a wet kipper as far as she was concerned. He was a great friend.

She stroked the cat on the table. Nick, in jeans, was jauntily stirring at something on the stove.

'Bugger chicken soup. No more chicken soup,' he declared. 'What we have here is a proper lunch. Did you have a good think?'

Molly nodded.

I can't marry you, she told him in her mind. What was I thinking about? Nick, I can't marry you.

It was a silent revelation which came as a great surprise. Only the night before she had set aside her doubts, and decided she would. But now a voice was drumming her head, and it was saying, no, no, no.

Molly took a stingingly large gulp of wine, and wondered how she might tell him. It was so cruel to curtail his happiness so soon. She tried to summon up every ounce of kindness within her. Everyone had always told her she was so kind. But she could not muster the kindness in herself to go ahead and marry Nick, and she hated herself for her selfish failure. She thought of her mother and her inability to be kind, and she began to feel sick. But she had to tell Nick.

He tasted the lunch in the pot, and Molly sat still, silent, watching, wondering. Only five syllables, she thought.

'I can't marry you,' she said, out loud. There. Such unspeakable, but unavoidable, unkindness.

She stood up and hugged him, and cried, and then she went away, leaving him with his cat, and his pot, and his solitude.

She returned home. Once again she was alone, and she felt the full force of her self-imposed isolation.

When Molly left him, Nick did not say a word.

Along the corridor, the front door clicked closed, she was gone, and he did not know what to do. It was a sunny Saturday afternoon. What did others do on sunny Saturday afternoons when they had been rejected?

He stood by the stove, completely still, because he had no idea how to move, in what direction. What next?

After a while, he became aware of a vigorous bubbling emanating noisily from the saucepan. He could turn the gas off, he thought. Stretching out a hand, slowly, he did so. But it did not take long, just turning a knob, so he was at a loss again. What now, he asked himself. Bugger lunch.

Ten minutes or so passed. Nick looked over the sink, through the window. He had never imagined that a sunny Saturday afternoon could have it in it to be so depressing. He did not want to stare out at it any longer. So he decided to go upstairs and wallow in his armchair.

The cotton bedroom curtains were closed. He was spared having to face the afternoon as it bore down on the street outside, so tactlessly sunny.

He spotted his alarm clock in among the old *Spectator*s on his bedside table, and snarled at it as he heard its wretched tick.

'You and your rotten resilience. Don't give up, do you?'

Nick decided, then, he was never going to give his alarm clock the pleasure of beating him again. He was in a mean-spirited mood.'I'll pip you to the post every morning from now on,' he informed it sternly.

The bed was unmade, but appeared to be more unruffled than usual. Nick leapt up, suddenly frantic, and straightened it out. He pulled up the sheets, and blankets, even puffed up the pillows. Almost unprecedented.

Then he sat down again, almost as quickly as he had leapt up, and leaned back into the armchair. He shut his eyes, and began to wonder about things. He knew he felt pain, but when he tried to place it, he could not quite pin down exactly what it really felt like, or where it was. It was a sort of emptiness, wasn't it? But maybe that wasn't the loss, maybe that was hunger.

Nick found it hard to admit, even to himself, that a woman had affected him so. He knew he was in love with her, no point in denying that. But other men, did they suffer like this? Perhaps they didn't admit it much, or perhaps they knew the suffering wouldn't last long: stiff upper lip, life goes on.

Of course, life would go on. Nick never doubted that. It was more a question of how long, exactly, the intangible, indescribable pain would linger?

Molly had rejected him. If it was merely a matter of loss of pride, he would not mind. But he was not a very proud man, and in this case any pride lost he couldn't give a fig for.

Far more painful was the simple, uncomplicated, practical loss of the one he loved. Molly.

There had been other losses in the past. Women had rejected him before. Not often, but it had been known. And the pain inflicted had been negligible in comparison, and anyway, swiftly remedied by a night of drunkenness with men friends in a pub.

But it was different with Molly. He had wanted to be with her for good, no one else.

Georgia had wanted to marry him. Had he caused her such pain when he rejected her? And Helen? What of them? That was something he had not really thought about before. He had vaguely imagined they would have been a touch sad, like he had been when rejected by other women. But it never occurred to him that he might have made them feel pain such as this.

Nick opened his eyes, lit a cigarette, and inhaled steadily. He hoped, by breathing the smoke out again, it might alleviate, to some extent, the agony.

'No such luck,' he mouthed when it had blown well away.

Then he sighed and tried another trick. With his hand, he touched his chin. He believed the afternoon roughness of his skin might remind him he had strength. Strength to overcome the loss, strength to look ahead hopefully.

After some minutes, Nick Winter slowly stood up. The pain remained very severe. But he knew what he wanted to do now, and he plodded downstairs.

In the kitchen, he sat at his big table. It was mid-afternoon. All the same, he began to eat the lunch he had made earlier, though he knew it would not assuage the real feeling of emptiness within.

When he had finished, Nick pushed his plate aside, sat back.

'Perhaps things aren't so bad,' he said out loud to try and convince himself. 'I have my bookshop, I could write a novel, maybe. I have my friends.'

He sighed, and addressed Molly in her absence, telling her that he loved her still.

'The pain'll persist a while,' he went on.

So saying, he took a swig of their wine.

'There're other fish, aren't there?' he asked himself. 'And there is time.'

Then he held his glass up to the light of the sunny afternoon.

'Fuel for hope,' he declared positively, as he stared at the dark red liquid inside.

Monday, as the weekend had been, was sunny.

Helen Hardy sat on a warm bench in Soho Square. In front of the pigeons and the lolling lunch-time sandwich-eaters, she opened her powder compact. It was a hot day. A shiny nose was not the thing with which to confront a distinguished publisher.

'Alfred,' she said under her breath, 'how do I look?'

She sat up straight and imagined him, wherever he was, assessing her appearance: the knee-length cotton skirt, the soft, baggy shirt, and the red shoes. He approved.

'And what do you think of the new hair?'

That morning there had been a revolution in Pimlico Perms.

Helen had been in a certain dither, anxious about her meeting with Orange later that afternoon.

When she entered the hairdresser's, the glossy receptionist had asked, as usual, if she would be wanting 'the usual'.

'Carol,' Helen had declared, 'no.'

That 'no' sprang out completely unexpectedly. It was too peculiar. Where had it come from?

'I can't be doing with another wash and set. I want a wash, a colour, a cut and a ruffle!'

Carol had willingly complied, endearingly excited by the idea of what she called Miss Hardy's 'new look'.

This 'new look' had taken longer than Helen had expected. She was not used to sitting there for more than an hour. But when she emerged, three hours later, she decided it was pointless to go to the library for the short while – by the time she had arrived there and settled – before her two o'clock appointment at Bedford Square.

Thus it was, with a little time to spare, Helen was now sitting in Soho Square with a pleasingly casual bob which had a light brown tinge and not even a hint about it of that former, rather ageing, rigidity of texture. She touched it lightly in disbelief and fancied Housman was telling her she looked ten years younger.

Cheerful, she glanced at her watch. If she began to stroll, very slowly, in the direction of C & O she would make her appointment at exactly the right moment: a courteous five minutes late.

She stood up and smiled at the greasy hippy lounging on the grass near her feet. The man had a green and purple waistcoat, and grey grime between his yellow toes. A can of beer rested by his stomach and his peat-coloured sandwiches protruded from a tin-foil wrapping.

He said, 'Hey man,' to Helen in a friendly tone.

That was always an odd form of address, she thought.

Then he suggested she should have a nice day. As she stepped over a few mangy pigeons, she thanked him and told him she would.

Helen began to wend her way across the square. It was littered with sunbathing bodies and apple cores, and it occurred to her that the decision to wear tights might not have been a wise one – the heat. But then she told herself that there again, bare calves were perhaps not the thing for signing contracts.

As she wandered along towards Bloomsbury, Helen resumed her conversation with Housman.

'If it wasn't for you,' she told him, 'I wouldn't be here now. I'm very grateful, you know.'

At the moment she reached Centre Point, she stopped, somewhat abruptly, with an anxious expression on her face. She was under the impression he was trying to tell her something. He had seemed quite jovial in Soho Square when she asked him how he felt she looked. But now his voice in her head seemed sad.

It appeared to be telling her that their association would have to come to an end, didn't she realise? When she completed the book?

A skinhead outside the tube station regarded Helen a little oddly, but she did not mind. Alfred's revelation inside her was a shock. She had not thought of it before.

Before she found a publisher, the writing of her book had been a task which had stretched ahead indefinitely. She had never seen it coming to an end. In the same way, her

251

association with Alfred was something, she presumed, which would continue for ever.

But, much though she loved him, she suddenly realised that he was right, and it could not be so. Spurred by Orange's enthusiasm, the book was progressing, the end of it was in sight. And then what?

Then, indeed, there would have to be new subjects. Housman would never be forgotten, of course not, but she would have to move on, wouldn't she? She could go on reading his poetry, she was entitled fondly to remember her close involvement with him, her silent companion, but she would have to move on.

He spoke to her again, and she could not deny his wisdom: there were, indeed, new territories, new beginnings which beckoned.

Helen started to walk again and turned into Great Russell Street in a daze. Housman began to suggest with such dignity, didn't he, that she was a woman of optimism. It was not a bad thing, perhaps, to bring things to an end. After all, there had been drawbacks in her arrangement with him, he suggested affectionately. Like the fact that he was dead, for example.

Could she hear him laughing? Could she hear him say that he would miss her, and that he would not forget her? Was he telling her that, of course, he would be sad, but that it was for the best?

And as Helen approached Bedford Square, she felt she understood. There was no bitterness. Alfred was doing it for her. Alfred was a kind and faithful, if softly spoken, non-tangible friend, and she knew he was right.

By the time she reached the Carruthers & Orange building, Helen did not feel so bleak about their mutual decision.

She admitted to Alfred, as she stood looking at the imposing front door, that she was a little nervous, but she detected that he was smiling and urging her on.

So it was that Helen was able to trot up the front steps, and she thanked him.

Once inside, she found she could go to Orange's door with a measure of courage, and she recognised that it was Alfred who had bestowed this upon her. She acknowledged this with a promise that she would never forget him.

252

Inside, the grand old man greeted Helen with a warm kiss of hello, and excitedly indicated that she should sit down.

'I'm so, so pleased, my dear Helen,' he said, standing behind his desk. 'When Bird rang me to tell me what you'd both decided, I was filled with pleasure.'

Helen told him that she, too, was thrilled.

'As I said the other day at lunch, I read those first chapters in a flash. I thought they were brilliant. Fascinating. I told you I had instinct, didn't I? And I was right. I loved it.'

'I'm so glad,' Helen muttered, slightly overcome. 'I never had much faith in it myself.'

Orange looked at her, puzzled. He clasped his hands together, and shook his head.

'You are too modest, my dear, I profess. It was excellent, and so the remaining chapters will be. I know it.'

Helen thanked him for his kind flattery.

'Well, no point in hanging about,' he enthused, sitting down. 'Here it is. The contract. *A.E. Housman: A Biography* by Helen Hardy. Why not use this?' he asked, leaning across the desk and handing her a heavy fountain pen. Then he edged the thick sheets of paper in her direction.

Helen bent over to sign. She watched her name glossily flow over the rich page, and felt exhilarated as she saw the ink seep into the distinguished document.

Having finished, Piers Orange stood up and walked round to her. Stepping forward, he congratulated the authoress.

And then he gave her an orange.

As he did so, he muttered the words, 'From your publisher!'

Then he reached his hand into his bowl again, and picked out another almost identical fruit. But it was rounder, brighter, more orange.

'Here,' he said, passing it to Helen. 'Something for you. Another orange.'

There was a pause, and he smiled at her.

'This one's a special one, though,' he remarked. 'This one's from me. This one's an orange from Orange.'

On the sunny Saturday afternoon that Molly left Nick's house, she returned to her flat, and stayed there, and wept.

She wept on Sunday, too.

253

On Monday morning, she woke up early. Her head felt foggy, and her eyes were stinging from all that crying.

It was seven o'clock. An hour and a half till she had to get up and go to work. Would she be able to go back to sleep?

Work. The word suddenly struck her. It was Monday morning, and on Saturday morning she had refused to marry her boss. What about work? Did she still have a *job*?

In her miserable confusion over the weekend, Molly had not put her mind to the bookshop much. She had vaguely, fleetingly thought that she might encounter a little awkwardness there at first, but that her basic friendship with Nick would ensure it would not last.

But now the day had come when she was meant to be going there as usual, when the circumstances were far from usual. And her mind was gripped with panic. For the first time it hit her: no longer could she remain an employee of Winter Books.

A gruesome, horrible loss.

Life in the bookshop, after all, comprised half of her existence. Indeed, now that Dominic had gone, it made for perhaps the most significant section of it. Winter Books was not only a place for her to go each day in order to make a living. The small emporium was infinitely more important to her than that.

It represented routine and security, certainly. But Molly was also deeply attached to it emotionally. With the owner, her friend, she had a sincere wish to make a success of it, and she enjoyed working extremely hard for that reason. She really cared about it. Every bit as much as her boss.

Christ, she loved it. The customers – those with 'catholic' tastes, the bossy ones, the quiet ones, the funny ones, the ones with legs like Perrier bottles. How could she bear not to come into contact with any of them again? Not to make coffee and chat to the friendly, regular ones? And the reps? How about not being able to humour them any more? No more arranging the window either, what of that? She never did graduate to anything more adventurous than wretched fans. But she would now miss even them.

As she lay in bed, Molly's thoughts eventually steered to Nick Winter himself. Not to see him every day would be terrible. But she couldn't just stalk into the shop this morning, assuming she was still his assistant. Even a man of the most generous-spirited nature would not want to work so closely with a woman who had turned him down.

What should she do? What course of action was honourable? Did he expect her to appear? Did he want her to, so they could carry on as if nothing had changed? And if she didn't go in, would it be tactless to ring, or cowardly and unforgivable not to do so? Perhaps a letter? But what to write?

Molly sighed, pained by the excruciating dilemma. Of course, whatever she did Nick would remain strictly stoical. That was in his nature. But which option, all the same, would inflict the least pain?

The red digits on the radio alarm clock were pulsating on: 07.43, 07.44. Time to make a choice rapidly approaching.

Meanwhile, headache rousing and beginning to put on an intolerably energetic performance. Going for its morning jog along the landscape of the frowning forehead, feet pounding the bone path, now just passing behind the bush of the left brow. Making sickening progress towards the right one, so smugly fit.

08.22: Molly decided to write to Nick. He would probably not want to talk to her or see her today. She would write a letter later. Tonight, or tomorrow. That was the wisest thing, surely.

She already missed him.

In her imagination, she watched him strutting and fretting about. She saw him charmingly chatting to Colette as she brought him cakes in the afternoons; she saw him humouring those customers with the dotty catholic tastes; she saw him ranting about *rigor mortis*, corpses and cotton-wool balls; she saw him raving about dippy passengers on the tube; she saw him face to face with Helen, smiling with her, devoid of the arrogance or air of superiority another man might have shown in the presence of a woman whose proposal he had turned down.

And finally, Molly saw Nick fondly teasing herself about her own silly or funny notions, and laughing with her and loving her.

Had she been wrong not to accept his offer, considering how keen she was to marry? Or rather, would it have been right to do so, just for the sake of being married?

No, no, she told herself, she had done the right thing. She had caused pain, yes, but he was spirited, Nick, wasn't he? And the pain would dissipate soon, she said to herself.

255

Soon, perhaps, he might even come to regard her unkindness as a kindness.

Molly smiled at the thought, and hoped, beyond measure, that in the end she would be forgiven.

Molly reluctantly forced herself out of bed just before nine. What was there to get up *for*? She padded into her kitchen, pulling the telephone with her, and switched on the kettle. A few minutes later, she sat at the table with a cup of coffee and a bleak face. Now what exactly?

Vaguely, her gaze flitted about her. The room, as yet barely lived in, but lived in enough to remind her of Dominic's presence there.

Her eyes tripped upon the small fridge beside the stove. It was white, blank. On seeing it, Molly's memory of her initial reaction to his untimely departure plumped itself on to her consciousness like a rough boy on to a beanbag.

When she had opened the little door and spied the two special strawberry cakes, the despair had not really hit her, had it? But over a week had passed since then. It was different now. She was feeling very alone. All she could hear was the screaming silence.

Molly bent down, as if doubled up, and picked the telephone up off the floor. She stared at it for some minutes, her mind blank as the fridge door.

Quite suddenly, she dialled some numbers.

'I'm coming home, Dad,' she told Rufus when he answered.

'How lovely,' his familiar voice enthused. 'Friday or Saturday, Mol?'

'Today.'

'At this short notice? You mustn't miss work, Mol, for me. I'm all right, I promise.'

'I don't think I am though,' she explained.

She wanted to tell him, to list to him, all those things she had lost. Not only Mum, she began in her mind, Dom, Nick, the job, the flat. But all she actually said was, 'I'm on my way, okay? I'm coming home.'

It was not a premeditated decision. It had not come about as a result of any weighing up, or by way of any logical process. The idea of going home had simply arrived. As Molly sipped her coffee, held the receiver to her ear, heard her father's sympathetic, comforting voice, there appeared to be no other possible course of action.

The next telephone call was to Sam, her landlord.

'I have to go back to Oxford,' she informed him, and he was surprised.

'Something wrong with the flat?'

'No,' she assured him. 'I can't be here any more though. Dominic's gone. It smells of him.'

'Where'll you live? Parents?'

'I think not. I'll rent a place.'

'What about your job? What'll you do?' Sam asked, concerned.

'Haven't thought. Blackwell's, maybe, if they'll have me. Won't be the same as Winter Books, though. Less personal. I could enjoy working there, I expect, but I don't think I could ever love it as much.'

He told her that, even so, it would be good to be in a bookshop, and then he expressed sorrow at her leaving the flat.

'I'll pay my rent to the end of the month, okay? And collect all my stuff before then.'

The voice on the end of the line wished her the best of luck, and told her to visit him. Molly thanked him for everything and they said goodbye.

When she had replaced the receiver, she hastily went to dress and pack a small bag.

It was over, she did not wish to be there any longer.

Afterwards, she locked up the flat, said goodbye to it and to Dominic's things, and was soon on her way to Paddington.

The 10.17 was not crowded, and Molly was able to sit on her own.

As the train drew away from the station, she looked out of the window and recalled that time on the bus when she had been going to work, listening to Ruth Etting. She had sensed a nostalgia for melancholy, and that same sense returned to her again.

Then she had viewed it from the privileged pedestal of happiness. This time, though, she saw it from a different angle. As the train swigged along, making its way out of London, she was looking up to melancholy from the depth of despair. On this occasion, she recognised that her desire to attain it was not simply some fanciful notion. Now her longing for it was

257

a justifiable and more urgent need to reach its comparatively sweet relief.

At Reading, a young couple in their twenties stepped into Molly's compartment.

They were an unprepossessing duo. He was wearing white trousers and an orange anorak, and he had an alarmingly pale face so, in fact, he was not entirely dissimilar to a motorway bollard. The girl had on a turquoise boiler suit of questionable elegance. The brims of her high-heeled ankle boots reminded Molly of dead rabbits – dead punk rabbits, at that, for coloured glass studs had been decoratively punched into the fur. They were the kind of boots, she thought, which seem to implore the question, why? Why had the girl deluded herself that they were attractive objects? Why, indeed, did they exist?

Molly was unable to answer, but then she looked into the girl's eyes. They seemed to sparkle like the studs at her ankles, and it no longer seemed to matter.

Her own eyes had doubtless sparkled likewise when she had last travelled on a train.

Dominic had been with her then. He had, she admitted to herself, read the paper and not talked much, but at least he had been there.

'Did you remember to buy some fags?' the boy asked his friend.

'I thought it was no-smoking,' came the reply in a whisper.

'Doesn't say so. There's no sticker,' he said.

The girl delved into her black wet-look handbag, pulled out a packet of Silk Cut and passed it to him. He drew out one of the cigarettes and lit it.

The Adam's apple bobbed up and down as he puffed. The girl giggled and gave Molly a glance to see if she, too, had noticed it.

'Don't do that, Paul,' she said fondly.

'Do what?'

'That thing with your voice-box. It looks funny.'

'I can't help it,' he protested reasonably, inhaling again.

Molly watched the happy pair and listened to the exchange, envying the intimacy of it.

'Fancy a Club? Raisin.'

'No, Anna. I've got this thanks.' Another drag of the cigarette. 'Silly.'

Anna fumbled in her bag again. She fished out a biscuit, unfolded the foil wrapper, and took a dainty bite. Paul looked

258

out of the window. His eyes, following the passing scenery, automatically twisted back and forth.

'I'm sorry. Would you like one?' the nice girl questioned kindly, holding up another biscuit to Molly.

Molly smiled and thanked her, but no.

'He's a chain-smoker, that one,' Anna revealed.

'I'm not!' the motorway bollard flashed, defensive and indignant, but only jokily so.

'I call forty a day chain-smoking,' the girl told him. 'Don't you? Does your boyfriend smoke?' she suddenly asked, turning to Molly.

Molly's expression went blank. It was taken to mean yes.

'All the same, aren't they? I tell him not to for his own good. But you don't take any notice of me, do you, Paul?'

'No, Anna,' he replied, still staring out of the window, 'I never take any notice of you.'

'It's a wonder we put up with it, isn't it?' she remarked to Molly again, in a feminine, confiding tone. 'Can't think why we do.'

''Cos you love it really,' her boyfriend told her, playfully poking her in the ribs. She giggled.

'Oh yeah?' And turning to Molly once more, still laughing: 'What'd we do without them?'

Fortunately the question was rhetorical, and Molly was extremely relieved she did not have to answer it.

'Please can you pass me my book, Anna?' Paul asked.

She handed him a thick, tatty paperback resting beside her on the grubby blue checked seat, and then wondered out loud what *he* would do without *her*?

'Disintegrate probably,' Paul replied, patiently but affectionately, teasing.

That, Molly said to herself, was just what she was doing, disintegrating, wasn't it? Without Dominic. Where was he now, she wondered gloomily.

Her thoughts were stubbed out by the aggressive swish of the door sliding open and the prosaic appearance of the ticket collector. She rummaged in her bag to find that silly bit of cream and orange card. Though she found it quickly, she was bored by the effort of the rummage. When she passed it to him, and he clipped it with his garlic crusher, she wondered why she bothered.

Everything she did was so trifling, somehow, and did not seem to be getting her anywhere. Everything she saw lacked colour.

Life was so pointless. Because he was not there, and with him not there, none of it mattered.

'Is your destination Oxford?' the uniformed man asked in British Railspeak.

Molly begrudged him a yes, but could not run to a smile.

When he went away, her mind returned to Dominic. Thinking about him was the only activity for which she had any enthusiasm.

Where was he now, she asked again, conscientiously carrying on from where she left off.

A little dot in the amorphous spread of the metropolis. Where, it was not possible to determine. But suddenly Molly felt nostalgic for London.

Perhaps he was in a street on a grey pavement? Maybe he was working at Colville Road? That was likely, more than likely. So what was he doing? Standing up, or sitting down? Was he wearing his faded old jeans, or the thin black trousers which felt so soft to touch? And in his hand? Was he holding a book? Which book? Or a pen? A cigarette? A cup of tea? The eyes, too, what about them? Were they fixed on to a person or a thing? Was he in conversation? Who with? What about? This very second, was he speaking, or listening? And what could he be touching? Tasting? Smelling? Hearing? Thinking? Her? In his mind, could he see her? Was he feeling guilty? Lonely? Sad? Missing her?

Molly wanted detail. She wanted to be not a fly on his wall, but a speckle of matter in his brain – something which she considered at present to be more fortunate than herself, because such a speckle would have knowledge, and she did not. She wanted the privilege of being part of that existence again, even the more mundane aspects of it, which, in his absence, had taken on for her a new importance.

The train rattled on.

In her mind Molly played back various scenes – not necessarily significant ones: when she and Dominic had been together. She tried very hard to see his expression, to hear his voice, to gauge his movements. But the picture was frustratingly unclear. At the time, she wondered, had she appreciated the reality?

She decided she must have done, but that it was poor consolation, all that appreciation then, just like the memories were now.

What was the point of them? What use was it recollecting Dominic's affectionate words or deeds if now they did not apply, if now they counted for nothing? What did it matter that he had loved her once if today he no longer did so? There was no solace to be gained from remembering how they were, for it would be a distorted, false kind of solace.

Perhaps, instead, I can look forward, she told herself, and hope one day he might return to me?

But Dominic would not return. She would not marry the man she loved. It was spoilt to suppose she might love again. And she would not marry for the sake of marrying.

In her mind, Molly perceived her parents: Cake's shoulders hunched with regret, Rufus's eyes dulled with misery.

No, she would not marry at all.

So, what was she left with? What had Dominic left her with?

Redundant memories. Vacuous conjecture. No wish to marry. Despair.

The train approached the grey cooling towers at Didcot. When it stopped at the railway station, the motorway bollard, gleaming, and the punk rabbits, twinkling, said goodbye to her cheerfully, and alighted.

Solitude.

There was a jolt as the train set off again towards Oxford.

She opened her book, and switched on her Walkman. The warmth of the summer glowed on her page, and the music was melancholic.

And for the rest of the journey, Molly found she was almost happy to be alone.